W9-ALN-072

A Hole
in the Heart

A Hole in the Heart

Christopher Marquis

St. Martin's Press ❧ New York

Grateful acknowledgment is given for permission to quote from *Now We Are Six* by A. A. Milne, illustrated by E. H. Shepard, copyright 1927 by E. P. Dutton, renewed © 1955 by A. A. Milne. Used by permission of Dutton Children's Books, a division of Penguin Young Readers Group, a member of Penguin Group (USA) Inc., 345 Hudson Street, New York, N.Y. 10014. All rights reserved.

www.stmartins.com

Library of Congress Cataloging-in-Publication Data

Marquis, Christopher.
    A hole in the heart : a novel / Christopher Marquis.—1st ed.
      p.   cm.
    ISBN 0-312-30630-X
    1. Women teachers—Fiction.   2. Loss (Psychology)—Fiction.
3. Fishing villages—Fiction.   4. Missing persons—Fiction.
5. Mothers-in-law—Fiction.   6. Married people—Fiction.
7. Mountaineers—Fiction.   8. Alaska—Fiction.   9. Widows—
Fiction.   I. Title.

PS3613.A768H65 2003
813'.6—dc21

                           2003040601

First Edition: August 2003

10 9 8 7 6 5 4 3 2 1

For my family

A Hole
in the Heart

All five of the world's loon species may be found in Alaska. The bird's distinctive yodel evokes insane laughter for some, implacable mourning for others. As much as any other sound, the cry of the loon is identified with the call of the wild.

—The Pemberton Guide to Alaska's Birds

*M*idafternoon on a Tuesday, it occurred to Bean Jessup that she was forgetting her husband's face.

She was working the slime line, one of a dozen people at the trough, facing a spout that spewed cold water onto a chopping block. On a conveyor before her, slippery, metallic hunks of salmon rolled past, their heads and tails removed, bloody wads of pinks and chums en route to the canning machine. Her job was simple enough: pull a fish from the belt, slash away the bits of fin and innards missed by the gutting machine, rinse it, and return it to the belt. Repeat. She wore a yellow rain suit against the splashing water; with pimpled rubber gloves, she gripped a dagger-sized knife.

Every few hours, Fat Al, the supervisor of the Northern Pacific Fish Co., strolled by to inspect the carnage. He had a squirrel's nest of a beard, Amish-style, and suspenders stretched drum-tight over a flanneled belly. His big slick pate reminded Bean of a chubby baby, but otherwise he was scary. His run-together eyebrows made him look permanently cross, and his left hand had only three fingers and a thumb. Bean had to remind herself not to stare at his hand.

The factory's screeches and clatter made threats useless, so Fat Al tried to boost productivity with surprise appearances and a few hard looks. Time was everything. Fish rotted.

It was early in the salmon run, two days after the Fourth of July, and everybody was pulling double shifts. Wrapped in rubber, Bean felt her T-shirt cling like yesterday's washcloth. The smell hung on her, too. But *smell* was too kind. It was the *stench* of blood and salt and fish heads, and not the fresh ones. By the end of the season she would have to throw away her shirts and jeans and probably her socks and underwear, too. She used skunk remedies on her hair.

The endless workdays threw everyone's clock off-kilter. You worked the line for seventeen hours and had the remainder to eat, clean, love, drink, laugh, and consider your life. It didn't help that the sun never set. After a while, you just believed whatever the clock in the break room said, though more than once Bean caught herself wondering whether it was morning or night. She stumbled home in the midnight dusk and was back by 7 A.M., trudging up the cannery's plank stairs in knee-high boots. All day, she and her coworkers toiled in unblinking fluorescence, wired on cookies and coffee, which Fat Al shrewdly furnished for free.

When she first worked the cannery a few years back, Bean had been appalled by how much slime got past her sleep-starved colleagues— prickly fins, chunks of gill, speckled bits of skin—and rolled right into the canning machine. Her instinct was to lunge after an errant piece of gristle, hoping to spare some Safeway shopper a rude surprise. But her reward would be to get water in her gloves. Or a dirty look from the guy who had already slimed the fish. After a week or so, she just let it roll by: the sinews and cartilage and entrails clinging to the precious salmon flesh. All that ever came out the other side were perfect cans with tidy green labels. It was someone else's problem.

With her hands leased out to Northern Pacific, Bean had lots of time to ponder. She wasn't a heavy thinker or a particularly organized one. Much of the time, thoughts fluttered through her head like clothes in the dryer. She suspected that most people thought that way—in loopy circles—even bosses like Fat Al. Sometimes she thought about her second-graders; she imagined them visiting her when she was old. Sometimes she dreamed up a new diet for herself; she would live on chicken and carrots, or drink so much water that nothing else would fit in her stomach.

Frequently she wondered what in the world she was doing in Eyak—so far from home—where it always rained and there were bears and there was no road in or out.

She forced herself to think ahead; no sense looking back now. But after lunch on Tuesday Bean had one persistent thought. It tumbled through her mind, pushed her eyes from side to side, and made her feel whimpery.

I don't remember what he looks like.

She glanced across the trough at Lois. Lois's face was tucked into a red bandanna; she hated getting splattered. Lois was tall, had eyes that said either "don't mess with me" or "fuck me," depending. She looked like an outlaw, which was pretty much how Bean saw her. Lois spoke her mind and drank whiskey and had blond highlights in her frizzy hair, even in winter. Bean felt lucky to have her as a friend.

Lois was sexy, too. Even now. Bean watched her work on a sockeye, slicing away at the gills, gore running up her forearms. She wore the same shapeless rain suit that Bean did, except Lois's was somehow cinched smartly at the waist. Her hips swayed slightly back and forth to whatever music was pumping from the Walkman into her ears. Her ears. Bright red fire hydrants dangled from each lobe. Only Lois would wear jewelry on the slime line. At twenty-eight, Lois was two years older than Bean, but next to her, Bean felt like a crone. Which was odd, because she had better breasts than Lois, and she didn't have all those moles. But Lois's face and body had an unimaginable asset: they had Lois as a press agent.

Lois looked up from her fish. She must have noticed Bean's idle hands. She gave Bean a slight nod and a good hard look, which was entirely illegible because of the bandanna covering her face. Bean shrugged and looked away. Lois couldn't help her with this.

Bean stared into the trough, at the blood swirling down the drain. It was horrible, yet oddly pretty, bright and thick, like finger paint. Her feet ached and she shifted her weight in her boots. Horrible pretty. As she rocked back, she bumped into a towering hulk behind her. It moved. She screamed and spun around, the knife in her fist poking at the intruder.

For a big man, Fat Al could jump. He hopped backward, clamped a meaty hand on Bean's wrist, and twisted the knife toward the ceiling. They stood there for a moment, looking at each other—Fat Al, a foot taller than Bean, clutching her upheld glove—like a pair of miserable dancers. She felt his breath full force on her face. Chewing tobacco. It was hard to believe a man could smell worse than a fish cannery.

"Jeez Christ," he said.

Bean's heart was still pounding. "Sorry," she whispered. She didn't want to look into his menacing face, and she especially didn't want to look at his abbreviated hand, so she dropped her chin like a bad dog. "Sorry."

Her apology didn't register. They were both wearing earplugs. It was like a conversation with her mother.

Lois was taking in the scene from across the trough, her eyes like Ping-Pong balls. Fat Al extracted the jagged knife from Bean's hand and placed it on the chopping block. For a moment, she thought he might smack her. But he just put his bush-beard next to her ear and shouted, "Fish ain't goin' to clean itself," then walked off.

Lois thought the whole thing was pretty funny. In the break room an hour later, she tossed lemon pretzel cookies into her mouth and shook her head. "I tried to warn you, honey," she said. "I really did. I can't believe you didn't feel him behind you. I mean, any closer and he'd have to buy you dinner."

Bean nibbled a cookie. "I'm distracted," she said. "You know that."

"You should've seen his face. His eyes popped out. He thought you were going to slime him, I swear to God."

"Maybe that's how he lost his finger, sneaking up on people," Bean said.

Back on the line that evening, Bean realized she could remember some things about Mick. Enough, for instance, to satisfy a police artist. His hair was brown and thick and he almost never combed it. He let Bean cut it now and then, and she shaved his thin white neck, taking care not to nick him. His eyes were brown, too. Gentle. He rubbed them when he was tired after he'd been out fishing. His body ran hot, even in winter. He sweated half-moons into his T-shirts before the morning was done.

Was that *it*, then? Bean wondered. Had she remembered him? Had she caught him before he slipped away? Everyone else seemed to think he was dead. There had been a service. But he had been missing for only a month. Some kids went to summer camp for that long.

How had his breath felt on her neck? Bean wasn't sure.

She reached for a fish and noticed the guy beside her, a college student with a ball cap that said OREGON STATE. He was talking to himself again. Just staring straight at nothing and chatting away. Maybe he was in some sort of religious trance. She wondered if she could piggyback on his prayer, so it would count for her and Mick. It would be like when an operator busts into a phone call for you in an emergency.

It occurred to Bean that she might launch a prayer on her own.

But she couldn't remember the words. She knew one that started "Hail Mary, full of grace." And it ended with "Now and at the hour of our death." But she was damned if she could remember what came in between. It was a prayer with the middle cut out, and the middle was what mattered. Like with this fish.

She spotted a slip of paper dangling from the water pipe in front of the college kid's nose. It was affixed with a blotch of salmon gut. He was reading something—memorizing it. By the shape of the words on the page, it was a poem. Bean wondered what it was about. She knew some poems. Well, rhymes really, stuff she'd learned as a little girl. Winnie-the-Pooh, Mother Goose. Her brother had read them to her, over and over. She remembered sitting beside him in the easy chair, cozily mashed together, shoulder to shoulder, hip to hip, as he turned the big pages in the book on their laps, she, safe and sleepy, sometimes dropping her eyes to stare at the blond down on his forearms. But she could never drift too far, because if he thought she was asleep, he would try to end the story in the middle.

"And they lived happily ever after," Chip would say, slamming the book shut.

"No," Bean would squeal, delighted that she had caught him in this trick. "No happy after." She would stab an imperious finger at the unread pages beneath his arm and command: "Read."

Bean hoped to read to her own child someday. She imagined only one: a curly-haired girl in sagging pants who played amid the daisies. You just had to smile to look at that little girl. Bean would bring her to her own best friend's house—a friend who baked her own bread, wore loose skirts, and finished Bean's sentences. On a lazy afternoon they would sit together on the porch, sip lemonade, and watch their children play.

So far, all she had was the porch. It was really just a deck that Mick built off the back door. Lois couldn't make bread and she said baby-making would ruin her hips. As for the curly-haired girl, Bean had stayed on the pill. Mick had wanted children, though. *Critters,* he called them. As in: "I wouldn't mind a few of those critters runnin' around on a Saturday morning." But she hadn't been ready. Too many things could go wrong. And now—now it might be too late.

As she yanked on a string of gut, Bean pictured the various snap-shots of Mick scattered around their house. Sleepy Mick in a thick brown robe cradling Fred as a pup. Skinny Mick in yellow trunks tugging a sailboat into the water in Cancún. Mick and Bean on the mountain, with surprised looks because the camera's self-timer had worked. She loved that picture. It was on the nightstand. Mick's soft eyes; her own pretty face, dark blond hair, her body luckily cut out of the frame so she didn't have to worry if she looked fat.

But she couldn't conjure Mick himself, make him stand before her, see him in the round as she had every day—jokey and excited, or bone-tired, or just there, with mussed hair and breakfast cereal. She couldn't recall the secrets of the lean body she'd hugged at night. What freckle where? Fingernails, flat or rounded? Second toe longer than the first? Bean wasn't sure. She recalled a scar across his eyelid where he'd hit a glass table as a little boy, and it made her feel a little better. But which eye?

The college boy recited his poem.

It felt terribly wrong. Mick knew her secrets; the least she could do was remember his topography. It had taken months of hurt feelings, stuttered starts and misfights over chores and money before Bean had managed to unfold herself to Mick.

When I was one, I had just begun.

He figured out her moods. He knew when to cajole. And he knew when to stand aside and wait for Bean to emerge, heavy-headed, from her lair of twisted sheets, children's books, and Ho Ho wrappers. Mick knew all this, but now he was gone.

And if she let him go, it would be as if the best thing that had ever happened to her—the *only* good thing, it seemed—had never been.

The Bald Eagle does not migrate. . . . During the harsh winter, when fish are not available, it remains attuned to the difficulties of larger birds, striking to kill at the slightest indication of weakness.

—The Pemberton Guide

*T*hey met four years ago, the year Bean finally decided what to do with her life.

Finding a job had kept her and Betty Chin, the career counselor at San Francisco State, on edge for quite a while. Six months after Bean had received her diploma, Betty dug up Eyak's desperate plea for a substitute teacher. No certification required, hardship pay, and a chance to make it permanent. "Take it," Betty said.

Bean got a long-distance call a week after they'd sent off the paperwork. A friendly voiced man from the school district wanted her on the next plane. Only then did she go to the library and pull an atlas off the shelf.

In fifth grade, when her class was making relief maps of the states, Bean had drawn Alaska from the hat. One afternoon she hurried home to mix a salt and flour plaster, arranged it on a cardboard tracing of the state and slipped it into the oven, hoping for the best. But her mother came home when she was pulling it from the rack, and it was all cracked up, like there had been a major earthquake. One by one, the Aleutian Islands slipped onto the floor, like turds.

Her mother was wearing a tennis dress. Which was lucky, in a way, because the kitchen counters were covered in white dust. Lately she was always wearing tennis clothes—wristbands, little white socks with tiny puffs over the heel—that seemed ridiculous. When the tennis club had slashed its dues in a desperate bid to shore up its finances, Bean's mother had pounced. Tennis was her new passion, and she was determined to spread it through the family. But Bean's dad refused to go. He said the club was full of fakers. He sat in his armchair and imitated them. It was a scream.

"What is the meaning of this?" Her mother had been shouting at her a lot recently. Maybe she'd gotten tired of shouting at her dad.

"It's Alaska," Bean said. Her voice shrank into a swallow. Why was her mother always around when she messed up? "It's due tomorrow."

Never mind that her teacher had assigned the maps two weeks earlier. Bean's interest in school had dropped off considerably. All she wanted to do was read books, but not the ones the teacher assigned. Her conference reports said Bean was "neglecting her potential."

Just then, the Alaskan panhandle, which had turned out pretty well given its odd shape, broke away from the main part and slid down the sloping cardboard, which Bean clasped with fat oven mitts.

They watched it hit the floor and break into crumbs.

Her mother arced her fingers around her temples and made a last-straw look. She stepped to the oven and peered in, as if it might contain a family of raccoons.

"I want this kitchen clean," she commanded. "This is all I need right now."

Bean made an imploring gesture, which the hand mitts made all the more dramatic.

"But I need a map," she begged. "I'll get an F."

It took forever to get everything down the drain.

———

After so many years, Bean was surprised at how familiar the shape was when she opened the atlas. The shelfy Arctic forehead, Kodiak Island, the Aleutian tusk. She stared at the map until the longitude and latitude lines ran together.

Maybe in Alaska it would be all right. A person could get lost there. Start over.

They lived better up north, she was certain. Nobody slept in the streets. They'd flat-out *die* if they did. In Alaska everybody had a home and a thick coat and drank lots of hot chocolate. Families worked; people stuck together. They had to. It took at least six people to kill and butcher a walrus. You had to respect that kind of cooperation, even if you hated hunting as much as Bean. Alaskans were like their sled dogs, pulling together.

Eventually, she found Eyak on the southern coast. It was so tiny that she locked her index finger on the spot. It was nestled amid speckles of islands, a thick blue river, blue stripes that meant glaciers, a splotch of green for forest, and lots of tight gray lines behind it, meaning mountains. It seemed like a lot of geography for a town of 2,500.

Maybe that was where a person could become somebody. Out in the woods, where there was nobody to tell you you were strange. Maybe it was a place where a girl could unblock herself. Something was holding her back—she knew it, she felt it—but she couldn't name it.

When Bean announced that she was moving to Alaska, her mother took a deep breath, as if a good argument needed lots of oxygen. She exhaled, then stared at Bean. "I don't know what you're trying to run away from," she said finally. Bean just gave her a look.

On a bright morning in February, feeling strangely peaceful, except for a jumpy belly, Bean caught a jet to Anchorage and a puddle jumper to Eyak. She pressed her forehead against the Plexiglas window as the atlas symbols became real, the ripsawed mountains, the oozing glaciers, the meringue-topped islands. The natural light had dimmed. She

sipped Florida orange juice served by a big-boned stewardess and realized none of them would ever survive a plane crash.

Maybe she'd never go home. Or she'd wait till everybody was dead.
Or at least really old. She'd come back one day, herself all wrinkled
and bleary-eyed, and walk stiffly over to the rope swing in the front
yard. And she wouldn't say anything. She'd ride back and forth and
pull the pins out of her scraggly, long gray hair so it would swing in
the breeze. And she would sing to herself as if all the years meant
nothing, and that would just freak the hell out of her mother standing
on the porch with her hand over her mouth.

For now, all that snow offered a convincing bulwark. Her plane
landed on a strip of asphalt gouged from the snowy forest and she
peeked through the oval window. The lights blazed in the airport, a
low-slung shed no bigger than a 7-Eleven. It was nearly dark. She
looked at her watch: 3:30 P.M.

The wind was strong. As soon as she stepped onto the rolling staircase, her clothes flapped against her and her hair went haywire. Cold
mist moistened her skin and stung her eyes. In the distance, darkened
trees bowed and bobbed frantically. She clutched the frigid metal railing
and stepped with an old woman's care down the steps.

The other passengers hurried across the slushy tarmac into the
building. Bean took a deep breath and slung her new canvas carry-on
over her shoulder. It felt ridiculously heavy, crammed as it was with
the last-minute addition of a few beloved books, thermal underwear
from the army surplus store, a box of Nilla wafers, and—embarrass-
ingly—six jugs of Finesse for dry hair, because who knew what they'd
have in Eyak? Somewhere in the bottom of the bag was a present from
her college roommate: a potent repellent called Bear Scare. There didn't
appear to be any bears on the tarmac.

From outside, she noticed a fur-lined parka lumped up against the glass in the tiny airport. It waved. Bean cast a quick look behind her to see if the parka meant her. She squeezed through the narrow glass door and the parka hurried over. Encased within was a stout, jowly woman with curly orange hair and thick pink cheeks. She was all hood and boots; she didn't appear to have any hands or thighs. Her voice was as high and excited as a gnome's.

"Oh, thank heavens," the woman said. Her obvious relief made Bean feel both proud—they needed her—and scared—they *needed* her. But then the woman yanked back a sleeve, magically produced a wrist with a watch, and explained. "I've got the four o'clock ferry, you see. Jiminy, it's going to be close."

Something about the woman reminded Bean of the White Rabbit; was it all that fur around her face? After hours of delicious inactivity— an airline passenger does so little, yet achieves so much—Bean felt herself sucked into this stranger's rush.

"Name's Rosalie," the woman said. She snatched up Bean's carry-on and crossed over to where they were piling up the baggage. Her coat was so long, you couldn't see her legs move and she gave the impression of floating. "Course, everyone calls me Feetie. Can't re-member why. Just the way it's been."

She scowled at Bean's bag. "What you got in there, bricks?"

"Shampoo," Bean said softly.

By then, Feetie had enlisted a gristly man in a ball cap to lug Bean's bags to the parking lot. Bean chased after her. She needed to finish the introduction. "My name's Celestine," she said. "But I go by Bean."

Feetie had the minivan door open and Bean thought she might whip out a cattle prod to speed up the bag man. "Bean?" she said distractedly. "That's odd."

Feetie peeled off her parka, as if skinning herself, and slipped be-hind the wheel. Bean jumped into the car before it left without her.

They sped down the two-lane road into town, hitting every pothole on the way. In the twilight all you could see was the stretch of road illuminated by the headlights.

Feetie talked as fast as she drove, and Bean—straining to see her new home—registered only every second or third phrase. Feetie grew up in Montana. "No one's really *from* here," she said. "Spent my whole childhood on the back of a horse, free as a bird. . . . Darrell rolls around and says, 'Hey, Feetie, you're twenty-two, time to get married.' And you know what? I did. Never thought I might say otherwise. Well, after two kids in two years, Montana is too crowded for Darrell. Imagine it. Montana, *crowded*. Suddenly, he can't *breathe*. We moved to Valdez— what?—nearly twenty years ago. Saw the ocean for the first time, learned to cut a fish. Two more kids. I'm thinking, well, we can build something here. Sure, make a home. But then Valdez got too crowded for Darrell."

Bean made a mental note. Val-DEEZ. Not the way you would say it in Spanish.

"Where's your husband now?"

"Beats me," Feetie said. "I mean, Jiminy, where do you go from here?"

Feetie swerved into an unpaved driveway and slammed on the brakes in a clearing. Three tiny trailers—bulbous, '50s models, with their rusted truck hitches sticking out—sat darkly before them.

Feetie stepped out of the van and tested a wood plank that stretched like a bridge over a mud puddle. She stuck her arms out, like a wire walker, and crossed slowly to the first Airstream trailer. Bean followed. The door was unlocked. Feetie squeezed aside, keeping her eyes on the plank, so Bean could enter. Bean sloughed her bags to the ground and stepped in. A mildew odor crept up her nostrils.

"There now," Feetie said, singing it. She pushed past Bean and tugged at some checkered curtains around the porthole window. "The school board pays for the trailer, but you're on your own for utilities." When she had taken in the smell, she made a vinegar face.

"Once you get settled, nothing you can't fix with a little Lysol, some air freshener," she said. "I think lilac is best, don't you? Heavens, the wildflowers we got in Montana." Feetie inhaled the memory, startled herself, then looked at her watch. She scurried off with a "jiminy" hanging in the air.

Bean clicked on the space heater, then sat on her bunk and pulled her knees up to her chest. The heater made the smell worse. She thought about lilacs. She sat still, feeling the room. She felt edgy, not right. Was the room too small? No, it was the silence, she decided. It was deafening. She sat there like a terrier, waiting to hear her master's keys in the door. Something. She had forgotten the sound of silence.

It was 4:30. She set her alarm for the next day, pushed aside the yellow comforter, and slid into bed.

Eyak Elementary was about the ugliest building Bean had ever seen. It sat on a denuded slope behind a field of river rocks instead of a lawn. The main building was a two-story box of corrugated white-gray metal that looked like it had been ferried over in prefab slabs and stapled together. Which it had been. But inside, the school was full of homey touches. A glass display case featured fishing flies the kids had made. Over that hung portraits of George and Abe. The auditorium was off to the right, with a huge mural map of the United States, and Eyak proudly marked by a star. The artist had sliced out Canada and pulled Alaska south, just like in the atlas. Eyak floated in the blue waters just west of Los Angeles, as if the Malibu wine sippers might view it from their decks. At the top of the staircase, there was another display case. It hosted a stuffed black bear, which was the size of a Great Pyrenees and had claws like the blades of a pocketknife.

Bean met all the teachers that first week. She tried to absorb their names and advice, but the introductions went right past her. They were big, solid people who spoke too loud, like when you used a cell phone. You could leave them out in any weather and they'd do all right. The women had big butts, which Bean secretly welcomed after all the anorexic types back home. There were only a few men. They seemed to go out of their way to look ridiculous to their students, sporting too-short pants, meticulous comb-overs, and furry ears and noses. They mostly kept clear of Bean, which suited her fine. But one math teacher, a beefy man who had lost the battle to tuck in his rumpled plaid shirt, shook Bean's hand and didn't let go. He held it up over her head, as if he expected her to pirouette. "Where's the rest of her?" he said. Then he sat down at the lunch table, pulled out a sandwich, and locked Bean in a wet, brown-eyed stare that made her want to crawl under the table.

Bean tended quietly to her lunch, but she was the news of the day. A chicken-necked teacher, who smelled like she was smoking even when she wasn't, sank into a chair across the table. She nudged the lady beside her, who just then was poking at something encased in Tupperware as if to make sure it was dead. Chicken Neck winked at Bean. "Pretty scary, huh?" she said. Her voice sounded like a toad burp. As if they were all pirates or snake handlers. Bean smiled wanly.

At the end of the table, another teacher—fifth grade, was it?— hadn't stopped talking since the break began. Something about a boy who was always trouble, chalk erasers, and Elmer's glue. Nobody was paying attention to her whiny ramble until she noticed Bean silently chewing her peanut butter and jelly sandwich and detected fresh material. "You know, dear, it's all right to have cabin fever at first"—a dramatic pause—"just be sure to take it out on the kids." Weary smiles all around.

At night, in her trailer, Bean struggled to come up with something to say at the lunch table—a story, an anecdote, anything to engage the others. The best thing would be to make them laugh, of course. They were always laughing at something. But she couldn't remember any jokes. Except silly ones that kids told each other. Big red rock-eater jokes. Hot cross bunny jokes. The baby in the blender. A really good joke grew out of the situation. You took something everybody was already talking about and made it funny.

The next day, as the sandwiches came out, she felt the thumping fear between her temples. She was going to speak up today if it killed her. It was raining. That affected everybody.

"Comin' down hard," someone said.

"Buckets," came a reply.

Now or never. Bean dove in.

"How long before I sprout gills?" she exclaimed.

The booming voice sounded foreign, even to her. Then: silence. Everyone looked away, as if she suddenly started to smell.

The chicken-necked teacher, Darleen, finally spoke.

"I hope you brought some good books, dear," she said. Bean could tell she was really talking to the others. "Now that we've seen you, we'll just let you be for a while. We'll check back in a bit, after you've had a chance to burrow in."

"Five years, that's the minimum," said the Tupperware-poker, who was auditioning to be Darleen's Ed McMahon.

"Five *winters*," Darleen corrected.

They chuckled like it was a practical joke that had to be played out. Bean smiled and looked at her hands. Then the talk turned to preparations for Sea Month, and Bean was forgotten. They ignored her. She sat in a way that would take up more space, took care to pack the same lunches that they did, nothing fancy. She groaned whenever anyone mentioned the superintendent and she bought her own art supplies at the Superette. But the conversations just eddied around her.

Sometimes when she walked into the lounge, they were all laughing and she felt the last giggles pop like soap bubbles. Darleen would wipe her eyes and change the subject. *They hate me*, Bean thought. *Or worse, they don't care.* The big-assed women and their Unabomber men. If only she'd made a better joke.

In her trailer at night, Bean cooked Campbell's soup on a hot plate and wondered if she would live that way till she died.

Jiminy, where do you go from here?

Bean started out substituting third grade for Rhonda Tatitlek. Rhonda was a short, 240-pound Native Alaskan with a leathery face and ink-hair she wore in braids, each as thick as a horse's tail. She had a heart condition that left her extremely weak most of the time. Rhonda blamed bad genes, but Bean suspected her diet of soda pop and frozen cinnamon rolls. When she wasn't teaching—which was most of the time—Rhonda spent her days propped up on pillows, surfing the soaps.

Rhonda lived in a two-room clapboard house near the gas station. You couldn't tell what color it was; the paint had long since cracked, curled, and fled. But inside it was tidy. Rhonda kept everything in reach of the daybed—the remote control, magazines, an impressive array of sweet snacks. She rested among her treasures like a queen bee.

"All I need is one of those little refrigerators," she said. "Then I wouldn't have to get up but to pee."

Rhonda's obesity fascinated Bean. She made a squishy noise when she walked and her arms hung out over the floor. Sometimes Bean looked up from the study plan to steal a peek at Rhonda's flabby elbow folds or wonder how she washed certain parts of her body. Bean's interest came from a nagging sense that if she wasn't careful with her own weight, she might one day be sharing Rhonda's minirefrigerator.

Rhonda and Bean worked out a system. Bean basically took over her class. Instead of notifying Bean when she was ill, Rhonda called her whenever she planned to go to work. Every couple of weeks, Rhonda felt the need to reassert her territory and Bean just waited her out, helping kids with their reading in the library. The principal was always begging Rhonda to take long-term disability. "No way, no how," she told Bean. "I guess they think I'm going to write my own pink slip. Ha. Ha. Ha."

Rhonda had her own sense of comic timing, and her staccato laugh shook the room.

Rhonda *knew* things. Eyakers would say almost anything in front of her, as if she were a chambermaid, or invisible. During commercials, she shared her intelligence with Bean. Take Darleen. Her husband was messing around with that massage lady in Seward and their fourteen-year-old daughter was pregnant by that deli kid.

"Which kid?" Bean asked.

"The one never washes his hands."

"Eeew," Bean said.

"Eeew is right," Rhonda said. "Spreads the mayo, pops a zit, says, 'Do you want a pickle with that?' Ha. Ha. Ha."

If it weren't for Rhonda, Bean would have had to wait for five years for such tidbits. Rhonda didn't care about those rules. As far as she was concerned, everyone but her own people were interlopers. Her people had *always* been in Eyak, and that, she reminded Bean, made the white folks nervous, especially when you were talking about fish. The salmon catch was regulated; if Natives demanded a greater share, the Feds were certain to take their side. And that meant cash from everyone else's pockets.

Bean liked teaching. She liked being around all the kids. She liked their goofiness. The way they never faked a smile. The way their heads were too big for their bodies, the way they turned their jackets into superhero capes, their delight in just chasing one another. The way they got tired after lunch and put their heads on their arms but kept their pencils upright. How different each of them was—the world hadn't stamped it out of them yet.

But they could be mean to one another, and even to Bean. One boy insisted on calling her "Miss Ketchup," because it rhymed with Jessup. The other kids found this hysterically funny. They raised their chubby arms: Miss Ketchup this and Miss Ketchup that. At first, Bean made a joke about "all you little hot dogs," but it got annoying.

And there was something else: their wide-open stares. They fixed their eyes on her like they were watching TV. It unsettled her. She felt that they were waiting for her to falter, to admit she was faking it— sure, with all her heart, but faking it nonetheless.

Bean's first winter felt like a lead overcoat. She waved good-bye as the third-graders rushed past the stuffed bear and trudged home in the gloom. She graded papers in the afternoon stillness for as long as she could stand it. As darkness fell, she gravitated to the classroom computer, a window to the outside world. She plucked keys idly at first, surfing the Web.

Some days, she plugged in her father's name—"Hank Jessup" and "Jessup, Henry W."—and watched the search engine spin. Once, it produced an advertisement from a community newspaper in Somerville, Massachusetts. Hank Jessup had received an award for selling the most insurance that month. But that was it. There wasn't even a picture. Even though she hadn't seen him in years, it bothered Bean that he had this new life that she wasn't a part of.

He used to call her Burt. She had insisted on it. When she was five or six, she declared that was her name and she wouldn't respond to anything else. It was when she was discovering the world around her, playing in puddles at Phoenix Lake and watching the herons fish for minnows. She came home caked in dirt and walked bowlegged into the kitchen for milk like a midget cowboy at the Black Oak Saloon.

If it was a Sunday, her father would be drinking beer in front of the TV. "Hiya, Burt," he'd say.

It drove her mother crazy. She'd drop the spoon against the pan of whatever she was stirring on the stove. She had a hard enough time calling her daughter Bean. Her real name was Celestine Josephine. And now this. "Hank," she said. Sharp, like the rest of the fight had already been fought.

After school, Bean walked back to her trailer in the dark with a squeezed-up heart. She bought a small used television and left it on for company. She watched reruns over and over and came to think of the actors as friends. She copied the more cheerful teachers who checked out novels from the library—thick paperbacks with flowers and busty women on the cover—but after a dozen pages, she gave up on the phony stories, and the books sat around the trailer, facedown, spines breaking.

She found herself looking forward to Saturday, when she could sleep all day. But by Saturday evening, disgusted with herself, she pulled out a notebook and drew up a list to keep her busy on Sunday: get up, laundry, groceries, swim, lesson plans. As the winter yawned on, the list shrank. Get up, laundry, lesson plans. After a while, she put the notebook away.

One stormy Saturday she phoned Jimmy, her oldest friend, in San Francisco. As soon as he answered, she had to tell herself not to cry.

"What's that racket?" he said.

"It's raining," Bean said.

"What?"

"It's *raining*."

"It sounds like you're trapped inside a snare drum."

"Yeah," Bean said. She tried not to gulp. "It feels that way, too."

They stopped talking and just listened to the rain for a moment.

"So, what's it like—all that *nature* everywhere?" Jimmy asked. "You livin' large?"

Bean looked across her trailer. A row of soup cans sat on the ledge above the sink, which was too small to clean a pot in. The space between the bed and the doorway was so tight, you had to be careful when you put on your jeans in the morning, or you'd tumble. There was a patch of blackish mold developing beneath the porthole window. She rubbed at it with a paper towel and some Windex.

"I just want a hot bath, is all," she said.

Jimmy knew his duty was to be upbeat.

"Seen any wild animals?"

"Well, there's this bear at school. He's dead though, stuffed."

"I dated a bear once," Jimmy said. "Same thing."

Jimmy had a way of getting his gayness into everything. Bean didn't care. It was just part of their palaver. They shouted over the rain a while longer until they both sounded drained. Bean assured Jimmy that she had not yet met a lumberjack.

"So, are you going to make it?" he asked.

Bean stopped scrubbing the mold. It wasn't doing any good.

"I don't know," she said. "How do you know if you're going to make it?"

"You're asking the wrong guy."

Jimmy had lost dozens of friends to AIDS in the past several years and was too spooked to get tested himself. He was dating a new guy, Peter, who was pushing him hard to take the test.

The rain stopped.

"Ahh," Bean said.

"Hey, Bean, whatever happens, you know, there's nothing wrong with you."

But it didn't feel that way, right then, in a trailer in a mudfield. It felt like plenty was wrong. And she had no one to blame but herself. She'd put herself there. That was the kicker.

"I guess," she said.

"I mean, hey, you rescued me," Jimmy said. "That's got to count for something."

Bean felt her breath catch. It was true: when Jimmy was lost, she had found him. It seemed so long ago. Now she felt herself adrift, and she doubted whether Jimmy or anyone else could return the favor.

Sleep was the hardest part. Falling asleep. Staying there. Bean had always wrestled insomnia. Often she thrashed all night, sometimes battling dreams. In college one of her roommates glimpsed her bed and demanded, "Who won? You or the wolverine?" Now the short days tricked her. She slept late on a Saturday and found herself drinking coffee at dusk. On school nights she'd doze off at about eight o'clock, then awaken with a start at midnight, with the lights and TV still on. Then the long vigil began.

She eventually found a book she liked in the town's lone bookstore: *The Pemberton Guide to Alaska's Birds.* It was full of paintings and photos and little essays about birds. There were hundreds of them, shorebirds, seabirds, songbirds, many of them migrants from as far away as New Zealand and Argentina. Bean liked to read about the birds that came to Alaska, their dances and appetites, their prey and nesting habits. She felt a kinship with them, and thrilled whenever she spotted a new one around town. The long-distance fliers charmed her especially. She thought about them, a few ounces of muscle, flapping dozens of times a minute, crisscrossing the globe, thousands of miles home to the same rocky ledge. On long nights Bean read a paragraph or two of the *Pemberton Guide,* then she dozed, almost magically. Her hand would slip and the book with its cover photo of an Arctic tern would rise and fall on her chest.

———

By the time school let out that first June, Bean had made some ad-justments. Her skin bore no trace of a California tan. She drank hard liquor. She had stopped watching the news. She was smoking again. All these things changed, but Bean knew she was still an outsider. She wasn't an Alaskan yet. An Alaskan was someone who took it and liked it.

Lois was her only friend. They met at Sheila's Hair Flair on First Street. Bean had dropped in, looking to have her split ends trimmed, nothing dramatic. She climbed tentatively into the swivel chair in front of the bulb-ringed mirror, when a tall, frizzy-haired woman unfurled a plastic smock and cracked it with a matador's flourish. Then she snapped it to Bean's neck.

"So what are you thinkin', hon? An Apache cut?" Lois held Bean's wet head by her fingertips as if it might roll off her shoulders.

"If you think it would help," Bean said.

"Well, let's start out conservative, and see where things go. You don't want to shock the hell out of this town all at once, you being new and all," Lois said. She pointed the scissors at the shelves in front of Bean's knees. An arsenal of gels and mousses, tints and wraps. "Now maybe after a few weeks, you might want to take a look into my bag of tricks."

Lois took forever to cut Bean's hair. She needed her hands to talk, and her scissors happened to be in her hands. Every time Lois had a point to make, she met Bean's eye in the mirror and flipped open the palm of her hand.

"And so I go, 'Thanks, honey. But it's going to take another round to make *you* good-looking.' " Lois had met some guy the other night. "And you know what? It did."

Bean blinked quickly as the scissors came round. Except for worrying about her eyesight, she was pretty content in the hands of this woman. Someone who didn't care how long she'd been there or where she'd come from. No probation.

Lois's boss was Sheila, a white-blonde, looking hard at fifty, with a taste for leopard spots and tiger stripes. Sheila would saunter into the shop late, and Lois would accuse her of having a "freshly fucked look." Sheila just laughed a croaky laugh. She was one of the few women who didn't mind Lois being Lois.

Despite her jungle outfits, Sheila was a businesswoman who was steadily expanding her empire. In just a few months, Bean had watched the salon morph into Sheila's Hair Flair, Frogurt, and Expresso to Go. "If you don't move forward, you die," Sheila announced one day. "It's like with sharks." Her latest sign, which she affixed with care so as not to scratch her newly painted nails, promoted hair wraps ("for a little something different"), facial waxing ("We don't have to put up with all those problems"), scalp treatments, manicures, ear piercing, and paraffin wax. Discounts for seniors and Coast Guard personnel.

Lois hated the sidelines. She was, after all, a professional. Twenty times a day she had to put down her scissors and become an "ice cream jerk," as she put it. Sheila tried to get her to put on a hat when she worked the frogurt machine, but Lois threatened to quit. As it was, all the swirling and spooning disrupted her concentration. She had already burned Nancy Keating's scalp while messing with jimmies and Heath bars for some girl. There were too many flavors, Lois said; women turned into complete idiots when you gave them a choice.

Lois was afraid of the espresso machine. All that hot steam and sputtering; she refused to touch it. "That thing's gonna blow one of these days, and it won't be pretty," she said. When Sheila wasn't around, she told people it was broken.

But Bean loved all the diversions. Sometimes, on a weekend, she'd sit with a magazine even when she didn't need a cut. Just spend an hour there, listening to Lois and Sheila parry, eating peanut butter swirl. It was a privileged perch—her seat at the Hair Flair—which she could enjoy as long as there wasn't a line. Half the town came through the door.

One rain-soaked Saturday, with no one around, Lois convinced Bean to work the cannery for the summer. The money was decent and Bean had no plans for a vacation, anyway. She quickly agreed. Lois talked to Fat Al, and they started on the slime line mid-June.

Locals usually shunned the canneries. They said there were easier ways to make a buck. Almost all the workers were foreign migrants, college kids, or Natives. But Lois made her own rules, always had, ever since the Coast Guard had transferred her father to Eyak a decade earlier. She said all that summer light was good for one thing, and you couldn't fuck all the time. So she gutted fish, and Bean did, too.

On their days off they pulled out a few big bills and went to the Alaskan Bar. It was a popular drinking hole for fishermen, and had a long burnished bar and a shuffleboard table. Upstairs there were ratty rooms for rent. When the salmon were running, the rooms were usually filled with crewmen between jobs or waiting on net repairs. Lois said she wouldn't go upstairs at the Alaskan unless she was really wasted.

Lois usually ordered a Diet Coke with Black Velvet, and Bean would make it two. Then they settled on bar stools and watched their effect on the men in the room, who outnumbered women four to one. Lois was a thrilling companion. She laughed too loud and always had a new story, even though she talked to Bean all the time. When guys came over to try their luck, Lois knew how to push them away and make them laugh at the same time. "Doll, you're making my *skin* crawl," she told one drunken suitor. She said it with a big smile. Lois also knew how to hook the ones she wanted. The women at the Alaskan kept their distance. They didn't like Lois, and they didn't like their men around her, either.

The way Lois explained it, single women in Eyak had two choices. They could hit the bars Saturday night, or they could do the church thing on Sunday. The town was split pretty evenly as far as that went. There were five liquor stores and three bars in town, and there were eight churches. It was a town in equilibrium, though anybody could see that the men chose the bars more and let their women pray for them. Bean wasn't much of a drinker. On the other hand, she hadn't been to church since she was a little girl. She chose Lois.

Sometimes she wondered what Lois saw in her. But Alaska was full of unlikely pairings—friends and lovers. Old guys with drooping pants and stained caps with pliable young women. Recycled husbands courting recycled wives. Friends who would have spurned each other in high school anywhere else in America. It wasn't so much choice as practicality. The winters were long and dark.

One night at the bar Lois told her about the annual footrace.

"Men in shorts," Lois gushed. She fanned her face with her hand and stroked her throat. Lois liked everything about men. She didn't even care if they smelled or had hair on their backs. "I'm only flesh and blood," she said.

The footrace was an Eyak tradition to celebrate the end of the salmon run. Bean decided to go because you went to everything in a town as small as Eyak. Something funny or unpredictable might happen and you would be hearing about it for weeks, so you might as well see it with your own eyes. Eyakers loved surprises; life changed little enough. When a bear wandered into one of their backyards, they didn't run for their guns, they fetched their videocameras and called their friends on cell phones. "I swear to God, he's here, right here, lickin' at the dog dish."

Two months after Bean started teaching, there had been a tsunami warning. The police drove around announcing it over loudspeakers. Bean wasn't sure what a tsunami was, but when some of the kids started shouting, "Tidal wave! Tidal wave!" she ducked out of class and raced down to the principal's office. *Ohmygod.* Was there an evacuation plan? But the office was empty, and so were some of the classrooms. Everyone had headed down to the docks for a closer look.

The Arctic Tern woos his mate by proving that he is a good provider. During courtship, he swoops past a female on the ground with a fish ostentatiously secured in his bill. If intrigued, she joins him on this fluttering "fish flight."

—The Pemberton Guide

*I*n the end, nothing surprising happened in the footrace—both blue ribbons for men and women went to kids from out of town who worked the canneries. The locals weren't much competition. The fishermen didn't go in for jogging. They claimed they got enough exercise loading and off-loading their boats. From the looks of them, they were dreaming.

After the race Lois headed over to the Hair Flair, and Bean found herself leaning against the hood of a truck, talking to a guy named Mick. He had messy dark hair, intense brown eyes, and lean, muscular legs. She couldn't tell if he was local. He was clearly feeling good about finishing toward the front.

"I guess you'd have to say I was the slowest of the fast guys," he said.

"Or the fastest slow guy," Bean said. There, a joke.

He smiled crookedly. "Ouch," he said. He had just walked up to Bean, wiped the back of his neck with a wadded-up T-shirt, and started talking, as if they were already in the middle of a conversation. As if they knew each other.

There was a long pause. Bean felt a strong desire to keep the conversation going. *Say anything.*

"I hate running," she said.

Another half smile from Mick. "You know, the truth is, so do I," he said. "It's murder on the knees. I don't know, maybe I walk wrong. I get this shooting pain sometimes. I listen to these guys talk about the runner's high and I keep wondering when it's going to happen to me."

This guy was a world-class talker. He got so excited; it was like watching electricity being made.

"But you know what I figured out? It's not about winning the race, or even the high. I know that sounds corny. But it's about putting one foot before the other. Never mind the pain. Or feel it, but don't let it stop you. You run into it until you hit the wall. Then it's just: Hang on, Snoopy."

Bean leaned against the truck, trying to look cool. She understood stubborn, if that's what he was getting at. All her life, people had told her she was stubborn; now someone had turned it into a policy. After a while she had stopped listening to this man—how old? late twenties?—and was taking him in through her pores. It was like watching TV with the sound off. She noticed the V of sweat expanding down the front of his ripped-sleeve sweatshirt. No ring on his left hand. The hair on his legs was slick with sweat. He wasn't that good-looking, but she was having a hard time meeting his eyes. It felt like if she held his gaze, he might see too much of her.

He had stopped talking.

"Sloopy," Bean said.

"What?"

"The song. I think it's 'Hang On, Sloopy.' "

He looked at her like she was nuts.

"If you say so," he said.

She was losing ground. She asked him if he was a fisherman.

"Yeah, I'm crewing a tender this summer," he said. "The rest of the time, I'm a carpenter. At least, that's the goal."

"Oh," Bean said. Why was she so edgy? Now what?

"Jesus was a carpenter," she said. *Ugh.*

Mick leaned toward her, and she felt her heart speed up. His voice turned confidential. "If you want to know the truth, I'm still learning. This table I've been working on since March? I don't know what happened. Spent a hundred bucks on the wood alone. Measured twice, cut once. Only . . ."

He ran his fingers through his dark hair, still oily from the race. Bean felt the urge to do the same thing.

"Only what?"

"It *wobbles,*" Mick said.

She could see it still bothered him. An impulse to make him feel better.

"At least you know when you mess up," she said. "Teaching kids, you never know a thing until it's too late. They do research on Hannibal Lecter and find out he got an A in your class."

She confessed that she was having a hard time breaking in with the teachers. He wiped the sweat off his forehead, kicked his running shoes into the asphalt.

"Folks here are damn misers with their kindness," he said.

It turned out he was from Vancouver, born in St. Louis. Still breaking in himself, after five years in Eyak. "People are waiting to see how you handle a few things," he said.

"Like what?"

"Winters, mostly. The dark. The isolation. They don't want to waste any favors on you."

"They want to wait and see if I wobble?" Bean asked.

A full grin. His teeth were unbelievably white. Like they were fake, or he used them only when drinking milk.

"Exactly," he said.

Bean said nobody gave her more than four words at the lunch table. She had tried to start conversations about the most banal things: food, weather.

Mick's face soured. "What did you say about the weather?" he asked.

"Just what everyone else said," Bean replied. "You know, how awful all the rain is."

Mick grabbed his ribs as if jabbed by a knife. "Suicide," he moaned. "Don't you see? It's not *your* weather. Not yet, anyway."

He wanted to be outside all the time. He invited Bean for hikes in the woods. They sat in a field of wildflowers and watched the bald eagles come home. One Sunday morning he called to say that a friend had lent him a boat. Bean raced around her trailer getting ready. She had already grown used to a dripping nose and knuckles scraped raw from cold. Now she stood at the sink and slapped mosquito repellent on her skin like toilet water.

She arrived at the dock with binoculars dangling from her neck and the *Pemberton Guide* stuffed into her slicker. Mick took over the wheel, and they set out. He sniffed in Alaska through gigantic nostrils. She scanned the islands for birds. Some cormorants, lots of pintails and shearwaters.

She lowered the binoculars and pushed the hair out of her face. The boat creaked. The air was salty. "Lovely," she declared. She realized that wasn't her word; it belonged to Mrs. Harper, her third-grade teacher, who had given her so much.

With the sun glinting on the water, she returned to Mrs. Harper's classroom at Old Mill School, next to the milk room where the teachers' pets loaded up the small orange cartons for lunch.

There were some ordinary signs of third grade behind the oak door with its stenciled number 7: the cursive alphabet strung along the walls, the lined green chalkboard, the high windows that were opened with a ten-foot pole. The children's desks sat in five rows, each with a glossy pressed-wood top that squeaked deliciously on the hinge, and chairs attached, where their fathers sat pinned like Gullivers on parent-teacher night.

In Mrs. Harper's habitat, you might not see her at first. She was small, fine-boned, and gray and usually surrounded by a huddle of children.

But you could hear her. She would inspect the latest specimen brought into class, a mollusk, say. When the mollusk flinched, or blanched or excreted or burped, she would throw her head back and exclaim, "Oh my heavens, yes!"

She dressed for action: knit sweaters, pedal pushers, Keds, and glasses draped from a chain around her neck. On days when there was no field trip, she dispatched her students into the unknown corners of suburbia—its creeks and canyons, the puddles and woodpiles. The next day Bean and her classmates offered up their treasures: Indian arrowheads, rattlesnake skins, deer antlers, spit bugs, abalone shells, daddy longlegs in jars with holes poked in the lid, polliwogs in various stages of evolution. They did it because Mrs. Harper would raise her half glasses and thrill to nature's cleverness, and by extension, their own. "Will you just look at that!"

Mrs. Harper was especially partial to birds. In the spring, she passed out construction paper and blunt red scissors and the classroom became a paper aviary. The real-life specimens showed up first thing in the morning, during home room. Usually, they were in trouble. A blue jay that crashed into the living-room window, a robin that ran afoul of a torturing cat, even a feathered lump that met the grill of a Ford LTD—these casualties were evacuated in shoe boxes and Baggies to

Room 7. Mrs. Harper would examine them and give the coroner's verdict. "Poor thing broke its neck," she'd say.

One day Rolfie Ferron, who lived in the part of town that always flooded when it rained, walked in with a shoe box and a triumphant look. Bean and the others crowded around Mrs. Harper as she lifted the lid. There was a nest inside, all soft grass, perfectly shaped. But it emitted a peeping noise. Rolfie reached in and with his fat thumbs pulled the nest half open. Inside were two babies, each no bigger than a pinkie, all purply with their eyes sealed shut, tiny beaks open.

Bean looked at Mrs. Harper—surely this was the best discovery ever.

But her teacher's mouth shaped an O of horror, and her eyes flashed. How could Rolfie do that? Hadn't he learned a thing? Once intruders touch a nest, the birds' mother will never return.

Rolfie dropped his chin, his prized show-and-tell a disaster. The rest of the children were silent. Bean knew she had just learned something important. But she didn't know whether to feel sorrier for Rolfie or for the motherless birds.

"Hey, Bean, what's the big one?" Mick was shouting over the boat's engine.

"What?" she said.

"The big one," he said, pointing overhead. "Up there."

She picked up her binoculars. He'd probably spotted a fat gull. Mick didn't know anything about birds. She looked at the patch of sky overhead and squinted. She saw a silhouette the size of a goose, but the wings—those narrow wings—seemed to stretch forever. The bird hung in the sky, effortlessly, scarcely moving at all. Marvelous.

"It's an albatross," she said. "A short-tail, I think. God, those are so rare. There's only, like, four hundred left in the world."

"What happened to them?"

"People hunted them for their feathers."

Her guide was in her pocket. She knew it all by heart. She felt Mick's eyes on her. He looked at her like he was thinking about buying something. She went on.

"They're the biggest, best fliers there are. They're so good at gliding, they can sleep in the sky. With the right winds, they can go for months."

"What's he doing?"

She studied the hovering bird—mighty enough to circle the globe without rest, yet on the brink of extinction.

"He's following us," Bean whispered. And for some reason, she felt like crying.

That evening Mick asked Bean to his house for dinner. She sat on the couch and talked to him as he broiled fish in the kitchen. When he finally emerged, he took forever to sit, like a dog spinning three times before lying down. She patted the space beside her and he finally settled in with a grunt, as if all that softness were painful. Then he put his arm around her and she leaned into him.

After dinner she walked back to her trailer alone. Mick had offered to join her, but she didn't want him to spoil her feelings about him by having him there. She walked down the middle of the dusky road. The summer nights were almost over, and she could see stars battling against the lingering light.

So this is how it feels. This was what they sang about on the radio. Funny how it seeped into your body. It didn't hit you in the head like an anvil. It oozed. It went on cool, like cream for muscle aches, then warmed and soothed more each minute. Once you felt it, you didn't want it to stop.

The night was still. She heard a loon cry. A swarm of mosquitoes tested her face but found it properly oiled and flew away. The giant evergreens on either side of the road stood like sentries. Around the bend, her little trailer awaited, with its reading light and the yellow comforter on the bed.

She had a secret—and not a bad one. All her life she had been on the sidelines. Tonight she was the main event. She was almost afraid to say it, but she knew she would explode if she didn't.

I'm saved.

Slowly, sweetly, Mick oiled her life.

He told her she had beautiful eyes and began to call her Little Blue. She loved him for giving her a nickname. He didn't say it a lot, but that only made her listen for it more.

When life's chores flummoxed Bean, Mick was there. Not that she was incompetent. It was impatience, really. Or maybe she was missing a gene. But small tasks stymied her, made her late, drove her crazy. The toaster had a mind of its own. Turtlenecks were made for people with tiny heads. The zipper got stuck in her jacket.

If it jammed, she forced it. If it didn't fit, she crammed it in. She opened jars the hard way, pounding the lid on the side of the counter to loosen them. She ignored the tabs on the cereal box and ripped off the top. She never balanced her checkbook, a red sock left in the washer turned her underwear pink, and she grinded the gears on Mick's truck. Most of the time Mick interceded gently. "No Beanie," he'd instruct. "Like this."

Sometimes she wondered if Mick stayed close because she was pathetic. Like in the magazines where "you can save this child for two cents a month, or you can turn the page." But Mick told her there was something about her that the other girls didn't have.

"What do you mean?" she demanded.

"You know how the Eskimos make jerky? Hanging out the seal strips on the line?" Mick said. "Eyak girls are like that. *Chewy.*"

"Chewy?"

"They put up a good fight. You're different."

Bean had spent her whole life trying not to be different.

"I can be tough," she said.

"Sure you can," he said. "But there's also something about you. . . ."

"What?"

"I dunno," he said, putting his arms around her. "It's like I want to roll you up in bubble wrap."

At school Bean arranged her first field trip. They would visit the Chitna River and watch the last of the salmon spawn. The kids were squirmy and excited about getting out of class, so she spent part of the morning reading to them while waiting for the bus driver to show up.

The children sat in the corner, facing Bean in her chair. They hugged themselves and their mouths dropped open as she read a story about a magical boy.

One of them stuck his hand in the air. Bean closed the book but kept her finger in it.

"Yes, Willie?"

"Are there, um, really wizards and sorcerers?"

"What do *you* think?" Bean said.

"I think . . ." He looked around at the other kids for support. "I think maybe."

Another boy protested. He was a Coast Guard kid. Three schools by third grade. "No way," he said. "It's make-believe. My dad says we should be reading about real things."

"Like what?" Bean asked.

The boy shrugged.

There was silence.

Then Wendy Rieger spoke up. She had a way of spitting when she talked, which she did rarely enough, because the kids covered their faces whenever she opened her mouth.

"I *like* reading about magic," Wendy said.

A couple of other kids murmured, "Me, too."

Bean rested the book on her knee. "If you were magic, what would you do?" she asked.

A crop of hands. "I'd fly to school," one boy said.

"If you were magic, you wouldn't have to *go* to school," the Coast Guard kid declared. "You could just *make* yourself smart."

Another boy, Petie, raised his hand as if he had to make an urgent trip to the rest room.

"Yes, Petie?" Bean said.

"If I were magic, I'd make every day Saturday—for the cartoons."

"Plus, there's no school on Saturday," another chimed in.

"Yaaay," the kids shouted.

Bean suppressed a smile. Once you got used to it, the children's honesty was disarming.

She raised her palms to quiet them. "Would anybody use their magic to make sure everyone had enough to eat?"

"Yaaay," the kids chorused.

"And to end all the wars?"

"Yaaay." Those were good ideas, too.

Bean glanced at the clock—where the hell was the bus driver?—then she noticed Mick leaning against the doorway, like he'd been there for quite a while. He had a clump of blue and white flowers in his hands.

"Miss Jessup, who's he?" one of the kids asked.

Mick's face was all beamy. Bean was glad she was sitting down because his expression made her feel off balance. Exposed, even.

The kids had to ruin it, of course. They saw the flowers and made smoochy noises.

In the hallway Mick explained that the bus driver, Larry Segal, was unable to make the trip. Larry was pretty good about keeping sober during the week, but he'd run into Lois at the Alaskan the night before and, well, just *seeing* her knocked him off the wagon. He had it bad for Lois. She had smiled at him across the crowded bar. He nodded, swallowed hard, and leaned over the bar to change his order. He slipped out the back door with a fifth of whiskey in a bag. That morning he had called up Mick with a fuzzy tongue and asked a favor.

Bean felt her field trip collapsing. All the permission slips had been signed, there were rangers waiting for them at Chitna, other teachers had adjusted their lessons. Then Mick offered to drive. "Sure, I'll take you," he said.

It was illegal as hell, of course. But it didn't take Mick long to figure out the yellow bus, which was more or less like the old milk truck he drove. The kids didn't care. At Chitna, the rangers explained the spawning process and the kids pointed at the leaping fish.

When they got back to the bus, Mick picked up the wildflowers from the driver's seat and handed them to Bean. Forget-me-nots.

They started having sex two and a half weeks after they met. Mick was playful and in no hurry. He had a mat of dark hair on his chest and a belly button that stuck out. The first time, they were on the couch at his house on a dark Sunday afternoon. He licked her nipples and she was warm. Not hot, but not cold. Warm wasn't bad. Later, when he released, she felt a surge of relief.

Sex was complicated for Bean. Sometimes just thinking about it made her weary—and a little sad. It was something that happened to other people—evidently, a *lot* of people. But for Bean it came wrapped in self-doubt.

When she was little, the boys and girls had divided up into their assigned genders, like teams. By the time she noticed, she was stranded in no-man's-land. She was a tree-climbing tomboy named Burt.

She shared her neutral turf with Jimmy, who early on had taken to raiding his mother's closet for clothes. He slipped into a housedress, turned a bath towel into a glamorous turban, and introduced himself as Ruthie. Burt and Ruthie stuck together. They played house. Their dramas focused on making dinner. They put in lots of fights, to make it real.

The years passed, and, one by one, the girls at school got their periods, sprouted breasts, and went boy crazy. Bean sat quietly at the lunch table—as they percolated with news and longing over the latest "TF," or total fox. Sometimes she took her lunch to the library and ate alone.

Her mother kept trying to have a little talk with her about what it would mean—to become a woman. She turned conspiratorial and gave a worldly smile. "You know, Bean," she said, "it's one of life's great mysteries." Whenever Bean felt the little talk headed her way, she either left the room or went catatonic. She might never need it.

A few months before her sixteenth birthday, it finally happened. She was so relieved when the blood finally appeared in her underpants. But by then, her face had erupted in zits and her thighs made rubbing noises when she walked. The mystery of life came with a hideous price tag.

She first had sex in a college dorm room with a guy from biology. He left his textbook open on his desk and climbed on top of her. From where Bean lay on the bed, she glimpsed the page that listed the functions of the cell. They had a test the next day. There were eleven functions in all.

Reproduction. Egestion. Movement . . .

Most of the time, she tried to put sex out of her mind. But it would not be ignored. It was the engine for human relationships. Everybody was looking for it all the time. No sex, no love. You spurned sex and you set out on a long, lonely march—sitting alone at the movies, ordering take-out meals, saving your laundry for Saturday night, and cursing the smugness of all the couples around you.

Some people exuded sex. Take Lois. The way she blew on her coffee and licked her lips. How she wiped away her bangs so you could see her face. The way she *smoked*. My God. Lois with a cigarette was positively X-rated. At the Alaskan one night, Bean came back from the rest room to find Lois on a barstool, telling a story, surrounded by guys, with a cancer stick in her hand. She left it unlit, putting off the moment of truth—as if she were teasing some guy's dick—waiting, waiting. Then she put up her hand, just before the best part. "And so I say, 'Get a load of you,' " she said. "And he looks at me real hard, and he says, 'Anytime, baby.' " And then, literally in a flash, her cigarette was ignited, and Lois heaved the nicotine into her chest, her face wincing with satisfaction.

The whole dance made Bean feel edgy. Sometimes, lying there with Mick, she just pretended. She wanted to love him, of course. She wanted to make him swallow just to look at her. She wanted to transport him to that rolly, next world after a man explodes the sticky stuff and turns sweet and philosophical. That's what couples did for each other. That would be normal.

One night she was totally dry but she just let him go on. After he pulled out, he noticed a small stain on the sheet.

"What the fu—— Are you *bleeding*?" he said.

Bean's heart pounded. She felt a sob coming on.

"Is it your period?" He was waiting.

"Bean, talk to me." Stern, now.

"It's okay," she whispered. She turned on her side, her back to him, and tried not to cry. She failed. "It's okay."

"The fuck it's okay, Bean," he shouted. "The fuck it is." He was somewhere between concern and anger. *Stay on my side*, Bean thought. *Don't leave me.*

But he was worked up, propped on his knees, naked in bed.

"I'll tell you why it's not okay, Bean. I mean, Jesus, apart from hurting you," he said. "It's like you made me a *rapist*, for chrissakes."

"I'm sorry," Bean said.

"So what is it?" Mick said. "I mean, what do you want?"

Bean shot a glance at the closed door. *I want to get out of here.* He was looking into her face in that X-ray way of his. She felt ashamed. She couldn't talk about it.

Maybe her mother had been right. Maybe she should have been more of a girl, worn all those puffy-sleeved shirts and pleated skirts her mother was always fighting for. *Cross your legs. Be ladylike.*

Maybe that time with Ronnie Romano had messed her up when she was ten. Maybe it was because she got her period so late. Whatever it was, sex felt a lot like staring at the sun.

Before Mick's penetrating glare, she tried to tell him these things.

"I think . . . I might . . . be broken," she said.

The rest of her life with Mick was so good. They had started to talk of a future together. He did most of the talking, being Mick.

She had learned some of his secrets. How badly he wanted to fit in in Alaska. How he tried so hard at everything, with few natural talents. How he kept such a tight rein on what he ate. She knew his radio code name for fishing. She knew his father was dead and his mother was practically a stranger.

She witnessed how this high-voltage man could shut down, like with the flick of a switch, and fall asleep, sitting up. He had rested his arm on her shoulder, as if seeking the reassurance of a touch, and he smelled like the sea.

One morning she leaned back against the pillow in the crook of his arm, watched a branch rub against the window, and listened as Mick spun out a picture.

"I think Mudhole will sell his license to me. I really think he might. Then, with a couple of good seasons, I could put something down on a boat. And before you know it, I'm out there doing it, Bean. Me and Mick Jr., we're pulling in the big haul."

"What makes you think we'd have a boy?" Bean said.

"Well, it's my dream, so I get to say."

Bean closed her eyes. He was eager for children, but that was a conversation she had so far managed to avoid. But this morning, with this light, that branch, this man, she told him they could have a daughter, too. She would have curly hair, and you would smile just to look at her, droopy pants and all. And they would sit on rocking chairs on a big wraparound porch and watch her play.

"Could you do that—build a porch, in case our house didn't have one?" she asked.

"Sure, I could," Mick said. "Build you a whole house, if you want."

Everything was possible. She loved him for his confidence.

With Mick at her side, she was going to be with the winners. She would shed a past of sitting alone in the cafeteria. She would not be sad or pathetic or lonely again. A spot had been reserved for her at the table, and she would claim it.

In early spring, after seven months, they decided to move in together. His house was the only option. It was small, but compared with her trailer, it was a palace. She was grateful to leave the mildew behind.

Mick's place was near the top of the hill above Second Street. It was bleached wood with orange and green trim, with an old hemlock tree in front. The yard was green ferns corralled by a fence that shed its pickets. There was a living room and galley kitchen downstairs, a single bedroom upstairs, and a deck in back.

While she was packing up her trailer, she called Jimmy in San Francisco. She felt like someone was daring her to be happy. "I'm doing it," she said.

"Wow," Jimmy said. "It's like that time you jumped into the cesspool."

When she was six, a bunch of neighborhood kids had gathered around a pit where crews were putting in a new sewage system. It was a hot summer day and they were bored. Most of them were older than Bean, except for Jimmy, who was exactly a month and a day younger.

The pit wasn't very big—the size of a small swimming pool. It had filled up with dark green brackish water and let off quite a stench.

The talk turned to whether any of them would jump in for a hundred dollars.

"A hundred dollars?" said one of the kids. "No way. Maybe a *million.*"

"How deep is it?"

"What are those things floating on top?"

"I'd do it for a thousand," an older kid said. "Sure I would."

"That's some weird disease floating on top there."

Bean peered over into the cesspool. It was just water and sludge. She was a good swimmer. All that stuff would wash off.

"A hundred dollars is way too high," she said.

The kids looked at her. She usually didn't say much. She usually just followed along.

"All right, Bean, let's see you do it for free." The other big kids got in the act. "Come on, I dare you." And: "I bet you're too chicken."

Jimmy had screamed when she jumped in. The water was warm and thick and she had to struggle to stay up with all her clothes on. Her shoes pulled her down. She hadn't counted on that. They filled up with water and it was like having rocks tied to your feet. She thrashed around a while and swallowed some sludge. The kids stood on the edge of the dig, laughing and cheering. Jimmy had his hand clamped over his mouth.

Finally, Bean kicked off her shoes and made it to the side. She pulled herself out, hitched up her jeans, every inch of her slime-caked and proud.

She walked home barefoot and the kids followed her, even the older ones. It was a sign of respect, she figured. But then they started talking about seeing her catch hell. Either way, they all scattered when Bean's mother stepped outside and took a look at her. Under her mother's glare, Bean's pride dripped onto the ground.

"Hank," her mother shouted. "Hank!"

Bean's father hosed her down, and waited for her to shower. Then he sat down next to her on her twin bed.

"Well, Burt, you've had a full day." They always talked to each other like they were eighty-year-old men. Lots of sighs and head nodding and talking about their lumbago and gout. It was the Burt and Hank Show.

"Yeah," Bean said. She stuck a finger in her ear and pulled out some goop. She wasn't sure what was coming. Bean's mother wanted punishment, and they both knew she would be listening for it from downstairs. The last thing Bean wanted was for them to go at it over her.

Would he spank her? That would break her heart. They sat side by side on the bed, looking at the wall for a while. She smelled beer on him. It was his smell.

"So, what were you thinking?" he asked.

"They dared me. They said I was chicken."

"Well, is that a good reason to do something?"

Bean shrugged. She knew the correct answer was no.

"It's just that . . ."

"Just what?" he said.

"I *was* chicken. The water was dark and there were things floating in it."

"So what came over you?"

"I thought about jumping my shadow."

Hank turned and looked at her face.

"You know," she said. "Like you told me."

Bean felt the ground firming up beneath her. He *had* told her that, more than once: Jump your shadow, Burt, it's the only way when you're scared.

Hank nodded a few times and sucked in his cheeks. Then he slapped his knees and stood up. It made Bean jump a little. At the doorway he turned. He was handsome even after a day and some beers. They could hear the stovetop fan whirring in the kitchen downstairs.

At last, he spoke. "Um, Burt, just do me this favor. Don't swim in the sewer anymore. It's too hard on your mother."

"Okay," she said.

The more time she spent with Mick, the more she saw Alaska through his eyes. He saw only its possibilities. The clean air, the untrammeled wilderness. He didn't seem to notice that so many other settlers had washed up in Alaska after their lives crashed. Most of them had fled something—bad marriages, taxes, the cops. Mick had left his share of trouble behind—a mother and sister in Vancouver who fought a lot and deserved each other. But coming into the country was not a defeat for Mick. It was an adventure, and Bean felt drawn into his game.

One evening they were walking back from pizza at Emilio's.

"Makes you want to whistle, doesn't it?" he said.

"What does?"

He opened his hand to First Street, the tidy houses, the Superette, the churches.

"It's Mayberry, Bean."

Bean had to agree; Eyak was the last American small town. "Who are we, then?" she asked.

"I'm Andy," he said. "You got a choice—Barney or Opie."

"Oh great," Bean said.

Little by little, he decoded the town for her. She could throw away her house keys, he said; nobody bothered with locks. "It's easy to trust when you can run down a thief at the ferry dock," he said. Phone numbers came in four digits because everyone already knew the prefix, never mind the area code. There were more banks (one) than traffic lights (none). Eyakers drove their cars fast, like bats after bugs, even though you could circle the whole town in ten minutes.

He brought home the weekly newspaper, and Bean made a habit of reading all twelve pages, from news to ads. The personals grabbed her. One had run for weeks. "Dottie," it said, "I will always love you. Please come home. Frank." Bean didn't know the sad story of Dottie and Frank, but every week she located the ad in the *Eyak Times*.

Some days she read the paper for the typos; it was edited by a harried Greek journalist who didn't have time to proofread. Not long ago, she found a classified ad for a house "with massive garbage." She showed it to Mick.

"Where would you park the car, with all that garbage everywhere?" he said.

The newspaper also listed meetings for the desperate: Overeaters Anonymous (Sundays and Wednesdays), Alcoholics Anonymous (every day but Tuesday and Thursday), Narcotics Anonymous (weekdays except for Wednesday), Marijuana Anonymous (Saturdays), Co-Dependents Anonymous (Fridays), Alateen (Thursday afternoons). Bean found the meeting list oddly comforting, even though she never found a place for someone like herself.

One morning Bean came down for pancakes and saw four little flapjacks sitting on the plate, not stacked but arranged like a square. She wiped the sleep out of her eyes and reached for the syrup. She had just poured some onto her plate when she noticed that what she had taken for a butter pat beneath a pancake was really a piece of paper. She extracted a Post-it. *Will*, it said. She looked up at Mick, who was tending the griddle and didn't seem to be paying her any attention. The pancake to the right of it yielded another slip of paper. *You.* She flipped the one beneath it: *Me?* One pancake to go.

"Beanie, you're supposed to go left to right, like a book."

"Oh," she said. She turned the last flapjack over: *Marry.*

Mick slipped into the chair beside her and held her hand as she looked at the message swimming in syrup.

"Will you me marry?" he asked.

Bean started to cry. She sat there, face running, staring at the plate. Mick pushed his nose against her head.

"Whatsa matter?" he said. "You don't like my cooking?"

They planned to marry in June, something small, a few friends. Mick said he would call his mother and sister in Vancouver to see if they wanted to fly up. Bean said she would call her family, too. But the days passed, and she just couldn't do it. In the end, it didn't matter, because in the last week of May, a friend got Mick a three-month slot on a seine boat. With any luck at all, that would cover their expenses for the rest of the year. So they moved everything up and held the ceremony that weekend. Lois wore a cocktail dress as Bean's bridesmaid. Mudhole Evans, the old guy who arranged the fishing gig, stood as best man. That night they all got wasted on Jägermeister.

Bean's new husband spilled humor and verve all over. It could drive you crazy.

There was the time she was late for school, and she sat flat on the floor trying to get her boots on. The boots she wore every day. They didn't fit, and not just by a little; she could get her foot only halfway in. She pulled her foot out, examined it—did feet swell?—took off her sock, and tried again, tugging hard. No luck. She picked up the boot and shook it. Nothing. She examined the sole, then the shank. Finally, she reached way up into the toe area and felt something fluffy. She pulled out a huge wad of tissue paper. How did that get in there? Then she heard a muffled laugh. Mick stood behind her in the doorway, arms folded, his face half shaved, watching her.

"How long you been there?" Bean said.

"Long enough," he said. His smile could look like the devil's sometimes. "What's the matter, Beanie, your feet grow too big?"

Mick couldn't help himself. Once he filled Bean's soup bowl and called it antler stew. He plopped wearily into the chair beside her. "You don't know how hard it is to get those things to boil down," he said.

His favorite thing was to sneak up on her. When she was watching TV, he'd pop up behind the couch. When she washed dishes at the sink, she suddenly felt a warmth behind her and it was as if she had sprouted two more arms. He took pride in these stealthy maneuvers. "Do you know how hard it was to get across that squeaky floor?" he demanded. "I hope you appreciate it."

Most of the time she did. His surprise embraces made her feel like he was always near.

The mournful song of the Golden-crowned Sparrow earned it the nickname "Weary Willy." Gold-miners, burdened by their own heavy loads, gave that moniker to the bird whose song to them sounded like "I'm so weary."

—The Pemberton Guide

Once the fish started to run, Mick came and went. A week, ten days—he just stayed out there for as long as the captain said. He spoke to Bean over a radiophone once or twice on a long haul. The scratchy conversations made her miss him more. She felt her life freeze when he left and lurch forward when he returned.

Winter came hard that year. Three feet of snow from a single storm. They canceled school. Mick had gone to Anchorage to pick up some tools and see some friends. He was snowed in. Everybody said it was a bad one.

The gloom invaded Bean's heart. She sat curled up in the easy chair, her bare feet tucked beneath her, staring wide-eyed into the darkness. Her fingernails kept growing—and her hair, too. The discovery appalled her. Everything felt dead.

One afternoon she lay on her back in bed with a tub of Ben & Jerry's on her belly. Chocolate syrup dripped onto her white flannel nightgown. It didn't matter. She pulled *Charlotte's Web* off the shelf and propped it open against her knees.

Some Pig.

Mick would be back tomorrow. They were clearing the runways, he said. He promised to be home for their eight-and-a-half-month anniversary. She would hide the trash, bathe in scented soap, put on clean clothes. He must never see her like this.

She was making her calculations when she heard the front door open.

"Where is she?" A happy voiced demanded. "Where's my wife?"

She bolted upright and started snatching up candy bar wrappers and cereal bowls from around the bed. In the shadows—the window shade was pulled down against the meager light outside—she glimpsed herself in the mirror across the room. Her hair was greasy; her eyes were cemented with sleep.

He tromped upstairs. She sank back into her pillows. It was too late. He stepped in, and his face fell.

"What's the matter?" he said. "Are you sick?"

She considered an acting job, but she didn't have the heart for it. He crossed to her and put a palm on her forehead. She shook her head sharply and slid down, pulling the covers higher on her chest.

He bent down and picked up an empty carton of Chunky Monkey from the floor. The spoon was licked clean. He looked at her like she wasn't human. Like she'd swallowed up his loving wife.

They fought, though Mick did most of the work. He had been busting his butt in all kinds of weather, he said. All she had to do was fight the winter. They hardly ever had sex anymore.

Then he said it: "Sometimes, you just suck the life out of me."

But he had no idea how she felt. She was drowning, and no one could rescue her. He slept that night on the couch downstairs.

The summer after third grade, Bean's teacher, Mrs. Harper, rescued a goose. A friend had found the bird struggling for life with a fisherman's hook in its neck. It turned up fighting cats for their food in open backyards.

Bean and a classmate, Tina Nessing, hopped on their banana seats and biked over to see it. Mrs. Harper gave them lemonade and took them out back, where her husband had assembled a chicken-wire pen. The goose was white, as tall as Bean's chest, and had eyes like beads. Mrs. Harper showed them a lump in its throat where the hook was wedged. She was waiting to hear from someone at the Audubon Canyon Ranch; they would know what to do.

After an hour Tina got bored and left. But Bean stayed with the bird all afternoon. The next day she came back, and the next, all week. She talked to the goose, coaxing it to eat applesauce and bread. Sometimes Mrs. Harper came out with lettuce. Sometimes she just waved from the window.

On Friday afternoon Bean was getting on her bike when Mrs. Harper called her to the side door. She sat Bean down at the kitchen table and put a few cookies before her.

The man from Audubon had called. He was going to send someone to pick it up over the weekend. Mrs. Harper sat down across the table. "That's a pretty shirt, Bean," she said. "I meant to tell you that yesterday."

She poured her a glass of milk and asked how everything was at home.

"Okay," Bean said.

Did her mother mind Bean being away in the afternoons?

Bean said she didn't mind.

Bean nibbled at her Chips Ahoy!, feeling Mrs. Harper's eyes on her. Would Bean tell her if something was wrong at home?

"Yes," Bean said. Meaning no.

Mrs. Harper tapped the table with her forefinger, the way she did in class to get everyone's attention. She wanted Bean to promise her that much, she told her. She wanted Bean to know that there would always be a place there for her.

Bean wondered what that meant. A place out in the yard with the goose? She pictured herself in a sleeping bag, curled up on the grass, surrounded by chicken wire.

On her way home, she imagined what it would be like to move in with Mrs. Harper. They would read to each other and rescue birds in their spare time. Bean would get pretty smart. After a while people might think of Bean as her daughter. Or maybe her granddaughter. Mrs. Harper was pretty old. Celestine Harper. Bean Harper. Would she get her own room? She hadn't noticed how many bedrooms were in the house.

That night Bean was nodding off in bed, lying with her head on one arm, holding open a book with the other. She heard steps on the stairs and sat up, thinking it might be her father. He'd been gone a lot lately; when he was around, there was a lot of door slamming. The door burst open and the overhead light blazed.

"What have you been doing?" her mother hollered. "What in the world are you telling your teachers? Do you tell them about your father and me?"

Bean sat up, eyes wide, and pressed her back into the pillow, knees up.

Mrs. Harper had called, her mother said. Her eyes were narrow as slits. She paced around the room. " 'I'm concerned about Bean,' she says," her mother spat. "*Concerned*. And she wants to know if things are all right here. Like she's talking to trailer-park trash. Jesus Christ."

She pointed a shaky finger at Bean.

"You will not go back there again," she commanded. "Do you understand me?"

Bean tried to sink lower into her sheets, absently clutching her book. Her mother moved to the door, then turned around.

"You know why she called, don't you?" she said. "She called because you're making a complete nuisance of yourself."

Mick thought Bean might feel less lonesome if they got a dog. She knew he was thinking a baby would be better. But they could start with a puppy and see how it went. It was their second year together.

They flew to Anchorage, where a friend of Mick's had a new litter. They were mutts—Labrador and beagle, the owner thought. Bean chose the runt. He seemed to need her the most. On the way home, he slept tucked inside her jacket. The little breathing lump of skin and fur against her breast overwhelmed her. A new life. It felt like hope. She cried quietly.

When Mick, sitting beside her, finally noticed, he turned tender and nudged.

"Whatsa matter, Little Blue?" he whispered.

"Nothing."

"Well, you got puddles of nothing coming out of your eyes."

She opened her mouth to laugh and all her emotions hopped out in a gasp. She elbowed him back, careful not to crush the puppy. Mick sighed and sat back in his seat.

"Too bad we have to take him back," he said.

"What, why?"

"Too messy. Him not even housebroken. You bawling all over the place."

The months passed. Bean spent a considerable amount of time teaching little Fred to do his business on the newspaper. Then he started to chew, and he went after the legs of chairs. Bean found some wood putty and did her best to cover up for him.

He was a good companion, but on some days the two of them were no match for life. School brought little relief. The whole town was dragging. Salmon prices were down and the canneries were faltering. Every morning, it seemed, the lounge was abuzz over a bar fight the night before. People were feeling bruised. They took vacations in the Lower Forty-eight, where the economy was booming, and they'd see their friends and relatives with nice cars and cleaning ladies. Then they'd fly home and fight.

The boys flicked spitballs and chanted, "Sub-sti-tute!" when Bean showed up in the morning. Rhonda's refusal to take disability—"I'm going to work forever," she said, "Ha. Ha. Ha."—made it virtually impossible for Bean to get any traction.

A lot of the kids were on medication to stay focused. The Filipino kids worked hard; they must have picked it up from watching their mothers scrub scales from the cannery tanks. And the Coast Guard kids bravely started over every time their fathers got transferred. But the fishermen's kids were lazy. Their parents didn't push them. During a parent-teacher conference, one mother smugly recited her family's possessions—satellite TV, a two-year-old Chevy Blazer, and by the way, did Bean have satellite TV in her *trailer*? All that without the benefit of a high-school diploma.

In time, Bean saw what happened. The kids tuned out, grew more bored with each passing year. When they hit high school, the girls got pregnant because they couldn't imagine a life beyond Eyak. The boys ran off, because they couldn't imagine a life within it.

In the fall, the principal offered her a second-grade class. She could start next semester. Her own class, full-time. Nobody was going to call her Miss Ketchup anymore. Excited, she called Mick from the pay phone in the hall. He was home, trying to be a carpenter; she'd left him in the morning bleeding over the sink.

As soon as the bell rang that afternoon, she hurried home with her news. She bonked her forehead on the front door; it was locked, for the first time ever. "Just a minute!" A muffled shout from Mick, then sounds of him scampering across the floor. When the door opened, the boom box thundered with "Pomp and Circumstance." She pulled her slicker around her neck like a cape and strode in, waving like the queen.

Winter came again. This time Bean was determined to fight it. The heavy snows hit in January. They pinned everyone down for a week. But school stayed open, and the kids managed to find their way, carving paths through snowbanks they couldn't see over. Bean had a hard time filling their days. She had lost the miracle of recess. Her lesson plan seemed to run out by 10:30 in the morning, and that left a lot of time until lunch. The children were hopelessly wound-up. She needed to command their attention, but how? Bribery? Hand puppets? She checked the TV listings: Jerry Springer and Queen Latifah. Which was really no choice at all.

Then she came up with Debbie the Duck.

Bean couldn't sing or play the guitar. Her art classes were a joke. She wasn't much for sports. But she could tell stories. She could rhyme. She'd done it all her life. Chip had taught her.

When I was two, I was nearly new.

That night, with winter groaning outside her window, she sat up till very late writing a rhyme about a stubborn little duck.

> *Debbie the Duck was dreaming away*
> *Of places she longed to visit someday.*
> *There was Paris, and Rome and Albuquerque,*
> *Bangkok and Bangor and Tangiers and Turkey.*
> *But at Phoenix Lake, which Debbie called home,*
> *A Goose full of gas told her she'd never roam.*
> *"You will live in this lake till the day that you die.*
> *Silly duck," said the Goose, "why even try?"*

"Not even Eyak, Alaska, will I ever see?"
Debbie asked the old Goose, who was forty-three.
Replied Goose to the Duck, "Your duty is clear.
It's not in Alaska, your place is here.
Your quacks must be quiet, no more than a hush.
You may waddle a little, but not like a lush."

Poor Debbie, who loved to quack just for fun,
And waddle a lot when she'd swum in the sun,
Said: "At least may I dine on my favorite dish
Of peanut butter and bread with herring fish?
The children, my friends, bring that tasty delight
To the Lake for picnics and give me a bite."

The old Goose to Debbie said, "Eat what you please,
As long as it's minnows and milkweed and peas.
As for the children, they're loud and absurd,
Tell them good-bye, after all you're a bird."

But Debbie hid in the reeds until it was late
And all of the fowl began to migrate.
Where they headed south, their sights on Cancún,
Debbie flew north by the light of the moon.
She dropped into Eyak and met a mallard named Matt
Who loved her at first sight, who'd ever think that?

Matt wanted to woo her and gave a big "QUACK!"
But Debbie gave only a quiet "quack" back.
"Well then," said Matt, "let's just waddle around."
But Debbie waddled a little, then just stared at the ground.

Matt asked her what kind of sandwich would please,
And Debbie said, "Minnows and milkweed and peas."

And the mallard named Matt looked sad as he said,
"All I have is herring, peanut butter, and bread."
And Debbie said maybe she'd try just a bite,
But so tasty it was, she gulped it outright.
Then she leaned back and let out a "QUACK!"
So loud to Matt's ears, it felt like a smack.

While Matt looked on her with love in his eyes,
Debbie the Duck did a little reprise.
She loved quacking so much, she decided to waddle.
She waddled a little, then she waddled a lottle.

When she told them the story the next day, the students sat blessedly still. As soon as she was done, they asked her to tell it again. After that day, Bean found herself thinking of Debbie at odd moments—while folding laundry, or falling asleep with the *Pemberton Guide,* or sliming fish. She wondered what was in store for that duck.

One wet morning in April an old college buddy of Mick's, Ron Grange, called from Anchorage. There was an expedition going up McKinley. A hotshot climber named Adam Rowe needed some crew to pull a bunch of tuna up to the top. That's what they called the tourists: tuna. "He's offering decent money," Grange said.

Mick knew Rowe by reputation. He always managed to get himself photographed in outdoors magazines, tanned, shirt off, teeth clenched, hanging by his fingertips from some previously untamed cliff.

Mick and Grange had summited the mountain once before, after college in Fairbanks, ten years earlier. Everything went smoothly. They were up and back in eighteen days.

The plan was to take six tuna up the West Rib. It wasn't the easiest way to the top, but it was less traveled. Rowe hated crowds.

People said summiting McKinley was like visiting the roof of the continent, but Mick said it was more like a trip to the bathroom. The actual summit was the size of a small room, he said, and hikers before them had felt compelled to leave a yellow splash of themselves behind.

Still, Mick said, it was a glorious place. And if Rowe was going to cover the expenses, he was in. He hung up the phone. "I'm gonna get paid to climb," he announced.

A surge of energy. Mick was the sort who needed a project.

"Hey, Beanie," he said.

"What?"

"I'm gonna get *paid* to climb."

"I heard."

Mick went off to take a shower. She heard the faucet squeak and the water flow. Within seconds his voice, exhuberant and flat, boomed from the steaming room. "Big ol' dog in a lighthouse," he sang, "don't carry me a-way today."

She sat on the sofa with her feet curled beneath her. She thought she recognized the tune. It was an old hit by the Steve Miller Band. "Jet Airliner." When Mick didn't know the lyrics, he just made them up.

He had taken the job without consulting her, but it was hard to be angry. He was so excited.

He would be gone for three weeks, maybe more. It was such a big chunk of time; if only she could use it well. She could find out where the red-faced cormorants were nesting. She could let Lois do something with her hair. She could rent some Cary Grant movies. She could try that ten-day rainbow diet, where you ate food according to its color.

She could read. How long had it been since she had surrendered to a book? When she was a girl, she plowed through all the Nancy Drews and half of the Hardy Boyses in a single year. Her mother couldn't understand why Bean's grades weren't any better, since she always had her nose in a book. But it was like a Chinese riddle: the question was the answer.

She was four years old when her brother taught her to read. It was their mother's idea. She was busy with errands and a part-time job at the florist's. Their father was traveling a lot for the insurance company. Chip was only ten, but their mother said it made sense. "Show your sister how to do it."

So after Chip got home from school, they sat together at the kitchen table or in the armchair and looked at the colorful pages. Chip pointed to the letters and Bean made the sound, then the word.

"Ka-oh-wa?"

He was serious but gentle. "*Cow,* Bean. Squish it together."

Eventually the smaller words became familiar, but when she tried to string them together, the meaning eluded. A sentence was impossibly long; she had to rest in the middle, and when she did, she forgot what she'd already read.

Then one day she broke through. Her stubby finger inched all the way across the page, and she understood. She looked up at Chip. "I can read," she whispered.

"Well, finish the page," he said.

But she slid off the knobby oak chair and ran out of the room. "I can read!" she shouted to the walls. Their mother was on the phone in the next room. She put her hand over the receiver and said that was wonderful.

Chip went upstairs and came back with something in his hand. He put it on the table and they looked at it. A Baby Ruth bar.

"Take it," he said. "Our secret."

Bean wondered how her brother was doing these days. She hoped he wasn't still taking drugs.

Anyway, with Mick gone, she could read as much as she liked—no distractions.

"Big ol' dog in a liiiii-ght house," Mick crooned from the shower. Bean leaned back into the sofa and shook her head.

The day before he left, Bean sat in the armchair, a magazine on her lap, watching Mick check his gear for the fourteenth time. Should she do it? It felt so silly.

His equipment was strewn across the thick oval rug—a mound of nylon and Gore-Tex and down. A shaft of late sunlight came through the window in the door and bathed the room in gold. He finished assembling his mess kit, his back to her. When he turned, his eyes were the color of coffee with cream and the hair on his cheeks was beautiful.

He talked to his equipment. A bungee cord was hooked to the wrong loop. "Oh, no, you don't," he said.

Then he started in with Fred. The dog had lumbered over to sniff the packs of dehydrated food. Mick swept him up and cradled him like a baby. Bean pretended not to watch.

"Well, Freddy boy, it's almost time to head for the tall and uncut. Got a big day tomorrow." His voice dropped to a whisper. "I want you to take care of old Beanie while I'm gone," he said. A lot of their communication went like that, through Fred. She had to hold her breath to hear it. "I don't want to come back and find out the two of you have been smoking."

Bean watched his mouth as he talked, saw his lips part, his teeth shine. She saw how spittle gathered in the corners of his mouth. She wasn't listening anymore.

She stood and went upstairs. She locked the bedroom door behind her. Hurriedly, from under the bed she pulled out an elegant blue box. The postmistress, Jen-Ann Klabo, had dropped it by on Thursday.

"Pretty light," Jen-Ann had said. Her job gave her a front-row seat into everyone's business. "What, all the way from Los Angeles?"

"Yep," Bean said. "Thanks." She took the package and eased the door closed. Not the sort of thing you chatted about with Jen-Ann.

Upstairs, Bean stripped off her blue jeans and sweatshirt. She heard Mick downstairs, still chatting with the dog. She took the lid off the box and held it up. It was pink and silky and it seemed awfully small for forty bucks. She'd ordered it from one of the magazines at the Hair Flair. She slipped it over her head and straightened the spaghetti straps on her shoulders. She went over to the mirror. She smoothed her hair.

His foot squeaked on the stair, and she saw the doorknob turn. It was locked. She hopped over to let him in, then stepped back against the wall. She sucked in her stomach, poked one leg slimmingly in front of the other, pursed her lips, and squinted dangerously. She ran a hand over her side. The teddy was still creased from the box.

Mick took in the tableau like a kid staring into a blurry aquarium. "Bean?" he said.

She stretched out on the bed and waited for him. She had stopped taking the pill.

"Let's make a baby," she said.

He left the next morning, two days before Memorial Day. She dropped him at the airport and watched him climb into the twelve-seater for Anchorage. He would meet up with Ron Grange and the others and drive north.

It didn't take long for Bean's plans to collapse. It bothered her how quickly her solitude undermined her. She tried book after book, but she couldn't concentrate. The words just kept rearranging themselves on the page. She took Fred on long walks down the cannery road. Mostly she watched television. Mick said television was evil; she might as well fill up now.

Ten days after he left, she was locked in a marathon viewing when someone knocked on the door. She clicked off the set; the screen felt warm, and it pulled at the hair on her hand. The door pushed into her when she opened it. It was a rare, dark night; the clouds were purple-blue, like carbon paper. A woman stood on the step, her hand clasping the rail to steady herself in the wind. She was dressed in jeans and a dark slicker. Everything about her said "man," except for the multicolored sash that cut across her chest. Bean had seen her before; she was a local. She had a frontier stare more powerful than Bear Scare.

"Paula Casey," she said, introducing herself. No intonation, no smile or handshake. Just as flat as tundra. "My husband was Ned. Ned Casey. Died fishing the Flats three years ago. Drowned."

The woman shifted her sash, and Bean heard a gurgle behind her. There was a baby hanging off her back, wrapped up like a papoose. Paula Casey ignored it.

Bean felt the blood rise in her face till her pores itched. She had heard about Ned. A terrible thing. But why was this woman telling her this? Did she want money? Was she a missionary? Please let it be about that.

"Can I come in?" Paula Casey said.

Bean nodded and they walked over to the couch, which was still rumpled from Bean's television extravaganza. Paula Casey sat down, knees apart, and pulled the baby around. It was Asian. Everyone was adopting from China these days. She lifted the baby before her, fixed her sagging eyes on its face, and sighed.

Inexplicably, Bean's heart raced.

"What?" she wanted to scream. "What? What?"

Paula Casey, apparently satisfied that the baby was alive, plopped it into her lap, and looked, wearily, at Bean.

"The police asked me to come," she said. "I'm afraid I have some bad news about your husband."

Everything in the room froze. Bean's insides went Ping-Pong. This ugly woman with the Chinese baby was going to give her some bad news. About Mick. Bean swallowed and sat up on the couch. She had been watching *The Simpsons; Friends* would be on in a few minutes. The woman spoke, and Bean heard the words, but Bean was somebody else. She was somebody sitting in a chair talking to a spaniel-faced man-lady while *Friends* was about to come on and her chest was going to explode.

Scientists caught 18 Layan albatrosses on Midway Island near Hawaii,
banded them, and split them up. The birds were crated and sent on
military flights to various Pacific destinations, as far away as
Washington State and Japan. Once released, all but four birds made
it back.

—The Pemberton Guide

ean stared at the window shade most of the night. The next day she caught the same flight Mick had taken, then rented a car for Talkeetna. She just put it on the credit card. Lois, who came over and slept on the couch, had offered to accompany her, but Bean needed someone near the phone. She made these decisions quickly, clearly. But everything felt underwater.

She drove toward Denali Park. She stared straight ahead and kept the accelerator pinned. Somewhere along the way, she blinked and realized her windshield was flecked with red spots. A mosquito graveyard. She pumped some fluid and turned on the wipers. But the blades smeared the mess across the glass so she couldn't see. She gasped and veered over to a rough stop.

Her underarms dripped despite the air-conditioning. She was just outside Talkeetna, the departure point for McKinley expeditions. The windshield cleared and she could make out a mountain range on the horizon. She saw the craggy peaks of two mountains, but a third, the farthest right, was hidden in a cloud.

Bean sat in her rented Geo, its engine heaving. All around her it was summer, green and hot. Shallow rivers crossed the rocky plain. A

Winnebago was parked crookedly by the side of the road before her. A family stood on the verge, pointing at a moose, which was grazing in the bog.

It made her think of Jimmy. He didn't believe in moose.

"They're make-believe," he said. "Like snipe."

Jimmy had come for a visit after she first moved in with Mick.

Bean, who had still not actually seen a moose, challenged him. "Well, how do you explain the MOOSE CROSSING signs all over the place?"

"That's just chamber of commerce bullshit," he said. "That's how you get tourists to come to a godforsaken place."

"Well, what about all those stuffed moose heads over the fireplace in the movies?"

"Taxidermy tricks," he said. "Horses with headgear."

"Somebody's out there cutting the heads off of horses?"

"Think about it, Bean. Have you ever seen a moose at the zoo?"

A lot of their conversations went like that. She loved Jimmy.

She had phoned him last night. He knew about crises. He'd lived in the Castro of San Francisco all this time, with AIDS picking off friends and lovers one by one. He said soothing things. There were long pauses. In them, Bean strained to hear the sounds of the city, a horn, a dog bark. Home.

"Bean?" he said.

She ran her sleeve across her nose. "Yeah?"

"I could come up."

"No, Jimmy," she said. "It's okay. My friend Lois is here."

"If you want, I could," he said. "I've got the time. I took disability last week."

Bean was stuffing clothes into a duffel bag. She had to be closer to the search. Only now did she register what Jimmy had said. *He's taken disability.*

She remembered the rest of Jimmy's visit. They were driving back from the lake one afternoon when he told her about his diagnosis. They pulled over beside a stand of spruce trees and cried. Then they pushed it aside. At night they watched videos and ate smores. Mick and Jimmy got along fine, though Mick had a hard time figuring out whether Jimmy was being funny or serious.

When they drove Jimmy to the airport, he threw his arms around Bean and declared: "Life is one long good-bye."

They both glanced at Mick. He looked bewildered.

"I guess so," Mick said.

Bean hugged her friend. "I swear, Jimmy," Bean said, "you're going to make me barf."

On her way to Talkeetna, the mountains ahead belonged to a foreign world. They were part of winter, as distant and foreign as Oz. Bean pulled back onto the road and drove as fast as her cheap car would go.

The ranger station was the only serious building in Talkeetna. All the others were huts, shacks, trailers, and run-down motels catering to starved and penniless hikers. Bean signed in at an A-frame lodge, dropped her bag in a stuffy room, and walked to the ranger station up the street.

On the way, she practiced what she would say.

My husband is Mick Linder. He's lost on the mountain.

At the station, two dozen tourists blocked the way to the reception desk. A ranger was briefing them on the McKinley climb. As Bean squeezed through, snatches of the briefing filled her ears. "Colder than the Himalayas . . . only half reach the summit . . . eleven to fifteen search-and-rescues every season . . . two or three people die a year . . . cornices, crevasses, cerebral edema . . ."

She reached the ranger at the reception desk.

"My husband is Mick Linder," Bean whispered. She couldn't remember the rest, and she couldn't talk anymore.

The ranger stood up and introduced herself as Beth. She was dressed in khaki and green, had a gentle voice, and looked like she never ate anything unhealthy. She took Bean into the back and showed her the task force they had assembled, introduced her to the chief ranger, let her listen to the radio chatter from the spotter plane and base camp. There were more than twenty people looking for Mick. All of them mobilized around her emergency. It was almost embarrassing. When Beth introduced her to the searchers, Bean wanted to say something encouraging, something that would make them look harder. She opened her mouth, but nothing came out. Beth told her to get some rest. They would call her as soon as they knew anything.

"I love him," Bean blurted. "He's my husband."

She went back and sat in her stifling room. It felt like a coffin. A mosquito whined around her head. After ten minutes she jumped into the car and drove to the airport she'd seen on the way into town. Its billboards advertised "flight-seeing tours." She put down $60 for a flight to the glacier, seven thousand feet up the mountain, which was where Mick had begun his climb. She crawled into a Cessna behind a Pakistani man with a videocamera and his teenage son, who complained when Bean got the front seat. After a nauseating ride through air pockets, the pilot pulled a lever that snapped skis over the wheels and they descended near a tiny hive of tents on the pocked ice: Base Camp.

They slid to a landing, and Bean stepped onto the ice. One of the last expeditions of the season was heading up, the pilot told her. She saw a group of nine or ten, roped together in twos and threes, slogging forward on skis, sleds with food and gear dragging behind them. Did they know what had happened to Mick? Would they go if they knew?

A flock of ravens picked through a pit of disturbed snow near the plane. They seemed out of place in the stark, treeless landscape. Bean had read about the mountain ravens. Climbers stashed food strategically along their route; if the caches weren't buried deep enough, the ravens ransacked them. The birds found natural prey, too. McKinley stood in the migration path of numerous songbirds. The Wolfson warblers and rusty blackbirds grew exhausted as they flew over the mountain. When they faltered, the ravens moved in for the kill.

Bean took a few steps toward the scavengers, hoping to scare them away. Instantly she sank up to her hip in snow. One wrong step. The birds ignored her.

"Found a crevasse, huh?" the pilot said. "You probably want to be walking where there are already tracks." He was smoking a cigarette and talking to Base Camp Molly, who appeared to be a kind of den mother to all the hikers. Bean wrestled herself out of the snow. She wondered what they would say if they knew Mick was her husband.

She watched as the string of hikers setting out grew smaller until they were ants lugging breadcrumbs. The first ridge dwarfed them ridiculously, making everything seem futile. She thought about the rangers looking for Mick. It felt strange that she was the only one who actually knew him. Mick's expedition mates had scattered. Rowe had called, from Anchorage. He'd wrenched his back getting the tuna down in a hurry and he was totally laid up. But if there was anything he could do, Bean should let him know.

Bean said she had been trying to get Grange on the phone, but there was no answer at his number. Rowe gave her another number to try: Grange's girlfriend's. She had dialed it over and over that night and twice the next day on the drive to Talkeetna. After midnight, in her motel room, she punched the numbers one more time.

"Hullo?" a voice said.

He sounded stoned.

"What happened?" she said.

Grange started to tell her how he'd meant to call her right away, but it was just so heavy, and they'd said the police were going to get word to Bean, and he sure as hell had hoped they'd find Mick meantime.

"What happened?" she whispered.

When she was in second grade and Jimmy was in first, he ran away. They had been listening to show tunes on his parents' stereo one Saturday morning. *The Sound of Music, Hello, Dolly!, The Music Man.* Jimmy especially loved *Oliver!* He thought the orphans led an exciting life. They lay on their bellies across the scratchy carpet and listened to the songs—Jimmy mugging occasionally with an invisible microphone. He was thinking of putting on a variety show. After an hour Jimmy's mother shooed them outside. It was a beautiful day, for heaven's sake.

It *was* a beautiful day. Too beautiful. The sun streamed into the family room, where Jimmy had forgotten to put back the records. While Jimmy and Bean had moved on to kicking a soccer ball in the driveway, a dozen LPs lay strewn on the carpet, baking like black pizzas.

That afternoon Jimmy disappeared. His mother, who had a blinking problem—blink, blink, blink—called the neighbors and his dad came home from work. Jimmy's dad was tough on him, always told him not to act like a little girl. He cross-examined Bean. But she wasn't hiding him. She didn't even know about the melted records.

They began to search the neighborhood. There were telephone calls and talk of bringing in the police.

Oh, Jimmy, Bean thought.

It was getting dark. The search party grew. You could hear "Jiiiii-meee" bouncing off the houses. Then it occurred to Bean: Midget Woods. It was an undeveloped hillside lot on the road to Phoenix Lake.

They played there sometimes. The dense low trees and the manzanita bushes gave it the feel of a miniature forest. You couldn't even get in there if you were grown-up. That was why they called it Midget Woods.

Bean led a couple of neighbors in that direction. It was almost dark when they got to the woods, and they followed the path by flashlight. Bean crawled in the entrance. One of the searchers handed her a flashlight. But she didn't need it. She could hear a soft voice, calm and sweet, singing a little tune.

"Weh-eh-eh-eh-ere is love?"

Jimmy was hunched under a manzanita bush, arms around his knees, because it was getting cold. He was wearing his pajamas, shirt, and shorts. It was an odd outfit for a runaway. He hadn't bothered with shoes, and his crew socks were filthy.

"Jimmy!" Bean said.

"Hey, Bean," he said. Like it was no surprise.

"Jimmy, whatcha doing? Everybody's looking for you."

"Oh, okay," he said.

Bean led him out of Midget Woods, and they headed for home. By then all the fathers had come home from work and the search had acquired a whole new level of seriousness. There were lots of shouts across the yards and more phone calls. Jimmy was okay.

That night Jimmy's dad came over and talked to Hank. The two men shook hands, and Jimmy's dad shook his head and rubbed his forehead. What he was trying to say was thank you, he said. Afterward, Hank pulled Bean into his chair.

"I'm proud of you, Burt," he said.

It was a different shift at the ranger station when she got back. Beth was gone, but there was still no news. The staff sounded as optimistic as the morning crew, but Bean felt like they were avoiding eye contact.

She rocked back on her heels, feeling dizzy, and realized suddenly that she couldn't remember when she'd last eaten. They told her about a pizza place in town.

The pizzeria was full of boisterous climbers. The din made her recoil, but she pushed through the door and found a table. The revelers had made it back to the land of beer and hot food, and they were celebrating. They laughed in a way that made Bean jump. Her stomach was still rebelling from the flight-seeing.

Their chatter was all about friends who had had narrow escapes on the mountain. The guy whose dick almost froze. The woman who was sure to lose her toenails to frostbite. The climbers who persevered despite altitude sickness. It was all merry. They were great friends in survival. Mick could have been one of these people. He would have had stories, too. Bean stuffed pizza into her mouth, trying not to listen. She hated these people.

Suddenly she felt a hand on her shoulder. It was an intimate feeling, a friendly touch. Hope was right under her skin, like a blush. She turned to see a woman whose face bore the inverse raccoon markings of the freshly descended. A stranger.

"Excuse me," the young woman asked. Her broad smile said *I can't believe I'm asking this.* "Do you know what day of the week it is?"

An impulse to punish her. "No," Bean replied, "I have no idea."

She got back to Eyak just before midnight. She shrugged off her jacket and hung it on a nail in the entryway. She pushed open the door and there was Fred, wriggling and wheezing. She exhaled heavily and patted him quiet. He was a strange little dog; he'd gotten the short end of a beagle and Labrador combination. There was a note on the counter from Lois: "Honey, call me whenever."

The house looked normal. Their lives were still wrapped together in the mail pile, the kitchen cabinets, the clothes hamper. He's no more gone than when I left to look for him, she thought. He's away. Just *away*. Except the rest of his team is off the mountain.

She had just splayed herself across the big chair when she saw it: a sheepskin slipper sitting in the middle of the living-room floor. It was a size nine, mailed from that place in Maine with the catalog full of hearth fires and foggy-breath mornings. She had ordered the slippers herself, a practical Christmas gift after she and Mick had been together for two years. They were still paying off their wedding rings. Their first Christmas, Mick had given her an expensive red sweater, which was too clingy and she almost never wore. And Bean had spent more than she should have on a toolbox for Mick. So for the next Christmas, it had been gloves for her and slippers for him.

Bean looked down at Fred. It was the third time he'd done this: removed one of Mick's slippers from the closet upstairs and brought it out to sleep with.

It was such a lonely sight, she felt embarrassed. "Oh, Fred," she said. The dog tried to hoist himself onto Bean's lap, but his weight and her altitude were beyond his stubby legs. She pulled him up and stroked his shovel-shaped head.

It felt like a good time to cry. Worth a try. She jabbed the air from her lungs with a small whelp. But there was nothing inside. She was too wrung-out.

"Hail Mary, full of grace," she whispered.

He'll find his way home, she decided. Penguins did it. Tens of thousands of them in a colony, and they always found their way, even though their mate and their little nest of rocks looked just like every other mate and nest of rocks. Nature delivered. But a penguin had to want to come home. And want it badly.

———

It would have been an awful call to make to the closest of relatives. But Bean had spoken to Mick's mom only twice before. Once on the day of their hasty marriage, when Mrs. Linder had offered a frosty congratulations by phone. And once when she had called Mick on Easter and Bean had picked up the phone.

As she dialed, Bean suddenly felt like a little girl. Guilty somehow. Mick had failed to invite his mother to their wedding, even though it was a rushed ceremony that culminated in a bender. Mick was ashamed of his mother, though he never said much about it. Bean gleaned it from the edges.

Now she had to tell Mick's mother that her son had disappeared at 15,000 feet. It was strange, her husband lying on an icy mountainside somewhere or trying to claw his way home, and Bean worrying over a phone call. She finished dialing the number, then hung up. Then she redialed and hung up again. She figured she'd do okay once she got going.

She dialed again. A ring and a small hello.

"Mrs. Linder? This is Celestine Jessup," Bean said. "Mick's wife?"

The voice said, "Oh?"

Bean had tried to picture this woman she'd never seen except in a snapshot or two. She lived alone in an assisted-care apartment in Vancouver. Mick said she had pretty bad arthritis in her arms. Bean imagined her with her arms in splints, sitting in a sepia-toned room, wondering whatever happened to her son, the one she had loved so.

Mick called his mother on holidays. He'd barely kept in touch with anyone from the outside. Bean figured it was an Alaska thing. She had never nudged him to do better by his mother. She was no one to judge about families.

But that morning, with Mick's mom on the line, she wished she'd called before this and just said hello. She wondered if she should explain about the wedding. Everything had happened in such a hurry. No, best to get to the point.

"There's been an accident with Mick," she said.

"Wait a minute." Bean heard the old woman put the phone down and walk away. After ten long seconds she came back. "I wanted to get my hearing aid. Now start over."

"This is Celes—"

"Not that part. Go on," she said. "What about Michael?"

"He's disappeared . . . on Mount McKinley."

"When?"

"Three days ago."

"Jesus, Mary, and Joseph," Mick's mother said.

His mother flew into Eyak the next day. Bean drove to the airport early to meet her plane. But when she got there, the old lady was already sitting in the one-room building, on a hard plastic chair next to the candy machine. Bean was surprised to see how small she was. Bean looked at her watch.

"Mrs. Linder?" Bean said. The only other people in the lounge were a couple of guys in overalls.

Mick's mom didn't stand or move right away. She looked Bean up and down. She sat with her hands on her lap, a handkerchief twisted in them. Her eyes were wide and vacant. "We made good time," she said. "We had a tailwind."

She stood up and Bean didn't know what to do—shake her hand, or what? She thought about hugging her, but they were strangers. Mick's mom just clutched her handkerchief for a while, then turned around to tend to her suitcase. It was one of those bags with the wheels and a pullout handle. Bean offered to carry the bag, but Mrs. Linder said no, she could do it. She extracted the handle all right, but then she tugged too hard and the suitcase flipped on its side. She gave it a stern look and jockeyed for a while. She looked like she wanted a fight, and Bean was going to let it be with her luggage.

Bean noticed her hands. They were slightly gnarled, as if they had been slammed in a few car doors. They had sagging flesh and spots, and the fingers curved in a little, like a claw. Bean stepped forward and righted the luggage. Mick's mom grunted and headed for the door.

There were three cars in the airport parking lot. Bean's was a big square delivery truck, painted blue. It was an old milk truck, with sliding side doors and a back that closed up with a rod and clamp lock. Bean helped her with the side door. When she was backing out, she saw the old lady looking for a seat belt; Bean wondered if there ever had been one in the truck. "Just hold on," she said as she guided the truck through the bumpy gravel parking lot. When it bucked, Mick's mom clutched the armrest with both hands.

She had offered to stay in a hotel. But that was ridiculous. The only place was the Alaskan, and even Lois was afraid of the rooms there. A few families advertised B & Bs in the *Eyak Times,* but they were merely kids' rooms made available as the need arose. The town could be very hospitable when there was money to be made.

Bean told Mick's mom that she could stay with her. She passed through town and gunned the engine up the little hill toward home. That night she gave Mrs. Linder their bed and curled up on the couch downstairs.

A kitchen clatter awakened Bean. She tried to ignore it, tried not to stir, girded herself against the need to visit the bathroom. Wrapped in a comforter on the couch, she had nearly recovered her slumber when a plate sang out again, slapped down on the counter. Bean lifted her head like a turtle.

"Good morning, Celestine," a voice said. "I hope I didn't wake you."

The racket could have been worse only if twelve monkeys had been playing catch with the dinnerware. Bean's back shot pain to her head. The couch cushions offered no support.

"What time is it?" Bean rasped.

"What?" The loud shout back made her wince.

Bean looked across the room, but all she could see from the couch was a tuft of white hair. Mick's mother was about seventy, shorter even than Bean, and hard of hearing. In the few hours they had spent together, she had shown a bent for talking—often at length—when she didn't have her hearing aid in. That way there was no danger of interruption. "I hear what I need to," Mrs. Linder said. "Everything would be fine if people didn't mumble."

"Never mind," Bean hollered. She wasn't going to shout small talk. They'd talk after the old woman was wired for sound.

"Oh, you're getting up," Mick's mom said, rattling some pans like a drunken galley cook. Apparently she had slept all right in Bean and Mick's bed. "I have some eggs just about ready to go. I have no idea how you ever find anything in this mess. There's some cheese in here as old as I am."

All Bean really wanted was coffee, maybe some cereal. The mention of eggs made her stomach jolt a bit. Mixed in with the buttery aroma pouring out of the kitchen was the stench of Benson & Hedges. Mick's mom was a steady smoker. It was almost jarring to look at—an old smoker—someone who ought to know better. She was the antidote to the Marlboro Man.

"Mrs. Linder, do you think you could wait until after breakfast before lighting up?"

The old woman looked in Bean's direction and waited a moment as if she were piecing together Bean's remarks from echoes she had heard. Without her hearing aid, Mick's mom was on a time delay, like the space shuttle. She reached for the ashtray, an overflowing abalone shell.

"Of course," she said. She spent a few seconds stubbing it out. "I guess already having my toast doesn't count."

Bean quickly began to dread Beth's calls from the ranger station. They occurred at 6 P.M., just before she left her shift. Which meant no news. Still, Bean arranged her day around them. She didn't have to worry about school. There was just a week left before summer vacation and Rhonda had rallied miraculously and was teaching her students in a combined class. "Don't you worry about a thing," Rhonda told her. "Don't you even be *thinking* about us."

But Bean wished she *had* something else to think of. All there was was this shriveled, deaf old lady sitting over on the couch, twisting Kleenex, watching her. To make things worse, she seemed to be flatulent.

She sat at the dining table and began watching the phone—actually staring at it—about 4 P.M. It was canary yellow, rotary, and sat on the kitchen counter with a cord that extended all the way to the couch but not to the back porch, unless you really stretched it. It was ugly and old-fashioned and she hated it. But it would tell her when Mick was coming back.

It might ring at any second. His voice would spill forth and he would tell her how lost he'd been and that all he wanted to do was hold her in his arms. Hope surged in her throat as she thought about how they would laugh about this for years. It would become a family story—the time Dad got lost—repeated over turkey dinners for a generation.

Bean's mother had cooked a turkey the Thanksgiving after Hank moved out. She pretended that everything was normal. Her eyes were dead-looking, but her voice was chirpy.

"There, now," she said, planting a butterball on the table. "I hope you're hungry."

Bean and Chip stared at it. She was ten. He was almost sixteen. Their mother asked Chip to sit at the head of the table and carve. But he shook his head. "I'm okay here," he said.

Chip had pretty much stopped doing anything anybody asked. He slouched and listened to his headphones and he smelled strange.

"Chip. *Please*," their mother said. She handed him the knife. She was trying so hard to make everything seem hunky-dory. Chip got up with a groan and wearily sat at the head of the table.

"That's Dad's chair," Bean said.

Her mother was dishing out candied yams.

"Not tonight it's not."

"It is. It's Dad's chair." Bean looked across at Chip, furious.

Hank had sent a postcard to his children. It had a picture of Boston Harbor. It said that he had to go away for a while to take care of some things and they could talk on the phone. He wished it didn't have to be that way, but it did. He added a P.S. for Burt: "Take care of that lumbago."

Chip had gotten to keep the card. Their mother said so, because his name came first on the address. Plus the fact that Chip always came first.

"Shut up, Bean," Chip said.

"You shut up."

Her mother put down the yams. "That's enough out of you, young lady."

She dropped her fork and knife on the plate and it made a noise. She crossed her arms. She thought about not eating dinner at all. But it was Thanksgiving and she was only pretending not to be hungry.

She must have fallen asleep. When the phone rang, her face was pressed against her arms on the table. She bolted up. The clock on the wall said 6:10. She answered.

"Hello, Bean? This is Beth. At the ranger station?"

Oh, *that* Beth. Jesus Christ.

"Yes?" Bean said. Her voice sounded hoarse.

"Well, I promised to call to give you an update, even if . . . even if there really isn't much new to say."

Then tell me something old. Tell me again about the guy who built himself a snow cave and called in the rescue plane by writing HEL *on the mountainside before he ran out of tea leaves. Tell me, goddammit, Beth from the ranger station.*

By now Beth was into a speech, designed no doubt to avoid awkward silences or, God forbid, tears. They were proceeding with the operation, everyone was in regular radio contact, the weather conditions were fair but subject to change.

Bean ignored the canned words. She strained to hear the noise *around* Beth. She wanted to hear doors slamming, microphones squeaking, helicopters ascending. She wanted to hear the cry of discovery. Instead, all she heard were radio hisses and bursts of scratchy bored voices.

Beth wrapped up her speech. Time to go home. She probably had a boyfriend waiting in the pickup truck out back. After all, it wasn't *her* husband. "So you can rest assured we're doing everything possible," she said.

Bean would never rest assured again.

"Only . . . ," Beth added.

"Only?" Bean whispered. She felt Mrs. Linder's eyes on her.

"You should know that after five days, the Park Service is obliged to reclassify the operation."

Was Bean supposed to know what that meant?

"Reclassify?" she repeated.

Beth paused. An uncomfortable break in her script.

"Um, you know," she said. "From a rescue to a search."

Swans mate for life. If one partner disappears, the remaining bird hunts for a new mate before the next breeding season.

—The Pemberton Guide

*T*he next morning it rained. Bean took Fred by the leash on their usual route down First Street. When she left the house, she had seen only drizzle and left her slicks on the nail. But now she regretted it because her umbrella wasn't doing the job. After a block or so, her shins looked like she had stepped in two buckets and Fred was soaked. But Bean kept on; she needed to leave the house as much as Fred did. She walked mechanically; when she passed the Copper Spike, the bookstore, the pizza place—all the little landmarks of their shared lives—she tried to push thoughts of Mick out of her head.

Walking the dog in town pretty much meant walking *across* town; Eyak wasn't much bigger than a movie set, especially if you forgot about the cluster of trailers a mile out the airport road and, past the lake, the smattering of cabins inhabited by men with long fingernails who did their shopping by the month.

Hard up against the snow-topped Chugach Mountains, Eyak and its harbor could be stunning. There were two versions of postcards of the town on sale at the Superette, though Bean had never seen anyone actually buy one. The first had been shot on a gloriously sunny day, so rare an event that shoppers sometimes admired the photo as an oddity, the way you studied a snapshot that showed the back of your head. In Eyak it rained 170 inches a year—more than 14 feet. Some gray days, while waiting at the checkout, Bean would stare at the sunny-day postcard—the glistening sound, the clumpy green islands, the brilliantly painted trawlers at anchor—and wish she lived there.

The other postcard was taken from the water. It showed Eyak as a seal might see it: nearly eight hundred boats at harbor, a set of waterfront canneries and processors, the low-slung clapboard buildings of First Street, all of it hunched at the base of a towering mountain. From that angle, Eyak looked as peculiar and lonesome as Pompeii.

Eyak was struggling, as it always had. These days the trouble came down to the price of salmon. Demand for the fish was as high as ever, but plenty of fishermen were having a hard time making ends meet. The way Mick had explained it, the world was crazy for salmon, especially the Asians. But they didn't want the stuff in cans; they wanted it fresh. And, if possible, they wanted it uniform—in size, quality, texture. That was where the Alaskans were getting hit: the fish farmers in Chile and Norway had developed cookie-cutter salmon.

Any Eyaker would tell you that a farm fish wasn't nearly as good as a wild fish, and no ordinary wild fish was half as good as a local sockeye that had to swim hundreds of miles up the Copper River to spawn. But shoppers in Tokyo and Toledo didn't seem to care about taste, and when Alaskan marketers printed "wild" on their labels, it seemed only to scare the customers.

There were other factors to blame besides competition. Sifting through them was a town pastime. Timber companies ran pulp mills that polluted the streams the salmon used to spawn. The state was always shutting down the fishing grounds because its river radar hadn't counted enough salmon in the spawning grounds to replenish the stock. The Feds pounced on any rule-breakers; they were itching to take control of the fishery from the state and give the Natives a bigger say.

Grousing about fishing, Mick had told Bean, was part of a larger Alaskan outlook. It involved taxes (too high), the general state of society (hopeless), drugs (bad, except for pot and booze), environmentalists (usually a pain in the ass), and breaches in their splendid isolation (why couldn't everyone just leave them alone?).

"So, basically, everybody hates the government?" Bean had asked.

"Well, they hate the Feds more than the state," Mick told her. "And they don't hate either one if they work for them, which is plenty of people. And the state starts to look okay when everybody gets their oil-kickback check. But then it goes back into the doghouse when it overregulates the salmon catch. Got it?"

Morning after morning, Bean awoke exhausted. There was a moment—a fraction of a moment, really—after she stirred but before she opened her eyes, when she felt the promise of a new day. But then a horrid snapshot pressed into her head: Mick, in a T-shirt, his arms wrapped against the cold. She got out of bed to make the picture go away. As soon as she stepped into her slippers, she began to plot an afternoon nap.

Her houseguest made it hard to sleep. Mick's mom turned up the TV news shows to dangerous decibel levels. Maybe she was hoping for some breaking bulletin. The house felt terribly small.

A couple of teachers dropped by with casseroles, and Bean felt the urge to flee. It was a nice gesture, of course, but Bean suspected they were on an intelligence mission. When she heard the visitors at the door, she locked herself in the bathroom, almost reflexively, and turned on the tub water. It was the only place she could avoid such people. No one knew what to say to her. There was no news. Everything was stuck. Mrs. Linder talked to the teachers. She asked them about their families.

Bean ended up taking two, sometimes three, baths a day. Her skin grew dry and her hair frizzed. She turned the water up hot till she was lobster red. She half fainted when she got up from her stew; for two seconds she felt weightless and giddy. Yet even in the bathroom, the old lady intruded. Mrs. Linder's toiletries, creams, and pills crowded every flat surface. When Bean reached for shampoo, she knocked a jar of ointment onto the floor.

Bean spent the day trying not to smoke, like she'd promised Mick, even as his mother kept filling up the abalone ashtray under her nose. When she crawled onto the sofa to sleep, she found forgotten wads of Kleenex tucked into the creases of the pillows. She picked up the perfumed clumps with fingers like tweezers and, arms outstretched, walked them to the wastebasket.

The days ended poorly, with no news. She turned off the deafening television and suddenly could hear the clock on the mantel. She missed her favorite television shows terribly—craved the morphine of all those pretty, witty people in New York with silly problems—but it wasn't right to watch a sitcom, not with Mick's mother there.

After dinner she looked across the dining table at the old lady, who sat there drawing invisible signs on the table with her clawed hand. Considering what a talker Mick was, he hadn't told Bean much about his family. She scrubbed her mind for anything he might have said. His mother hadn't been around much; she'd worked after Mick's dad died. To Bean, it felt like picking through a musty card catalog. So far, she had retrieved only one card, and she couldn't use it.

It was a story Mick had told her a couple of years ago, on Mother's Day, after he'd hung up from the obligatory five-minute call. Bean hadn't called her own mother, but that was another story. Mick lay on his back on the sofa, Bean sitting at his ankles. He stared at the ceiling, as if the past were projected there, and told her about something that happened when he was ten years old.

Mick's family lived in a town outside St. Louis then. His father drove a truck, his mother was a housewife. In the fourth grade Mick had joined Cub Scouts.

His mother had agreed to be the assistant den mother, which meant she would help run the weekly meetings. The day came when Mrs. Barry, the den mother, left town with her family on vacation, and Mick's mom was in charge.

Things were rocky at home. Mick's father had been diagnosed with lung cancer, and was severely weak. He hardly spoke, lay around in his bathrobe staring at the TV, didn't say hello or good-bye; and family life limped along around him. Mick barely knew his dad; ever since he was small, his father had been gone half the week on the run to Detroit. Now he was home all the time, and Mick thought it was unfair. His friends all had healthy, active fathers who threw footballs and went to work every day, and he had this zombie dad he wished he could hide from his schoolmates. Before that week's meeting, Mick had asked his mother half a dozen times: "What about the Cub Scouts?" As if she could wave a wand and make his father healthy, or disappear. She told him not to worry, everything would be fine.

On the afternoon of the den meeting, Mick came home in the carpool with three other Scouts. They wore their blue uniforms and their yellow kerchiefs and played keep-away with one another's caps.

When Mick and his friends entered the two-bedroom rambler, his mother was nowhere to be found. There were no sandwiches or chips on the counter, no punch in the refrigerator. All that greeted them was the canned laughter of an afternoon TV show. Mick stopped short, but the other boys spilled around the counter and saw a man wrapped in flannel moving painfully to an upright position on the couch. Medicines sat before him on the coffee table and there were wads of tissue everywhere.

Mick looked at the dead-faced man and froze. He said nothing. The other boys stopped their joking and stared at him. He pushed himself to his feet, breathing with his mouth wide open. He moved to gather up his medicines, thought better of it, then decided to cinch his robe, which hung open, exposing cotton pajamas with stains all over his chest. Mick's father looked back at the boys, with hollow eyes.

"Hello, Mr. Linder," whispered one of the Scouts, Tommy Cross.

Mick's father didn't reply; he just turned toward the bedroom. The boys were still watching him when Mick's mother burst in through the kitchen door. She had two big bags of cookies under her arms. She greeted the boys, eyed her retreating husband, and yanked open the cookies. She pulled a little too hard—her hands had been giving her trouble—and some gingersnaps sailed across the counter onto the floor.

Mick scooped up the cookies, and the meeting began. A few minutes later the phone rang. Mick jumped on it; his father hated noise. It was a manager from McCormick's supermarket. Was his mommy home? Mick called his mother, who was reading to the boys from the handbook. As soon as she picked up the phone, Mick could see there was a problem. Her free hand went to her throat, her eyes got wide, and she spoke indignantly.

She hung up, patted her hair, and went back to the table. She came up behind Mick and whispered in his ear: "I need you to do something for me."

Fifteen minutes later Mick had left the meeting—in his own house!—and was at McCormick's, looking for an office he'd never noticed before. A cashier directed him past the window where they sold stamps and took film. He walked past a big safe. A balding man in a striped, short-sleeve shirt and a wide tie sat behind a small Formica desk.

"Oh, jeez," the man said, looking Mick up and down. "Hey, Murray, get a load of this. Lady sends a Boy Scout." The man who sold stamps popped his head around the partition and stared at Mick.

"And who are you supposed to be?" the striped shirt said.

Mick said who he was. He held up a fistful of money. For the cookies. There had been a mistake.

"Yeah, we wondered about that ourselves, when she left with the first bag," the man said, throwing a look at the stamp seller. "But you see, then she came back."

Mick didn't want to cry. Cub Scouts were supposed to be brave. He put the wad of money on the desk. The man picked through it, then handed him back a couple of bills.

"Now, you Boy Scouts have rules against stealing, right?" he said, winking at the stampman. "You got all kinds of rules. Like the Ten Commandments, right?"

Mick couldn't say anything. He just nodded. The man jerked his head toward the door, and Mick left. He took an hour to walk home.

"Maybe it *had* been a mistake," Bean had said when Mick told her the story.

Mick shook his head. It wasn't the last time.

"You mean she's a thief?" Bean said. "Why would she steal cookies?"

Mick just stared at the ceiling.

"I can see it if they were Pepperidge Farm," Bean said. "But gingersnaps?"

Mick plainly was done talking about his mother, so Bean shut up.

Now Bean worried that this secret she knew about Mrs. Linder would somehow slip out. She might somehow blurt out "cookies" or "shoplift."

In time, she realized that Mick's mom was also at a loss. She knew next to nothing about Bean. She called her Celestine, for chrissakes. Nobody called her Celestine. They were strangers in every way, except they both wanted Mick back.

Bean had never learned to cook. Her mother had always prepared meals for nutritional balance, and they tasted like it. But even those ancestral skills were wasted on Bean. By the time she was of an age to learn how to caramelize onions or mix a meatloaf, her mother and she barely spoke. At college Bean relied on the cafeteria, a microwave oven, a can opener, and the guys at Joey's Pizza, who knew her as Pepperoni and Mushroom, Thin Crust.

Even so, food was her best friend. If you bought snacks in boxes or air-puffed bags, it was always the same—perfect Pringles, phosphorescent Chee-tos, swirl-topped Hostess cupcakes. And if you planned ahead, food was always there. She stashed the treats in her dresser at home and stuffed the wrappers in her book bag to throw away later. That kept her mother's hectoring to a minimum. "Do you really *need* that cinnamon roll?" she'd say. And Bean would jam it into her mouth. Of course she needed it.

Nobody would call her fat, really. Solid, certainly. Plump. No one would mistake her for a ballerina. Her hips were too wide; her sizable breasts gave her a round look. Her calves barely tapered at the ankle. Sleeveless T-shirts and two-piece bathing suits were out of the question.

She had dieted since freshman year of high school. She swiped her mother's magazines from the coffee table and studied the advice. Liberate Yourself with Cottage Cheese! Eat Your Way into the Body You Want! Halfway through an article, she made her way to the kitchen. She returned with a bag of Ruffles and some onion dip. All that talk about food made her hungry.

Her culinary illiteracy appalled Mick. On one of their early dates, he showed up at her trailer with a bottle of wine just in time to see her slip a box of spaghetti into water over the stove. He waited until she had poked it a few times, then suggested boiling the water first. Bean, who had bought a second box of noodles in anticipation of trouble, dumped the pasta lump and started over. "You distracted me," she said.

Ever since, the kitchen had belonged to Mick. After she moved into his little house on the hill, Bean stationed herself at the table and watched him cook. To her, it was sorcery. A bag of groceries from the Superette turned into pork chops with applesauce, linguine with clams, arroz con pollo, or Mick's famous lasagna. She loved to sit and watch him at the chopping block or over the stove. It was almost as good as eating what he made. And Mick loved an audience; he waved his spoons and knives around, talking, dicing, stewing.

Now, with his mom, Bean had felt compelled to display her incompetence up front, so they might reach an early understanding. The night Mrs. Linder arrived, Bean attempted pork chops. The meat soaked up plenty of the grease, but it clung to the pan anyway, and when she pulled the chops off the flame, they were still pink inside. She popped them into the microwave and served them with frozen succotash and charred french fries.

Mick's mom poked at the food enough to rearrange it on her plate. The next day she told Bean she would like to pitch in by cooking if Bean would get some groceries. Bean went down to the Superette and stocked up, and Mrs. Linder worked the family magic.

Soon the oven was disgorging casseroles. Mick's mom wasn't a creative cook, certainly not a daring one. She probably had eight or ten recipes she rotated through. And she was the noisiest chef Bean had ever met. It was because of her hands. The pot handles slid out of them and clanged on the stovetop. She dropped a glass. Bean heard it smash, followed by a curse—a hushed but unmistakable "shit"—and she rushed in to sweep up the shards. Bean became an apprentice in a way that Mick, so jealous of his kitchen turf, would never have allowed. She opened jars, stood on a chair to fetch cans from the high shelves, and even became taster-in-chief. Mrs. Linder didn't think her buds were reliable anymore. The two of them added up to a competent cook.

On the morning of Day Seven, the front door sprang open. Bean was in her sweats, sipping coffee in the big chair and staring out the window. Fred was curled up on the couch. Mrs. Linder sat over half a piece of toast at the dining table. The surprise caused Bean to scald her tongue. Fred hopped to his feet and let out a sharp bark.

So much depended on that door.

Mrs. Linder, who lived in a deeper silence, was the most afflicted. She grunted and slapped her palm over her chest.

Lois swept into the kitchen, oblivious to the shock caused by her sudden entrance, and began pulling groceries out of two bags. She stuffed the food into the cupboards.

"I've got some chicken here. You can eat that tonight. And here's a can of peas and if you want, you can make mashed potatoes," Lois said. She looked at her watch. "Crap. I gotta go, honey. I've got a nine o'clock at the Hair Flair." She paused at the door and gave Bean a last instruction. "You better make sure the chicken is defrosted before you try to cook it."

Bean didn't have time to say anything but thanks.

Mrs. Linder pushed her toast away from her. She was still recovering. "What did *she* have for breakfast, I wonder," she said.

Bean half smiled. That was just Lois. Her friend. "She's kind of manic," Bean said. "And bossy, too."

"I have a daughter like that," Mrs. Linder said with mild distaste. " 'Remember to defrost the chicken first.' Honestly."

Bean carried her jitters into the street.

That afternoon Darleen from school came out of the hardware store and threw an arm around her.

"Any news?" she asked. Bean shook her head. Darleen squeezed her neck, clucked twice, and shook her head. "Tragic," she said. "You let me know when you're ready for a good cry. Promise?"

Bean nodded. She wondered if Darleen's husband was still getting massages from the lady in Seward.

Other people avoided Bean—crossed the street, peered into their purses, dug deeper into conversations—as if she was bad luck. It felt like the whole town was watching her.

Still, she felt herself drawn outside. It was silly, of course, searching for Mick in Eyak. But she couldn't help it. His old trick of sneaking up on her had left her raw, expectant. Whenever anyone tapped her shoulder, she jumped.

Plus he was everywhere. The lithe man buying cigarettes at the gas station had his shoulders. The fisherman coming up the hill was wearing his watch cap. Mick could have been any one of the guys at the docks in head-to-toe raingear. Her heart surged and crashed hourly. Fred fell for it, too. He practically tore her arm off straining the leash when Neil Samson got out of his old bread truck wearing a jacket like Mick's.

Mick even occupied her dreams. One evening she pushed open the thick door of a cabin in the woods and there he was, tending the stove. He barely glanced at her.

"Oh hey, Beanie," he said.

Relief coursed through her. "Mick, what happened? We thought you were dead."

A blank look. "I made macaroni," he said.

———

The morning after the macaroni dream, Bean realized she had completely forgotten the birds. She threw a poncho over her head, claimed an errand, and drove to the lake. It was a mile out of town, ringed by trees and fed in one corner by a stream. She climbed across the mud-clumped hillside and down the ravine to the creek. She pulled her poncho across her backside and squatted down. There were only two of them today. The rest would be out scavenging.

A dozen trumpeter swans nested at the lake. From a distance they were the most beautiful birds Bean had ever seen, enormous, downy white with sleek black bills and legs. But Bean knew they were clowns. They squawked and crapped, tangled their necks with one another and—when they were hungry, which was most of the time—sounded like a seventh-grade band. Their majesty had enchanted Bean when Mick brought her to the hidden place, but it was their crassness that endeared them. It was like watching Queen Elizabeth shake her booty.

The birds came right up to Bean. They were almost tame, which was part of their problem. They were marooned in Eyak. They had forgotten how to migrate. Either that or they'd given up on the rest of the world. When the winter closed in, and all sensible birds took wing, the swans toughed it out somehow.

One of them parked itself two yards from Bean and honked. It stretched its neck toward her like a retractable crane. Bean reached into her pocket and pulled out a bag of goldfish crackers. She made a pile of orange fish and watched them eat.

She wasn't supposed to feed them. Mick had said that from the start. "You feed them and you're messing them up even more," he said. "They have to learn to leave."

But there were too many dangers in Eyak—predators, floatplanes, the cold. Bean visited them secretly. She understood that the swans should learn their lessons. But she also knew they were stubborn and might die without her.

That afternoon, Bean swam. She stuffed a towel and goggles into a knapsack and walked down to the municipal pool. She emerged after a few laps, feeling lighter, with her hair dripping onto her sweatshirt and achy arms hanging at her sides. The improvement was brief. As she crested the hill on First Street, she saw Paula Casey—papoose in tow—talking to a lady in front of the bookstore. Bean turned abruptly to walk back the way she had come. But Paula Casey had spotted her. She dropped her conversation, overtook Bean, and grabbed her wrist.

"We've been wondering when you might be having a service," she said. "For your husband."

Those eyes: pink crescents below the eyeball. Like they'd gazed right into hell. Bean looked at her shoes.

Fuck you.

"I don't know," she said.

"Sometimes the best thing you can do is have a ceremony," Paula Casey said. "To put it behind you."

Bean mumbled that she had to get home. Paula Casey finally let go of her wrist. The question stung. You didn't dwell on things on the frontier. You put things behind you. She imagined Paula Casey digging Ned's grave in the permafrost.

That night Bean set the table while Mick's mom tended the frying pan. She was talking about the search for Mick. It was nothing they hadn't already discussed fifty times. Mothers had to say everything over and over.

With the hissing skillet and her poor hearing, she shouted into the dining room, where Bean fixed the place mats.

"My friend Enid said there must be private people we could hire," she hollered.

On the other side of the room, the television news had given way to *Wheel of Fortune,* cranked up to a wincing volume.

"IS THERE A G?"

Bean paused while setting the table. She studied the plate in her hands. It was so clean, round, perfect. The cradle for how many of Mick's specialties? She ran her thumbs around the rim, felt its thickness.

"But who knows what that would cost?" the kitchen bellowed.

With her free hand, she pressed the maple table with the tips of her fingers. Slightly, but unmistakably, it wobbled.

"I'D LIKE TO BUY A VOWEL, PAT."

"I mean, where would we *find* that kind of money?"

Suddenly, it was as if someone else held the plate. Someone who lifted it above her head. She squeezed her eyes shut as it slammed against the edge of the table. It exploded in every direction. Mrs. Linder burst out of the kitchen, with alligator-shaped potholders over her hands, her mouth agape.

"LADIES AND GENTLEMEN, THE LOVELY VANNA WHITE!" Cheers and bells.

The plate had not broken cleanly. It shattered into a thousand shards and left a puff of white dust that hovered over the bowl of green beans. The sound had been satisfying, but Bean had hoped for more. Eyes unfocused, she moved over to the television and clicked it off.

"People are wondering when we might have a service for Mick," she said.

Her voice sounded dead. She kicked a few pieces of the broken plate.

Mick's mom sat down at the table and began serving herself, ostentatiously ignoring the mess. She stuck a spoon into the bowl of potatoes and pulled out a shard of china. A long silence.

"I guess I could fry them," she said.

"Huh?"

"Got too many potatoes here," Mrs. Linder said. "Would you eat them fried for breakfast?"

Bean slapped the table. It teetered. "Did you hear what I just said?" She was at a loss over what to call Mick's mom. She kept forgetting her first name. Hanna? Yes, Hanna. She stuck with Mrs. Linder.

"We could use some more eggs," Mrs. Linder said. "Is the store still open?"

Bean was talking to a wall. She leaned forward, almost enjoying the confrontation, exaggerated the moves of her mouth, and shouted: "I said, people are asking about a service."

"I heard what you said." The reply was like a knuckle crack. The spoon clanked on the side of the bowl. "What *people*?"

"I don't know," Bean said. "The townspeople."

The townspeople. What a word. A mob of villagers chasing Frankenstein with torches.

Mrs. Linder peered into the potatoes as if they were the most distasteful thing she'd ever seen.

"He's been gone a week," she said. The way she said it, you'd have thought he just ran down to the drugstore and got delayed.

"Eight days," Bean corrected.

"What?"

"It's been eight days," Bean whispered.

Another poison look from the old lady.

Bean made a pile of the plate shards on her paper-towel napkin. "I'm just telling you what people are saying, is all."

"People are saying that he's dead?" Mrs. Linder was working herself up. "Is that what *you* think?"

Bean looked at her hands. "I don't know."

"Why should he be dead? They haven't found a thing."

Bean rubbed her face.

"No body. No trace . . ." Mrs. Linder stood up and snatched up the dinnerware with such violence that Bean was sure something would hit the floor.

Just before she stepped into the kitchen, she said: "And, besides, how do we know he didn't just leave?"

"What do you mean?" Bean said.

"I mean *leave*. Just leave. Men leave women all the time."

Bean turned around in her chair.

"What are you talking about?"

Mrs. Linder had the sink running now and was flicking scraps into the drain. "I'm just saying, how do you know that's not what happened? Happens all the time."

Bean glared at her through the kitchen doorway.

"Maybe they leave *you*," Bean said. She stalked over to the coatrack, yanked down a jacket, and headed for the door.

But Mrs. Linder was behind her now. She was practically shouting as Bean stuffed her arms into the sleeves.

"If I were lost on a mountain for eight days, trying to stay warm and eating God knows what, I wouldn't want to know my wife had decided I was dead," she said.

Bean only made it across the street, to the old schoolhouse. In the yellow evening light, she leaned against the brick wall near the steps and hugged her chest.

It could have happened, couldn't it? Now that somebody else had said it, she had to admit it as a possibility. He'd had enough. It was all part of a plan to start over. It happened. She'd seen it in the papers. There was that electrician from Fairbanks who disappeared on a hunting trip and completely vanished till one of his sons bumped into him on the surfing beach in Santa Monica. Things like that happened all the time in the movies. She brought this on herself. Mick had practically said so.

A pack of schoolboys rode by on skateboards, and Bean found herself wishing for darkness.

It was chilly, and she put her hand in her pockets. She felt a lump. In her rush to leave the house, she had grabbed Mick's barn coat. She pulled out half a roll of breath mints. She extracted one, smelled it, and popped it into her mouth. She imagined a kiss.

In the morning Bean had cereal for breakfast. Her molars ground over the oatmeal squares in her bowl, and Mrs. Linder's knife noisily scraped butter over her toast. Nobody mentioned the white dust on the tabletop or the crunch their feet made on the floor. When they finally spoke, it was after noon.

They scheduled a service for the third Saturday in June. Mick had been gone for two weeks, and everybody was asking about it. Paula Casey took care of everything. She turned Bean's shrugs and grunts into decisions. "Just you leave it to me," she said. She seemed to be enjoying herself.

Mick's mom wanted it at the Catholic church, and Bean said all right. She realized with embarrassment that she didn't know Mick's beliefs. They had never talked about God; what *had* they talked about?

Mrs. Linder called Mick's sister, Franny, in Vancouver. Bean sat in the living room and listened as the old woman grew more and more agitated. They were going ahead with a service, she told her. No, there was no body. Whether to fly up was entirely up to Franny.

Lois came over the day before the ceremony to pick up some snapshots of Mick. She wasn't wearing any makeup and she looked pale, even for Lois. "People need something to look at," she said.

Bean pulled a few photos from dusty film sleeves—she'd never gotten around to making a scrapbook. She went upstairs and brought down the picture of the two of them on the mountain.

When she entered the church the next morning, Lois's handiwork sat in front of the altar. From a distance, it looked like a psychedelic, fuzzy inner tube propped on an easel. On closer inspection, she saw it was meant as a wreath, woven with reeds and wildflowers and lots of baby's breath. Mick's photos were arranged on a board in the center of it.

Bean sat down next to Mick's mom in the front row. The priest was a young man who split his time between Eyak and a church in Valdez. There weren't enough priests to go around. Bean had seen him at the pool. He swam slowly and barely kicked, so his back half sank, especially in those big flowered shorts. It felt strange seeing a priest almost naked. Lois just said a man was a man.

When the priest opened the floor for people to talk about Mick, everyone who really knew him hung back. Bean certainly wasn't going to go up there. Her job was to sit up straight, thank people for coming, and look like a brave widow. Mrs. Linder wasn't going to say anything, either. They'd put a fresh battery in her hearing aid; she came to listen.

There was an uncomfortable silence. One of the fishermen nudged Mudhole, who had treated Mick like a son. When Mudhole didn't move, the fisherman elbowed him again. "Fuck off," Mudhole snapped. The words flew down the aisle, and the priest raised his bowed head to make sure Mudhole didn't mean him.

Finally, Ron Grange, Mick's climbing partner, sprang out of his seat and stepped up to the altar with the balky stride of a heron. He hitched up his pants and smiled and nodded at Bean. All she could think of was spending hours trying to get his phone number and hearing him on his girlfriend's line, stoned.

He cleared his throat.

"What can you say about Mick?" he said. Everyone waited for the answer, including Grange. He seemed surprised when it didn't come. "Well, uh, he was our friend," he said at last. "And now he's gone, we're going to miss him."

It was either the most plainspoken tribute ever made or the stupidest ad-lib Bean had ever heard.

Grange was unbelievably tall, with bad skin and a thick mustache. He'd met Mick at college in Fairbanks. They took chemistry together and were assigned as lab partners. One of them had knocked over a Bunsen burner and created a small fire. Each blamed the other. They climbed McKinley that summer. They had been friends ever since.

Grange was still talking. He raised his hand as if to settle the room, which was already graveyard quiet.

"While everyone's here, I just got one other thing to say," he said. "I know it may not seem like the best time and all. But, look, we were partners. And we looked out for each other on the mountain." Grange took a deep breath. "And I just hope none of you thinks otherwise. Because I know there's been some talk."

Bean hadn't heard any talk. Grange shifted on his feet and tugged at one side of his mustache. The rest came out in a rush. "Because I told him a million times, if I told him once. Don't ever go anywhere without your ice ax. And he's thinking, I'm only going to take a sh—— I'm only going to use the facility. And, you know, everybody bends a rule here and there. And that's your choice. But look what happens when you do."

Everybody was getting uncomfortable with this lesson, but Grange was just getting oiled up. Suddenly a handsome, wide-shouldered man about Mick's age stood up. Adam Rowe, the famous climber. He walked stiffly up to the lectern and displaced Grange. Bean felt like she was in a movie.

"We're here today to honor a man who died doing what he loved,"

Rowe said. "We should all be so blessed." He clasped both sides of the pulpit, as if it were his.

He talked about how Mick was singing on the last day of his life. They had been pinned down in their tents for days, and Mick was singing.

"We wanted to kill him," Rowe said. "Man, what a tin ear. It got worse when we started fighting over the words. He swore it was 'Loosely in Disguise with Diamonds.' Bet me twenty bucks. Said my way didn't make any sense."

Even Bean laughed at that. Rowe bowed his head in deference to a wager he wouldn't collect on. Bean lowered her eyes, too, hands still clasped on her lap, and let herself cry.

When it was over, people hugged Bean and patted Mrs. Linder's hands. Bean was walking out the door of the church when someone tapped her on the shoulder. She turned to face a prim, clean-shaved man in a khaki shirt who had sat in a pew all by himself. He was the fish counter from the Park Service. "Low Count" Lowenstein. Bean didn't know his real name. No one did. He was the enemy, always restricting the catch. You didn't talk to Low Count; you hit the brakes and shouted at him: "Fix your radar, Low Count."

She had an absurd notion that when he opened his mouth to talk, numbers would come out. But his words were soft and deep.

"I was proud to be his friend," Low Count said. That was it.

Goddamn you, Mick.

Mick's mom said almost nothing until they got back to the house. She tried to open a can of soup. Bean saw her struggling with the opener and took over.

"All that talk about Mick loving the outdoors was true, right?" she said.

Bean said, "Yeah, he was a maniac about the outdoors. It was all about breathing the cold air."

Mrs. Linder pondered. "I can't help feeling like he was trying to get away."

"From what?"

Mrs. Linder and Bean looked out the kitchen window into the twilight. But the lights were bright inside and they couldn't see past their own reflections.

The next morning, just as Bean got up to clear the breakfast bowls, the old lady said, "I could help you with Michael's things."

"What?" Bean said.

Mrs. Linder was all hepped up with the idea. "It might take a while," she said. "Good heavens, there's so much to do." She wasn't ready to leave. She locked on Bean's eyes.

"Please," she said quietly.

Her look said, *I'll beg if I have to.*

Bean moved into the kitchen. She didn't know what to make of Mrs. Linder's companionship. Sometimes she felt lucky that she didn't have to face it all alone. Other times she wanted to fall apart but couldn't, because she had company. It made her want to scream.

She found it hard at first to accept that Mick's mom was not going to tell her how to dress or eat or live her life. Or that they could talk without getting mad. They could sit quietly with their own thoughts and pain.

It had been different with her own mother. She had been so determined to fix everyone else. Her father with his drinking. Chip and the stash of marijuana under his mattress. Bean being Bean.

When Bean was twelve, her mother had arranged an outing. The Ice Capades were in town. "Just us girls," she said. Bean was determined to hate it. She read a book on the drive over, and she clutched it on her lap when they settled into their seats.

"Isn't this nice?" her mother said.

"Yeah," Bean said.

"Aren't they pretty?"

The whole day seemed designed to get Bean to want to lose weight and wear a tutu.

During intermission Bean wanted some caramel corn. But her mother nixed the idea—it would spoil her dinner. The tutus returned with a skating Goofy.

"Isn't this fun?" her mother said.

If there was one thing Bean couldn't stand, it was her mother trying to be nice to her.

She went back to the slime line. It would fill her days, and now she might need the money. On that Tuesday after July 4—the day she almost gutted Fat Al—she got home at midnight and found Mrs. Linder asleep in the easy chair. Her mouth was open and her reading glasses were askew, and Bean wondered if she had suffered a stroke. But on closer inspection, she was resting comfortably, her little bird chest rising with each breath.

Bean peered into the ashtray to make sure she hadn't left a cigarette lit, then she slipped quietly into the kitchen and opened the refrigerator. She squatted in search of a Diet Coke, snagged the last one, then remained on her haunches, looking at the back of the refrigerator. She pulled a large piece of blue Tupperware from the bottom shelf.

In the glow of the refrigerator light, she peeled off the lid and inspected the contents. It was lasagna, with spinach and ricotta. Mick had made it the night before he left. The noodles were brittle, of course, but she couldn't see any mold.

How was it possible that his leftovers could survive him? Ridiculous, she thought. Just the other morning, when she was brushing her teeth, she'd glanced at the new toothbrush Mick had bought at the drugstore, still sealed in its plastic case. How was it that a slip of plastic and bristles of his had endured? *Who are we,* she thought, *that we are mourned by our casseroles, survived by our toiletries?*

She had left the new toothbrush on Mick's side of the sink. And now, after checking the lasagna, she slid it back into the refrigerator. It was well past edible, but she liked it there.

Bean closed the refrigerator door and found herself, in half-light, looking at a third-grader's drawing. It was the product of one of Bean's disastrous first art assignments as a substitute teacher. One day after school Trudi Hite's mother had come in and slapped it down on the table.

"What the hell is this?" Mrs. Hite had demanded. She had a round head, wide eyes, and a bobbed haircut. Her head swiveled on her neck like a short-eared owl.

"It's art," Bean said. "And science. We made posters for Sea Month."

Bean looked at the drawing. A big fish jumping upstream beneath a rainbow. Written in the rainbow were the words *Save the Salmon.*"

Mrs. Hite poked one finger at the offending message and scowled. The salmon run was low, and the Feds were threatening to shut everybody down.

"We fish salmon," Mrs. Hite said, her last shred of patience in play. "We *all* fish salmon."

Bean looked again at the picture. "I don't think Trudi meant *you,*" she said.

Mrs. Hite's little beak was practically touching Bean's nose.

"Just teach her how to read, okay?"

Bean made herself sit up straighter. Hold your ground, Mick had said; otherwise, they'll walk all over you.

"I *am,*" she replied. "Look, she even got the *l* in there."

Mrs. Hite narrowed her eyes at Bean like she were a wise guy.

"Where you from, anyway?" she asked.

"California," Bean said.

"California," Mrs. Hite repeated. As if that figured. "You don't get it do you?"

"Get what?" Bean said.

"Salmon are paying your salary."

For months after that, Bean pictured a big chum salmon with a green visor on its head signing her checks. When she told Mick the story, he winced. "Oh, man," he said, clapping a palm to his forehead. "Save the Salmon. In *Eyak*." He asked for Trudi's drawing. It had been on the refrigerator ever since.

Bean moved softly past Mrs. Linder as she dozed, and crept up the stairs. She hadn't spent much time in her bedroom since turning it over to Mick's mom. She stood outside Mick's closet and yanked on the light. She took a deep breath and stepped in amid his dangling shirts and folded sweaters. She smelled the cedar blocks tucked among the clothes. She ran a browser's hand over the shirts, selected one, and pulled its sleeve to her cheek.

Almost methodically, she bent down and touched his shoes. She examined his buckskins, noting how the outside of the soles had worn more than the instep. She lifted a suede shoe to her nose and inhaled.

A voice from the doorway startled her.

"I must have fallen asleep," Mrs. Linder said. "They called. The Park Service. They found Michael."

As Bean rose, she let go of the shoe and it hit the floor.

*H*is body was frozen solid by the time they got to him. One of the bush pilots had found him, near the trough of a steep rise, at 10,000 feet. The pilot was working one of the flight-seeing tours, taking three passengers in a swirl around Foraker and McKinley. He spotted Mick's red jacket and dipped down for a look.

Bean had already pieced together an account of the accident from the rangers, Grange, and Rowe. Now she had the ending. The team had been six days into the West Rib climb. They reached the Bergshrund camp without incident. The tuna were adjusting pretty well to the altitude, though one man vomited a few times. The winds kicked up as they were setting up their snow walls and tents at 14,800 feet. Base Camp Molly warned by radio that weather was coming in. Grange marked off the perimeter of their camp with rope, and they all settled in.

They waited four days at Bergshrund. It was wind and snow and wind again. All day their tents made a racket, snapping in the wind. But they were all right. Just bored and cranky. Except Mick. Everyone else got sick of one another's stories, weary of the novels they'd ripped up and passed around, tired of all the granola. Really pissed whenever someone farted in the tent, which was often because of all the granola. But Mick didn't seem to mind. He was having fun.

Then just before 10 P.M. on the fourth day, Mick left his tent, telling Grange he was going to use the toilet. It wasn't much of a facility, an exposed fiberboard throne the size of a dishwasher perched on a lip just inside the rope perimeter. Beyond it, the ridge gave way. Grange didn't remember even looking at Mick as he left, so he didn't notice that Mick had stepped out without crampons on his boots and had left his ice ax behind.

Sudden winds had stirred up whiteout conditions and you couldn't see more than twenty-five feet. It was disorienting. You had to think about which way was up or down.

When Mick didn't come back in ten minutes, Grange suited up and went to see if something was wrong. By then the snow was coming pretty hard, but he could see Mick's tracks. Yet when he got to the toilet, there was no trace of Mick. He peered over the side, but the snowfall was blinding. He went to Rowe's tent and they hastily organized a search of the camp.

No one had heard anything, which was not hard to believe. The snapping tents made quite a racket. People almost never shout when they fall, anyway, one of the rangers said. Those long decrescendos are pure Hollywood. When someone plunges, he usually does it silently, after a little groan of surprise.

The nearest help was at the ranger camp on the West Buttress at 14,200 feet. Molly radioed that they would send out searchers as soon as the weather broke.

Rowe had paced around the toilet area in disbelief. There should have been two gullies where Mick had slipped and tried to dig in his arms to stop sliding. They would need those gullies for a search, to know which direction he fell. But the snow kept falling.

It turned out that Mick had tumbled nearly a mile in elevation.

Nobody had guessed he would fall that far. The plunge itself probably killed him, the rangers said. If it hadn't, he probably died overnight, where he lay. If not then, well, a man in his position couldn't be expected to last more than three days without food or water.

Bean wanted to know why it took them nearly four weeks to find his body. They'd had a high-altitude helicopter, all those air taxis, two search teams on the mountain. Why hadn't they found him before? The rescuers were stumped. Their best guess was that he'd been buried in two or three feet of snow, and it took all that time to melt.

Beth had put the chief ranger on the phone.

"Wouldn't be the first time," he told Bean. "There are lots of 'em on the mountain never been found. More than thirty, I'd guess. Even if you eventually find one, there's no guarantee."

Sometimes a recovery was impossible. A climber had died more than a decade ago near a crevasse on Mt. Hunter. "Everybody knows him," the ranger said. "You can fly by and see him dangling from a rope, upside down. Can't get him, though. Too risky."

Frozen solid, the unrecovered dead were monuments to themselves.

Bean took the afternoon flight to Anchorage and rode a taxi to the office of the medical examiner. Ron Grange was sitting on a bench just inside the door. He looked like a schoolkid serving detention. He sprang up when he saw Bean; he was so tall, she had to stand back to see his face. "They asked me to wait here, for you," he said.

Grange started talking fast and Bean looked for an escape. She noticed signs up the steps for the National Guard and the highway patrol, which shared the building.

"I'd a done it, Bean," he said. "Some people, it might give 'em the creeps. But I seen worse. Car wreck out near Chugiak two years ago, and I was the first guy there. I mean before the cops, ambulance, anybody. Serious shit. And hell, Mick was my best friend."

Low Count, now Grange: everyone was Mick's best friend.

"But once they found out you were coming, they told me just to sit tight. Out here. And here I am."

Bean nodded. They'd told her on the phone that the identification was just a formality. Mick hadn't been carrying a wallet. She could have someone else do it if she liked. No, Bean said, she would come.

She took a big breath and walked up the rubber-coated stairs, past a mounted moose head, and stood before a receptionist who wore a metal tag over her breast that said LT. MARY CRUMM. She looked busy answering phones and transferring calls. But mostly she was apologizing, apparently because the people she transferred kept getting cut off.

"Whoops, bear with me, sweetheart, I've got a new switchboard here," Lt. Crumm said into her telephone headset. In between calls, she kept a conversation going over her shoulder with a highway patrolman, who was sitting behind her, sipping coffee. It was confusing. Bean stood directly in front of Lt. Crumm but couldn't tell whether the receptionist was talking into the phone, to the cop, or to her.

Their eyes met and Bean opened her mouth.

"That's what I'm telling ya, if you'd just hang on a minute. They brought her in this morning." Lt. Crumm held up a finger to Bean. Her switchboard bleated. "Coroner's office? Sorry, darlin', just give me one more try here." She pushed a button and leaned back toward the cop. "So they fished her out of the creek, back of the Wal-Mart. The doctor says he don't know, but it looks like blunt-force trauma. Well, if you ask me, that *trauma* is named Mr. Frank Chulig.

"Yes, dear?" Bean stared stupidly at her a moment, then she spoke up. Lt. Crumm buzzed the coroner and sent Bean and Grange down the hall.

Dr. Julius Feinberg wasn't what Bean expected. He didn't look at all like Dracula or a mad scientist. He had a red face and cheeks like hams, and looked like he spent a cozy life among the living. When they entered, he sneaked a last bite of an egg-salad sandwich from the remains of lunch at his desk. He wiped his fingers and lips with a napkin, missing a bit of egg in the crevice of his thick lips, and stated just how sorry he was.

Bean said thanks. She watched his eyes stray greedily back to the crust of sandwich. Then he wrestled into a lab coat and asked Bean to follow him. Grange trailed them. Feinberg pushed the button for an elevator.

"Now, as I said, he's mainly in good shape," Feinberg said. During the early summer McKinley was as good as cold storage, he told her.

Except he's dead.

But she stayed quiet. Her insides were pounding. She didn't know how she would feel when he lifted the sheet. There would be a sheet, right? In the movies, there was always a sheet and a table that slid out from the wall.

The elevator opened; its floor was tiny, a square yard. As they boarded, Feinberg pushed B and kept talking. "Of course, you can't remain out in the wilderness for that long without some damage," he said.

Bean was crowded up against these men, her face even with their chests. She could smell Feinberg's egg salad. Grange drummed his thighs absentmindedly. It made her feel panicky, and for a moment she thought she'd be sick. She didn't say anything.

Grange said: "What kind of damage, Doctor?"

"Well, frostbite mostly." Feinberg paused. "And some evidence of a carnivore."

Oh God.

Bean didn't say anything. So Grange did.

"You mean some *animal* got to Mick?" Grange said. "Shit."

There was a long pause. It was a slow elevator. Then Grange said, "What kind?"

Feinberg shrugged. He didn't know. Bean stared at the elevator buttons. The back of her neck itched, and she felt a drop of sweat work down from her underarms. She had to get out of there.

"I'll bet it was a grizzly," Grange said. "No, wait, they don't eat dead things, do they? Unless he was *alive*."

Feinberg shrugged. That was out of his field. The B lit up and the elevator doors cracked open. Bean wanted to scream. She burst out and smashed her shoulder on the still-opening door.

Grange noodled it some more. "I suppose it could have been the ravens," he said. "Depending on what they went after."

They came to flapping double doors. Feinberg held one open for Bean. She was instantly overcome by a chemical smell; disinfectant and something else, something from seventh grade, when you dissect frogs. Grange saw himself blocked by Feinberg. "Don't you want me to come with you, Bean?" Grange asked her. "I'll come with you if you want."

Bean shook her head no, and followed the coroner toward another set of double doors. She leaned back on her heels, inching forward with her toes, as if walking up to the side of a cliff. Feinberg poked his head behind the door and told whoever was in there that a civilian was coming in.

"Um," Bean said. She stopped and swallowed.

"Yes," Feinberg said.

"Will there be a sheet?"

"Do you *want* a sheet?"

Bean nodded. She really wanted a sheet; Mick deserved a sheet.

Feinberg slipped in first while she waited. Moments later he propped open the door for her.

There were two stainless-steel tables. Both were lumpy with what Bean was certain were dead bodies.

Hail Mary, full of grace.

Two men in gloves and surgical gear stood in front of the nearest table, making a human fence. They clasped their hands before them and looked at their shoes, which were clad in paper booties. They wore guilty looks, like boys caught looking at dirty magazines.

Bean could make out behind them a mound of opaque plastic casing, like a garment bag. She tried not to look, but she couldn't help herself. Through the sickly, yellowed membrane, she discerned an elbow, hair—jet black and straight, like a Native's. The body appeared to be on its stomach, and one arm was crooked over the head, as if protecting it. *Mrs. Blunt-Force Trauma*, Bean thought. She started to take a deep breath, but then the room's chemicals flooded into her nostrils and she knew she would puke if she finished it. She squinched her eyes so she could barely see, but even then she noticed the fist stretching against the plastic and, on one finger, a ring.

Bean edged toward the other table, where Feinberg now stood over another lump. With a sheet. Her lump. Her sheet. Mick. The coroner shuffled his feet as if to make way for Bean.

The sheet was basic white, very clean, a little too starchy. Like they'd just pulled it out of the package. Probably a twin. Mick's bed had been a twin before she moved in. Then he replaced it with a queen—the one they had now. It had been really hard to get up the stairs.

The body was too long, judging by the contours, and Bean felt a surge of hope that there had been some horrible mistake. But just as quickly she realized that Mick had always pretzeled up when he slept; she'd rarely seen him lie flat on his back like this. She took a step and felt a shiver.

She always got cold first. On a dark night after a dark day, they would slip under the fluffy comforter and he would let her warm her toes in the crook of his knees. Mick always had heat to spare.

Feinberg waited, with his guilty assistants standing by. Bean stood

six feet back, her knees locked. Something Mick had said echoed now.
Sometimes you suck the life out of me, Bean.

Her chin fell to her chest. She hugged her ribs and she felt a tear splash on her arm.

"Oh God, Mick," she said. "I'm so sorry."

Feinberg held the corner of the sheet and looked to Bean to say it was okay to lift it.

The sandwich crust was gone from Feinberg's desk. She sat in a chair across from him as he asked what she wanted done with the body. She tried to think. But she felt him staring at her, and her mind just kept erasing itself. He asked her if she wanted some water. She must have nodded because the coroner slowly escorted her back to the waiting room and put a paper cone cup in her hand. Grange was waiting there. He sprang out of his chair like a toy.

She leaned her head against the wall. She refused to focus her eyes on Grange.

"Did he look . . . okay?" Grange said.

She noticed the moose head and considered whether it was in fact a horse.

"Please go away," she whispered.

Grange was determined to stay and help.

"But Bean . . ." he said.

She snapped back into consciousness, sat up, and waved her arms. Water sloshed out of her cone cup.

"Get a-*way* from me!" she shouted. Everyone in the room stopped what they were doing to look at Bean. Lt. Crumm put her hand over her mouthpiece and peered out from her window. "You left him. You left him on the mountain. And then you went home to your girlfriend and smoked a fucking joint. Your best friend."

Grange took three steps back like a spanked dog.

"It wasn't like that," he said quietly, tugging at the watch cap in his hands. "It wasn't like that at all."

Bean twisted on the hard plastic chair and turned her back to him. A few minutes later, when Feinberg came back, Grange was gone.

The first thing people usually decided on was burial or cremation, Feinberg said. He spoke in confiding tones, like a priest. Normally that sort of thing was handled by a funeral home. But Eyak had no funeral home, Bean knew. Along with all the other things it didn't have.

Bean had thought about a grave. A place she could visit. Flowers. Birds. Maybe even a view. She could go there and talk about things.

Eyak's cemetery was pretty, with lots of white headstones on a hillside overlooking the sound. But she didn't know if she wanted Mick there. The town seemed so small and mean for eternity. Mick might get stuck next to Ned Casey, and Bean would have to share her visits with Paula. Paula Casey probably parked herself graveside for hours, knitting and whittling and letting her Chinese baby run free. The other option was cremation. It was such a harsh word, right up there with *decimation, obliteration*. Wasn't there a gentler way? He died in the cold; now he had to burn? Perhaps she was making too much of this. He was dead. What she needed was for him to lean into her from behind and whisper the answer, even if the answer was that it didn't matter.

Feinberg's beeper went off. He rose and looked at Bean. "What do you think?" he said.

She pushed open the front door to their house, brushed past Fred, grabbed a chair from the table, and carried it into the kitchen. It was a good, solid, store-bought chair, and she stepped on it. Mick's bottle of scotch was in the back of the high cupboard. She pulled it down and poured some into a juice glass.

"I *thought* I heard someone," Mrs. Linder said, coming down the stairs. She looked rough. She wore a quilted housecoat, periwinkle blue with cigarette burns over the thighs.

Bean sipped the amber liquid and hoped it would kick right in. She sifted among the day's images, trying to figure out what she could tell a dead man's mother. There was nothing, really. Not about the elevator. Not about the sheet. Certainly not about the carnivore.

But Mick's mom sat down at the round table, and she stuffed her hearing aid into her ear. She bowed her head like she was waiting for grace.

What to say? He looked taller, all stretched out on the metal table. His eyes were flattened and his nostrils seemed frozen in mid-gasp. His skin was pimpled up and sandpapery. And cold. So cold, when she rested her palm lightly on his cheek. Only his hair was the same, the thick fur she used to cut on the deck. That was all. When Feinberg pinched up the sheet and asked Bean if she wanted to see the rest of him, she just shook her head. She had done her job. This had been Mick, this man she loved. Here he was, this dead thing.

Now she leaned against the kitchen counter, holding the scotch near her chin.

"When Mick started going out fishing with Mudhole, he brought along a book, for the down times," she said. "It was the story of a storm—the storm of the century, they called it. It wiped out a fleet of fishermen on the East Coast. Well, Mick had rough seas at first, so he spent his first few days with Mudhole puking over the side of the boat and spooking himself with that book."

She took another sip.

"Then," she continued, "when he started training for the McKinley climb, he picked up a book about a bunch of guys who'd died on Mount Everest. He spent his days doing chin-ups, and running all the way to the airport, and at night he just freaked himself out reading what went wrong on that expedition."

Mick's mom blinked a few times, like she was watching a TV ad she didn't care about.

Bean kept her next thought to herself. Nobody was going to write a heroic book about Mick. He was the guy who went to the toilet without spikes on his shoes.

"You saw him?" his mother asked.

Bean nodded.

The scotch warmed her, throat to belly.

"Where is he?"

"Still at the coroner's," Bean said.

"In Anchorage?"

Bean nodded.

"You *left* him there?"

"He's frozen solid," Bean said. "The doctor told me I have a week. I don't have to decide anything until he thaws."

Mick's mom stared at her hands. "Did they let you . . . *keep* anything?"

Bean sighed. Day after day the old woman had gathered Mick's things to her bosom. She sorted his junk mail as soon as it arrived, washed and folded all his sweaters, carefully stacked the condolence cards. Now she was asking for more, some souvenir from a man who'd been frozen on a mountainside for a month.

"They gave me his wedding ring and his watch," Bean said. "They said I could have anything I wanted. I took the ring and the watch."

Bean sat down at the table and opened the manila envelope. She pulled out Mick's ring, the one she'd picked out at the jeweler's in Anchorage. She slid it over her middle finger. She wasn't going to part with that. Then she pulled out the watch. A Timex Triathlon. She bought it for Mick's birthday last year. He used it to time his runs.

She inspected it. Takes a licking and keeps on ticking. She felt the eyes on her.

"You want the watch?" Bean said.

Mrs. Linder sat up.

"If you're sure you don't want it," she said.

Bean had never known what all the buttons were for, anyway. "It's yours," she said. Mick's mom looked hard at the watch's digital face, then tried to fasten the band around her wrist. Bean reached over and clasped it.

A moment later the old woman yawned. Then it occurred to her to look at Mick's watch. She didn't have her glasses on, and Bean was certain she couldn't read the little digits without them. But she studied her wrist a moment, then announced she was heading for the tall and uncut. Just like Mick used to say. Bean swallowed the last of her scotch and snapped on the TV. Reruns of reruns.

"Good night, Mrs. Linder," Bean said.

"Good night."

The old lady stopped with one foot on the stair, poked her head back into the room.

"I was just thinking," she said

"What?" Bean asked.

"I was thinking . . . you could start calling me Hanna."

That was a relief. It was awkward saying Mrs. Linder this and that when Death was there, sitting with them in the living room. Bean had stopped calling her anything at all.

"Good night, Hanna," she said.

Mick's mom started up a step, then stuck her face in again.

"Celestine?"

"Bean," Bean said.

"Bean," Hanna said. "I was just thinking. We could bury him in Vancouver."

Bean walked home from the Superette lugging two plastic bags of groceries. She was just about to head up the hill when a pickup pulled up beside her and a man with a face like cracked leather bent around at her. It felt like Mudhole had been waiting for her.

"You want a ride?" he said.

Mudhole was an old sourdough. He had five children, four girls and one son who broke his dad's heart by moving to Seattle to study design. Mick had filled the hole. He crewed with Mudhole for a couple of seasons on the *Sea Scout* and began to learn Mudhole's tricks. You couldn't buy experience like that. It was worth more than a $125,000 boat, gill nets, or a license. Mudhole knew where the fish were.

Bean shrugged, her arms weighted by the bags. She rested the groceries on the floor of the cab and slid onto the front seat. It was silly to ride for such a short distance. But what the hell.

They drove the hundred yards up the hill in silence, and Mudhole put on the brakes. He never wasted words. Didn't sugarcoat them, either. If you wanted it sweet, then you stayed away from Mudhole. Mick had worshiped him. He said Mudhole was a true Alaskan. "That man can do anything," Mick had said. Bean felt shy around him.

"He ever tell you what he did to my nets?" Mudhole asked.

Bean remembered the night Mick had come home, his skin welted up from mosquitoes, looking like a kid with acne. He had gotten seasick as usual on the boat, but then he made a cardinal mistake. After he threw up, he had dozed off, with Mudhole already asleep down below. The unmanned boat spun in the current and all the nets tangled together in a horrendous knot. Such a mess, they had to cut them loose. Nine hundred feet of gill net, some of it wrapped around the rudder. Four thousands bucks for the nets. All the fish were lost in the nets.

"Yeah," Bean said.

She looked at Mudhole out of the corner of her eye. She felt sheepish for Mick. Why bring that up now? "I lost the catch," Mick had told her. It was the only time she'd seen him cry.

"Some people just know how to work a boat," Mudhole said. "Not him. No stomach for it. All thumbs." Mudhole stared out the windshield and Bean waited.

"Still, I never saw a kid want to learn something so bad," Mudhole said. "I'd a sold him my license, too." Bean knew there was no heir for the *Sea Scout*.

She looked at her hands, then noticed the Ding Dongs in the bag at her feet.

"Wanna go somewhere?" she said.

Ten minutes later they were at Bean's hidden place, where the stream met the lake. Four trumpeter swans waddled up the bank. They squawked as she opened up the box of cakes and pulled away the cellophane. She handed one to Mudhole, then began tossing chunks to the swans.

"They catch you, they'll fine you big for feeding 'em," Mudhole said. He squatted, like a fisherman would—couldn't see fit to planting his butt on the ground.

Bean shrugged. "No skin off my nose," she said. Then she glanced sideways at him. "You won't tell, will you?"

"Why would I do that?" Mudhole ripped up a cake. White cream oozed onto his fingers.

"I don't want them to starve," Bean said.

"These birds'll never starve," Mudhole said.

"Why's that?"

"If I tell you, I'd be telling, wouldn't I?" Mudhole said.

Bean bit into a Ding Dong.

"More likely to die from heart attacks," he said. "Look at 'em. Fat as turkeys."

They did look well fed.

"Saltines," Mudhole said.

"Huh?" said Bean.

"That's what they really want: saltines and oats." Mudhole used a bunch of leaves to wipe the cream off his fingers. "You're wastin' their time with these."

"What makes you think he wanted to be cremated?" Hanna said. "Did he tell you that?"

They were washing dishes. Hanna rinsed, Bean dried.

"No, but—" They hadn't discussed it. He was thirty-two years old. He didn't even have a will.

"When you don't know, you bury," Hanna said. "That's the way it's always been."

Hanna plunged a plate into the suds. She was pretty sure of herself. But this was Bean's decision; everyone told her so. The coroner. Lois.

"I mean, what would you rather have: a nice headstone in a park? Or ashes? You can't visit ashes."

What a choice. The hard relics of a man with so much life in him, he drummed his fingers on Sunday morning.

Bean rubbed a glass till it squeaked. "Look, Hanna, I don't know what he wanted. I don't even know if he believed in heaven."

A surprised look. "Of course he did," Hanna said. "How could you not know that? He was confirmed in eighth grade."

Bean shrugged. Their lives had been sewn together by meals, walks with Fred, departures, reunions, sex, thoughts of children. For all she knew, Mick thought God was a big old dog in a lighthouse. "We never talked about it, is all."

"You didn't talk about it?"

"No."

"How could you not talk about it?"

It was a fair question. Bean remembered the night of the comet shower when everyone climbed up to the ski run and had a picnic in the cold. They had huddled together for warmth. Mick said seeing the galaxy made him feel big and small at the same time.

It wasn't much.

Hanna was scrubbing the sink. "Well, I know my son. And he wanted to be buried. He wanted a headstone and trees nearby and a bench."

A bench. She had gone too far.

"How do you know he wanted a bench?"

"What have you got against a bench? You've got to sit somewhere."

If it wasn't about Mick's wishes anymore, what did Bean herself want? It seemed like she was always facing that question. Was his body still Mick, or was he already gone? If he was gone, where did he go? If he was in heaven, would he want to watch himself decompose? The questions spooled out endlessly from the big question: God. She wanted to believe, and she envied people who did. But He felt so far away.

A burial would have to be soon. It would be here or in Vancouver. She wasn't sure where she was headed and she didn't want to leave him behind.

"I'm leaning toward cremation," Bean said.

Hanna wrestled the taps off and pressed her lips together so tight, her mouth went vertical.

———

After four days Bean called Dr. Feinberg and made it official. Mick would be portable until she was sure of the place she wanted to settle down. The coroner said he'd arrange it.

Two days later Jen-Ann, the postmistress, stopped at Bean's house on her way home from work. She handed Bean a box that was the size of a small TV. It had stickers all over it, saying PRIORITY and HAND-DELIVER. Jen-Ann said she figured it must be really important, what with all the insurance on it. Bean just said thanks, and did Jen-Ann need a signature? Well, Jen-Ann sure did, what with the precious cargo inside, so mysterious and all.

Bean took the box inside. While Hanna watched, she stripped open the lid, picked through the Styrofoam peanuts, and extracted what looked like a big brass trophy.

She put Mick on the mantel, over the fireplace he used to tend.

At the cannery, Yoshi, one of the Japanese supervisors, told Bean she could crate roe next season. That meant she could get off the slime line. Packing eggs was coveted work. It was clean and dry and paid better because a lot of the job was quality control. You delicately packed the little pine boxes and nailed them shut. Japanese importers paid a fortune for them.

"Great," Bean told Yoshi. Next year seemed awfully far away.

School would start up in a couple of weeks. The principal, Marty Keene, had already tucked two notes under Bean's door saying he hoped Bean would renew for the fall. A three-year contract sat on Bean's kitchen counter. It had an orange-juice ring on it.

She felt physically ill at the thought of committing to anything.

Was this enough for a life? It seemed so meaningless now.

One night she sat down on the edge of the bed and stared into Mick's closet. She tugged open the top drawer of his dresser. Just peering into it made her think of Mick's manhood: the way he stood sometimes in silent praise of his own hard body, his thick wrists covered in fine hair, the rumble of his voice.

She pushed aside a heap of boxer shorts and explored. A Swiss Army knife—she marveled at its ingenuity. A box of inlaid wood; inside there were gold cuff links and a tie clasp—his father's? She knew so little about his family.

She sighed and put the box back and was about to close the drawer when her wrist grazed a cardboard box. She pulled it out. Condoms. What were those doing there? Her heart raced while her mind struggled to keep up. They didn't *use* condoms. She had always used the pill. She examined the box with the silhouette of the kissing couple. It was open. There were ten condoms inside. That meant two were missing. She shoved the box back into the drawer, beneath all the underwear.

On the couch that night, as she twisted her blanket into a knot, she heard the box screaming at her from upstairs. Or maybe it was laughing.

After a stormy Friday, Eyakers awoke to a blessed sight: sun. Word poured out over the public radio station: it was a glorious day—and on the weekend, no less. Mothers pried their unblinking children from morning cartoons. Women invented outdoor chores; suddenly it was time to pull weeds and wipe windows. Men stared at their muddy pickups and leaky rooftops and wondered where to start.

The Dominicans and Hondurans living in cannery housing spilled out of their cramped quarters, beer bottles and wheels of fried dough in hand. Down at Shelter Cove, hippies, college kids, dropouts, and dopers all stumbled from their tents into a blinding light. Within moments their squatters' village—nestled in a tree-ringed lot behind a seawall—had turned itself inside out. Socks, underwear, boots—

everything that had clung to these workers' flesh for weeks, never getting dry—found a clothesline, a rock, a tree, and stretched in the healing warmth.

A brisk breeze kept the temperature hovering in the sixties, but the light beckoned and a few dozen souls found themselves drawn to First Street to verify such a fine thing as a sunny day.

Midmorning someone pounded on Bean's door. Still in bed, she thought at first it was Hanna, perilously cooking. But she could hear the radio blasting upstairs, so she suspected Lois. Bean didn't want to see Lois. She didn't want to see anybody.

She had to think about the condoms and what that meant. But every time she started to think about it, her mind jumped away like it was a hot stove she'd leaned on.

Lois wasn't easily denied. She opened the door and stalked right up to where Bean lay in a heap on the sofa.

"See, I knocked like you said," Lois blared.

Bean had asked Lois not to burst into the house because it might give Hanna a coronary.

"Outside," Lois commanded. "C'mon, Bean, you don't want to miss a day like this."

Bean groaned and pleaded fatigue. Lois sat down on the sofa's arm and started to tug on Bean's naked toes.

"This little piggie went down to the pier," Lois said. "I'm telling you, honey, you'll thank me later."

Bean pretended she was emerging from a coma, then gave up, put on shorts and a T-shirt. She was startled to see how milky her legs looked. She put Fred on a leash and followed Lois into the light. The water on the sound was like cellophane, catching the sun in tiny ripples. Mothers loaded their kids into vans to go look for bears. Gardeners fixed their tulip and daffodil beds. Men and women looked each other up and down.

Lois was ready for it. When they got to the pier, she crossed her forearms, snatched the bottom of her sweatshirt, and pulled it over her head. She was wearing a bikini top. "That's more like it," she said, arching her back toward the sun. At first, Lois's skin puckered up with goose bumps; there was still a chill in the air. Lois didn't care. She flipped her hair over her shoulders, looking for an audience. There were a dozen people on the pier, mostly kids on bikes. Her gaze landed on a handful of college guys, sitting splay-legged with their shirts off. They were huddled close and passing something around.

"Whaddya think?" Lois asked.

I think my husband may have been cheating on me.

"About what?" Bean asked. The sun felt good on her shoulders, her stray hair making a gilt frame for her view of the sound and the mountains beyond. Fred snuffled at her feet.

That was what you did in a town with no mall. You made things happen. You stirred the pot. Mick was always telling her to make her own fun. Too often she felt like a kid in a playpen whose mother hands her the measuring spoons instead of a real toy.

"About what," Lois repeated, in mock disgust. "Honey, I know you been through a lot. But don't tell me now you're going *blind.*"

Lois walked toward the college boys. Bean got up to follow, pulling Fred along. She felt uneasy. Like most year-rounders in Eyak, Bean tended to stay clear of the seasonal workers. They lived in tents or hollowed-out school buses, rarely shaved or showered, and had a free and easy way about them that made her nervous. They smoked grass, danced in a mob on Saturday nights, and talked about ashrams in India.

"So, you guys make good money this summer?" Lois asked. The boys turned to look at her. Bean could tell that Lois had already decided on the one she wanted: he had longish sandy hair and was wearing loose blue jeans over a tight body with muscles all over his belly.

"Some," he said, since Lois was staring right at him.

"Well look at this," cracked one of the other two guys, turning to note the altitude between Bean and Lois. "A shot and a double."

Lois ignored him. "Whatcha drinking?" she asked Blue Jeans.

In minutes, Lois and Bean were sitting with them on the pier, passing around a pint of Christian Brothers brandy. The guys were all from Seattle. Two of them were college kids; the one Lois liked was on his own.

Lois nodded sympathetically. Bean could see how quickly, in her friend's mind, Blue Jeans was becoming the rebel, the dropout, James Dean. Lois, who never made it to college herself, sat next to him and arched her back so her breasts plumped inside their green halter. The next time Blue Jeans tried to hand her the brandy, she took it from him with both hands: contact.

Bean cast sideways glances at the other two guys. The wiseguy was the better-looking of the two, tall, red-haired. But Bean knew to avoid someone who was snide to strangers. She peered at the other guy. He had dirty blond hair and a beard on the underside of his jaw. His unkempt appearance reminded her of her brother, Chip, after he stopped washing and their father kept telling him to just try to look like a human being. This guy looked slightly anemic, like he could use a week's sleep or a dozen milk shakes.

Lois unfurled her long legs and stretched, as if she were an overgrown ballerina worried about her hamstrings. The guys lounged cowboy-at-the-campfire-style, each trying to look more relaxed than the next. Bean saw that Lois's proffered foot had landed just centimeters from Blue Jeans's crotch. Then Lois decided to work on her calves, poking her cloth sandal even closer. Blue Jeans rearranged his legs to lean toward her, but he didn't even look at her.

"I'm so tight," Lois said.

The prospect of sex hovered over them both like a blue mist; everyone else was fascinated, but they pretended not to notice.

Bean stretched her legs a bit, pointing her toes, groaning a little. No one seemed to care. The other two guys, like Bean herself, were riveted by what was happening between Lois and Blue Jeans.

Bean had always been mystified by how these fires started. So easily. So unself-consciously. Lois and Blue Jeans were like movie stars born with their lines memorized.

Bean shifted her position to move closer to Anemic Boy. She didn't care so much about him. Lois was feeling sexy. Lois was having fun. Bean arched her back a little. She wanted to feel what Lois was feeling.

For a searing moment, Bean wondered if she would ever experience the cool flirtation, the easy pickup, the zipless fuck. She had sweated the high-school dances and avoided drunken college parties, and it had taken so long getting used to Mick.

Mick. *All this time, had he loved someone else?*

"How 'bout it, Bean, do you want to?"

Lois waved a hand in front of Bean's face and rolled her eyes at Blue Jeans. "They've got an Indian sauna going down at the Cove," Lois said, pulling her to her feet. "You want to check it out?"

Bean squinted an eye and was ready to beg off, using chores as an excuse. Before she did, Lois yanked her aside and hovered over her. She used her height to bully Bean.

"I'm only going to say this once, so listen to me," Lois said. "*He* died, Bean. Not *you*. Now don't be stupid."

It was a challenge. Bean felt she had no choice. Lois had some sort of power over her. She always knew what she wanted. It was seductive. The only thing worse than doing what Lois wanted was the prospect of being abandoned by her.

They walked down the dirt road to the Cove. There was a shed with smoke coming from an aluminum pipe in the middle. Bean tied Fred to a tree. They crawled through a small door with a canvas flap and were enveloped by heat. Rocks the size of melons crackled over a white-ash fire. Bean's face took the heat, feeling singed, but her body welcomed the dry embrace. They huddled in a space no larger than a Buick's interior. No one knew who had built the sauna. Probably some hippie kid who'd overdosed on indigenous culture in college.

Lois, who should have been pretty limber by now, started stretching again. "Oh, yesss!" she said. She reached behind her back with both hands and unclasped her halter. It fell into her lap, and her breasts swung free. She closed her eyes and tilted her head back so everyone could have a look at her rack.

Bean sat there in T-shirt and shorts and looked at her friend. She was pretty sure Lois was her friend, even though she knew a lot more about Lois than Lois did about her. Of course, she couldn't blame Lois for that entirely. Bean sometimes wondered why Lois hung out with her. After all, Lois could get anything she wanted. Wasn't Blue Jeans proof? It wasn't that she was a beauty. With her lips parted, you could see an overbite. Her head was too small for her body. But Lois knew how the world worked. She knew what people wanted. She never gave up, even when people got cross with her.

Sometimes Bean caught herself looking at Lois like a man might. Not because Bean was that way, really. She just felt that if she could bury her face in those frizzy curls, or maybe share a deep kiss with Lois, or more, then she'd retrieve a secret. She might belong on this earth as much as Lois did. She could be dirty without feeling dirty. Be free. But Bean wasn't going to start something on her own. There was too much to lose.

Wiseguy had wandered off, which Bean figured was a plus. Anemic Boy and Blue Jeans had stripped down to their boxer shorts. Blue Jeans sat next to Lois, and Anemic Boy turned his shoulder to Bean to poke at the hot rocks with a stick. Even with her eyes closed, Lois was managing the stage. She reached out a hand and ran a long finger over

Blue Jean's bicep, saying something about not wanting to get too hot. Blue Jeans gave a half smile and looked hard at Lois.

Bean watched this through slitted eyes, pretending to relish the warmth. The heat made her sweat, and she felt self-conscious about pools under her arms, between her legs. She looked at Anemic Boy. He was almost bluish, like a fetus in trouble. But he was muscled and trim in his boxer shorts. Bean sat, shoulders slumped a bit, sweating and waiting for him to drop the stick and make a move.

Lois and Blue Jeans started to kiss. She seemed as cool as dew. He was slick with sweat, but it looked good. Bean's eyes stung as sweat puddled in their corners. Lois started to groan lightly, like when she ate chocolate. Blue Jeans was enjoying himself, too, from the look of his shorts. Bean wanted to insert herself into this tableau unfolding three feet away. She wanted the middle. She shifted her weight on the bench.

Something brushed her hand. Anemic Boy was stroking it with a finger. Bean turned her sweat-streaked face toward his and felt his mouth clamp on hers like a limpet. He licked the corners of her mouth, and his spittle mixed with sweat from her upper lip. She wondered when her next breath would come. He put his palms on her cheeks and she suddenly felt a surge of fear. She tried to raise an arm to push his wrists away. But she felt too weak, as if her blood had drained away in the sauna. She glanced at the little door and realized she would never have the strength to make it out.

Anemic Boy was back with his tongue in her mouth. Bean wrenched her head violently away. She burped the brandy they had slugged down on the pier, and the taste was so revolting, her breakfast started to cascade out. With her back to Anemic Boy, Bean vomited the only place she could. It landed on the hot rocks with a sizzle. Suddenly the sauna was unbearably rank.

"Holy shit, Bean," Lois hissed.

The two guys fled the sauna like rabbits, trying not to retch before they could suck in clean air. Blue Jeans's handsome mouth was snarled. Anemic Boy looked seasick. Lois held her breath; she had to struggle first with the tangled straps of her halter top. She plunged out finally, followed by Bean, who crawled out on all fours.

"I'll say this for you," Lois said as Bean gulped the cool air. "When you kill a moment, you shoot it right in the head."

At first, Bean had been reluctant to let Hanna go through Mick's things. She imagined trash bags full of Mick's treasures flying out the window, and she wasn't in a hurry to see Mick go. She liked having his adventure books on the shelf, his camping gear in the closet under the stairs. The toolbox she gave him that held tools he'd never used. His fishing boots standing guard, like silent black geese, on the porch. And his clothes—the T-shirts, slightly yellowed under the arms, the socks frayed at the heels, the belts with creases at different holes.

But after a while Bean realized Hanna wasn't discarding Mick's things. She was *visiting* them.

Bean came home one evening and found Hanna sitting on the couch with sheaves of nostalgia all around her—stacks of curling photographs, a high-school yearbook, a recipe binder freckled with drops of grease.

Hanna looked up.

"Oh, hello," she said. "I've just been going through some things."

Once Hanna's plan was understood, Bean helped her. She brought out things for Hanna to look at—a shoe box full of postcards, Mick's fishing codebook. Mulling and shuffling, they built little memory piles on the dinner table, on the kitchen counter, on the window ledge.

Mick would have hated all the clutter. As it turned out, Hanna didn't discard anything. She folded it, rewrapped it, bagged it, boxed it, or jammed it into a drawer.

The kitchen became a monument to thrift. Mail-order catalogs fought for room with pickle jars and egg cartons on top of the refrigerator. There was an impressive economy to it all. In the knife drawer there was a thatch of twist ties held together with a twist tie. A plastic bag filled with plastic bags hung on the pantry doorknob.

The shelves of the refrigerator were populated with the smallest pieces of leftover food. Chunks of fruit, bites of chicken—you couldn't really be certain—were carefully wadded into cellophane packages no bigger than a finger and stowed away. Then there were the odd items from nature. Hanna returned from her walks with oddly shaped driftwood, an eagle's feather, a rock with quartz in it. She didn't feel the need to comment on her discoveries, she just found a place for them inside.

For all her hoarding instincts, Hanna didn't share Bean's inability to part with Mick's ashes.

Bean overheard her on the phone one night, talking to Enid, her bridge partner back in Vancouver. Hanna was sitting at the dining table, staring straight at the urn on the mantel, her back to the front door, when Bean stepped in.

"I have no idea whether it's a sin or not," Hanna shouted into the phone. "That would be worth looking into. It really would. But I'll tell you this, it's not right. It's not right. It's not even *sanitary*. I'm telling you, they're just sitting right here. Like a jar of potting soil. I'm just beside myself."

Bean pulled back and came through the front door again, this time making noise. Be patient, she told herself. The old woman would be going home soon.

———

The next morning Bean noticed that Mick's urn had moved to the end of the mantelpiece and a large pinecone sat in its place. Hanna was upstairs, going through Mick's filing cabinet for the third time. Bean put the urn back in the center.

After a while Hanna came down with an armful of papers. Receipts for lumber. *Auto Repair for Dummies.* She was really scraping the bottom now. But then she turned up a snapshot.

She stared at it, then passed it on to Bean. Mick was wearing a college sweatshirt with the sleeves ripped off, and you could see his muscles. He looked sleek and sunburned, with his thousand-watt smile.

The woman next to him wore an oversize denim shirt and a half-bored movie-star look, like Cher. Their eyes were reddened by the Polaroid's flash. It made them look drunk. Or like devils. Sexy, drunk devils. Mick's right arm was draped over her shoulders. It was Lois.

"When did you take this?" Hanna asked.

But that was a problem. Bean hadn't taken it.

When Lois wrapped her fingers around an idea, she poked you with it until you gave in. So when she insisted for the fourth time that it was time for Bean to go on a date, have some laughs, Bean said okay just to shut her up, and Lois got to work.

All her life, people had told Bean she was pretty, though never in a way that gave her confidence. They'd always said it with a certain surprise, as if finding fetching colors in an oily puddle. "You're actually quite pretty," a high-school boy once appraised, pushing back her unruly hair. Bean shrugged it off. With her unreliable weight, any confidence she took from such remarks ran out at the neck.

Those thoughts skittered through Bean's head as she stood at Lois's elbow and heard herself described as "outdoorsy." She wondered what that meant. Outdoorsy like fresh air, or outdoorsy like a plow horse?

Lois was leaning into the pay phone, plugging her open ear with a finger, using her *Let's Make a Deal* voice to talk the guy into it. A friend of a friend, the guy had only two days in Eyak before heading back out on a salmon tender for three weeks, and, well, he had to be choosy.

Lois's expression said, *Give me a break.*

Bean pretended not to listen to this bargaining over her, and the grinding sounds of the fish factory that August afternoon pretty well smothered Lois's conversation. She had told Lois four different ways she didn't need a date. But now when the time came, she found herself intrigued by her friend's sales pitch and huddled near.

"Not tall, but not too short," Lois said, staring down at Bean. "Uh-huh. I told you—blond." Lois peeked at her friend's hairline, concealed by the yellow fisherman's cap Bean always wore in the drippy plant. "Dishwater blond," she said.

Bean stood there in the employee lounge, bathed in fluorescent light, her thick-gloved hands hanging at her sides. She looked at the clock nailed on the plywood wall. Any minute now Fat Al would round the corner and wonder why the hell they weren't back on the slime line with the others.

"How old are you?" Lois whispered, hand over the mouthpiece. Bean figured that meant, *How old do you want to be?*

She just told the truth.

"Twenty-six," Bean whispered back. She was starting to get interested in the negotiations. How would it end? Would she marry him? Was this how you got on with your life? The suspense was killing her. She noticed a piece of salmon gut stuck like pink yarn on her bib. She flicked it away.

"Twenty-six," Lois said into the phone. "I told you, she's *working.* They barely give her time to pee. So, do we have a date?"

Lois hung up and looked at Bean.

"Oh, he was just loving *that,*" she said. " 'I have to be careful. I'm only a few days in port.' " She was aping the guy.

Bean thought about the picture of Lois and Mick. Her hair had been a little straighter in the snapshot. What they were wearing—it had to be summer. But when? Four years ago? Or last August? By which she meant, *Before me, or after me?*

"Lois?" she said.

Lois was still on a tear. "Earl. Earl the Pearl," she said, looking like she'd just swallowed her gum. "Any man in Eyak would line up to go on a date with a knothole, and we get Earl the Pearl. Oh well, you gotta start somewhere."

"Lois—" Bean said.

Lois stopped rolling her eyes. "What is it, honey?"

"Did you know Mick . . . before?"

"Before what?" Lois stopped playing.

Bean felt pinpricks behind her eyes. But she mustn't cry.

"Before me," Bean whispered.

"What a question, Bean," Lois said. "Yeah, I knew him. Like I knew a lot of guys in a town so small, you bump into your own ass dancing."

"But you met through me," Bean said. She was speaking slowly now. *Take your time, Lois, get it right.* She had introduced them at the halibut bake behind the cannery after that first season. They'd said things like "pleased to meetcha."

"What?" Lois said. "Well, yeah. I guess it was through you. Officially." Lois turned to her, standing wide open like a wheelbarrow. "So what?"

Bean backed down. "Nothing," she said. *Officially?*

Lois turned away. "Honey, I'd love to stay here and chat, but Fat Al will have our asses if we're not back on that line."

Lois tugged Bean through the flapping doors onto the factory floor.

A blast of screeches and bells and running water punched their ears as they headed back to the slime line amid catwalks and forklifts and zombie workers in yellow and green slickers.

Bean picked up her knife and started in on a sockeye. After a minute, she glanced over at Lois. Her face was masked by a red bandanna.

Bean decided to go ahead and meet Earl, a fisherman from Valdez. Maybe Lois was right. Maybe it was time to meet someone, get out of the house, hear some new lies. She didn't have to feel anything if she didn't want to. She could just go, have a drink, and leave.

On Saturday afternoon she announced that she was going out that night with Lois. It felt strange lying to Hanna, but she might see a blind date as an insult to Mick. Lois made things suspicious by calling three times within a couple of hours.

"Want to borrow my fuck-me boots?" Lois said. "Or Lopez. I could let you wear Lopez."

All of Lois's clothes had names. Lopez was a blue button-down shirt. It was named after the movie star, Jennifer Lopez, who would have filled it out better than Lois, if not as enthusiastically. It was Lois's favorite shirt, and it went well with Rock Star pants.

"I could lend you my cap," Lois went on. "But you gotta use it carefully."

Men loved her Mariners cap. Lois had a theory as to why. "It's like a big magnet," she once told Bean. "They figure you're into sports, and they're thinkin', 'Hey, a twofer.'"

"I dunno," Bean said at last. "What difference does it make?"

Lois wouldn't sleep with Mick, would she? It was too much to think about. The doubts clogged her head, and she could barely talk. But then again, Lois had this weird morality when it came to sex. It was exercise. Or a ride at the amusement park. The harness came down and bam: ninety seconds of thrills and chills. Then it was seeya, don't forget your pants.

"What?" Lois barked into the phone.

Bean snapped back. "Jeans," she said. "I thought I'd wear jeans. Is that all right with you?"

"Geez, what crawled into *your* panties today?"

"Just jeans," Bean insisted. "And a sweat—"

"Don't move," Lois said.

"No, Lois, I don't want—" But the phone line was dead.

A few minutes later Bean heard Lois's brakes squeak outside. You tended to forget how short the distances were in Eyak. The weather kept everyone so bottled up, you didn't think twice if you hadn't seen her next-door neighbor in a week or if you only talked to people by phone for days.

Bean stood by the bed, staring at a heap of clothes. She heard Lois shout hello to Hanna and clomp upstairs.

"You didn't scare her, did you?" Bean said.

Lois shrugged. "Just once I'd like to visit during the half hour of the day when she can actually *hear* something."

Lois looked at all the clothes on the bed.

"Geez, don't you believe in hangers?" she said.

"I like things where I can see them," Bean said. "Out in the open."

Lois gave her a look—what*ever*—and began picking through the tops and jerseys. She stood in front of the long mirror and held a couple against herself.

"What else you got?" she asked. She stepped behind the closet door and said, "Whoa, Nelly."

From behind the door a come-hither finger poked out. Lois was playing around. A twist of a wrist. Then a hip, swathed in pink. Lois hadn't been there five minutes and she was already in the middle of a burlesque. The teddy. Bean couldn't stand to look at it; it was a reminder of everything that had gone wrong. She let out a bellow and stalked over to the closet. She yanked the negligee away from Lois, but it was still on the hanger in Lois's hand.

"Hey, you ripped it," Lois said. "Honey, what's wrong?"

Bean shook her head. She felt herself skidding down two paths at once, like when you learn to ski and each leg has a mind of its own. One rut ran into a lonely, black scream. The other way involved this girl before her, with a bewildered look and a hanger in her hand—her only friend in Alaska.

Bean sank onto the bed and curled up on the corner where there were no clothes. She stuck her wrists between her ankles, balled up, facing away.

"Bean," Lois whispered.

Bean was weeping softly, not bothering to mop the liquid from her face as it seeped out. Just lying on her side like roadkill.

When she spoke, her voice was gulpy. "He said I sucked the life out of him. He did. He said it one time."

Lois, who had been staring at Bean like a time bomb, slowly lay down beside her. She curled up close until they spooned. Bean wasn't sure she wanted Lois to touch her. But when she did, it felt all right.

"He loved you, honey," she whispered. "He said he'd never seen anybody tame a roomful of kids like you. Said it was like you cast a magic spell."

Bean was still crying, but softly so she could hear.

"He even liked it when you messed up. Like that time you left the truck in neutral on the cannery road? He loved telling about that, him chasin' after the truck, and all the slimers standin' there with their mouths open."

Bean shuddered a few times, then felt exhaustion behind her eyeballs. Lois seemed to know an awful lot about Mick's feelings. Was this what it had come to? Had Alaska left her with so little? She fell asleep in the arms of the Other Woman.

When she woke up, it was still light out. The curse of Alaska in summer: you mourned in never-ending daylight. Lois hurried her.

"We can call it off, if you want, honey, but you gotta let me know."

Bean rubbed her face. The fisherman. She pulled herself to her feet. "I'll go," she said.

"These guys get kinda nasty if you stand 'em up." Lois was almost apologetic.

"I'll do it," Bean said.

From the pile on the bed, she picked up a white sweatshirt with mirror chips sewn in.

Lois's face said veto. "You might as well just wear your slicks from the cannery," she said.

In a flash, Bean was a fourth-grader in the changing room at the Emporium. Laura Branigan sang "Gloria" in the background. Bean waited in her underpants as her mother handed clothes over the plywood half door. The shirt was a green sleeveless turtleneck. What was the point of that? Next came some striped pants. They were too small.

"They're too small," Bean said after tugging them up to her thighs.

"Let me see," her mother said.

After some more back-and-forth, Bean finally emerged. She couldn't get the top button to snap, so she held her hands there. A saleswoman stood at her mother's side. Other shoppers paused for a look.

"Oh, those are too small," the saleswoman said.

Lois picked up the red sweater Mick had given to Bean and draped it over Bean's front. They looked in the mirror. "Wear this. It's perfect."

No, Bean told her. She never wore that sweater.

"You look delicious," Lois said.

"It makes me look fat," Bean said. You could see every Ding Dong she had ever eaten in that sweater.

Lois stood behind Bean and stroked her hair till it lost its electric surge and rested compliantly on her shoulders. "Girlfriend, are we looking in the same mirror? Because the lady in mine is *hot*."

Holding the sweater in place, Lois touched Bean's cheek with the back of her other hand. "Look at this skin." Mercifully, her acne days were over. She had smooth skin and naturally rosy cheeks. Her face was broad, almost heart-shaped.

"I can't wear that. It's slutty," Bean insisted. "I can't wear the same things as *you*."

Their eyes locked in the mirror—Lois, a head taller than Bean. They stared at each other, and Bean tried not to blink. Suddenly Lois erupted in laughter. It came from down deep, and Bean couldn't help smiling.

Lois rubbed her eyes, as if hit in the head with a mallet. "Well, that about says it all, I'd say."

She picked up the sweater again.

"Bean, what's the point of holding back?" Lois said into the mirror. "I mean, you get ten, twelve, maybe fifteen years if you're lucky. Then you've popped out a bunch of babies, you got saddlebags for hips, an ass like cottage cheese. By the way, honey, you really should start moisturizing now," she said.

Lois plastered the red sweater on Bean's chest. "The way I see it, you're a big fresh birthday cake all lit up," she said. "Now, go find somebody to blow you out."

Male ducks undergo the most spectacular makeovers in preparation for breeding. Whether mandarins, eiders, or harlequins, they acquire the most dazzling colors in summer. Within weeks of breeding, they moult their brilliant garb, resuming a more drab appearance.

—The Pemberton Guide

*A*s soon as she pushed open the saloon doors at the Copper Spike, heard the throbbing music, and saw all the people, she wondered if she'd made a mistake. Keith, the science teacher, sat at the end of the bar, sipping a draft. He saw Bean, raised his glass to her, took a sip, and wiped his upper lip with a cocktail napkin. Everyone had decided that Keith was gay—he tended his mustache too much; he spent his summer vacations at his mother's in Alabama—but no one ever bothered to tell Keith. "Might as *well* be gay," Lois said.

The Spike was filling up fast and Bean ordered a beer. It was the usual weekend crowd: fishermen in red-and-black-checked shirts and thermal underwear tops, some with beards down to their ribs, ponytails, a few hoop earrings, swelling bellies absorbing boilermakers. She felt hemmed in by water buffalo at the drinking hole. When did everybody get so big? Drinks were being passed over her head, ashtrays swiped from behind her. Everybody had horns and an attitude on, it being Saturday. The men moved slowly because of the booze, stiff muscles, heavy boots on their feet. It wasn't a good idea to rush things at the Spike on a Saturday night. Drinks got spilled, accidents happened.

Of the three bars in town, the Spike had the finest view of the harbor, the best nachos, and the most fights.

Bean caught a glimpse of herself in the strip mirror behind the bar. She was surprised to see how normal she looked. Bright, like someone with a future. Her hair, after a heavy conditioning, had fluffed up nicely and fell shiny down her shoulders. The red sweater was pretty, even though it made her breasts look huge.

With her back to the room, Bean leaned on the oak bar and watched people through the mirror. The men were standard-issue fishermen. They slouched in the dark, drinking therapeutically, as the evening sun poked through the blinds. They didn't waste any movements, didn't smile or talk more than they had to. It was early yet.

A cluster of women sat by the door, smoking. They had lean faces that told of hard nights and rough sex. Bean wondered if she would end up looking like that. A Filipino woman came into the bar on a fisherman's arm. She wore a loose sweater and shorts that could only be called hot pants. Hair teased up, eyes blackened, lips on. She smiled, a little expectantly, a little self-consciously, and made her way over to the women. She became instantly fascinated by their conversation, but Bean knew she was just handling all the eyes on her, letting the guys adjust to the sight of her. Bean was grateful; it took the pressure off.

After half an hour, she got tired of looking busy. Then he showed up.

"Are you Celestine?"

A huge man stood before her. Six-three, easy, maybe 230 pounds. Bean wasn't sure about her estimates, but her eyes met him in the sternum. A voice like a foghorn. She nodded.

"Earl," he said, introducing himself.

"People call me Bean," she said, sticking out her hand. She did her best to look at his face, but she made it as far as his bushy chin.

"Bean, huh? Now why's that?"

It was a dumb story, but it gave her something to say. Her mother had named her children in a fit of Catholic pomp. Her brother, five years older, had been Christopher William, and she was christened Celestine Josephine.

"Syllables were cheap back then," Bean said. No reaction from Earl.

"But you couldn't expect a little kid to lug around a name like that," she said. "When I tried to say it, the best I could do was Bean. My brother became Chip."

"Chip and Bean," Earl said. "Sounds like a snack."

Earl gulped two beers while Bean sipped hers. When he turned to go to the men's room, she watched his back in its sleeveless green jacket, broad enough to play Ping-Pong on.

Men and women were different species in Eyak—like kings and silvers—and they ran mostly with their own. Both had their rites and secrets and hobbies. Both found the other fascinating, if ultimately mysterious. They knew so little about each other's lives. The fishermen left on trips for three days, a week, or a month; had adventures; caught fish; cheated death; and came home just wanting to eat, sleep, screw. The women ran their homes, took on second jobs, minded the children, and watched their men in awe. The women worked harder, but they contended with sheets and groceries, not nets and squalls.

Fishing could be dangerous. The salmon ran through the Copper River flats, where the deep currents from the Gulf of Alaska hit shallow water. Sometimes the weather turned snotty—big winds, tricky swells. The little boats from Eyak Harbor flipped over. Every year one or two fishermen died from exposure or drowning. Nobody worked in their safety suits—they were too bulky. Everyone fished in jeans and a slicker and just accepted calamity when it came.

The men treasured the risk. "There's a thin line out there between coming back and not coming back, and even though it scares the shit out of you, you want it," Mick once told Bean. "It's like breathing cold air on the mountain."

Bean suspected that the men also liked fishing because it was so close to loafing. They could disappear for days, eat and drink what they wanted, wear the same clothes, pee off the boat, tell stories, play with their radios and secret codes, and fish. They could earn enough in three months to support themselves for the rest of the year. Not bad when you figure they spent twenty, maybe thirty days total with their nets in the water. The rest of the time, they painted, puttered, worked wood, went hunting, drank and smoked, tomcatted around, and drove their wives crazy. It was a pretty good deal.

The men were civil to one another because they needed one another—you couldn't live off the sea in a small town and be otherwise. When things went wrong out there—anything from a stalled engine to a capsizing—the nearest boats were honor-bound to yank up their nets and go help. Any fisherman who didn't would probably have to leave Eyak, if they let him live.

Still, the men were fierce competitors in the water. They looked over their shoulders when they set out in the morning and guarded their secret spots. They made sure to complain about their luck. Anybody who didn't was just asking for a tail. And that meant trouble, because once you dropped your nets, the only thing keeping another guy from laying his right in front of yours was common decency. If the second guy went ahead with it, he'd "corked" you. Mick said most fights at the Spike involved corking. That and women.

The fishermen were mostly loners, but they banded together in small radio networks of half a dozen guys. They talked among themselves in code. They told one another where the fish were running, how many they were pulling into their nets. "I got a retarded avocado in Philadelphia" could mean "I caught fifty kings in thirty feet of water off Grass Island." The codes changed all the time.

Contrary to what was said in the bars, a man's radio buddies actually knew when he was having a good season. Everyone else found out later, after his wife blabbed or they came back with tans from a vacation in Hawaii.

Mudhole Evans got Mick into a radio group. Bean remembered the day Mick came home, flushed with excitement, like a sorority pledge. Now he could sit over coffee with the clusters of men who wouldn't bother to spit on a stranger, and talk about currents and mechanics and wind. He was in because Mudhole said he was in.

He studied the codes as if cramming for an exam. His call name was Lindy.

Bean listened to him practice. She interrupted him with a question that had crossed her mind more than once. If all the best fish went up the Copper River to spawn, why did they need a fishing fleet? Why not just install a big gate at the delta, let X percent through to replenish the stock, and scoop up the rest? They could divide all the profits evenly in town. Easier, safer, and with a fraction of the manpower.

Mick looked at Bean like she was speaking Swahili. That was the craziest idea he'd ever heard.

"A big gate," he said. "Only a woman could come up with an idea like that."

Bean said she didn't see why it was such a dumb idea.

Mick opened his mouth, then shut it.

"Well, among a thousand other reasons, because a guy needs to leave the house in the morning, that's why," he said. "He's got to do something hard. Use his wits."

"So then, fishing is just a macho ego trip," Bean said. "It has nothing to do with economics."

"It's a way of life," Mick said. And he didn't want to talk about it anymore. "A gate," he scoffed.

Bean looked around the Copper Spike at the women, who were dragging on cigarettes and theatrically ignoring the men. Lois had taught her about the women. Before they'd gotten tangled up with the fishermen, they had been single and in demand. They could be choosy. Some of them went for the older guys, who were maybe a little gentler, a little more grateful, or had their boats paid off. After a divorce, the women were still in demand. But they were less picky.

It was a hard life. There were losers out there: guys who never shaved, rarely bathed, couldn't talk about anything. And that wasn't even counting the violent types. "The odds are good, but the goods are odd," Lois told her. Lois pretended to find some men disgusting.

Earl came back. He took her outside to see his new truck. He'd ordered it a few months back, when everyone was still banking on a good season. Working the tender was hard labor—loading and off-loading salmon around the clock. Earl flicked at a bird dropping on the hood. "I figured I deserved it," he said.

In a town with two roads to nowhere, a truck had limited uses. One road ran around the west side of the lake then turned into a Forest Service trail. The other road ran past the airport fifteen miles east of town, went gravel, bisected, then ran into two glaciers, one to the north, dark with grit, the other out east, translucent blue. The road to the glaciers hugged a path carved by the old railroad. When the copper mines played out, the railroad fell apart, and Eyak lost its land link to the outside world. The only way in or out now was by ferry or plane.

Some people said that saved the town, kept the ills of the world at bay. Others complained they couldn't get enough tourists in, or fresh fish out, without a road to connect them to the rest of Alaska. But they'd have to cut through federal forest to build that road. And nobody could agree on that, in town, in Juneau, or in Washington.

"Brand-new truck and I can't put any miles on it," Earl said with a look of disgust. "Had to put it on the ferry from Valdez. I mean, what is this—the Belgian freakin' Congo?"

Bean rather liked seeing progress turned back. Where she grew up in California, the fields she'd played in as a girl were now carpeted with strip malls and anonymous developments. "I kind of like not having a road," she said.

Earl grunted. "Oh, you're one of *them*," he said.

Bean shrugged.

"Hey, you got fingernails?" he asked.

"Huh?"

"Fingernails."

Bean looked at her hands—some chewed up, some intact. "Yeah, I guess, a little," she said.

"Wanna help me with this?"

He reached through the truck window and handed her a decal. It was of a little, spiky-haired boy with a mischievous smile. An arc of urine spouted from his pants. Bean peeled off the backing and they spent five minutes finding the right place for it on the truck.

Earl stepped back to take in the masterpiece. He rubbed his hands. "Now what?" he said.

They decided to drive toward the glacier.

Bean fiddled with Earl's CD player as he drove. It was past eight on Saturday night, but the light was still golden afternoon. They rode past ponds with lilypads and beaver huts, past geese that cried like spoiled children. The roadside was purple-flecked with wild lupine. She relaxed a bit and drank in the smell of the new truck, felt it handle the rough road, looked up to a wide sky with heavy cumulus clouds.

Earl was quiet, which suited her fine. Mick had always been talking about three things at once. Earl was so much bigger than Mick. He was like a grizzly, dark hair sprouting everywhere, even on his knuckles.

She wondered when she should tell him about Mick, or if he already knew.

After thirty miles, the road simply stopped. An abandoned bulldozer, yellow paint flaking off, sat at the end, engulfed by bushes. You could practically hear some highway construction worker saying "fuck it" and walking off the job. Man was always slamming up against nature in Alaska. Sometimes nature won.

They sat in the truck looking at the blue sheet-cake glacier that oozed down from the coastal peaks then crumbled in little avalanches. The glacier was as tall as a twenty-story building and it made popping sounds. Blue ice chunks broke off and bobbed downriver like drunken whales.

Bean sat next to Earl in the truck. She liked the silence. But did he? She couldn't think of anything to say. What would Lois do? She cast a sidelong glimpse at his furry face. But she couldn't see enough of it to read him. Should she talk? Should she tell him now, about Mick? What was he thinking? If only she could get inside his head.

The glacier popped again.

"She's burping a lot today," Earl said.

Bean quietly agreed. With a grunt, Earl draped his arm across her shoulder. He pulled her chin up toward his face. "You'd be quite a looker if you held your head up," he said. He put his scratchy beard up to her cheek and poked his beery tongue into her mouth. Bean let him do it; she closed her eyes, tasting the kiss. Salt and beer. Not too bad.

His free hand began to explore her chest, stroking and squeezing. It's a birthday cake, Bean thought. A birthday cake with the candles lit. He was under her sweater and his hands started to hurt. He leaned into her, pinching harder. She didn't feel like a birthday cake.

My husband is dead. Tell him.

"Um," she said.

Her stomach rebelled. He leaned into her, pinching harder.

"No," she said.

"C'mon," he said. "You want it."

She closed her eyes. She looked over his shoulder, to the vacant ceiling of the new cab. And then she was looking down on herself, jammed up against the passenger door, eyes squeezed. She had to help that girl.

She stirred up a cyclone of arms and knees.

"No!" she bellowed. "No no no!" One fist grazed his jaw. Another knocked the rearview mirror askew. The bear backed up.

"I can't," Bean said. "I'm sorry."

His lips curled and his eyes were glassy.

"What are you," he said, "some kind of a lesbo?"

They drove back in silence.

When she came in just before midnight, the old lady was in bed. There was a message in her cramped hand on the dining table.

"Lois called," it said. "Wanted to know how it went with Mr. Pearl."

After Bean's father left, her mother went once a month to see an accountant. She worried a lot about money, and you could tell by her nerves when the visit was drawing near. One night, it was an accountant night, but Chip had plans. He said he couldn't stay home and baby-sit Bean.

"Then take her with you," their mother said.

Chip howled. That was just sooo ridiculous. He was almost sixteen—he could drive, he was a *sophomore*, for godsake. His friends would never let him hear the end of it. Hanging out with a baby ten-year-old.

"I'm not a baby," Bean said.

"Shut up, you."

"That's the deal," her mother said. "Take her along, or stay home."

They were standing in the hallway by the front door. It was crowded because there were moving boxes lining the wall. They were full of things Hank had missed when he packed up. Clothes, mostly.

They waited in the driveway for Chip's buddy to pick them up. "Thanks a lot, Bean," he said.

She wished it could be like before, when he read to her in the easy chair. Everything would be so much better if they were friends. But it was hard to believe he was the same boy. He had become surly. He lay on his back in his room with his headphones on loud. Sometimes he went out with friends. They drove around in their parents' cars and talked about how much they hated their parents and their cars.

Chip's friend Eddie showed up in an Oldsmobile station wagon. They went to pick up two other guys, Ronnie Romano and David Barnett. Each time somebody got in the car, he looked at Bean and said: "What's with the kid?" and Chip had to explain all over again.

Bean sat in the backseat, next to Chip and Ronnie. They drove down Paradise Drive and parked in a vacant lot overlooking the bay. Chip made Bean get out of the car while they smoked. At least he didn't tell her not to snitch.

It was chilly out, the air was full of brine, and the ground was mucky underfoot. But there was a lot of moonlight, and Bean went out into the flats and looked for crabs. She saw a few, but they were too fast to catch. She went back to the car.

She tapped on the car window "Chip?" she said. It was foggy inside.

The window rolled down. A punch of sickening smell, like body odor wrapped in horse manure. "Shit, Bean, I told you to wait."

"I *been* waiting."

"Well, wait some more."

"I'm cold."

She had gotten her T-shirt wet when she picked up a shell and it drained down her front.

David Barnett exhaled and giggled. "I can *see* that," he said. Like it was the funniest thing.

"Perky cold," Eddie said. "Sassy cold."

She looked into the car at the teenagers with red, glazed eyes. She didn't even have breasts.

"Shut up," she said.

Then Ronnie Romano offered to wait outside with Bean. "Won't hurt to stretch my legs," he said. They walked over to a grassy slope and sat down and talked. He had a Marlboro. He seemed to like talking to her, even though he was older. When she started shivering, he put his arm around her.

Ronnie was a good-looking guy. When he talked, people listened. He had almost made the swim team last year, but he got cut at the last minute because he'd missed a few practices. It was so unfair.

Ronnie tightened his arm around Bean and she realized she wasn't cold anymore. He put his cigarette in front of Bean's lips, so she could taste it. She sucked on it, then spit out the smoke. She couldn't believe how nice it felt, sitting there in Ronnie Romano's arms.

He touched her chin and told her she was beautiful. With his other hand, he fumbled at her jeans. When the top button suddenly popped open, they both laughed. He slid a hand down her pants. She let him do it. He was breathing hard and seemed to know what he was doing. It hurt a little as he poked her with his finger. He nuzzled her neck. Then the car horn blared; time to go.

"Shit," he said. "Come on." He didn't even wait for her to pull her pants up.

Monday was the worst day of Bean's life. People in school knew. Ronnie had bragged about it. Bean Jessup went to third base. A couple of sixth-graders came up to her and winked and jabbed their elbows at each other. "How was Paradise?" one of them said.

Bean thought all the attention might kill her.

Please God, don't let my mother find out.

Chip came home from high school. He didn't even ask her how it happened. It was her fault. "Jesus, Bean, what were you thinking?" he said. "This is the most fucking embarrassing thing on the planet."

The wind was a real roof-ripper that night. The hemlock tree in the front yard thrashed madly. Bean finally fell asleep on the couch, a notebook on her chest.

When Debbie was little she dreamed up a song
To sing while she swam, it wasn't too long.
But dark clouds appeared as she sang in the Lake
The sky crackled with lightning, the hills seemed to shake.
All the Lake's creatures ducked under the trees
They hid 'neath the branches and pulled up their knees.
And it rained and rained and rained.

At first, it rained like dogs and cats,
Then like mooses and gooses and giraffes with hats,
The animals watched as the Lake water rose
Then a turtle swam over, and he blew his nose.
"I've come from below, where I'm sorry to tell
There are cracks in the dam," and he hid in his shell.
And it rained and rained and rained.

"If the dam breaks," all the animals cried,
"We'll lose our home in one giant tide!"

A weasel named Wally blamed Debbie, said he:
"She sang a Rain Song at a quarter to three."
The animals crowded young Debbie to scold:
"Make it stop," "How could you," and "My feet are so cold."
And it rained and rained and rained.

Debbie the Duck knew they were wrong,
The storm wasn't caused by her little Swim Song.
She ran to her mother and buried her head,
But her mom pushed her back. "Make it stop," she said.
Debbie looked at the heavens and with no more delay,
cried, "Stop!" But then her dad flew away.
And it rained and rained and rained.

Debbie moved north, where it rains all the time.
The people there know there's no reason or rhyme.
The storm stopped back home, and the dam held. What luck!
The only thing broken was the heart of a duck.

Hanna was on the back deck, smoking, when Bean came into the kitchen. Bean pretended not to see her through the glass door and sat down at the table Mick built. Before she noticed what she was doing, she was gently nudging it back and forth on its legs, feeling the wobble. She glanced outside where Hanna sat, stock-still, in a cloud. The deck was covered with twigs and wet leaves.

Bean stepped onto the deck, silently daring Hanna to say the wrong thing.

Wordlessly, she picked up Hanna's pack of B&Hs, shook one out, and lit it. The ember flared and she scorched the back of her mouth. It felt good. Her muscles eased with the first rush of nicotine. What an efficient drug. Mick had hated cigarettes.

Hanna, it turned out, had her own thoughts. They sat together in silence for a while, feeling the remorse of a Sunday afternoon. From their lawn chairs they could see Eyak's harbor. Crews scrubbed and unloaded a few beat-up salmon boats.

"Michael's father died twenty-one years ago this year," Hanna said. "Lung cancer. They found a spot after Thanksgiving. He was gone by August."

"I'm sorry," Bean said. She paused to see who would take the next drag on a cigarette. Hanna did; she raised her bent hand to puckered lips and sucked till every line in her face jumped into relief.

"Michael was just eleven," she said, exhaling now. "His sister was even younger."

Hanna's husband had been a proud man. He liked the nicer things. He bought his dress shirts at Brooks Brothers. Trucking kept him in dungarees all week; he said a fellow had to feel his own man on Sunday.

Bean stared at the boats.

"When he got the bad news, something clicked off inside him," Hanna said. "He just turned his face to the wall and waited to die. That was it. No Christmas. No Easter." They had celebrated the holidays around him, as if he were part of the furniture. Mick joined Little League. Franny had her first Holy Communion.

All Mick had ever said about his sister was that she gave him a headache. Franny had married a software designer in Vancouver and produced a kid a year, four times over. Now she scheduled everyone's life—soccer games, piano lessons, Little League—like Mussolini. She complained about how much work it was, but she wouldn't slow down and she wouldn't let anything slide. "She thinks she invented motherhood," Mick had said. Everybody in Franny's life was a little incompetent. That was her cross to bear.

"We had the kids late in life," Hanna was saying. "You can't just turn them off when they're so little. But Jack didn't want any of it. He was done."

Hanna was going to talk herself out. Bean wondered if she would mention the Cub Scout cookies. She felt a bit buzzed from the first cigarette but took a fresh one anyway and held it in her hand.

"He was done with me," Hanna said. Their marriage—everything she had shared with a man for ten years—just stopped. She became nurse and cook and counselor, she didn't know what all. But she stopped being the one thing she knew how to be: a wife. He didn't let her talk about what was happening, even though it was happening to all of them, she said. She changed sheets, rinsed pajamas, drove him to the doctor. But she never got to say good-bye.

Bean suddenly remembered something Mick had said about his mother. They had been strapped almost immediately after his father's death. The union had paid for the funeral, but the benefits went quickly. Hanna's brothers had taken up a collection that covered her house payments for a couple of months. Then she went to work as a telephone operator.

"Nobody ever gets to say good-bye," Bean said. "Not really."

Hanna didn't say anything. Bean glanced over to see if her hearing aid was in. It was.

Bean leaned back and took in the deck where they sat. The wooden railing had subsided in the past couple of years. But the floorboards were flat and solid. It wasn't much of a deck—ten feet by twelve feet—but she loved the view. Just months ago she had loved their house, with its green and orange trim, on the hill across from the old school, now a boardinghouse. She had planted nasturtiums. Now it was just a house that needed work.

"Mick built this deck," Bean said.

Hanna got interested in the deck. Bean gave all the boring details she could remember.

"It's warped," Bean said. She pointed. "Here. And there. See?" It would have driven Mick crazy, if he found out some crook had sold him green wood. Hanna surprised Bean with a laugh, then she brushed imaginary tobacco flakes from her lap. Bean figured it was a good time to confess.

"Hanna, about last night," she said. "I didn't go out with Lois in the end."

"I gathered that," Hanna said. She stared at her hands in her lap, and Bean couldn't see much of her face.

"Have a nice time?" she asked.

Bean didn't hear any bitterness in Hanna's voice. Now she felt like crying. She looked away, out over the harbor and the clumpy islands in the sound.

"No," she whispered.

A tall figure in a yellow slicker slid through the glass door and appeared on the porch. Bean and Hanna both jumped. When would they stop expecting Mick? Lois closed the door behind her and faced Bean. There was something strange about her. Not just the hangdog face. She was lumpy.

"Hey," she said.

"Speak of the devil," Bean said.

"Honey, I'm so sorry."

Sorry for what, Lois?

"I know," Bean said. She didn't want to talk about Earl. She pointed at Lois's belly. "You about to give birth or something?"

Lois drew one of her bad-girl looks from her wide repertoire. Then she lifted the bottom of her slicker jacket. A fin as wide as her foot poked out. She kept rolling upward, in a disgusting striptease and each inch uncovered a slimy, spotty wad of flesh.

It was a king salmon, worth a couple hundred bucks retail.

"I brought a friend," Lois said. "You know what goes good with this? Soy sauce and brown sugar, in a glaze." She looked at Hanna.

Hanna took the cue, stubbed out her cigarette, and headed into the kitchen. She didn't care much for Lois. Before long she was banging dishes. Lois plopped the fish onto the deck.

"Men are assholes," Lois said.

"They're not the only ones."

Lois stepped closer, put her hands on her hips. "Spit it out, Bean."

"Okay, I will."

"Go ahead."

"Did you fuck my husband?"

For all the buildup in Bean's head, it was plain that Lois hadn't been expecting that one. She opened her mouth, then closed it, like the force of the question made her stupid. It probably didn't help that Bean was crying.

"Oh, honey," Lois objected. Like there was a long version of the story.

But now that she'd said it, Bean wanted an answer.

"Well?" she said.

"Well, when you put it like that," Lois said. "Yeah."

A duck reared in isolation feels the impulse to migrate, but is at a loss as to where it should go. While males tend to follow different mates to different destinations each year, females are strongly drawn to their birthplace each spring.

—The Pemberton Guide

hen Bean came back from walking Fred, Hanna was on the phone.

"Well, two for me was more than enough, I'll tell you," Hanna said. "I can't imagine trying to handle a hundred."

A hundred kids? Who was she talking to? Then she knew. Marty Keene, the principal. Bean had been dodging his notes and calls. He wanted her to sign that contract.

Hanna looked over at Bean, who was hanging her jacket on a peg. "Oh, I think that's her coming in," she told the principal.

Bean frowned and waved her arms at Hanna like a train switchman facing trouble. Hanna looked flustered.

"Oh," Hanna said. "No, I guess I was wrong. It was . . . the dog . . . back from his walk. Hello, Fred."

Hanna promised to give Bean the message as soon as she got back.

Bean sank into the couch.

She loved her students, of course. Last year, before vacation, the kids had given her a good-bye hug and she burst into tears. When one of the boys insisted that Bean was faking it, they all inspected her face. "No, they're real," someone insisted.

But the children needed education, not sentiment. She felt so in-effective.

Despite her best efforts, Wolfie Hagen still hadn't learned to read. His parents were no help at all. When she had assigned an essay based on a story about Debbie the Duck, Wolfie had turned in a paper with just a few lines: "In case of a fire emergincy, walk do not run to the nearst exit." It was copied from the sign over the door. Before long, Wolfie would be an emergincy himself.

Or take Brittany Miller. Bean had asked them to report on what they had learned during the course of the year. Brittany had apparently forgotten all about counting by twos and threes, figuring out money, the field trip to see the salmon, and reading *Charlotte's Web*. "I learned to sit up in my chair and write neatly," she wrote. Neatly.

Bean imagined her legacy after thirty years on the job. She saw six hundred middle-aged men and women with tidy penmanship who sat up straight and walked away from fires.

She decided to go for a swim. She did some of her best thinking in the pool, with its wraparound mural of palm trees and beach scenes. The chemicals cleared her sinuses. Before long, it would be cold again. Swimming was so much harder in the winter.

She was alone in the pool, except for the lifeguard, a gangly teenager with hair like topiary. She started slow, a solid crawl, waiting to see how much might was stored in her arms today. Some days she tuckered after a few laps. Other days she felt like she could swim forever.

She plowed along, arms slicing and gliding, her breathing timed perfectly to the stroke. She neared the tiled wall, accounted for the optical illusion that made it seem farther off, hurled her body over her right shoulder in a flip, landed her feet flat on the tiles, and gave herself a ferocious push forward. It was a forever day.

She pulled herself through the thick water, lap after lap, until her triceps ached. She paid for the Twinkies, repented the cigarettes, and swam on. After half a mile, her thighs added their burn to the pain in her arms. But she knew it would ease again.

The swimming allowed only for five-second thoughts. If you were counting laps, you had a few moments after the flip turn to let your mind drift. Bean wondered how she looked to the lifeguard; had he ever seen a swimmer like her? *Forty.* Flip. She was positively aquatic. She was a sea creature, come to swim a thousand miles in an afternoon. *Forty-one.* Flip.

It wasn't just the teaching. Everything had gone sour, turned crooked. Without Mick, Alaska was just a lie people told themselves. All that hearty-ho, make-do bravado. Rain, you say? What rain? And isn't it swell that you can dress a deer with nothing more than a Swiss Army knife? Big deal. The rest of the world has Price Club.

Forty-one. Forty-three? Shit.

Had they all forgotten a world where it was light in the morning and dark at night? Where children didn't swing from the jungle gyms at midnight, howling their hearts out like baboons? A world where, every now and then, the sun, not meaty mosquitoes, tickled your neck?

Could they admit to a longing for beaches and Slurpees and baseball diamonds and movie stars and fireworks and Rollerblades and swimming pools and bike rides and roads that led to other roads?

They could not. The whole tableau would come crashing down.

Or maybe it was her. She had failed spectacularly. It all seemed impossible now. Without Mick to cheer her up with a bowl of antler stew. *Forty.*

Without Lois to confide in. She couldn't talk to Lois anymore; she kept imagining her together with Mick, and it made her want to throw up. The stories Bean told herself to keep from disappearing—they didn't work anymore. It was the worst kind of lonely: losing people. She had lost, and now she had to get out of there. That would mean saying good-bye to Mick. Really good-bye.

Jiminy, where do you go from here?

She popped her elbows over the side of the pool and hauled herself out of the water.

When she got back to the house, the phone was ringing. Hanna made a play for it, but Bean snatched it up. Somehow she knew it was for her and she needed to hear it. It was Jimmy in San Francisco. She filled him in.

"Sounds like you need a vacation," he said.

Mick and Bean had taken exactly one vacation. Last March they had flown to Cancún. It was a package deal—they were trying to economize. They ended up sharing a balcony with a bunch of drunk frat boys on early spring break. They ate dinner at Señor Frog's, and when they got back to the hotel, the frat boys offered them Jell-O shots. During the day, they sat on the beach and sailed a Sunfish. Mick sang to her in a corny Spanish accent.

"Or better yet, why not just come home?" Jimmy said.

She'd been waiting for him to say that, of course, but when she heard it, she went mute. "You've had the power all along, you know," he said.

"Huh?"

"Just click your heels three times."

She remembered sitting on an overstuffed couch with a little boy, his soft brown eyes riveted to a television, and within it, a world that changed from gray to brilliant color.

They had watched the movie and had been tucked into warm beds. Back when their families were whole. When the world worked. When the wicked things melted away, and you could run out of the room during the scariest part.

"I thought I'd strap myself to the back of a flying monkey," Bean said.

Jimmy moaned. She knew those flying monkeys had always scared the shit out of him.

Bean and Jimmy spoke more and more often. She, standing on the back porch in a B&H haze, amid an eternal blast of crickets, beneath a sky studded with stars. He, sitting in the kitchen of his flat in the Castro, poking absently at his computer keyboard and, she was sure, driving his lover Peter crazy with their marathon calls.

Jimmy urged Bean to end her exile, and Bean allowed herself to think of what she might recover. She tried to assemble the most enticing visions of home—the house she grew up in, with its rope swing and wide porch; the lovely mild sun on Mt. Tamalpais in October; Old Mill School, with Mrs. Harper's gentle face lighting up the third grade. Would she still be alive? How much would remain?

Her mother would have a new life by now. New friends, a better job. Maybe another man. She was indestructible. They hadn't spoken in so long. Not really since Bean became a teenager and ended every fight saying she wanted to go live with her father.

Her brother was a question mark. He could be a big-shot business guy or a crack dealer. Every day was like starting over for Chip—all that wired-up energy. Could they become friends? She hadn't seen him in years; she feared she might not recognize him.

Jimmy was on the line. "Just remember, Jelly, wherever you are, you're going to have to deal with real life," he said. "Try to run *to* something. Not just away."

"You should talk about running away, Mr. Pajamas in Midget Woods."

Sometimes, Bean decided, it didn't matter if it was to or away from. You just had to run.

———————

In the years immediately following the divorce, Hank saw his children a handful of times. It was always last-minute—a call would come, he had a business trip to the Bay Area—and he would show up in a rental car and honk the horn. Usually just Bean went; the last thing Chip wanted was a lecture from a dad who didn't even live with them. Bean loved the visits. They went to Clown Alley for cheeseburgers and spoiled her dinner.

She asked if she could visit him in his new home in Massachusetts. He said he would like that very much. But he was traveling an awful lot and he needed to wait until things got settled in the new house. He had remarried and they had three-year-old twins.

There were only a few slurps left in her milkshake when she asked him again. It was a warm day and they were sitting at a little plastic table. Cars whizzed past.

"Hey, Hank," she said, "how's about I come to see you?"

"I dunno, Burt. My gout's been acting up. Specially when it rains."

It was never the right time.

During Bean's sophomore year in high school, her mother signed her up for tennis lessons at the club. She had no chance to protest. "They're paid for, and you're going," her mother said.

There was plenty of room for sullenness, though. For her first lesson, Bean wore baggy shorts and a Grateful Dead T-shirt. The pro was named Steven. He had nut-brown legs and a hank of tawny hair that covered his forehead. He stood behind you and almost hugged you to check your grip. For the next lesson, Bean put on a better T-shirt.

Bean's backhand improved, and though her mother might not have noticed it from her one-word offerings in conversation, her outlook did as well. Steven was a total fox—all the girls said so. But for Bean, he was more than that. The way he tossed his hair, the way he picked up balls effortlessly with his ankle, the way he said "Bean." Steven was a creature from a better world. Sometimes when he crossed the net to give her a tip, she couldn't hear anything; he was too close.

One afternoon Bean's mother came to pick her up at the club. She sat in the bleachers watching the class, wearing her pleated white mini-skirt, even though she wasn't going to play. After the class, when Steven was corralling balls, Bean's mother walked over to him. They talked for a few minutes as Steven punched the balls into the wire basket. He must have said something hysterically funny because Bean's mother squealed and threw her head back and laughed. Then she reached over and grabbed Steven's forearm and offered some kind of reply. On the other side of the court, Bean and the other girls zipped up their rackets and watched the two of them.

During the car ride home, Bean didn't say a word until her mother said: "What's eating you?"

Bean said it was embarrassing how her mother fawned over the tennis pro. "Oh, Steven," Bean mimicked in a high voice, fluttering her hand to cool her face.

At a stoplight, her mother looked over. "I never thought I would see it," she said. "You're jealous."

"What?" Bean shouted.

"I told him, I told Steven, watch out, there's a crowd of cow-eyed girls watching his every move. He'd better be careful."

They carried the fight through the front door. Bean announced she couldn't take it anymore. She was going to live with her father.

"Call him up," her mother insisted. "Call him up. Go to him. See what you get. Go. Go."

Later that night Bean snapped shut the door of the den and dialed Hank's number. A woman answered. She sounded sleepy. Suddenly Bean remembered the time difference.

The woman's name was Margie. The *g* was hard.

"Is something wrong?" Margie asked.

Jimmy called one night before Bean had assumed her telephone pose. The cigarettes were distressingly out of reach.

"Hey, Jelly Bean," Jimmy said. "Listen to this: 'SF school district seeking teachers, bilingual, grammar school, all levels. Will help certify.' That's you, isn't it?"

Bean agreed it could be her.

After they hung up, Bean went back to the table, where Hanna sat.

"I'm thinking of leaving here," Bean said.

Hanna had picked up last week's newspaper. She looked at Bean over her glasses.

"Oh? Where would you go?"

"Home. San Francisco."

Hanna blinked about ten times.

"There are some teaching jobs opening up."

"Oh, what grade?"

"All grades."

Hanna stared ahead, looking shocked. She didn't think they would live there forever, did she?

"I see," she said. She looked around the house as if the movers were at the door.

"I mean, it's where I'm from," Bean said. It felt like an apology.

Hanna took a deep breath and lit a cigarette.

"When?"

"I dunno. I'm just thinking."

They were practically whispering. Was this how you started to say good-bye? Bean had gotten used to having Hanna around these past few months, however much she groused to herself about the imposition. She liked seeing her face in the morning. It was a good face, without any tricks in it, at least not when it came to Bean. It sagged and looked like it might actually flap in a strong wind, but it was a face that made you feel a little better about life.

She had learned to work around Hanna. Picking up her Kleenex, replacing the battery in her hearing aid. Living with the clutter of a hoarder. She turned the TV up extra loud even when Hanna wasn't in the room.

Bean wondered what Hanna was thinking. Sometimes she sat among Mick's things like an achy woman taking a hot bath. Was she worried about losing that? Bean didn't know.

"It just seems so sudden, that's all," Hanna said.

Bean had nothing more to say. After a while Hanna sighed and stood up.

"I've got some boxes tucked away that'll come in handy for a move," she said.

By the end of her sophomore year, she was drowning in school. Classes were deathly boring. She didn't care about football games and pep rallies. The zits appeared and she scrubbed her face so much that it looked like hamburger. Her clothes didn't fit right. The worst part was that everybody else seemed to be doing just fine. They knew what to say, what to do with their hands, where to go at lunch. They divided up effortlessly. Almost instinctively, they knew where they belonged: the drama kids, the athletes, the brains, the burnouts. Bean hovered.

She missed Jimmy. His father had sent him to the Mountain Academy; he said it would make a man out of him. They made you march every morning.

She got terrifically hungry by lunch. But the cafeteria food was so bad, she relied on the vending machines. The fruit pies had actual fruit in them, so they counted as lunch. She lined up to put her quarters in, a novel tucked under her arm. The girls her age breezed by. The pretty ones were outlandishly happy and bold. The not-so-pretty ones were funny and loyal. They all knew about clothes and lip gloss and boys. Bean was working her way through *The Bell Jar*.

One. gray day she had piled up a plastic-wrapped meal. Her hands were overloaded with soda and pastry and books and coins and there was a long line behind her, so she rushed. Everything fell to her feet. Some of her quarters rolled under the vending machine. When she bent over to pick them up, one of the boys behind her mooed. A long, nasal cow sound. She cut sixth period that day and walked home.

But Hank called that night and said okay. Bean could visit that summer. They would spend two weeks in Somerville, then they'd take a family vacation on Cape Cod. He had a week off.

A family vacation.

Bean's days brightened. She measured time backward from the day she would land in Massachusetts. She loved the word, and she said it a lot around her mother to punish her. "When I go to Massachusetts," she'd say. "Do you think it will be cold in Massachusetts?" They barely spoke anymore.

At night, lying in bed, she wondered how big her father's house was and if she would have her own room. If she had to share with the kids, that would be okay, *temporarily*. She wondered if the high school was close by. She wondered if she could lose ten pounds before school started. She could enroll in Massachusetts as a whole different person. She might even change her name.

———

Hank picked her up at the airport in a station wagon with toys and juice cartons sliding around in back. There were heavy bags under his eyes, and Bean figured he was probably drinking pretty hard. He was still handsome, in a beat-up way.

He hugged her and opened up the hatch. "Hiya, Burt," he said.

The traffic from the airport was slow, but Bean didn't mind. While Hank honked and swerved, she told him about everything she could think of. She really talked a streak. It was so good to be there.

Margie came out to the car when they finally pulled up. She was about thirty. She was TV–thin with short, frosted hair and a way of sounding cheery even when her face looked hard. She had one of the boys on her hip. Before the twins, Margie had worked as a dental hygienist. That was how she met Hank—he blew a crown one morning eating a nut muffin. She looked tired. Raising twins was hard work. Bean suspected Hank wasn't much help in that department.

Bean got to know the twins right away. It was a little weird thinking of them as half brothers; she already had a brother, and these were practically babies. But they were good kids—clumsy and loving and eager to share their toys. After she saw they hit it off, Margie started using Bean as a baby-sitter. She had so many errands to catch up on.

Hank came home at night and went straight for the refrigerator. He never liked to talk after work. "I talk to people all day," he once told Bean's mother. "Talk and listen, nice as pie." He popped open a bottle of beer and settled in to watch sports. Bean had been cooped up in the house all day with the twins, so she had nothing to contribute. She wished she hadn't told him about her life all at once, coming from the airport. But they could connect later, she figured, on the family vacation at the beach.

Margie had plenty to say. But it was strange with her. She seemed grateful for Bean's help, but she resented it, too. Bean decided not to piss her off.

They were in the tiny backyard on a warm afternoon, watching the kids play on a plastic jungle gym.

"It's nice and all that you like the kids," Margie said.

"They're great kids," Bean said.

"I was just wondering if you missed your friends. I mean, people your own age? Sixteen is such a wonderful time. What are your girl-friends doing this summer?"

Jimmy was working as a stagehand in the touring version of *Annie*. He got up early every morning and took the bus into San Francisco. He said it might lead to a big break—you never knew. There weren't many other friends to worry about. Bean had made some headway getting to know this girl named Sarah, who was pretty funny and knew lots of other girls.

"Well," Bean said. "There's this one girl—"

Margie was staring at her children, crawling on the gym. "Not too high, Ethan," she said. Ethan and Eric. Bean couldn't tell them apart. She called them both Tiger.

Bean waited to see where Margie was headed. They were silent awhile.

"What's your mother like?" she asked.

That was the last thing Bean wanted to talk about. She shrugged.

"She's pretty mad a lot, I guess," she said.

Suddenly, she felt bad about tormenting her mother with all the happy talk of Massachusetts. Now she was talking about her to Margie, her replacement.

"Is she . . . seeing anyone?"

"I really don't want to talk about her right now," Bean said. "Sorry."

———————

Two days before they were to leave for the Cape, Bean put the kids in the double stroller and headed down the bikepath to the marsh. Margie had gone to Jazzercise, and Bean was craving some fresh air. It was a long walk, but they were rewarded by several herons feeding in the reeds.

It took a while getting back, because the twins insisted on pushing the carriage, first one, then the other. When the orange sun slipped beyond the horizon, Bean decided to stuff them into the buggy and speed things up. But the fork in the path near the Alewife T stop confused her. She guessed wrong, and they ended up having to find their way through the busy city streets.

When they finally made it home—stopping dog-walkers for directions, bouncing curb to curb—Margie was waiting on the porch. She was still wearing a sweatshirt and leggings from her class. The front door was open behind her, and lots of bright light spilled into the drive. She was on the phone and the line stretched taut back into the house. It looked like she might break it.

Margie hung up and swooped onto the carriage. She started to pull out the boys. They got stuck, but she yanked on them anyway, until they were free. She angrily swatted at their jackets, as if they needed dusting.

"It got late," Bean said.

"I am *not* speaking to you," Margie declared. But she was. "We were worried sick. Just sick."

Bean saw that her father's car wasn't in the driveway yet, so Margie really meant herself. *She* was worried sick. Unless she had phoned Hank at work. That would be bad.

Margie shooed them up the front steps. "What kind of a person disappears in a strange city with three-year-olds? And past dark. You are truly unbelievable."

"We took a wrong turn," Bean said.

Bean waited a few minutes before following Margie into the house. She went to her room and shut the door.

That night Margie and Hank had a fight. It sounded different from the way her parents used to fight, largely because Margie kept hushing them both to keep from waking the kids. It was a warm night, and Bean sat near her open window with the bugs hurling themselves into the screen.

They were careful not to say her name.

"It's only one more week," Hank said. "You're working yourself up over nothing."

But Margie was on a tear. "*Nothing,*" she hissed. "That's perfect. That's just great. Do you have the slightest clue, Hank, what holds a family together? The slightest clue?"

A car with its radio on pulled into the driveway next door. Aretha Franklin's "Freeway of Love." It was harder to hear.

"Show some spine. . . . Living her own life, not grafting herself onto ours . . . Hard enough raising twins without hosts from your old life."

Hosts? Bean didn't quite hear it. No, it was *ghosts.*

She was a ghost.

The morning Hank drove her to the airport, Bean couldn't believe it was happening. All week at the Cape, she had let the kids bury her in the sand, even though her face got horribly sunburned. She had swept the porch when they dragged in sand and walked into town for juice when they'd run out. Now it was over. And her father was going to let her leave. She would stay if he only asked. They would work it out with Margie. But she was a ghost.

He threw his arm around her at the gate and kissed her forehead.

"See ya, Burt," he said.

———————

She knew she was pushing her luck with the milk truck. A college kid had driven it up from Portland and sold it to Mick for a few hundred bucks. Now its odometer was stuck, and there was no telling how many miles it had clocked. But Bean was going to try to coax it through one last trip down the Alaska-Canada Highway, to San Francisco.

The truck wore a thin coat of light blue paint; if you looked hard, you could still see CLOVER emblazoned on its side. It had been outfitted to live in. The college kid had put in two beds, nicely tucked into the sides, a hot plate, sink, even a bathroom, though Bean hoped to avoid using that as much as possible because then it had to be cleaned. It gave a springy ride, as any big block teetering on wheels might, but Bean liked the view from the driver's seat, the sliding doors, and the way people looked at her expectantly when she pulled up. As if she were the last milkman alive.

It had plenty of room for their things. Bean had decided to keep Mick's table and give away most of the rest of the furniture. That was how she and Mick had furnished their home in the first place, through giveaways. Charity begot charity. It kept life bearable. Give now and give large, the frontier motto said, because soon enough you'd be needing a hand yourself. It was solid advice in a place where the salmon run could dry up and milk cost five dollars a gallon.

On the last day, she put Mick back in the box with the stickers on it. Hanna had saved the Styrofoam peanuts, and Bean sprinkled them around the urn. She placed the box between the seats, behind the gearshift.

Rhonda made a rare appearance that day. She showed up at the house, wheezing, in flattened flip-flops that squished with each step. She needed to sit right away after that hill. Hanna put a glass of water in front of her.

"Do you have RC Cola?" Rhonda asked. "No? Well, no harm in

asking. Listen, Bean, I'm just gonna say 'so long.' That's what my people do. I figure you'll be crying your eyes out as soon as you get wherever you're going and eventually you'll come crawling back. So: so long. See you real soon. Ha. Ha. Ha."

It was the weirdest good-bye. Bean taped up her last box.

"I guess that's it, then," she said. For months she had wanted so badly to leave, to be somewhere else. But when the moment came, she just felt like a failure.

A pickup tore up the street and pulled over. Fred scrambled to get out of the way.

Lois got out and walked slowly up to Bean, back straight, eyes up, like it was the bravest thing she ever did. Heart pounding, Bean shifted her feet and waited.

Lois pulled a parcel out from behind her back. It was wrapped in the *Eyak Times*.

Dottie, I will always love you.

"It's not the prettiest thing," Lois said. "But it's from the heart."

Bean stared at her gift, not knowing whether to reach out and take it. Lois gently took her hand and put it in.

"If I ever thought it would hurt you, I'd've killed myself," Lois said.

Bean looked at Lois. She looked tired. Another few years and Lois would be a fixture on a corner-stool at the Alaskan. After today, they might never see each other again. Lois would never leave Alaska; it was a part of her.

She had been Bean's protector. She had held Bean's hand. Bean remembered it all. "I couldn't handle another death right now," she said.

Bean told Lois to stand there, she had to get something. She climbed into the back of the truck, rifled through a duffel bag, and stuffed something into a paper sack.

"This one looks worse," she said, handing Lois the bag. "Still . . ."

Lois reached in and pulled out a wad of pink silk. The teddy.

"I fixed the strap," Bean said. "It's practically brand-new."

Lois had tears in her eyes. That was a first. "Thanks, honey," she said softly.

Bean ripped the newspaper off of Lois's gift. It was a children's book. She could have told you that before she even looked. It was the one where the elephant hatches the egg.

"I figured since you like birds," Lois said. "You don't already have it, do you?"

Of course she did. Lois was always getting things wrong. Blind dates. Espresso machines. Sleeping with her husband. That morning Bean had lit the Polaroid on fire; she held it till her fingers got singed, then dropped it into the kitchen sink.

Bean shook her head. She reached up, slipped an arm around Lois's neck, and held her. "I can't wait to read it," she said.

I meant what I said and I said what I meant, an elephant's faithful one hundred percent.

None of Mick's friends showed up to say good-bye. Not the radio guys, not even Low Count. Mudhole had agreed to sell the house for Bean, so she left the door unlocked and the keys on the mantel. Bean knew why they had stayed away. Mick had told her: people who left Alaska were turncoats. They made everyone feel left behind.

The truck was loaded and Bean had Fred's bowl in her hand when Hanna started coming out of the house with more stuff. Boxes and folders. As Bean crammed them in, she realized they were things that she had put in the trash. Mick's fishing license application, furniture plans, letters he'd kept, old sweatshirts. Hanna said nothing, just kept handing her more. Bean knew better than to say anything. They could always find a trash can later.

When the truck was clamped shut, Bean pulled Lois aside and asked to borrow her wheels. "You cuttin' out on your own good-bye party?"

Lois was impressed. Bean took her keys, stopped at the Superette, then rode to the lake. There were no swans today. Maybe they were out swimming in the last light of summer. Bean opened up a box of saltines and crumbled the crackers into little piles atop dry leaves. She stuffed the wrappers in her pockets and looked side to side.

She was about to run off when the soft light glinted on the opposite slope. She crossed the creek and made her way through the fir trees until she came to a shed. She was surprised that she had never seen it before, with its metal roof that caught the sun. She crawled through a hatch. Inside, there were chicken-wire roosts piled with grass. There were two large plastic bowls on the ground. It stank to high hell in there, but it was warm. There were wispy white feathers everywhere.

It had all been put together by serious hands. Mudhole. He didn't want the swans to leave any more than she did.

The plan was to drive Hanna home to Vancouver, then head down to San Francisco. It was two thousand miles and a lot of rough road. Bean had never driven the Al-Can before.

Fred needed a little boost getting into the truck, and Hanna needed some help with the door; it took a firm wrist. Bean sidled onto a couch cushion to improve her altitude, yanked the big floor stick into gear, heard an unsettling grind of grit and complaint, and eased down on the accelerator. She heard Mick's voice, clear as water.

"Just remember, Beanie," he said. "Spit and toilet paper. That's all that's holding it together."

Me, too, Bean thought. The gear engaged.

They rolled the truck off the Valdez ferry and stopped for coffee. Bean ordered them to go and for some reason it made her smile. They were only ten miles down the road when Hanna spilled her cup. It slipped right out of her hand, "the bad one." Bean couldn't tell which hand was worse than the other. Hanna looked embarrassed. Bean found a towel in the back and helped pat Hanna dry. Fred sniffed at the little puddle under their feet.

It was rough going. One mile in four was unpaved. The harsh brew of winter ice and summer rain chewed up pavement faster than anyone could fix it. The upside was that they didn't need directions. Take the only road, everyone said; head south.

Coming out of a Yukon town, they noticed a diner. It was made up to look like an Eskimo trading post, with a brightly painted totem pole out front. Hanna asked Bean to pull over, there was something she needed to pick up. Bean eased the truck off the road; it didn't so much turn as float when she rolled the black steering wheel, which felt as big as a hula hoop.

Bean let Fred out to pee in the parking lot. Hanna was back out in a minute, clutching her purse.

Bean asked her what she had bought.

Hanna unsnapped her purse. Two fat rolls of bathroom tissue were tucked neatly inside. They'd run out, she told her.

"Hanna," Bean said, "toilet paper only costs, like, a dollar."

Hanna snapped her purse shut and tucked it beneath her feet. She made a sly face, like a carny. Bean feared she might wink at her.

"A little larceny is good for the circulation," she said.

They drove in silence for almost an hour. Bean quickly tired of her music: dusty cassettes from high school. *The power of love is a curious thing.* People's musical tastes froze in high school; it was scary.

Minutes later she was painfully hungry. She wished Hanna had swiped cookies instead of toilet paper. Maybe it wasn't hunger. There was something thumping around in Bean's dryer. It had bothered her for miles. She took a deep breath.

"We didn't always get along, Mick and me," she said all of a sudden. Both of them stared straight ahead. Lots of nothing.

"No one does."

"There were—problems," Bean said.

"There always are."

Bean sighed again. Drove.

"What is it, child?" Hanna asked.

Bean squinted at the horizon. "You don't think I killed him, do you?" Her voice was high-pitched. Hanna looked at her.

"Why would I think that?" she said.

"I don't know," Bean said. "You just don't know me that well."

"I think I know a thing or two."

"I don't mean *killed* him killed him, like with a knife," Bean said. "But like . . . you know. Drove him away. Made him a little crazy. Like he had to go climb some mountain."

Hanna said that nobody had made Michael climb a mountain. They couldn't if they tried. She stared at her hands. "Sometimes there was no talking to that boy," she said. "You couldn't tell him a thing."

Bean recognized that. Eating one meal a day. The codebook. The training runs for McKinley. "Like when he got really excited, right?"

Hanna nodded.

"And you couldn't tell him a thing?" Bean said.

Hanna shook her head.

"He became obsessed," Bean said. "Like, the day before he left, he lined up all his equipment and kept inspecting it. Just poking at this and that. And he kept checking the weather reports. Every hour. I thought he was going to explode, or something. He sweat through his T-shirt. I mean, I can't even imagine what he'd be like as a kid, waiting for summer camp."

The conversation comforted Bean. But when she stopped talking, she noticed that Hanna had tears in her eyes. It was worse than a crying baby or an upset friend. Seeing an old person cry was the loneliest thing you could think of.

There was nothing to say.

"There's a truck stop in fifteen miles," Bean said.

Hanna just stared wetly through the windshield.

"He didn't let me love him," she whispered.

Bean chose her words carefully. "That was just his way," she said.

"The thought of him alone on that mountain . . ." The image haunted Bean, too. A knife in the gut.

"Look, Hanna," she said. "Mick wasn't alone. We were with him on that mountain. You and me. I figure it's like when he was a kid and you sent him off to school. He ran off with his lunch in a bag but, for him, you were still there. You were in the bag. And in his sneakers. And in the air all around him. Same thing when I watched him head out on a fishing run. I was there. He knew that."

If only Bean could believe it herself.

"I wanted to take care of him," Hanna said. She reached into her purse, tore off a wad of toilet paper, and wiped her nose.

"You did take care of him. And when he came to me, I took over from you." All Bean could think of was how Mick had taken care of her. But surely she had done the same for him.

"Wanna know a secret?" Bean said.

Hanna swallowed and nodded.

"He was kind of a klutz. He was always bumping his head or dropping something on his toe. Used to make him so mad. He thought of himself as—I don't know—some Paul Bunyan type. I ended up keeping the cotton balls and peroxide in the kitchen, just to have them handy."

Hanna took a deep breath. She looked over at Bean, reached out, and squeezed her arm with a withered hand. "He was lucky to have you," she said.

———————

Bean drew the line at smoking in the truck, so they had to stop frequently. When another nicotine fit rolled around, Hanna absently clicked an empty lighter in her hand until the noise drove Bean crazy. They hopscotched from truck stop to gas station to fat places in the road where Hanna could light up.

After one of those butt stops, a few miles out of Prince George, Bean shifted on her seat and stretched against the steering wheel. Something was gnawing at her, and there was nothing but bad music and the chunky highway to distract her.

She asked Hanna how old she was, if she didn't mind the question.

Seventy-one, Hanna replied.

Bean stared at the road.

"So, why do you think we're here?" Bean said.

Hanna bunched her eyebrows. "I thought you said there was only one road."

"No, I mean here, capital *H*."

By which Bean meant on this planet, in this century, a freckle on infinity's rump.

Hanna sighed. "I don't know, child," she said. "I'm not even sure we're supposed to know."

"Don't take this the wrong way," Bean said, "but I thought old people figured that stuff out, being closer to death and all."

Hanna thought a bit.

"Maybe we're here to make each other feel a little better about things," she said at last. "About all the things we can't figure out."

But Bean couldn't see how life could matter and then just stop. It made no sense. If it didn't matter, then death was no more tragic than cutting the grass. She could bend her mind around that. But what if it did matter? Mick had been more alive than anybody. On his last day in Eyak, he was up all night, chattering away and packing his gear and making lasagna and wrestling with Fred. Bean still had the lasagna. It was in the van's minirefrigerator.

"It's all shit," Bean said.

Hanna pinched her hearing aid and said, "What?"

"*Shit,*" Bean intoned. "I was just saying it all feels like shit."

"Like a hole in the heart," Hanna offered.

That was it *exactly*. "Yeah," Bean said. "I guess."

"I've lived a long time," Hanna said. "And you know what? It doesn't get any easier. You'd think it would get easier. But it doesn't."

Bean paused a moment, then looked over at Hanna, expecting her to say something comforting. She didn't. She just shut her mouth tight.

"That's it?" Bean protested. "How do you keep getting out of bed in the morning?"

Hanna expelled another sigh and faced Bean. "After a while, you get to know your little holes," she said. "You can put your finger in them, feel the inside, know how deep, what's still tender, what's scarred over."

Bean stared at the horizon.

"This might sound strange, but it's true," Hanna said. "It's as if they become your friends. They're yours, and nobody can take them away from you. Your little heart holes."

Bean gripped the wheel tighter. A lot of green and brown flew by. "Do you think this could be my last hole, please?" she said. "It feels like enough."

"Probably not," Hanna said. "But try to think of it differently. Like a badge."

"A badge," Bean repeated.

"That's right. By the time they call your number, you want a heart full of holes," Hanna said. "What else you gonna have to show for your life?"

With a mere 15-inch wingspan, the Arctic Tern manages the most astonishing migration of all birds. It flies 25,000 miles in a given year between Alaska and Antarctica in a huge figure eight that takes in Europe, Africa, and South America. It is thought to spend more time in daylight than any other creature.

—The Pemberton Guide

*T*hey reached Vancouver in six days. Bean's lower back ached as she downshifted, pulled off the highway, and rumbled toward town. It was hard when you had to do all the driving yourself. All she could think about was taking a hot bath and sleeping in a real bed.

Hanna had traveled well. She kept Bean alert without tromping too heavily on her thoughts. Their conversation had floated like leaves on a breeze. She never complained. She talked to Fred like he was a wise old Buddha. She made instant coffee in the morning over the hot plate, easing the uncertainty of waking up by the side of the road.

As soon as they caught the Vancouver turnoff, Bean assumed that Hanna would take over with directions, barking turn left, turn right. But as the neon motel signs flew past, Hanna stayed mostly silent, one hand cupped over the other, staring beyond the parkway. When a major intersection approached, Bean asked her what next.

Hanna frowned. She wasn't sure. "Can't we just drive a little more and see?" she asked.

"For Pete's sake, Hanna, how long have you lived here?" It had started to rain and cars were swishing by them.

She had lived in Vancouver for fourteen years, since the year Mick had graduated from high school. But in the suburbs. She moved in to an apartment downtown a few years ago, and she sold the Plymouth at the same time. Franny had insisted; she said Hanna had no business being behind the wheel. "When you stop driving, it's harder to remember your way around," Hanna said. "Funny thing." Bean could tell Hanna didn't think it was funny.

She drove on, following signs toward downtown.

Before long, Hanna began muttering to herself and pointing a timid finger at some of the buildings. She'd been to that store, knew that intersection. They scanned signs for Hanna's street until Bean discovered they were already on it. By now, Bean was ready to hurl herself out the window.

Hanna leaned back into the black upholstery and let Bean follow the numbers. She looked old.

When they were just a few blocks away, Hanna sprang to life. "We're here," she declared. She told Bean where to turn. They pulled into the circular driveway of a six-story apartment building. Fred hopped out to pee in the impatiens in the middle of the driveway, and Bean gave a quick stretch in the drizzle, then walked around the truck to open Hanna's door. Hanna was already sifting through her bottomless purse, looking for keys.

Bean clipped a leash on Fred and headed toward the building, then stopped short. The box with Mick's ashes was wedged behind the gearshift. It had a brown stain on it from where Hanna had spilled her coffee. She decided it was all right to leave Mick alone in the truck, but she fought an impulse to crack a window for him.

Bean, Hanna, and Fred stepped into the brick building. The long hallway, the steel doors of the elevator, the bland colors, all reminded Bean of a visit to the dentist. Two brown-skinned women in immaculate smocks walked by, joking quietly in another language. They emerged on the fifth floor. A woman in a blue muumuu labored behind an aluminum walker in the hallway. Bean and Hanna walked up behind her, careful not to rush her or scare her, as she crept along the carpet, staring at her own feet. She finally reached 5A, turned around to see who was behind her, tilted her head back for the bifocal effect, but then said nothing. She fished a key from a string around her neck, jammed it into the lock, entered, and shut the door. It closed solidly, like a bank vault.

"New neighbor?" Bean asked. Five-A was seven feet from 5C, Hanna's door.

"No, that's just Mildred," Hanna said.

She pushed open the metal door to 5C, and led Bean and Fred into a stuffy, curtained room. She opened a couple of windows and pulled the drapes, presenting what might have been an inspiring vista had it not been for the twin building across the courtyard, which blocked everything.

Hanna faced Bean across the room, cream walls, beige carpet, a sofa. She lit a cigarette. "Nice, isn't it?" Her voice was flat.

Bean hummed affirmatively, then she started looking around the room. Something wasn't right. The coffee table had two *Newsweeks* on it, that's it—no old newspapers, doilies, store coupons, cigarette detritus, box tops, tea bags used only once. The sofa looked naked—no wadded-up tissues in its cracks. Bean shot a glimpse at the kitchen; she was sure there wasn't a single stack of egg cartons beside the fridge. This couldn't be Hanna's home.

While Hanna fiddled with the kettle, Bean wandered over to a door next to the hallway. She turned the knob, half expecting to find a Fibber McGee closet that would spill the treasures of Hanna's life. But there were just three coats on hangers.

"It's so *neat*," Bean said as the kettle started to whistle. It wasn't a compliment. The place had just been vacuumed. Dust would feel lonely in a place like this.

"What, dear?"

"Where's all your stuff?"

Hanna prepared the tea and explained. The old house had been too much for her after Franny moved out. Fanny insisted that Hanna needed an assisted-care facility, because her arthritis was only going to get worse. She came over one night with a brochure.

" 'Let's face facts,' she says. Bossiest girl on the planet," Hanna said.

Hanna moved in three years ago next November. At first, she had wanted to bring most things, then a few things, then just her favorite things. But it had been like trying to cram an elephant into a bird's nest. The nurses and janitors couldn't do their jobs in clutter, and the supervisor handed her a list of what she could keep. The day of the move, Hanna spent most of the time with her hands wrapped around an old shirt box from Brooks Brothers that was full of photographs. Franny and her husband, Sam, swept in and made huge piles for Goodwill and the dump.

It was late, and Bean asked Hanna if she could take a bath. As she lay in the tub, her big toe playing with the dripping faucet, she heard Hanna play the messages on her machine. There were about six, three of them from a high-voiced woman who had so much to say she interrupted herself. It must have been Franny. Having a daughter like that probably didn't do wonders for your confidence. Bean wallowed in the hot water and listened as Hanna made a phone call. It was so easy to eavesdrop on Hanna.

"Hi, it's Mom," she shouted. "If you're there, pick—Hi . . . About an hour ago. . . . She's here. Mm-hmmm. Spending the night. Heading out for San Francisco tomorrow . . . All right, I guess. My arms, a bit. Listen, Franny, I'm tired, we can catch up in the morning. I just wanted to call you because of all those messages about holding a service here. I really don't want that. One was enough. It really was. . . . Well, if you want to get your friends together and do something, that's fine. . . . No, we're not going to get the parish involved. I told you, I've had enough of that, all those sad-sack faces and people who never even knew Michael. . . . Your *what*? . . . Well, *my* grief process says that one was enough. . . . I'll tell you what selfish is. Selfish is not finding the time to come to Alaska in the first place. . . . Well, we asked you to. . . . He's your brother, for heaven's sake, you make things happen. . . . Enough of this, I'm at my wit's end. I really am."

Hanna snapped, "Fine," then hung up.

Bean stared at the islands of her rosy knees.

Minutes later, her skin still steaming, she slipped into Hanna's queen-size bed. The old woman had fallen asleep with the light on. Bean felt the nice rebound of the mattress, the crispness of the sheets, and burrowed her damp hair into the pillow. As she matched her own breathing to Hanna's, her last thought was, *I can't leave her here.*

In the morning Bean padded toward the kitchen, thinking of breakfast, and stepped into a cloud of stale smoke. Hanna's ashtray had a few butts in it already and the creases under her eyes stretched deep into her cheek. Her paintbrush of gray-white hair, usually indestructible, was dented in the back.

She wasn't reading or watching TV or listening to the radio. There was no plate for toast. As far as Bean could tell, she'd spent the past two hours or so puffing away and sipping coffee. A rough breakfast for a seventy-one-year-old, though Bean supposed a body could get used to anything. Mick's triathlon watch drooped on her left wrist.

Bean headed for the coffeepot.

"Did Michael ever talk about me?"

Since leaving Alaska, they had been in one continuous conversation, beyond greetings and transitions. Bean poured her coffee carefully.

"Oh sure," she replied.

"What did he say?"

Bean took a sip. It burned her tongue, but she needed the time.

"That you lived in Vancouver . . . that he wished he could see you more often."

Hanna took a drag.

"Did he ever say anything about the police?"

"Oh, you mean the thing at the supermarket?"

"What supermarket?"

Bean wondered if she had taken a wrong turn. Couldn't this wait until after her coffee? But there was no going back. "You know, the cookies?" she said tentatively. "For the Cub Scouts?"

Hanna lit up with recognition. She shook her head slowly and inspected the fingernails on her gnarled hand.

"Oh *that*," she said. "That was when Jack was dying." And that was that. Hanna looked at Bean sidelong. A beat. "So . . . nothing about the police?" she asked.

"No," Bean said truthfully.

Hanna grunted and stood up. "Should I make more coffee?"

Suddenly, a bell went off and a thunderous voice filled the room. Bean jumped. The voice poured in from intercoms throughout the apartment. It was scratchy and deep like God's voice, except it had a Caribbean lilt. Hanna, for once, was unfazed.

"Good morning, Mrs. Linder," the voice said. "We were just checking to see if you needed anything."

Or if you've fallen down in the shower, Bean thought. Or forgotten who you are. The place was starting to give Bean the creeps.

"Morning, Louis," Hanna told the walls. "I'm still breathing."

She didn't even have to push a button.

When Hanna went in to shower, Bean hopped up and dashed around the apartment like a daffy mother hiding Easter eggs. This was no place for Hanna. You came to a place like this to die. She arranged her props in the living room. Who could have thrown Hanna away like this? Bean rebuked her dead husband and Mick's sister, whom she'd never met. If her ruse didn't work, she'd just have to rescue Hanna outright.

Hanna emerged from the bathroom looking exactly the same as when she went in. After a certain age, you didn't get much of a boost from water and soap. Hanna had two eggs in the refrigerator and she insisted on frying them up for Bean. Bean ate, then stretched extravagantly in her chair. "Well, I guess I should get started," she said. "Don't want to fall asleep at the wheel."

Hanna poured her more coffee. "Now, you remember to pull over and sleep when you need to," she said.

"I will, if I can," Bean said. "It's different when you're driving by yourself. You want to get there."

Hanna looked through her cupboards, probably to offer Bean something to eat on the road. "Well, don't forget about the oil," she said.

"What oil?" Bean said.

"The motor oil. It's low. You said so yesterday when the light came on," Hanna said. "You're making me worry."

"Oh yeah." Bean rubbed her face a minute. "I bet I can make it to Seattle on what I've got."

Hanna picked a box of saltines off the top of the refrigerator. She pulled out an unopened sleeve and gave it to Bean. Bean put the crackers in the top of the twine-handled kitchen bag she was using as an overnight case.

"I guess I'm all set," she said.

She stood in front of Hanna but made no move to leave.

Hanna had red eyes. Bean couldn't tell if it was due to lack of sleep or her leaving. She looked like you could pick her up and crack her over your knee. Bean thought of them calling her on the intercom every morning to find out if she was still alive.

She stuck her hand out to Hanna. Hanna took it with her crooked hand and put it on her chest, pulling Bean closer, to hug her. Bean's forehead rested on the white tuft.

After they pulled apart, Hanna spied something on the floor. "Good heavens," she said. Fred's bowl sat in the middle of the carpet. "You can't forget that. Poor Fred."

Hanna snatched up the bowl and handed it to Bean. Then she bent down to pet Fred, who was alert because people were saying good-bye.

"Well, I guess that's it, then," Bean said.

Hanna turned toward the door, then she saw something on the kitchen counter: Bean's sunglasses. She announced them, then recovered them, shaking her head and grumbling. She couldn't believe Bean could be so careless. There was all that glare on the road.

"I guess my head isn't screwed on right today," Bean said.

Hanna asked her if she was sure she was okay to do this by herself.

Bean paused a millisecond, then shrugged. The sunglasses weren't that important, she said. They were too dark, anyway. She couldn't see a thing with them in the shade. Not to mention tunnels. She avoided wearing them after noon.

Bean moved glacially toward the door.

Hanna looked like she was considering something.

"Well, I guess that's it," Bean said.

The old lady finally erupted. "I'm coming with you," she said.

Bean protested. "No way, Hanna," she said. "I couldn't put you out like that."

Hanna said it was no imposition.

"What about all that stuff you gotta take care of?" Once the fish bit, you reeled it in slowly. That was the fun part. "All those chores you been talkin' about since Whitehorse?"

Hanna changed the subject. "Michael's sister wants to hold another service," she said.

"Too bad she missed the first one," Bean said.

"That's what *I* said," Hanna said. "I've got some phone calls to make, but I could do that from anywhere."

"Well," Bean said, "I could use another pair of eyes on the road."

By now, Hanna was worked up, like Fred got when you had a biscuit in hand. "I could get you settled in," she said. She started straightening up the dining table, brushing away breakfast crumbs. "I could help you get on your feet."

She headed for the kitchen, spun around, and came back. "You know, the good thing is, I don't really take up much space. Just a little corner is all I need. I barely sleep, anyway." Another spin. "I'll have to pay some bills first. Where did I put my glasses? It might take an hour. We could do a couple of loads of laundry in the meantime. Do you have any whites that need doing? It's settled, then. Not another word about it. I'll go talk to Louis. Have you seen my glasses?"

Bean watched her rush out the front door, then moved quickly to the coffee table in front of the sofa. She scooped up her wallet, which she'd placed there. She went over to the breakfast table and reclaimed the western states map she'd left in plain view. With the rest of her props in hand, she awaited the return of her copilot.

They decided to ride along the coast for a while. There was no rush. The winding road hugged the hillside and took a lot of concentration. If Bean didn't pay attention, the milk truck just went where it wanted.

The views were worth it. Squadrons of pelicans flew alongside as they passed the dock-front dives that sold fried clams. The sun set off to her right, a flattened ball doused by the Pacific. An orange glow suffused the dry-grass hills, the stretches of beach, and even Hanna's drained skin.

The scenery put Bean in a mellow, confiding mood.

"So, Hanna, what happened with the police?"

Hanna had spent the past few hours staring at the road ahead, barely looking at the golden tableau off her right shoulder. Her crunched hand gripped the armrest on the door. The cliffs unnerved some people.

"So he *did* tell you," Hanna said.

"He didn't tell me anything," Bean said. "*You* did."

Hanna let out a sigh and stared ahead.

When Mick was in high school, she'd been arrested, she told Bean.

"For what?" Bean said.

"Nothing," Hanna said. She fiddled with the seam on her black stretch pants. "A huge misunderstanding."

"Over what?"

"Wait a minute and I'll tell you," Hanna snapped. "You got a train to catch?"

Back then Hanna and her children were living in the suburbs of St. Louis. She'd managed to put a down payment on a three-bedroom corner lot in a decent neighborhood. It was before real estate prices took off, and they were comfortable. Mick was graduating from high school, with fair grades and a lot of friends. He was a nice kid, a sense of humor, upbeat. Franny was the serious one. "She studied too hard, if you ask me. If that's possible, in this day and age," Hanna said. "Worried over everything. Classes, clothes, making friends."

"So when do the cops come in?" said Bean.

"I'm getting there. Now, are you going to keep butting in every five minutes?" Hanna said. Bean mumbled an apology. Hanna glanced at the flimsy-looking guardrail separating her from the Pacific Ocean. She leaned back in her seat.

The story obviously made her cranky. But if she was going to tell it, she was going to tell all of it. She unleashed a tide of background information that Bean was sure was irrelevant, all about the house, the neighborhood, Mick's plans for college.

Then she got to it: the time Mick decided to throw a party during his last week of high school. He invited all his friends, about forty kids. Hanna had ordered a ham and a roast beef. There was going to be a cake.

After most of the kids had arrived and everyone was feeling pretty good, Hanna had pulled Mick aside, gave him a hug, and led him into the laundry room. She swept off a towel to reveal a bottle of expensive champagne sitting on ice in the sink. A huge bottle. "A magnus, I think."

"Magnum," said Bean.

"Huh?" said Hanna.

"A magnum. It's a really big bottle."

Anyway, Hanna went on, Mick had been delighted. It was the perfect gift to open before all his friends. Dixie cups were passed around. Then Mick unleashed the geyser. There were toasts of triumph and farewell.

When the police rang the doorbell, apparently none of the kids thought twice about it. Mick went to the door, apologized for the noise, and said they'd keep it down. There were two officers. One of them, the older man, asked Mick if he minded stepping out for a word. Mick said sure. After he did, the other officer asked the kids in the doorway if he might come in for a look around. They obliged; they were nice kids.

"Uh-oh," said Bean. She thought this was going to be a story about underage drinking. What an unfair thing to be busted for. Every high-school graduation had alcohol.

But the older cop told Mick why they had come. The owner of J.B.'s had filed a complaint. Said he'd sold a keg of beer to Hanna, then went in the back to fetch it. He'd loaded up the keg in her car, then he came back to the store and a magnum of his best champagne had disappeared. Then he remembered Hanna carrying something heavy, wrapped up in a coat, as she'd said good-bye. He had even offered to help her carry whatever it was, given that her hands weren't so good. Hanna had just smiled, the cop told Mick. Now that smile was really burning up the guy at J.B.'s. Said nobody was going to make a monkey out of him. He was going to press charges.

About five minutes later the older officer walked out of the house holding Hanna by the elbow and the younger officer had his fist around an empty bottle of Don Perry Non.

"Pérignon."

"Huh?"

"Dom Pérignon," Bean said. "It's champagne."

"Whatever," Hanna said.

Franny was crying by then, pleading with the police and making quite a ruckus. The music had stopped and all the kids watched the terrible spectacle.

Hanna took a deep breath.

"After that, I can't remember the next time Michael looked me in the face."

They had moved to Canada the next fall. Franny was so upset about leaving before her senior year that she all but stopped talking to her mother. Mick moved out of the Vancouver house after a few months; he worked and enrolled in a junior college. After a year he transferred to Fairbanks. He never mentioned the champagne incident again.

Hanna recounted this last part to Bean as if in a trance.

"All because of a misunderstanding," Hanna said.

But Bean felt like she had earned some honesty.

"How do you *misunderstand* a magnum of champagne into your raincoat?"

Hanna was quiet for a long time.

"It's not like I robbed a bank," she said.

Bean agreed it was not like Hanna had robbed a bank. She looked over at her passenger, perched on the black, cracked vinyl seat. She was like an Alaskan frigate, a fast-flying bird that steals desperately to build her nest. A nest in which, soon enough, she finds herself alone.

Another day of hard driving would get them there. But Bean decided to pull over and feel her return home. Her new life—the one that she had designed—had blown apart, and she wondered if it had merely been a dream. Now she was coming back—quietly, on backroads—to start again.

She had always loved the golden hills, with their great basset hound folds, soft wrinkles upon wrinkles, curled up against the sea. It was a fierce sea—not a hemmed-in Alaskan sound full of driftwood—but a roiled, primal ocean. So big she could shout at it, bathe in it, pee in it, swim in it, and it would always be the same. Bigger than her. Mightier, moodier than her. Always there.

They spent the night in the van parked at Limantour Spit near Point Reyes. Bean lay awake for a time, curled in her bunk. Hanna, close enough to reach with an outstretched arm, breathed evenly. Bean wondered if her arthritis was still troubling her; she never mentioned it. She thought of her story of the arrest. She imagined Mick as a teenager, mortified to see his mother being led off by police: "Jee-sus, Beanie, you'll never know how bad it was." But she also thought she understood Hanna's impulse. Life stole so much from us as it was. A little larceny was good for the circulation.

Bean listened to the crashing waves. She had been swimming at this very beach with high-school friends. It was a few weeks after she came back from Massachusetts.

The girls were blossoming, giddy with their changing bodies, drunk on Big Plans. They witnessed their own power over boys and they shared giggly stories about giving head. They sang "California Girls" about themselves. Bean sat there in a bathing suit that bulged in the wrong places. She hoped they wouldn't notice that she had nothing to add. All she could think of was Ronnie Romano putting his hands down her pants. The jerk.

After one truth session that day, Sarah Berkowitz—who thought humor was the same thing as saying whatever popped into her head— announced they would be "best friends forever, until we die or get married. We're a team."

"I'll be the head cheerleader," said Maggie, who was pretty enough for it.

"Me too," said Shelly. That was what she always said.

"Who's our captain?" somebody asked.

The girls who already had jobs looked at Bean. Then Sarah said: "It's Bean. Bean's our captain."

"All right, Bean!" The girls laughed and clapped their hands.

Sarah apparently sensed good material. "Bean is Captain V."

The nickname stuck. Bean was Captain V for a month, until they forgot about it. *V* for *virgin*.

Bean reached down and snapped for Fred. He lumbered over to her hand, dopily. She dropped her arms like ice tongs, embraced him, and pulled him up to her bunk. Her sciatic nerve, strained from so much driving, flared for a moment, then the pain eased. Fred snorted and settled in by her side.

———

It was a few minutes before eight on a Saturday morning. Bean double-parked the truck on the hill outside Jimmy's house. The pavement was still wet from the street sweepers. She pressed the buzzer and Jimmy came down all disheveled. His shirt was buttoned wrong and his short hair was flattened in back.

Jimmy's lover, Peter, stood behind him. He was dressed tidily in a pullover and khakis, loafers, and a belt. His black hair was tamed with something shiny and he looked like he'd been up for hours. Bean had never met him, even though, through Jimmy, she knew his underwear preferences.

Jimmy hugged Bean in the doorway of their Victorian flat. She noticed over his shoulder that the milk truck, splattered from fender to roof with mud and gravel, was heaving oddly. Suddenly, it coughed up a cloud of black exhaust. The cloud lingered over the truck. It reminded Bean that Peter worked for the Sierra Club.

"It does that sometimes," Bean said. "I know what you're thinking: the Beverly Hillbillies, right?"

The passenger door opened and Fred hopped out onto the sidewalk. He sniffed twice, then fertilized the junipers in front of the house. Then they saw Hanna, struggling a bit to step down from the truck, which was parked on a slope.

"Oh my God," Jimmy whispered. "And there's Granny."

Bean made a guilty face. "Guys, I brought a friend," she said. "I hope it's okay."

From the top of the stoop, they watched as Hanna—now free of the truck—took a look at the house, and all the steps leading up to it. She climbed into the ceremonial garden, planted herself on an ornate Japanese bench, and lit a cigarette.

Jimmy and Peter rushed down to meet her.

After they'd unloaded what they needed and stashed the truck on a side street, Hanna napped, and Jimmy and Bean headed to the Patio Café on Castro Street.

Bean and Jimmy looked at each other across the table. She saw a gaunt man with a buzz cut, with long expressive hands poking out from too-short sleeves. His soulful brown eyes sat in dark sockets. Bean registered this and forgot it. Jimmy would always be the excitable boy who gave himself away when they played sardines.

"So, how ya feeling?" she said.

"Shouldn't I be asking *you*?"

"You first," Bean said.

Jimmy was doing all right, he said, all told. His numbers were in the toilet, but that had been true for two years now, and here he was, defying the laboratory analyses, still getting up every morning. The virus was mutating around all the drugs he was throwing at it, like some oozing thing from a sci-fi flick. When he got down to ten T cells, Jimmy said he was going to name them.

Things were okay with Peter, though Jimmy often felt he couldn't talk about his fears, his aches and pains. Peter turned everything into a grand political statement. He was ferociously liberal. Bean knew the type. He bought his politics by the pound, loved humanity, hated Republicans. When Peter was watching, Jimmy felt cornered into the role of heroic AIDS patient. It didn't leave much room for bitching.

Peter had insisted that Jimmy get tested when they started getting serious three years ago. When the bad news came back, Peter figured they would get by, with all the strong medicines coming down the pike.

Jimmy was less optimistic. He once told Bean he hoped he wasn't the last man in America to die of AIDS. That would be pathetic.

"Do you know how boring it is, Bean, to be the only guy who isn't getting better?" he had said. "You see your friends who looked like scarecrows just a couple years back. Now they're out dancing all night, doing Ecstasy. And you just sit there, feeling lucky if you got a good night's sleep or have a decent shit. I can't even talk to those people anymore. I'm a bad memory."

Now Bean saw how the light died in his face. She wondered what it must feel like. Here he was, chatty as ever, with this terrible knowledge. At least his Jesus period was behind him. That was some consolation.

After the initial shock of his diagnosis, Jimmy had tried to reorder his life. He greeted the sun in the morning and the moon at night, he hugged his friends, he pointed out the marvels of cell phones and Sondheim, Ziploc bags and microwave popcorn. He pointed out metaphors in movies. He claimed to enjoy chores he'd always avoided, noticed the garden, took out the garbage. He didn't mind waiting for the bus to work. He'd gotten a death sentence, and he was going to cherish the hell out of life.

He told Bean about his new outlook in long phone calls. She felt like she didn't know him anymore. He was Jesus.

"Have you ever looked at an egg, Bean?" he said one day. "I mean, who would have thought it was something you could eat?"

It was like he had joined a cult. He stopped going out nights. He shepherded his energy, worried that if he did too much, it might flit off, like a bird. He didn't want to miss the morning. Didn't want to waste any time.

Then one morning he was lugging groceries home from Lucky's and a taxi cut in front of him as he was in the middle of a crosswalk. The driver plowed right through before hitting the brakes. Jimmy shouted, but the cabbie just grinned and gave him the finger. Jimmy boiled over. All those months of being serene had left him a volcano. He dropped his bags in the street and walked over to the cab—still stuck at the light—and thwacked the driver's side mirror with his palm. It shattered, and shards flew all over the street.

The driver went purple, got out of the car, and flagged down a cop who happened to be passing by. Jimmy just stood there, his hand dripping blood, creating a biohazard on the street, his box of Froot Loops on the asphalt. The cabbie lied about giving the finger, and Jimmy was literally red-handed, so the cop made him agree to pay for the mirror.

When Jimmy sheepishly told Bean of the incident, she secretly rejoiced. Jimmy had stopped being Jesus. He was like everyone else: cursing, messing up, losing it. He was going to live like the rest of us, Bean thought. Lots of boredom, a little terror. It was the only way. You had to act like you were going to live forever.

The waiter poured more coffee. Bean wondered how Jimmy arranged his life. Life was all plans. With death hovering over, what was the point? Did you bother to plant bulbs in the garden? Did you go to the dentist? Meet new people? Wear a seat belt? Go to a class reunion? Did you save, or spend? Obey the law, or break it?

She remembered the rest of their conversation.

"Sometimes I see someone like me, across the room, at the gym, on the street," he'd said. "He has the same sunken cheeks, glassy eyes, and it's like looking in the mirror. I'm so grateful."

"What do you do?" Bean asked.

Jimmy had paused.

"It depends," he said. "Sometimes, I sleep with him."

Now Jimmy had Peter.

"He seems nice, Jimmy," Bean said.

Jimmy smiled. "Kinda cute, too, in a *Gilligan's Island* professor-ish way, don't you think?"

Jimmy said he was taking a class at the junior college. "It makes you feel like God," he said. Now he wanted to buy a wheel and a kiln to make pots at home. But it was such a production. All the clay and glazes and tools. You were talking a couple of thousand bucks.

"Get the wheel, Jimmy. Get it all," Bean said.

Jimmy rubbed his face.

"Maybe if I wish hard enough," he said.

"What?"

"Maybe then it'll come to my door in a big truck. And a clown will deliver it. With lots of red balloons. And all the little kids in my orphanage won't have leukemia anymore."

Jimmy was smiling. Bean rolled her eyes.

He reached down into a Macy's bag he'd brought from the house and pulled something out that was wrapped in newspaper.

"So, anyway—here," Jimmy said.

Bean pulled the paper aside and extracted a ceramic piece, approximating a cup. Or was it a saucer? Its rim was wavy and uneven like a piecrust, and it was covered in a sugar-white glaze, except for some random blue spots.

"What is it?" Bean said.

"An ashtray," Jimmy said.

Bean considered it.

"You snuff out your cigarettes in them," he said.

"Oh."

"It started out as a mug," he said.

"It's nice," Bean said.

"But so far everything ends up as an ashtray."

"Ashes to ashes," Bean said.

"I need to find more friends who smoke," he said. "Do you think Hanna would want one?"

Bean tucked the gift back in Jimmy's bag. It was her turn to talk.

"You know how it is when you've got the flu?" she asked.

"Stomach or all-over?"

"Stomach," Bean said. "And you feel so miserable when the pressure builds up inside your belly and you know you're going to have to throw up, but you don't want to retch? You just *know* you need to stick your finger down your throat. It's the only way to feel better. You have to vomit."

A queasy look crossed Jimmy's face and he put down his cappuccino.

"Yeah," he said.

"Well, missing him feels like that. Either I'm about to cry, which is bad, or I'm crying, which is worse. But it's this physical thing I have to work through. There's no break, except for sleep."

Jimmy had lost three former lovers. He shook his head slowly.

"Don't fight it too much, Jelly," he said. "They're counting on us to remember them."

A busboy in tight jeans cleared the table. Jimmy was distracted for a minute, then he changed the subject.

"So, what's with the sidekick?" he asked.

"Hanna? She's helping me get settled."

"Don't you think moving in with his mom is kind of . . . weird?"

"What's weird about it?"

"Well, for one thing, Mick never hung out with her, right? And you guys eloped. So as far as you're concerned, she's just one step removed from some old lady off the street."

"She's a good cook," Bean said.

After they found Mick's body, having Hanna around had been a guilty pleasure. She had the same expressions as him. Their eyes wrinkled the same way. They both sliced their sandwiches diagonally. There were a hundred things she did just like Mick. But now it was more than that.

"You're going to have to learn to let go, Bean."

"Jimmy, I swear, sometimes you sound like a bad episode of something," she said.

Never mind that he was right. As a toddler, Bean had loved a stuffed dog to ruin. Its button eyes popped out, its stuffing scattered, and one disconcerting day, a floppy gray ear came off. Bean's mother had swooped in to discard the unsightly toy. But she overlooked the remnant. After that, Bean cupped the woolly appendage to her face. When they put her down for a nap, she cried out for "Ear."

Jimmy snapped her back. "Hello? Earth to Nanook. I'm talking to you."

"I heard you. I was just waiting for you to make sense," Bean said. "I've been letting go of things all my life. Seems to me the only thing I never let go of was you."

Their mood lightened as they stepped out onto Castro Street. Bean slipped her arm around Jimmy's and they walked toward home, feeling stronger as two.

At the corner, they waited for a man in an electric wheelchair to scoot onto the sidewalk. His front wheel had snagged on the indented curb. The man jiggled the control at his wrist, and the chair's battery wheezed with the strain. Finally, he jostled over the bump. Bean exhaled.

Jimmy leaned his mouth to her ear and nodded at the paralyzed man in the fancy chair.

"Some people have everything," he said.

When they got home, Peter and Hanna were in the kitchen, drinking tea, a pile of cookbooks open between them.

Tufted Puffins are notorious thieves. Fishermen are wary of their ability to snatch bait right from the hook.

—The Pemberton Guide

Bean found an apartment in three weeks—a miracle in San Francisco—but that was only after Jimmy and Peter had enlisted half of the gay community in the search. Tips poured in from the East Bay, Noe Valley, and, of course, the Castro. They were mostly rumors or comments on the advanced age of a certain tenant; there were no actual vacancies anywhere.

Then, one afternoon, Jimmy got a call from Nan, a friend who worked in advertising at the *Chronicle*. She read him a listing from the next day's paper.

"You da man!" Jimmy hollered into the phone. Nan the Man; only in San Francisco.

Jimmy hung up and rushed to Bean with his notes.

"It's perfect," he said, as flushed as a prospector with nuggets in the pan. "I know that neighborhood. There's tons of lesbians. You'll always be able to find a plumber."

Bean couldn't tell who was lesbian and who wasn't. But she liked Bernal Heights and quickly signed the lease for the one-bedroom apartment over a garage on Bessie Street. The sidewalks were full of kids from the Catholic school in their ties and plaid skirts. There was a park nearby for Fred. And Hanna liked the neighborhood. No big hills, a few benches in the park, a view that swept across the bay on a clear day.

The day they hooked up her phone, Bean picked up the receiver and felt the need to call someone. She had a new home. She was back. She found herself dialing her mother's number. It was the same since Bean was a girl. The answering machine came on and Bean hung up. The phone worked fine.

Hanna was putting contact paper in the kitchen drawers.

"Who were you calling?" she said.

"Nobody," Bean said. Hanna could be so nosy.

Hanna was deft at settling in. Within a week, she had found a Laundromat and a vegetable man she liked. The owner of the café on the corner would give her coffee grounds for compost—she just had to ask. If only she had some plants. At least once a day, Hanna disappeared with Fred to Precita Park. They were gone for hours, it seemed. Bean suspected that Hanna went there to smoke. She had outlawed cigarettes in her new home, with the notion that she herself would smoke less—or even quit—if it was too much of a hassle.

Bean hadn't even taken all of her socks and underwear out of the suitcase yet, and here Hanna was, practically a local.

They pulled the mattresses from the truck to sleep on, and Bean bought a fat gray couch for $30 at a nearby thrift store. The apartment—up a flight of tired, wooden stairs—had decent light. The rent was steep; she'd have to find work pretty fast. She was in no rush to furnish the place; the emptiness suited her mood. She put Mick on the mantel. She silently apologized for the fireplace. It was sealed off with drywall.

Bean quickly realized she'd lost her urban skills. She crossed streets without looking for traffic, carelessly relying on her ears. All the extra noises made her jumpy. On a crowded sidewalk one morning, a woman in clickety shoes matched Bean's stride for an entire block—"walk faster or walk slower!" she wanted to scream. When she broke down and tried to light up one of Hanna's B&Hs in the café, an antismoking Nazi pounced on her.

A few days after their move, Hanna proposed a crime. She had seen some lovely black-eyed Susans in the park. And there was a tiny, vacant plot next to their stoop. They were just the thing to brighten up the place. It would be a housewarming gift to themselves. Did Bean have a shovel?

Bean did. But why not go to the nursery?

Hanna looked at her like she was crazy.

"What if we get caught?" Bean asked.

Hanna made a face, her eyes wide as buttons, her mouth a tiny pucker of surprise. "I'm just a confused old lady."

"With a shovel?"

"That's the confused part."

"What about me?"

Hanna puzzled. "You can be my idiot daughter," she said.

Just after sunset they set out for the park. Hanna gave Bean her raincoat to slip on, because she was taller. If Bean held the shovel head over her chest, she could almost walk normally.

"I guess nobody's going to notice I have three legs," Bean said.

Nobody did. Once they reached the flower garden, Hanna stood sentry as Bean started to dig. "Get the roots," Hanna instructed. "The roots!"

"I am," Bean said. Nothing like taking orders when you're doing all the work.

They extracted a huge bush, four feet tall, roots and all. Bean did her best to cover the hole while Hanna unfolded a sturdy sack she'd pilfered from Alaska that said POLAR PROCESSORS on it. "Hurry up," she told Bean. Like a scoundrel working a cracked safe, Bean stuffed the plant and a good chunk of soil into the bag.

They waddled off, carrying the plant between them. Bean wished she'd done a better job of covering up the hole, but Hanna had coaxed her away. Bean juggled the shovel with her free hand, trying to keep it under the raincoat. The flowers rubbed up against Hanna's face. Every few yards they had to stop and rest to give Hanna's hands a break. They drew a few stares on the crowded sidewalk. But Hanna affected a no-nonsense look, as if she were a flower medic.

When they got back home, Bean closed the door and leaned on it. Hanna sank into a chair.

"You sure look confused today," Bean said.

"Where am I?" Hanna said. She let out one of her laugh-wheezes that made Bean smile until it turned crackly and alarming.

A few days later Bean came home to find a letter with an Eyak post-mark waiting on the floor beneath the mail slot. The address was written in a literal hand that could only be described as penmanship. It was from Rhonda.

"Dear Bean," it said. "I thought you'd want to know the class has been asking about you. Or at least about your duck. Today, we were practicing writing letters and Wendy insisted on writing to Debbie. It's been solid snow here since forever and the kids have me climbing the walls. Maybe I need to come up with a make-believe animal. Right now, all I can think of is a bear that eats children. Ha ha. They've got me doing third grade now. Am feeling a little stronger, though I still need to stay off my feet. Hugs, Rhonda."

Rhonda's note was wrapped around a beige sheet of wide-ruled paper. As Bean unfolded it, she wondered when Rhonda was going to use the classroom computer. Most of the children already knew how it worked, but Rhonda always missed the training classes. Bean opened Wendy's letter.

> *Dear Debbie Duck:*
> *How are you? I am fine. I am Wendy R. from third grade, Eyak*
> *Elementary School.*

Bean pictured Wendy. She had thick glasses and a way of sloshing— sort of half spitting—when she spoke. Say it, don't spray it. That's what the kids chanted.

> *I am writing to you because it is snowing out. I was wondering*
> *if you know that it has been snowing here for a long time in a*
> *row. My dad is in a bad mood, and my mom is mad too. We did*
> *not have school for three days. But now we do. And this is home-*
> *work. Oh well.*
> *I am wondering if you are having any new adventures*

Rhonda had stepped in on the big words with red pen corrections.

> *Things are quiet up here and there isn't anything on TV and*
> *I am bored. Miss Tatitlek said you migrated and that someday*
> *you'd be back. And I wanted to ask. Is it warm there. Do you*
> *wear your duck mittens. I hope the people are feeding you fish*
> *sandwiches. Please write to me. I also want to know if you still*
> *love Matt the boy duck.*
>
>   *Love,*
>   *Wendy R.*

After Hanna went to bed that night, Bean sat on the couch, a notepad against her knees, with Wendy's letter at her side. She wanted to say something important to Wendy, something the little girl could use later on. Wendy had remembered her.

She started to write.

> *Dear Wendy R:*
>
> *Thank you for your letter. Debbie asked me to write to you to let you know what she has been up to. She heard all about the snow-storm and she hopes you have your duck mittens on.*
>
> *Debbie landed in San Francisco. She lives near a pond where the boys and girls come by with peanut butter and herring sandwiches after school. Sometimes they put alfalfa sprouts in them, because it's California. A big foghorn blows so loud it shakes the trees. On sunny days, Debbie goes Rollerblading and works on her tan.*
>
> *Debbie still loves Matt. But she isn't with him anymore. He stayed in Alaska.*

Bean chewed on her pen.

> *He flew too high one day.*

She scratched that out.

> *God took him.*

No.

Bean looked up at the mantel. Mick had moved all the way down to one end. A vase with a bunch of black-eyed Susans sat in the center. Bean put her pad down, walked over, and switched them back.

*Debbie has a new friend. Her name is Old Shirley. Old Shirley
is a magpie. Magpies like to chatter a lot, but Old Shirley's hearing
isn't very good.*

The job interview on the following Monday went well enough. Bean
was walking home from the bus stop when she found herself stepping
around pieces of furniture on the sidewalk, about ten yards from her
door. As she slalomed between a coatrack and bureau, a tea table and
several rickety chairs, she guessed that someone was being evicted and
would come home to find the battered antiques placed on the sidewalk
as a landlord's final fuck you.

But then she saw that the items were coming in, not leaving—
heading up the very steps to her apartment—and a truck parked halfway down the block seemed prepared to disgorge plenty more. A big
man in jeans and a half-tucked shirt said, "Excuse me, miss," and
pressed past, toting an unfortunate bookcase and a stand-up ashtray
with a pink glass cup.

Bean opened her mouth to say something but ended up just stepping aside as this man—Bob, according to the decal on his shirt—
huffed up the steps to her home. Bean dumbly ran her fingers over a
metal sewing table on the landing and followed. When she squeezed
through the open door, she saw Hanna at the other end of the room,
looking tiny against the mover and his burden.

"Just put it down," Hanna said, looking at the bookcase apprais-
ingly. "Ooh, nice deep shelves. We'll have to think about what to do
with that."

Hanna gave a satisfied grunt and pulled the cup from the ornate
ashtray. She patted the pockets of her housecoat but didn't turn up
any cigarettes.

The entryway, which doubled as their living room, was so crammed with old furniture, it looked like somebody had emptied out their entire garage. What's more, it was strange furniture. Beat up and mysterious. Bean knew the use of some of the pieces—the rattan chair-throne, the '70s trumpet lamp—but others took imagination. Was that a spittoon? Umbrella stand? Baptismal font? She had no idea.

Hanna couldn't see Bean at the door. But Fred detected her arrival and tried to beat a path to her. It was nearly impossible. He bumped around the maze like a cheese-starved mouse.

Eventually Hanna noticed. She peered around a Chinese screen with a tear in it and said, "Well, hello there." Her face brimmed with excitement, the flush of a high roller.

"Jesus, Hanna. What is all this?"

That morning Hanna had gone to an auction in the parking lot of the Cow Palace. She'd taken two buses. Bean had barely registered her plans; she had been so preoccupied with her job interview. But Hanna had mentioned that it was time they got a few things for the place. Bean had thought that meant a spice rack, or maybe a paper-towel holder.

"You want me to bring up the piano desk next, ma'am?" the mover asked from the doorway.

"That would be fine, Bob," Hanna said.

The mover looked Bean over. "I could use a hand with it."

Bean was still trying to figure out how angry she was going to be. She anchored her hands on her hips and stared at Hanna. "Well, which is it," she barked, "a piano or a desk?"

Hanna made "stop right there" hands like a cop and started talking fast. "So, I'm standing on the blacktop and I put up a bid on the desk," she said. "Which, by the way, is gorgeous. Wait till you see it. Before I know it, they're telling me what else I bought with the lot, quote-unquote. Well, I say, I'm an old lady and I took the bus. How'm I going to get all this stuff home? And they say: a mover comes with the deal."

She clapped her hands: jackpot.

The man who came with the deal was waiting on Bean.

"I was just as surprised as you are now," Hanna said. "That very same look."

"Hanna, where are we going to *live*?" Bean held out her hand as if appealing to the furniture.

But Hanna had that almost all worked out. "I just need a schematic," she said. She seemed a little drunk. "Isn't there a pen here somewhere?"

"How much is all this gonna cost me?" Bean said. She didn't even have a job yet. Maybe she could slip Bob a few bucks to take it all back.

Apparently, that was the question Hanna had been waiting for all afternoon. She found her cigarettes on the hearth and poked one into her mouth. She held up a crooked finger, thumbed her lighter with the other hand, and took a good pull.

"Guess how much," she said, exhaling through her nose. "Go on, guess."

Bean felt her mood breaking down. She hated looking for work, being all perky with strangers. Her no-smoking rule had been crushed, and now she craved one of Hanna's cigarettes. She wondered if this avalanche of stuff meant Hanna was planning on becoming a permanent fixture herself. She just wanted somewhere to sit down.

"I dunno, Hanna," she said. But the old lady was waiting for her moment. What the hell. "Seven thousand dollars?"

"Hah," said Hanna, opening her arms like Eva Perón. "Sixty-five bucks."

She was going to show Bean how it all would fit, too, by drawing a plan. Hanna tugged open the tiny drawer of what Bean took to be a stationery caddy, leaning against the trumpet lamp. It had tiny, chipped wooden cherubs on it. Hanna pulled out a wad of cloth. "Oh my," she said, unfurling two velvet, elbow-length black gloves. "Opera gloves," Hanna exclaimed. "Isn't it wonderful?"

"Those'll come in handy," Bean said. She felt the mover staring at her, so she went outside to help him with the desk piano, or whatever it was.

While she waited to hear about a job, she walked the streets of her new neighborhood. There was a lovely park on Dolores, but she avoided it because it was always full of couples sucking face. It annoyed her when couples made out in public. It was like they were showing off.

She wondered if Mick was watching her start over. It made her try harder, thinking he was. But everything was more difficult without love to grease the skids. The world was a mass of bland faces. No one stuck out. No one floated above the rest, like they were seven feet tall. That was what love brought to it. No one looked her way or gave her a popcorn feeling in the chest.

With Mick, it hadn't always been easy. And she wasn't forgetting the bad stuff. The loneliness even in marriage, the fights over her sadness, the rocky sex. But the more Mick was dead, the more she loved him.

The school district came through with an offer: $28,000 to start. It wasn't much, but she still had a few thousand in savings, and Mudhole was making progress on selling the house. The best part was that the district didn't require her to get certified. They saw she had studied Spanish in college and that paved the way.

Mornings, she got up at six, walked Fred around the block, then showered and got ready for school. By 7 A.M. she was on the bus, riding the dozen blocks to César Chávez Elementary in the Mission District. The school walls were a brilliant aqua blue and covered with vast Mexican-style murals—full of blazing oranges and bloody reds—which showed muscled brown-skinned men; nurturing, raven-haired women; frolicking children; Aztec gods; and lots of fresh fruit at the feet of their patron, César Chávez, the farmworker leader.

The murals made Bean feel heroic. And that eased her sense of being a bit of a sham. She was the replacement for a bilingual teacher who had left midterm on maternity leave. But Bean's Spanish was no match for the kids'. They spoke rat-a-tat fast about all kinds of subjects. It was nothing like the tapes in the language lab, in which Maria patiently explained when, why, and how she was going to the fiesta.

Bean wasn't expected to teach in Spanish, just to understand the kids. She was part of the English experience. Fortunately for her, most of the kids were in the process of rejecting their native cultures outright. They were only too glad to adopt the language of Walt Disney. Every day, her Spanish-speaking colleagues struggled mightily to engage the children in their native tongue. But the kids just rolled their eyes. To them, everything important came in English. Bean secretly rejoiced.

The children nevertheless were hungry to learn. Their day began on the playground, when Mr. Gutierrez, the principal, reminded them all they were part of a *gran comunidad*. A midsize man with a few strands of hair plastered against his large head, Mr. Gutierrez always seemed cross with Bean; she wondered if she was too blond for his agenda. After the principal's greeting, someone—usually Elena Ortiz—sang the school song. Elena was a third-grade teacher, built like a barrel, with a head like a soccer ball and a bowl haircut. She held the microphone like Madonna and sang so sweetly, Bean sometimes wanted to cry.

"Para los niños de todo el mundo, queremos paz y libertad . . ." Elena sang. Some mornings it was worth getting out of bed just to hear Elena.

Yet, soon enough, confusion and indiscipline reigned. Before lunch Bean called a halt to the mind-numbing drills of her plain-speak English. She told the kids to gather on the rug around her plastic orange chair in the corner for a story. They pressed together, like puppies proud of a new trick. She loved it when they raised their hands with questions, bursting with curiosity. Afterward, she would have them write compositions: all those thick pencils in pinched fingers, writing tales inspired by hers.

Even the children who didn't understand much English enjoyed the stories. Bean used inflection. She popped her eyes. Her arms drew pictures in the air. Sometimes she told a story she'd mapped out the night before, when she couldn't sleep. Sometimes she invented one on the spot.

Old Shirley was a collector, no doubt about that.
On Tuesday she flew home with the brim of a hat,
Some tinsel, a glove, the lace of a shoe—
All of it excellent, though none of it new.
But Debbie complained that the nest was too small.
"Oh Shirley," she cried, "where will we put it all?"

"We'll find a broom and make some room," Old Shirley said.
And she did.

The next day, Old Shirley brought two friends to stay.
She fed one of them berries, the other ate hay.
The first was a skunk, you knew by its funk,
The other, an elephant, from the looks of its trunk.
Debbie groused and grumped and felt the floor creak,
But Shirley declared, "It's just for a week."

"We'll find a broom and make some room," Old Shirley said.
And she did.

On Saturday, Old Shirley stayed in bed.
Her wings were sore, she ached in the head.
The nest was bursting, but the magpie grew sadder
Until Debbie came home with a firetruck ladder.
Debbie let out a whistle and Shirley sat up to see
A herd of buffalo climb in for tea.

"We'll find a broom and make some room," said Debbie the Duck.
And they did.

On Wednesdays Bean had yard duty. She stood at morning recess among the screaming kids, their jackets slung low around their elbows, working off their sugar-frosted breakfasts, chasing one another on pencil legs, playing freeze tag, screaming, bouncing brick-colored balls. Usually, they played pretty well, though Bean noticed how they divided up by skin color; all that started early. They brought little treasures to the playground—Aladdin, Pinocchio, Pokèmon, and Rugrats—anything that McDonald's or Kmart could jam down their throats.

There was one kid who seemed entirely out of sync, an island of sobriety in all the mayhem. One sparkling morning Bean watched him. Martin. Mar-TEEN, the Spanish pronunciation. She couldn't remember his last name. He was a new kid in school, small for second grade, with ears that stuck out like handles. His jeans were slightly stiff with grime. Oblivious to the flying balls and crack-the-whips around him, Martin managed to find something of interest in the dreary lot with its dried-out trees and rubber matting and jungle gym. He crouched before a denuded maple and used a stick to poke at the bark chips near its trunk.

Bean wondered what he saw there. Was he discovering a new world, or fleeing an old one? Did he feel like a giant, or one of the termites? Was he content in his solitude, or was he aching for someone to ask him to play tag? She fought off the urge to talk to him. Getting chatted up by a teacher wasn't any kid's idea of recess.

"Yard-duty, Yard-duty!" One of the third-grade girls, her round cheeks flushed from exertion, tugged on Bean's hand. Bean wondered how long it would take before the kids knew her name. The chubby girl pulled her to the rings. Another dispute that required the wisdom of Solomon, or at least the authority of Saddam Hussein.

"She keeps cutting in line," the girl said, poking an accusing finger at a slight girl with a ponytail, her hair black and unbelievably thick for such a little head.

"You're crazy," Ponytail said. "Fatty Fatso."

The plump girl stood her ground. "No cutting."

"Fatty Fatso. Fatty Fatso," Ponytail chanted.

Bean grabbed Ponytail by the jacket and was just about to spank her on behalf of everyone who ate cookies after midnight. Then she realized a dozen children had gathered round her and were waiting to see her mete out justice on the spot. She remembered her teachers' briefing. Kids around here had their own lawyers. It wasn't like Alaska. "Enough," she declared, and let Ponytail go.

As she stepped back to the chain-link fence, she looked left and right and wondered if she could get away with smoking a cigarette. No smoking in front of the kids; it was in that same briefing. But if she stood right up against the fence and held the cigarette behind her, it would be practically the same as if she were a passerby watching the kids from outside the yard.

Then she realized someone was doing just that. On the other side of the jungle gym, a bulky man with thinning hair—maybe in his early thirties—had his fingers hooked on the fence links. He seemed to be in no hurry. Dressed in nondescript blue work pants. Just looking at the kids. Something in her bristled. Bean stared at him—a warning glance. He caught her gaze, then looked down at his feet. He shifted his weight a couple of times and stayed.

Bean took a deep breath and walked over to him.

"You need something?" she said through the fence.

"Hello," said the man. Brown eyes. Arms like hams. He stood up straight and jammed his hands into his pockets.

"This is school property," Bean said, toughening up.

"I know," he said. "I—I just thought I'd come by."

"Who are you looking for?"

"I . . . um . . . thought I might—"

Something about his retreating manner made her suspicious. "You thought what?" she said.

"Whoa," he said. "We met. The other day."

Bean narrowed her eyes at him, certain they'd never met.

"I'm Bob."

Bean drew a blank. Then suddenly she pictured the name decal on his shirt, which must have been there still, hidden beneath his jacket. The furniture mover. She felt a little embarrassed, but she'd been distracted by all that stuff pouring into her apartment. Besides, lugging a desk together hardly made him an old friend. How did he find her here?

Hanna.

"Don't tell me she's been to another auction."

Bob smiled and looked relieved to be recognized.

"No," he said. "Nothing like that. I just thought, if you're interested, we might go out for dinner sometime. Eat something. Talk."

———

She rode the bus home later than usual one drizzly evening after a teachers' meeting. As soon as she sat down on the crowded trolley, her thoughts started to drift, another day behind her. She listened as the wheels whished along the pavement. Then she noticed a man seated three rows in front, his ample back to her. In the half-lit reflection beside him, she saw the line of his chin, a clump of stubble, a bit of nose. He sat rigid, facing forward.

The bus crept down Folsom. Bean leaned against the plastic seat and stared at the back of his head. His straw-colored hair was short and soft-looking. A hint of a white collar beneath a loose black sport coat. The natural divot at the base of his skull must have been a challenge for the barber.

She sat up a bit.

So many times, she'd wondered when she would see her brother again, after all these years. She had seen him only a few times since high school. Command appearances arranged by their mother. He would be in his early thirties now.

He would have gained weight since then, gotten taller, like their father. Like this man before her. And he would dress more carefully now; this man was almost stylish.

His hair looked lighter than she remembered it. His ears were bigger; maybe it was the haircut. Or maybe it was just time, rearranging things. She thought of them reading together, and the secret of a candy bar. She thought of fighting over their father's postcard. She thought of Ronnie Romano—"the most fucking embarrassing thing on the planet."

When he suddenly stood up, Bean realized her temples were pounding. She couldn't move. A fat woman with shopping bags had trapped her in the window seat. Bean's hands clenched the bar before her.

"Chip?" she whispered.

He threaded among the straphangers—so tall, was it possible?—

and headed for the front of the bus. Bean jerked her head back and forth, but she was blocked by the crowd.

The bus stopped at the corner. As it pulled out, Bean twisted around and half rose to see through the sealed window. Her heart felt like she had run a mile.

"Chip!" she said.

Then she saw his face as he turned on the sidewalk: a forehead too broad, eyebrows too thick.

"What, honey?" The fat lady with the bags. "This your stop?"

Bean looked at her hands. They were still squeezing the bar. She shook her head.

Dignified in flight, the Sandhill Crane is quite another thing during the mating season. The dance ritual of this three-foot-high game bird is one of the more bizarre performances of any American species. It begins with the stately bows of a minuet, but ends with the flapping frenzy of a cheap burlesque.

—The Pemberton Guide

On their first date, Bean and Bob had a quiet spaghetti dinner Saturday night in North Beach. Afterward, she felt comfortable enough to propose an outing the next day. The Palace of Fine Arts had a good-sized pond with lawns all around. It was full of ducks and swans, and Bean hadn't been there in years.

In the warm afternoon they sat on a bench across from the great domed structure with its friezes. Next to it were dozens of columns that supported nothing. The palace had been built ages ago for the World's Fair, and Bean thought it was the most beautiful piece of architecture she'd ever seen. It was a modern ruin whose only purpose was to please. The Romans had to wait thousands of years for such exquisite decay.

Bean told all this to Bob as they sat nibbling Cracker Jack. Every now and then Bob threw a kernel to the fat ducks that grunted just out of reach. The swans were too grand to beg, but they kept an eye out, nonetheless.

Bob was one of the quietest people Bean had ever met. When he talked, he told jokes on himself. He looked at his hands and shoes a lot, as if his digits might suddenly explode.

Some children sailed model boats in the pond. Someday, Bob said, he was going to build himself a sailboat. Nothing too big or flashy, just enough to sail across the bay. "Been thinking about it for years, and I'm tired of just talking about it," he said.

Bean leaned back against the park bench. It felt nice to have somebody listening to what she had to say. She felt safe. His reticence emboldened her. She wanted to tell him about her life, about what happened in Alaska.

She was trying to figure out where to start when a hefty swan flipped over to feed on something underwater. They stared at its downy ass and its wedged feet bicycling skyward.

"I feel like that sometimes," Bean said.

They waited for the bird to right itself. And waited.

"How long can they stay under like that?" Bob asked.

"A long time," Bean said.

"What do you think one of them weighs?"

Bean was gratified. These were questions she could answer. It was delightful to know something for sure on a warm afternoon in San Francisco.

"The biggest ones—trumpeters—can weigh forty pounds," she said.

"I had a twenty-two-pound turkey once—for Thanksgiving," he said. "Last time I used the oven."

After a while Bob asked Bean about her family. She looked away from him.

"What do you want to know?"

"I dunno," he said. "Where are they?"

Bean took his Cracker Jack box and emptied the crumbs on the ground. The ducks moved in. Some seagulls circled overhead.

"They're all over the place," Bean said.

———

Bean sat with Jimmy at the Patio Café on a Sunday afternoon. She had eaten her eggs Benedict and was picking at the Canadian bacon from Jimmy's plate. He had barely touched his food.

"What made you think it was Chip?" he said.

"I don't know. It looked like him. Or how I figured he'd look."

"Like what?" Jimmy said.

"Bigger, taller."

"Where's he living now, anyway?"

"I don't know. I don't know anything about him."

"What does your mom say?"

"I don't know," Bean said. "What difference does that make?"

"You haven't talked to her?"

Bean noisily dropped her fork on the side of her plate and leaned back in the wire chair. All around was the merry chatter of Sunday brunch, gay men draping their arms around each other's shoulders, taking snapshots, laughing, clinking mimosas.

"I don't see why it's up to me to get in touch. *She* should get in touch. I mean, I'm the freakin' widow," Bean said.

"Jelly, have you ever thought she might not even know that Mick died, or that you came home?"

Came home with failure written all over my forehead, Bean thought.

"Well, maybe if she called my house in Eyak, someone might tell her. Jesus, Jimmy, whose side are you on?"

"I guess I'd better be on your side, because it looks pretty lonely."

Bean considered firing back. What did Jimmy know about families? His father had turned him out, and his mother let him do it. Jimmy said his dad might have been able to handle the homosexuality or the AIDS, but not both. Now they were strangers. Bean stabbed a piece of pork.

"I think you should be talking to somebody, Bean."

"I'm talking to you, aren't I?"

"I mean somebody professional. You've got too much going on."

She'd been to a therapist once. Freshman year in college, he put her on an antidepressant. It made her feel dizzy and numb, and she couldn't read her assignments. So now she was going to be sad *and* stupid. She had tucked the bottle of pills in a suitcase at the top of the closet.

Jimmy picked up the shreds of the Canadian bacon on his fork and deposited them onto Bean's plate.

"I've decided to get the pottery wheel," he said.

"Do it, Jimmy."

"And the kiln."

"Do it," Bean said. It was the best news she'd heard in a while.

"I told you, I'm going to," he said. A table of gay men erupted in laughter. Jimmy glanced over.

"So what's going on with Bob?" he asked.

Bean sighed. "Well, he's really sweet. And he really likes me."

"Uh-oh," Jimmy said. "But . . . ?"

"I don't know," Bean said. She rubbed her eyes. "Did you know there are men who fold their underwear?"

"Peter does that," he said. "Boxers *and* briefs."

"Does he show you his all-holy sock drawer, because it's so tidy he can't stand it? Does he alphabetize the canned vegetables? Does he call you on the phone and then just sit there, waiting for you to do the talking? Does he start getting ready for a football game, like, half an hour early by putting a six-pack in a cooler at his feet, remote here, Tostitos here, salsa here?" Bean's arms were flailing like an octopus. "Then does he sink into his chair with a minute to spare and make this loud *aaahh* sound?"

"It's hard breaking in someone new, Bean. Try not to get too spooked."

"I just don't think I could stand that *aaahh* sound for the rest of my life."

Bob had small tastes. He made regular pilgrimages to the Dream Fluff bakery on Sanchez, where he invariably selected a glazed doughnut and a bear claw. He dipped the doughnut carefully in his black coffee, steam swirling about his fingers, watched with satisfaction as the sugar eroded into the dark brew, withstood the temptation five seconds longer, then pulled it up to his mouth, sank in his teeth, poked out his tongue in the search for errant sweetness, and smacked his lips. It was gone in three bites.

There was a certain Bobness to his days. On weekends his life map was a few blocks large: the Dream Fluff, the video store on Twenty-fourth Street, Paddy's sports bar, and the hardware store in between.

"Why would you want to ruin a Saturday, running all over creation?" he said.

It was different during the week. Bob's job as a contract mover sent him everywhere, and he was quite an expert at getting around town. Bean would mention that she had run an errand, and his first question was how she had gotten there. Which streets, which trolley, why hadn't she cut through the park?

Bob liked country music and he got Bean to like it, too. He would put a few discs in the player and let Patty, Clint, Garth, and Dolly cheerfully weep all over the floor. From the start, Bean *understood* country music. It assumed something would go wrong. You just waited till your man cheated, or the sheriff came after you, or you lost at poker. You had a helluva sad time. Then, if you could carry a tune, you moved to Nashville and wrote a song about it and got rich.

————

Bob and Bean helped Jimmy and Peter pick up the ceramics stuff from a lady in the East Bay. She had about ten cats and lots of frizzy hair and had decided she was going to become a watercolorist instead. The wheel and kiln weighed a ton. There was a huge bag of clay, a dozen jars of glazes. It was quite a production, and Jimmy looked a little intimidated. But Peter had cleared a place in the garage for him, and Jimmy was going to have a hobby.

They loaded everything into Bob's truck, then Jimmy and Peter followed them in their Celica. On the way home, they stopped for pizza. Bob had given up on trying to have a conversation with Jimmy and Peter. Whenever he brought up the 49ers or the Giants, they looked at him like he was an alien. Now, he sat hunched in his chair and barely said anything.

Is it the gay thing? Bean wondered. Bob would have to get over that; this was San Francisco, for Pete's sake. And Jimmy was her best friend.

Then she realized that Peter had been talking for most of the past half hour. The latest political outrage was a plan for a housing project on some land recently ceded to the city by the federal government. The Sierra Club wanted a park there, and Peter was geared up for World War III against the developers.

"They're just stuffing their pockets," Peter said. "They don't care whether the children have somewhere to play."

Bean heard the hint of a Cat Stevens song in her head, then Bob mumbled something. He had been staring at his hands while Peter riffed.

"What?" Peter said. The joint was noisy.

"I just said, people gotta live somewhere," Bob said. "People need houses."

Bean didn't know if Bob was speaking from a philosophical conviction or from his own financial interest, as a furniture mover.

Either way, he had a point.

Peter looked troubled. "Yeah, well, they can put their houses where there aren't two-hundred-year-old trees. Funny thing, you never see the developers living in their own cookie-cutter projects. No, they're all spread out on lakes in Colorado and Idaho."

That was true, too.

Bob took a gulp of beer. Peter was going to get his debate after all.

"It just seems to me that some of these rich, Green people who already have nice houses might want to think about a working family before they lie down in front of the bulldozers," Bob said. "I mean, who in hell has half a million dollars to buy a decent house?"

Peter did—after his mother gave him the money for a down payment.

Bean and Jimmy, who had both grown up in houses where disagreements ended badly, watched their boyfriends spar. It got tense. Bob didn't call Peter a self-righteous elitist, but it sounded like it was in the back of his throat. Peter didn't call Bob a shortsighted clod, but the sentiment was just a few parries away.

When the waiter passed by, both Bean and Jimmy scribbled in the air for the check.

On the sidewalk Bean slipped her arm through Jimmy's and they walked on ahead.

"Who put the nickel in those two?" he said.

In time, Bean realized they had an implied date for Saturday night. The thought irked her during much of the week, but comforted her on Saturday afternoon. Life with Bob felt like lounging in a hot tub or an old beanbag chair, so easy to slip into, so hard to leave. When he put his thick forearms around her, she felt life-proof.

His apartment on Church Street was immaculate, dominated by a big-screen TV, a bookcase crammed with Stephen King novels, and a kitchen full of cans. For all their yin-yang, Bob was just as much a foreigner in the kitchen as Bean. He used the oven to store his shoes, neatly arranged on three racks. They ordered takeout a lot, Chinese and pasta.

Like novice actors, it took Bob and Bean a while to learn their roles. But soon the plot emerged: Bob would hew to order and Bean would do her best to usurp it. She would leave the house without her keys, pat her pockets, wondering where they'd gotten to; Bob would dangle them over her head. She would insist on dressing lightly, succumb to shivers, then finally accept the coat Bob had offered four times.

She secretly enjoyed disrupting Bob's world. It was too organized, too clean, unmarred by the chaos that trailed her. She remembered how Mick had wanted to roll her up in bubble wrap. Maybe she had needed a hand back then. But now, she was sure, it was Bob who needed a dose of reality.

She knew he was waiting for sex. "I just need to take it slow, Bob," she told him. He said that was fine, and he shifted his weight back in his chair.

Even before they had actually done it, Bob began talking about them like they were a couple.

"Sweet, isn't it?" he said one Saturday night, after the video on his big-screen TV ran through the credits, then left a blue screen. They had watched *The African Queen*—Bean, for the first time. She was still captivated by the rapids and the humidity and the leeches.

"What is?" she said. She lay against Bob's chest, her belly overly full from Chinese spareribs. He sat against the corner of his sofa, his bicep cradling her head, a beer dangling from his fingertips.

"This," he said, sleepily. "Our life."

Had it happened that quickly? Bean wondered. Had two lives merged? Were she and Bob one simply because they had eaten too much and the sofa cushions tended to suck you in?

"Our lives are okay," Bean said.

Suddenly Bean feared that Bob had decided that they were Hepburn and Bogart, embarked on one of the great romances. This couch, this magenta sofa with the sagging springs and the arm protectors that always slid off, this was, in Bob's mind, their *African Queen*. They had braved the cruelest heat and turbid rivers since dinner, and now they could push a button, sip a beer, and say, "Sweet, isn't it?"

Bean struggled to sit up. "I mean, it's not like you ever had leeches," she said.

He mumbled something about that being a good thing, too. Bean wasn't so sure. Bob sipped his beer.

"You know, Bean, I wouldn't trade places with those poor souls. All right, so our life isn't as exciting. Well, that's life, right? It's not the movies. You get up in the morning, make some coffee, get dressed, and go out and have a day. You do it ten thousand times, and then, one morning, you're too sick to wake up. Or you figure out you don't have to anymore. You're old. That's life. It's not all vacations and Coke ads and rides down the Zambezi."

Bean wasn't leaning on Bob anymore. He still had his arm draped over hers, though, and his free hand was tracing along her forearm.

"Most of life is boring," he said. "I never understood why it takes some people forever to figure that out. I guess that's why there are so many drug addicts and gamblers and musicians. They fight it. But if you know that life is mostly ordinary, you can see how sweet it can be. When you find your tools sitting on the bench just as you left them. Or when you catch all the green lights on Gough Street across town. Or when you go to just another day on the job, and you find someone on the other end of a piano desk and you realize you want to wake up to her for the rest of your life."

For a quiet guy, Bob sure was getting chatty. By the time he stopped talking, Bean had resolved to go home alone that night. In an hour, if not sooner. He was too strange a creature—satisfied, unhurt. His life was so unruffled that it allowed him to be ordinary, yet fancy himself a romantic. He slapped Old Spice on his cheeks before they went out and even whistled the song. He put on a beret, cocked it at a jaunty angle, and walked around like Pablo Neruda.

One night at Bob's, about three months after they'd met, Bean knew it was going to happen. They had finished their takeout and he came back from the bathroom smelling like mouthwash. It was before nine, too early to plead fatigue. He had asked her how she felt, and she carelessly replied, "Fine"—which meant no headache, no PMS. Anyway, she was tired of wriggling out of his grasp. Tonight was the night.

"You mean it, Bean? You're sure you're ready?"

"I said I was, didn't I?"

It was hot. A front had stalled over the city. Bob was sweating even more because of the Thai noodles. Mick used to sweat, too, but in a lovable way.

"Can you believe it?" Bob said. He held his soggy hands like Jesus. "I showered just a half hour ago. I'm telling you, it's *genetic*." An image of fifteen sweaty babies.

He snuggled next to her on the couch. "Do you want me to shower again?" he asked. He said it with a sexy French guy accent. He sounded like Pepe LePew. "Or do want me au naturel?"

It was a rhetorical question. You had to be careful. Men could be so dense and so touchy at the same time. Lois might have come up with something clever. She'd say, "I'll get wet if you do," and pull him into the bathtub. But that was Lois. Bean softly replied that a shower wasn't necessary, it being kind of late and all.

They went to the bedroom and Bean sat against the pillows, fully dressed. She watched Bob peel the clinging T-shirt from his blocky shoulders. He dropped his shorts, and the appendage came out.

"Bean?" Bob was waiting for applause from the house.

"Oh, Bob," she said, giving a sexy stretch to his name. Already it felt like a lie.

Bob had been installing a new ceiling fan and Bean lay back, willing it to life. He sank heavily into the bed beside her, reached across for her hip, and pulled her onto her side. His kiss was warm and sloppy, and saliva gathered in the corners of her mouth. With his balding head and furry body, he reminded Bean of a Saint Bernard. They were good dogs; they rescued people.

Carefully, he began to remove her clothes. Just as earnestly, she began to concentrate on images that might ignite her, transport her. It was a tricky business. Once you peered into the box, anything at all might come out. George Clooney in his hospital scrubs. Dom DeLuise eating a napoleon. It was like that board game, Mystery Date.

Gently, he rubbed his groin against hers. At first tenderly, like a brush with a stranger. She thought she might feel something: a stirring. Then he settled down on her harder and his cock became a probe, catching on the lips of her vagina, mashing her pubic hair. He was breathing faster, was rock hard. He wanted in.

There was a stain on the ceiling, next to the fan. It was V-shaped and it reminded Bean of the stylized way her schoolkids drew birds on the wing. They drew V after V, and suddenly they had a flock. The birds flew over perfectly arched rainbows and houses with chimneys that emitted smoke in coils shaped like mattress springs. The houses were inhabited by dangerously thin people with large, round heads who stood side by side and smiled.

She wondered how her swans were doing. Was anyone feeding them? What if the creek froze over? How would they survive? "These birds'll never starve," Mudhole had said. She hoped he was looking after them.

She twisted her back a bit; it had been bothering her since the drive down. Was she getting old? "Take care of your lumbago, Burt."

Bob was really wet now. He was working hard. But suddenly he slid off her a bit and looked into her face. It was a huge violation of the rules—far more intimate than putting his thing inside her. He managed a smile.

"How're we doing?" he said.

Bean moaned. It was an ambiguous sound. It could have meant anything: I'm hot for you. I'm hoping to become hot for you. Stop asking me questions and get off me. Men usually took the first interpretation. Lois admired them for it.

"They get all beaten down by life, have a couple of terrible seasons, lose their hair, grow all mooshy around the middle. But they still think they can make you squeal in the boudoir," Lois had said. "You gotta respect that."

Get out of here, Lois. Get out of my head.

Bob rolled off Bean, yanking the sheet all the way off her as he turned. She heard the drawer of the nightstand slide open. He pulled out a blue box. It was the same brand that Mick had used. It made her feel sad.

Mick had been proud of his abilities. She loved him for his silent pride, in the way his muscles stood out, the way his thing got hard. Bob was on his knees in front of her, struggling with the condom wrapper. His fingers were too big. Everything about him seemed inflated. Maybe he'll never get it open, Bean thought. *Sorry, Bob, time's up.* He looked like a bear picking grubs from a log.

Success. He flashed an excited, naughty-boy grin. Bean smiled politely.

Mick had been smooth and compact. It was all that exercise. He was positively manic about running. Funny how he took such good care of his body, and it betrayed him in the end. His body was as sleek as beach glass and he smelled of sea. It was like having the outdoors in bed with you.

Bob managed to sheath his cock. It was in that bouncy middle stage where it would get rock hard with the slightest encouragement. He moved between her legs and put his palms on her knees, which were slightly raised.

From her back, her thighs looked like twin hams. She needed to get more exercise.

"Are you ready?" he said. Another grin. Men spent their lives trying to replicate such moments.

If he asked her that again, she'd scream. But *was* she ready? She rubbed her legs together. Two sticks trying to kindle a fire. She would settle for an ember. A twinge. But she had been distracted. All these strange thoughts. Now it was going to happen, and she wasn't at all ready.

"Yes," she said.

It slipped in easily enough. It was short but thick. He leaned his bulk on top of her. She felt the wet, matted hair on his chest against her skin. He began to thrust and withdraw. She tried to share the rhythm. *George Clooney,* she thought. *George Clooney.*

Paging Dr. Ross.

He came quickly. And she made it sound like she did, too. She wondered if it was believable.

On weekends they went for walks in Golden Gate Park. Bob liked to hold hands as they strolled under the eucalyptus, meandered the twisting trails, watched the bison graze. They went to the movies. During a tearjerker about a little girl from a dirt-poor town who always wanted to dance, Bean caught Bob watching her face instead of the screen.

Bean showed him the tide pools at Duxbury Reef, each one a world in a thimble.

Sometimes they took Hanna along on their outings. Bob liked her a lot. "She's got a lot to say, that one," he said.

"You're not kidding," Bean said.

Lately Hanna had taken it upon herself to get Bean to phone her mother. Hanna tried to nudge softly, but Bean saw it coming a mile away and cut her off.

"I'm serious, Bean. She knows things."

They were walking along Bolinas Beach. Driftwood, crushed shells, and the smell of kelp.

"She *steals* things," Bean said.

"What do you mean?" said Bob.

"Little things. She takes them. Toilet paper, cookies, plants."

"What, just picks them up? That's not stealing. That's just using."

"A two-hundred-dollar bottle of champagne."

"You're kidding."

Bean shook her head.

"Maybe she's just hoarding. You know, because she lived in the Depression."

Bean subtracted back to the 1930s. Hanna had been barely alive then.

"Well, what do you think it is?" Bob asked.

"I don't know," Bean said. "What's strange is, you should see her place in Vancouver. There's nothing in it. It's like one of those spooky movie sets that's supposed to be homey, but everything is fake. They don't let her have things, because they get in the way of all the janitors and nurses."

They reached Bob's truck.

"Has she taken anything from you?" he asked.

"That's the funny thing," Bean said. "My house just keeps getting more and more stuff in it."

———————

They took Hanna to the Marina to watch the people fly Chinese dragon kites. They took her on the ferry to Sausalito and had cioppino. When a couple of Bob's friends came over to watch the 49ers—*aaahh*—Bob invited Hanna, too.

Hanna hung back a little at first, fiddling with the sink as the men spread out on the living-room furniture. She looked a little nervous, and Bean couldn't figure out what the problem was. After the first quarter, Steve the Roofer got up, stretched his arms and legs till he was ten feet tall, and said he was going to step out onto the fire escape for a cigarette. All of the guys spoke in booming voices that Hanna could appreciate.

"Do you want some company?" Hanna said.

So that was it, Hanna was jonesing for a smoke. She must have left her B&Hs at home. Steve said sure, only all he had were Camels.

"Wonderful," Hanna said.

Bob opened the window to the fire escape, and Steve helped Hanna step through it. They were still out there when the game resumed. When they climbed back in, trailed by an acrid smell, they were laughing. By halftime, Hanna had been offered the best seat in the house, the center of the couch. She was practically one of the boys. Bean sat on a stool behind them.

After his friends left, Bob announced that he'd gotten something exciting in the mail and he just had to show somebody. Bean was at the sink, washing dishes, and she started to dry her hands. But Bob sat Hanna down at the coffee table and told her to close her eyes. He came back with some blueprints rolled up into a cylinder. He lay the drawings on the table before her, and told her to open her eyes.

"That," he said, "is my boat."

Hanna blinked at it, then exclaimed: "Oh, a schematic! It's beautiful, Bob."

Bob had sent away for the plans from a site he found on the Internet. They were expensive: $400. He rolled his eyes. His boat was already a money pit, he said, and he hadn't even bought a stick of lumber.

Hanna was all oohs and aahs over the blueprint, which got on Bean's nerves because there was no way she could see the details without her glasses.

Bean watched from the kitchen counter and managed a smile when they both looked up. Bob hadn't been around as much lately. He'd stopped talking about their life together.

She went to the cupboard for a coffee mug. She noticed a new box of cereal. Honey Bunches of Oats. For all the time that she had known him, Bob had eaten Grape-Nuts. Now he had replaced them. She closed the cupboard and forgot about the coffee. The new cereal worried her.

She woke up at 4:15 one morning and couldn't fall back to sleep. Flat on her back, eyes open in the dark, she worked on the Debbie story she would tell later that day.

> One day Debbie was swimming in Phoenix Lake and she saw a Hunter. He was tall with big boots and a gun.
>
> When Debbie saw all the other animals flee, she grew alarmed. The Hunter came up to her and pointed his gun at her nose.
>
> "I want to make duck soup and you are a duck," the Hunter said. He cocked his gun, and Debbie was scared.
>
> "But I'm not a duck," she said. She rolled over and sat up and wagged her tail. "Bow wow," she said. "I would certainly like a biscuit. Bow-wow."

The Hunter lowered his gun and looked at Debbie. "If you are a dog, let me hear you howl," he said. "You are a duck and I am going to eat you."

Debbie tried and tried, but she couldn't howl. Just when the Hunter put the gun back in her face, she said, "Moo."

"Did you say 'moo'?" the Hunter asked.

"Why would you shoot a dairy cow?" Debbie said. "For surely that is what I am."

The Hunter looked confused for a minute and lowered his gun. "If you are a cow, give me some milk," he said.

Debbie tried and tried, but she could not make milk.

"Ah-ha!" said the Hunter. "You are a duck and I am going to eat you."

"You can't eat me," Debbie said. She sat up prim and proper and batted her eyelashes at the Hunter. "I'm your daughter."

The Hunter dropped his gun and scratched his head. "If you are my daughter," he said, "let me see you hunt."

Debbie picked up the gun and pointed it at the Hunter.

"I am Debbie the Duck," she said. "I am not a dog or a cow or a girl. I may be little, but I'm a smart duck."

Debbie pointed to the road. "Now, you'd better leave Phoenix Lake," she said. "Because I have a recipe for hunter soup."

The Hunter ran away lickety-split, and all the animals came out from hiding and clapped for Debbie.

At recess, Bean saw Martin Lagos sitting on a bench, staring ahead as the kids ran around him.

She grabbed Emily, a popular girl, and told her to go ask Martin to come over.

Emily drew a blank. "Who?" she said.

"Martin, over there."

There was something worse on the playground than being called fat, a faggot, or all the racial stuff. It was when no one ever learned your name.

Martin, glum-faced, walked over to Bean. He didn't say anything, just looked up at her with soft, brown eyes.

"Hello, Martin," she said.

He stared at her knees.

"*Hola,* Martin," she said. "*¿Te gustó el cuento?* Did you like the story today?"

Martin nodded seriously. He put a finger in his mouth, and shifted his feet. Bean saw she wasn't getting anywhere.

She lifted a hand to touch his bristle-cut hair. He took a step backward. She let him go.

Later, in the break room, Bean mentioned to Elena Ortiz, the third-grade teacher, that she was worried about Martin. As far as she could recall, Bean had never heard him utter a word. She guessed it could be some sort of developmental thing. She'd heard it could happen. A kid was shy. He wasn't ready to speak. Then—*bam!*—you couldn't shut him up. She wished she had a file on him; but as with so many of the immigrant kids, there were no records to check.

"I forget," Elena said. "Which one's Martin?"

When Bean got home, Hanna was sitting in front of the television. Fred was by her side on the couch. The sound was at its usual decibel nightmare and Hanna was mesmerized.

A young man in New York was on the telephone with his mother. His soccer team had won. The mother was in Italy—cobbled streets, donkeys, the whole bit. She slapped her cheek and shouted, "*Bella!*" Her eyes were all watery.

So were Hanna's. She produced a tissue from nowhere and wiped her nose.

A long-distance company flashed its rates on the screen.

"Hanna," Bean said. "It's an ad, for Pete's sake."

Hanna blew her nose. "I know it," she said.

Bean really had to start thinking about having a place of her own.

Bob had been acting strange lately. Could he lose interest so quickly? She was trying to enjoy the sex. Things might work out if she just had more time. But there were no guarantees. Sometimes things didn't get better.

They had just eaten their egg rolls at Garden Palace when Bob got an antsy look to him. He shifted in his seat and his leg started jiggling uncontrollably. His conversation was distracted. Bean wondered if she knew him well enough yet to ask whether it was any of a number of embarrassing maladies.

"Feeling okay?" she said.

Bob nodded gravely, which did little to reassure her. He shifted his bulk again and said, "Bean, I need to talk to you about something."

Bean flinched. She had just spent the entire day with Bob—from coffee and eggs till now. She had to think hard when she had not last been in his company. Which meant something had been brewing.

"Okay," she said slowly, "what's up?"

Bob fished in his jacket pocket and pulled out a little velvet box.

Oh shit, Bean thought. It was the next worst thing to being dumped.

He put it on the table and gave it a tiny nudge with his finger.

Bean looked at it. Her heart started to beat fast, and she tried hard to organize the features of her face into calm control. But everything seemed to be acting independently. Her brow furrowed, she squinted, her mouth smiled blandly.

Her arms were at her sides, and she let them hang there. She leaned over the teetering table with its red rubber cloth and stared at the box as if it were a rare but poisonous caterpillar.

She looked up.

"What did you want to talk about?" she said. No point in making it easy for him.

Bob exhaled, realizing he was going to have to work some more. She wasn't even going to touch the box. He looked left, then right, like someone who wanted to call in reinforcements to untangle his tongue, spritz his throat, and prompt him.

"Bean, how long we been going out now?" he said.

Nice move, Bean thought; *make it a dialogue.*

"Four months," she replied.

"Four months," said Bob, as if the rest of his case were Perry Mason–clear.

"Just four months," said Bean.

They looked at the little velvet box, navy blue with gold piping on the rounded edges.

Bob took a sip of water that lasted longer than it should have. He was going to do this. She had seen him sometimes with unwieldy pieces of furniture that looked like they'd never make it through the door. He had the same look when a guy in Noe Valley wanted that oak armoire in a fourth-floor walk-up with tight stairs. Bob had strapped on his hernia belt, called his buddy Steve to help out, and gotten it done. The job had been so painful, they kept talking about it afterward, like skiers recalling a challenging slope. "Could you believe that second-floor turnaround? It wasn't tight enough? There's gotta be a bicycle locked to the radiator there?"

Bean felt heavier than the armoire.

"Bean, I'm not sure I'm going to say this right. But I'm thinking that we go good together—I mean, we're great. I like waking up to you. I like hearing you fall asleep. I want to be part of your life—and you be part of mine—always."

Bob was looking between his thick fingers and her face, apparently getting little information from either. Bean felt that her eyes were screaming, "No, no," but he was undeterred. He was going to do it. The full monty. If the restaurant tables hadn't been so cramped, he'd be jostling for knee space.

"Celestine Josephine . . ." Bob began.

"Bob," Bean said.

"I'd like you . . ." he said.

"Bob, stop," she said.

But he'd come too far. He decided to blurt it out quickly. "To-be-my-wife."

Bean slapped her palm hard on the table. "Stop it, goddammit," she shouted.

The water glasses and silverware hit a high note, and the little velvet box hopped. A couple sharing kung pao at the next table over froze, chopsticks in midair. The roiled ice water tinkled in its glasses for what seemed like an hour.

Bean looked Bob flat in the eye. Another time she might have worried about hurting him or arranging an artful reply. But she was still in mourning. Everybody knew that. Now he was driving over her feelings in a truck.

She sat up in her chair, hoping to look taller. She realized that a waiter was standing behind her with two plates of steaming food. He was waiting for her to remove the little velvet box.

"No, Bob," she said. "Not now. Maybe not ever. But definitely not now. It's too soon."

Bob stared at her for a full ten seconds. Then he fished his 49ers jacket off the back of his chair. He was going to leave. The restaurant was so small, it took some doing. He half stood, gently pushed the table away from his chair, then over to the left so he could pass the next table, a rhino doing the job of a jaguar. Even though it took a long time, he didn't look at Bean, didn't explode or complain. Gingerly, he pulled a twenty from his wallet, slipped it under the egg roll platter, picked up the little velvet box, and left without a word.

Bean stared ahead.

The waiter with the plates moved in. "Szechuan shrimp?" he said.

Bean pointed to the abandoned place mat.

"That would be his," she said.

Bean walked home quickly. Was she doing the right thing, or was she throwing away her chance at happiness? With each stride, the answer came up differently. She was fond of Bob—didn't want him to disappear—but her finger still had a ring on it. She needed to sort it out. She needed to talk to Hanna about it. Hanna would know what was best.

But when she pushed open the front door, she saw that Hanna had company. Her guest was over eighty. She wore a blue flowered dress and hose that ran out below the knee. "Hello, dear," Hanna said. "This is Marguerite." Marguerite lived four doors down and co-owned a consignment shop on Precita Street. Hanna had met her while she was out window-shopping. They'd gotten to talking about children, and the lady blurted out that her boy, Buddy, had been killed in Vietnam.

So Hanna invited her over for tea.

As soon as Bean stepped into the room, she realized that the only thing familiar in it was Fred. Hanna had painstakingly arranged all the auction purchases around the room—a desk here, a clock there—until every nook, every inch of wall space bore a knickknack, every table had a lamp, every chair sported a doily or a pillow. It looked like a platoon of grandmothers had lived there for thirty years.

Despite all the clutter, Bean had an immediate impression that something was missing. Of hers.

They were seated at the wobbly table, talking over empty cups. It was the first time Hanna had brought someone home. Bean dripped annoyance. Having a stranger in the house made her think of all the things she couldn't do just then. She couldn't sit around in her underwear and eat Rice Krispies treats. Plus, Hanna had made a friend before Bean did.

She sat on the couch and tried to read a magazine. She struggled to ignore their conversation.

Old women were sloppy talkers. They spun out the story slowly, lots of background, lots of history, lots of family tree. Sometimes they spent so long negotiating the branches of ancestry, they forgot who they were talking about. Then came the admission—"I'm out here on a limb"—then the recapitulation. "Well, you were talking about so-and-so." "No, before that." "Before that?" "Yes." "Hmm. I don't know." "Me, either." Then the sigh, "Oh well," and the attempt to move on. Then came the recovery, "Oh, I know what it was." Then the story. Then the verdict. "That just goes to show you," or "I don't know what you can do with them at that age." Then the slow shakes of the head, the fingering of a teacup, the attempts to sound wise or feisty. Then a little chuckle. Then an expectant glance upward. Then "That reminds me of the time . . ." and the whole thing began again.

Marguerite had begun a story about a distant cousin who raised rabbits. The cousin had terrible diabetes. Lost her left leg, and the doctors had doubts about her right one. She lived in Portland, or was it Eugene? The story fanned out until Hanna's guest was on a skinny branch. She looked like a bewildered squirrel.

Bean slapped her magazine down on the coffee table. She walked into the kitchen and started opening cupboards. There were some Fig Newtons around somewhere, she was sure.

"Help you find something?" Hanna asked Bean.

It was the last straw. Marguerite had started a stupid story she couldn't finish, Bob was tromping all over her grief, and now Hanna had colonized her house and made her feel like a guest.

"No thanks, Hanna," Bean shouted. "Can I help *you*? That's the question." She tugged open a drawer, not knowing what she would find. "A spoon from my kitchen, maybe?" She slammed the drawer shut, and yanked open the refrigerator. "Some yogurt from my refrigerator?" When she slammed it closed, a chopping block slid down and crashed onto the counter. It startled everyone.

"It *is* my stuff, isn't it, Hanna? I mean, I gave you money for it. It's not like you *stole* it or anything, right? I mean, you don't do that anymore, do you?"

Hanna looked like she'd swallowed a bug. Bean glanced at Marguerite, who would have disappeared if only she could remember the magic words. Then Bean noticed what was different. Mick's ashes. From the mantel. They were gone.

"Goddammit, Hanna," she thundered. "What have you done with Mick?"

Owls do not build their own nests; typically, they settle into the abandoned homes of hawks.

—The Pemberton Guide

*B*ean woke up late on Saturday. Whatever weekend plans she'd had died at the Chinese restaurant. Bob had talked about driving down the coast; the kind of thing fiancés did. She yawned and got up to feed Fred.

He was waiting in front of her bedroom door, wagging his tail. She reached down and patted the sides of his belly. He felt full. She picked him up. He definitely already had breakfast in him.

Bean walked into the living room and saw that Hanna was up and dressed. Her daybed was made tidily. There was a note on the table that said "Bob called."

Hanna waited for Bean to say something. Bean's head was still foggy. She mumbled good morning at last, and got one back. Hanna had her back to the table; she was working the sink.

In her ornery state, Bean half enjoyed the strained silence.

"Pee yet?"

Hanna gave her a look. Bean jutted her chin at the dog.

"Yes," Hanna said.

"Poo?"

Hanna shook her head. That exhausted the neutral topic of Fred.

Bean's eye fell on the mantel. The tchotchkes that Hanna had arranged there were shoved off to both sides. Mick's urn once again had pride of place.

Hanna walked over to the table. She was dressed more carefully than usual. Her hair was puffed right and she had shoes on. Her chin jutted out, pulling up the loose flesh on her neck like a tent pole.

"There's a casserole in the freezer," she announced to no one in particular. "Macaroni and hamburger. The stew in the refrigerator has to be eaten today; tomorrow at the latest."

Bean tried to make her face a big question mark.

"Why are you telling me all this?"

"Because it's time I head back home."

Oh brother, Bean thought. *She's bluffing.*

"Just like that?" she said.

Hanna continued to wipe the sink, keeping her eyes down. "Hard to believe it's been five months," she said. "Setting up a new home takes time. But you're set. It's time for me to get back."

Bean looked around the room. The statue of the little boy flying a kite from the garage sale. The silly refrigerator magnets from the dime store. The ceramic bowl full of plastic apples and bananas. The piano desk. It was all Hanna. Bean had rented the space, but Hanna had made it a home. Bean remembered the blank walls the day they had moved in. She thought of the two of them painting. Fred had stepped on the paint lid and made tracks across the floor.

It was time to back down. "Okay, Hanna," she said. "I'm sorry about last night. Something must have come over me."

But the old woman waved her off. "Oh, that," she said. "Everyone's entitled to a little cabin fever." She wiped the counter for the twentieth time. "No, really, it's just time," she said. "I have a lot of things to look after."

Bean stood up. Couldn't they talk after she'd had a cup of espresso?

This was absurd. Hanna would give in. And if she didn't—wasn't this what Bean had hoped for: her freedom, a life of her own? It angered her that Hanna had shrugged off her apology.

"Like what, Hanna?" Bean demanded. Her voice sounded harsh even to herself. "What's so important? What's waiting for you back home? You've got nothing."

That ought to bring a little clarity. But Hanna's chin just popped out farther. Her little snap eyes were wide against her corrugated face. She was digging in.

"Like I said, there's plenty to do," she said. "You needn't worry about that."

"What? Like hurry home to fight with your daughter?"

Hanna said that was quite enough. She had booked a 3 P.M. flight and had already reserved a cab. Now, she was going to take Fred to the park to say good-bye to anybody they knew. She'd see Bean later. She picked up Fred's leash and was out the door before Bean could say anything more.

There was nothing to do but go back to bed. She dozed for an hour. Lying on her mattress, she felt one of her dark moods coming on. If she didn't plan carefully, she might slip into a funk for days. There was plenty of time to talk Hanna out of leaving. But first she would go to the YMCA for a swim. Maybe the water would give her a second chance.

She was halfway through her routine at the Y, using the kickboard to work her legs, when she noticed an athletic young man beside her. He was kicking, too, sharing her lane, goggles up on his forehead, looking around. The splashing sounds, the shrieks of children playing in the kiddie pool, all vaporized into a generalized din in the middle of the pool beneath the high ceiling. Sun streamed in from the street and brightened the water.

Bean blinked several times to clear the chlorine from her burning eyes and see if he was looking her way. He seemed to be intent on his dolphin kicks. Bean saw his strong shoulders and the triceps that popped right out of his arms. When she passed sideways, she glimpsed muscular legs and a round butt tucked into his Speedo.

She began to frog-kick, enjoying the sensation of splaying her legs. The muscles on the inside of her thighs purred at the stretch. Her breasts rubbed against the Styrofoam kickboard as she pushed on. Soon she abandoned the board for a final ten laps of crawl. She pulled the goggles over her eyes and spotted him in the middle of a flip turn, his body a muscled coil exploding off the wall.

After her shower, she stood in front of the drink machine and fumbled for change. A long mirrored panel ran the height of the machine, and Bean glimpsed herself in it. She poked in her change purse but was distracted by what she saw. She wore a tank top and khaki shorts. Even after all that exercise, her arms looked flabby. She really should avoid tank tops, she decided. She raised one elbow in search of definition on her tricep. Maybe if she swam more frequently. Someone walked up behind her. She pretended that she was wringing water from her hair.

It was the guy from the pool. His curly hair was wet in little ringlets; his eyes still bore the imprint of his goggles. He asked Bean if she had change for a dollar. Bean said she'd look, though she seemed to be short herself. She poked in her bag a minute.

"Weren't you in my lane?" she said.

"Oh, was that lane yours?" he said. A hint of a smile.

Bean gave up looking for coins she knew she didn't have. What she said next surprised her.

"Why don't you let me buy you a real drink?"

He smiled, swiped a quick look at her up and down, then read his watch. He stood there, comfortable in his good looks, his fleece sweatshirt and nylon sweatpants. He looked twenty-one, maybe twenty-two. He reminded her of a leopard or some other lean creature from the Nature Channel. She suddenly realized she was drunk on adrenaline and endorphins—a potent combination of lust and fear. She was shaking slightly. She licked her lips.

"What did you have in mind?" he said.

She didn't know the neighborhood well enough to come up with something quick. She only knew that she wanted to be near him. She wanted him to press against her. She wanted to lick the chlorine off his neck.

"I don't know, where's a good place to get a beer?" she said.

They took a few steps.

"My name's Andrew," he said. He stuck out his strong hand, his mouth curled in an amused look.

Bean took his hand. Her blood began to tickle beneath the skin. *A birthday cake, all lit up.*

"I'm Lois," she said.

Andrew knew a place nearby. As they left the Y, Bean realized how a commonplace action—she pushed through these doors twice a week—could suddenly become infused with thrills if one dared. She thought for a moment of Bob, but erased him quickly. This was hot and unpredictable. This was not a day with Bob. This was about the pulsing between her temples and her legs. This was about Andrew.

They walked for three blocks, Bean trying to keep up the display of confidence. Then Andrew pulled out a key at the door of an apartment building. It looked like a decent building. But she balked.

"C'mon," he said. "I've got some cold ones upstairs."

Everything told her to turn around and walk away. Everything, except what mattered.

When they got to the third floor, Andrew unlocked a door. He stepped in, threw down his gym bag, and casually pulled off his sweatshirt. "Hot, isn't it?" he said. He crossed the dreary room with a flaking radiator pumping out too much heat, and disappeared into a kitchen of grimy, white tiles. He returned with two bottles of beer.

Bean took one and clinked out a toast. She realized now that something was going to happen with this stranger who stood before her, shirtless, all sinews and muscle. She tilted her head, and he leaned forward to kiss her. It sent a wave of heat bounding through her veins. She had to break off the kiss to breathe. He returned, kissing her more deeply, putting a hand around her back and pulling her close.

He started to tell her this was not what he had expected going to the gym today.

"Don't talk," she said. She slipped her shirt over her head and stood before him, her breasts at attention. He stared at them like a hungry child, then moved in and buried his lips around a nipple. He placed a hand around her hips and pulled her groin in toward him.

Bean closed her eyes and heaved with desire. She saw the rounded muscles of his arms like oranges and the cords of his neck as he licked and fingered her breasts. She thought for a moment to suck in her stomach, but then he bit her nipple—ever so gently—and she threw her head back and forgot about how she looked.

He raised his head and pulled her into the bedroom. A double bed, a chair, a mound of dirty clothes on the floor. She tugged at his hips and felt his hard prick through the nylon pants. He peeled off her shorts. She saw his eyes turn foggy with desire—blank and unaccountable—it was almost alarming. But she sank back into the bed, watching him fumble with a condom. And then he was inside her, and she was so thrilled to feel someone so sexy plunging into her, drunk on her. He worked his narrow hips, pressing deep into her, driving himself to a near scream of pleasure when his face turned stony and all his might and life blood flowed to his engorged prick and exploded into her now, and again, and more still.

She reached down while he still shuddered above her and teased this nameless, animal pickup into her groin. Until it felt like she had crossed a sea and there would be no return, just the insistent prod of this finger—her own finger!—beckoning, pointing the way. She groaned when she came.

This stranger—Andrew, was it?—grinned, kneeling over her like a conqueror, with the battlefield haze enveloping them both. Bean lay on her back, arms and legs wide, her mind serene. She knew she was the victor.

She showered in a dirty tub and dressed hastily. When she emerged, Andrew was sitting up on a futon couch, wearing his nylon pants, finishing her beer. She walked over to him, planted a wet kiss, and moved wordlessly toward the door.

"Hey, wait," he said. "What about your number?"

He tore a corner from a pizza menu and wrote his number down for Bean. She borrowed his pen to write down her own. But something compelled her to make the one look like a seven, the way they did it in Spanish-speaking countries. Lois was going to disappear while she was ahead.

When she reached the street, she adjusted her T-shirt, wrung her hair, and walked toward the streetcar. A homeless guy sat with a hat out on the curb. She pulled a bill out of her pocket and dropped it in. Six steps later, she realized she hadn't even bothered to see how much it was.

———

Riding back, her head was remarkably clear. Sunlight streamed into the streetcar. She found herself humming. She was freshly fucked. Her watch said 2 P.M. Now she would straighten things out with Hanna.

The car climbed into a tunnel. *This is how it's supposed to be,* she thought. This is why women spend hours toiling over their appearance, make their lips look like vaginas, tease up their hair, shave their pits, and smooth out their panty lines. This is what makes men empty their wallets, suck in their guts, and run up to women hopelessly out of reach on the chance that just maybe—in the right light, on an off night—the women might shrug their shoulders and say what the hell.

It was a delicious secret. Bean smiled to herself. She wondered if the Asian woman with the see-through purse across the aisle knew it. Could she tell that Bean was different, somehow *changed*? Wasn't it obvious? Two seats down, a bearded man in a leather vest sat cross-legged, doing needlepoint. Surely, he could tell; all you had to do was look at her. Lois would have sensed it immediately. And Mick.

They emerged from the tunnel and headed toward the Mission. *Oh God, Mick.* Her triumph bled onto the floor. *I should have given you this. I could have been captivating, brought you release. The way things are supposed to be. Instead, I stalled and faked it. I hated my body. I was scared. I forced you away.*

When Bean got home, Hanna and her bags were gone. Hadn't she said she was leaving at three? Slowly, it dawned on Bean that her *flight* was at three. Hanna would have left for the airport an hour ago. She felt her stomach turn over.

Bean ran three blocks to where the van was parked. A ticket sat on the windshield. She snatched it up and hopped in. She chose the shortest route, straight over Sutro Hill. It was a steep climb, a dangerous gambit for the truck. The engine groaned. The brakes screeched. As soon as she cleared the summit, she saw the freeway to the airport: it was clogged, bumper to bumper.

After half an hour locked in traffic, Bean exited and parked outside a Taco Bell. She put her head on her hands at the wheel, and cried.

That night Bean sat in front of the television watching a video. A pint of Häagen-Dazs Vanilla Swiss Almond was perched on her belly, her pants were unbuttoned, her neck was bent uncomfortably. Mick used to lecture her about milk fat. He was such a Nazi when it came to food.

She was watching *Breakfast at Tiffany's*. When Holly Golightly kicked the cat out of the taxi cab, Bean put down her spoon. She looked over at Fred. He was all eyes on her, muzzle on paws. Did everyone have to stare at her? She tried to cry with the movie. But she'd played herself out at the taco stand. She scooped some more ice cream.

Every now and then she looked at the phone on the table, next to the message in Hanna's script that Bob called.

After the credits, she got up, picked up the phone, and dialed Vancouver. Hanna's answering machine picked up. It greeted the caller with a formal, reedy voice that betrayed a suspicion of the machine.

"I just wanted to make sure you got home okay," Bean said.

Martin was not in school Monday or Tuesday. On Wednesday Bean went to the office to see if there was news of him. The attendance secretary said that she had spoken with his aunt just yesterday and that he was home, sick.

Bean asked for his number. She figured she could send him some homework or something to read. When she called, a tiny voice answered the phone.

Bean introduced herself as Martin's teacher. Could she speak to his mother?

"She's no here."

"How about his aunt?"

The voice sounded a bit confused. "That's me. I'm her."

"How old are you?" Bean said.

"Eleven."

"Is Martin there?"

"*Sí.*"

"Can I talk to him?"

"*Quieren hablar contigo.*" She called him to the phone.

"Heh?" said a shard of a voice.

"Martin? It's your teacher."

"Heh?"

"I was wondering if you're okay. Are you sick? Do you want me to bring you anything?"

Silence.

"Martin?"

"No." A whisper.

Bean tried a bit longer, then gave up. When would she see him back in school?

"Heh."

"Martin, do you know who this is?"

"*Sí,*" he replied. "Meese Daybee." Miss Debbie.

Bean hung up. There were dark clouds hovering over Martin's house, and she didn't know what to do.

She waited several days before calling Bob back. She suggested that they drive to the Cliff House to look at the sea lions. When she was a little girl, all those flabby, clumsy creatures had fascinated her. Her father had taken her there once, after a trip to the zoo. The sea lions sat on a wickedly craggy rock a few hundred yards offshore, and they were always jostling one another for a better perch. They were so big and gelatinous, a nose nudge from one could upset the delicate balance of another and pitch him into the water. The toppled lion would get up a good steam underwater and spring back onto the rock to contest the spot once more. A junior lion, outraged but fearful, would bray to the heavens. That would set off the whole colony.

From the cliffs of the mainland, people gazed with longing at the chaotic world of Seal Rock. Fathers propped daughters on their shoulders, sons cadged quarters for the goggle-eyed telescope, and they all wished they were closer.

Bean and Bob didn't talk much on the drive to the ocean.

When they arrived at the restaurant, with its wide cliff terrace, Bean was immediately struck by what she didn't hear. No barks or howls. She walked in silence to the overlook. A few brown pelicans swept by, heading for the tiny archipelago.

She gave Bob a sharp look. He shrugged. He hadn't taken the seals.

"Do they migrate?" he asked. "They couldn't have *died*, could they? I mean, wouldn't there have been something on the news?"

A couple taking pictures overheard them. "Try Pier Thirty-nine. They're all down there," said the man. Pier 39 was a big tourist complex off Fisherman's Wharf. It meant the sea lions had been turned into performers, Bean thought. They'd gone pro. Everyone in this town had an act.

Bob's face showed things weren't going well. "Well, let's go down to the wharf and find them," he said.

"It's not the same," Bean said. "They're not wild anymore."

"They're still seals, aren't they?" he said. "Tell you what, we'll swing by your place and we'll pick up Hanna. She'll get a kick out of it. Then we can drive over—"

"Hanna's gone, Bob."

Bob stopped short. "What?"

Bean gave Bob an abbreviated account. Hanna had decided to go home; she'd said it was time. Bean left out the parts about the scene in front of Marguerite, her morning with Andrew, her dash to the airport.

"Just like that?" Bob said. Bean guessed he meant that Hanna hadn't told him good-bye.

"We had words," she said.

"About what?"

"It doesn't matter."

"Well, you see, Bean, it does," he said. "It really does. Because I, for one, liked having her around. She's an amazing woman."

"How do you mean?"

"Not everyone could pick herself up after a husband like that."

"Because she loved him so much?" Bean asked.

Bob looked at Bean like she was nuts.

"Because of the debts, Bean. *His* debts. He died owing a bunch of money in two states."

"Oh," Bean said. Hanna hadn't told her about any debts.

Bob looked at her. "You don't know the story, do you?"

She shook her head. It made her mad that Bob knew something about Hanna that she didn't. *Goddammit, Hanna.* After all, Hanna knew everything about Bean. She was a star witness to Bean's ripped-up life.

Bob was ginning up a story. Before he got sick, Mick's dad was a truck driver. A steady route: St. Louis to Detroit, every few days. Twice a week he said good-bye to Hanna and the kids. Then he went to see his other wife in Detroit. They weren't actually married, but they might as well have been. When that got boring, he went out with the guys and played poker. From the sound of it, he was as bad at gambling as he was at being a husband. He died owing several thousand dollars to some pretty ugly people.

"What did Hanna do?" Bean asked. Why wouldn't Hanna tell her about that? Had Bean forgotten to ask? Had she been so hopelessly self-absorbed?

Bob went on. "She didn't know about it until after he came home with spots all over his lungs," he said. "She started getting calls. From department stores in Chicago, from friends who'd lent him money, from the uglies. He wouldn't talk about it. He just lay there. Let Hanna deal with it all."

Bean remembered that part, about how he'd just turned over on the couch. Bean pictured Hanna trying to raise two young kids, getting hit up for gambling debts and presents for a mistress. She thought of Hanna with no one to talk to. Not even Mick had known about this, Bean was certain.

Bob was still talking. "So she takes a job as an operator at the phone company. Split shifts, so she can see her kids when they got home from school. But then her hands start to give her trouble and they switch her to nights. She's too slow, with the arthritis. It was before there were laws. Didn't see much of her kids after that. Just tried to put food on the table."

Bean thought of the gingersnaps and the champagne. She thought of Hanna's stripped-down apartment in Vancouver and the daily death-watch by intercom. She thought of Hanna's excitement the day of the auction, with Bob's truck parked outside.

Bob had asked a question.

"Huh?" she said.

"I said: you know how she's been looking out for you, don't you?" Bob said. "Maybe that's why she didn't tell you. Figured you had your own heartbreak to deal with."

Bean didn't answer. She wanted to walk on the beach.

They plodded in the sand for twenty minutes.

When Bob made another pitch to Bean, she was ready for it. She felt so strange, so wrong, inside out. He had her by the shoulders.

"I know everything's not perfect, Bean. But I love you, and I'd treat you real good," he said.

Bean managed a smile. If she said no, would she have to spend her life alone? That morning when she rose from bed, she'd felt so overwhelmed by the silence, she skipped breakfast and went to the Park Bench Café for a latte.

"I know you would," she told Bob, leaning into him. Was that enough? she wondered. He felt so safe. But the better she knew him, the more impossible it all seemed. He was dragging her into a life she couldn't sustain. She would end up frustrating him and feeling miserable about herself.

"Bob," she said.

She'd given up looking him in the eye. Now it was getting harder and harder to say his name.

"Bean, I—"

"Just let me talk, okay?" Bean said. "Jesus."

She saw him gulp.

"We're in different places," she said.

"What do you mean?"

"Different places. And you're flying out there way ahead." She fluttered her hand like a drunken bird.

"So what if you join me?"

He wasn't getting it.

"You're falling in love by yourself, Bob."

He didn't say anything for a long time.

"Oh," he said.

He wiped his face with his hand. She couldn't look at him anymore.

Later that week Jimmy went into the hospital. He had been incapacitated by headaches and was extremely sensitive to light. After scarfing Tylenol with codeine in a dark room for two days, he agreed to go to the emergency room. When they ran tests, a doctor took Peter aside

and told him the bad news: Jimmy had a large brain tumor, precipi-
tated by his HIV infection. Surgery was out of the question. It was a
matter for chemotherapy and radiation.

Peter tried to keep as much of the prognosis as he could from
Jimmy. Words like *tumor, cancer,* and *brain* combined to sound even
worse than AIDS.

When Jimmy called Bean to fill her in, he was matter-of-fact. Bean
knew that the maladies had been piling up on him lately: CMV, which
threatened his eyesight, required regular injections to the eyeball. Re-
current thrush in his throat had made it hard to swallow his food. His
twice-daily mouthful of pills made him nauseous.

She knew that when he told her about the mass in his brain, she
had to treat it separately from all the other problems. Otherwise, she
would be acknowledging a systems failure. The *Titanic* was going down
and all she could talk about were the leaks in the cabin. She asked him
questions about how it was treated. A nurse had told him that one of
her patients was still alive after facing a similar tumor. Bean didn't ask
details; she knew Jimmy didn't have them.

Facing illness makes accomplices of us all, Bean thought. There was
only so much mortality any of them could confront at once. You
peeked at it, then lowered your eyes. You talked about what was cozy
and near, like pioneers around the fire, with winter coming.

Bean realized her hand was trembling as it gripped the phone.

"Bean?" Jimmy said.

"Yeah?"

"I'm scared."

Everything that she had forbidden herself to say flooded her mind
at once.

"I know, Jimmy," she said. "Me, too."

————

Mudhole called. The picket fence had fallen down in the last storm. "Who put that thing together?" he grumbled. Mick had always found new ways to jury-rig the fence, keeping it upright for another season. Mudhole added some new two-by-fours.

"Gutter over the door took some fixing, too," he said.

Bean listened to the rumble of his voice, the whiskey and salt and phlegm in it, the economy of his words. He was a capable man. It was soothing just to know he was on her side.

Fix my life, Mudhole.

With Alaska behind her, she was free to miss it. Not the whole state. Not the crushing wetness of it. But the small things. The times she'd fallen asleep in front of the fireplace. The view of the boats from the deck. Her boots standing next to Mick's in the entryway. She missed her life as it was. The house with the orange trim. The hemlock tree. Mick singing nonsense. She wondered if she would ever dare to have such things again.

"I almost forgot," Mudhole said. "Reason I called."

He thought he had a buyer for the house. A guy from Anchorage was looking to relocate. "Don't think he's a crook."

Bean paused. Her heart sped up a bit. The orange trim. The hemlock.

"So I told him I'd have to check," Mudhole said.

Mick.

"Tell him okay," she said.

Jimmy was awake and watching TV. Beside him, there was a tray with some breakfast cereal eaten. He'd barely touched his fruit bowl.

"Not good, Jelly," he said.

Bean said it didn't sound good.

They sat and talked for a while, and Bean picked at his fruit. A muted talk show played overhead. Bean could hear the second hand ticking on the wall clock across from her.

This is life, Bean thought. *Hours of boredom punctuated by moments of terror.*

Mick and the others had been pinned down on the West Rib for four days. They were stuck in their tents, waiting for the weather to clear. Someone had brought along a copy of *Moby Dick* and they ripped it up and passed the sections around to read. They were bored out of their minds. Then one ordinary night, Mick left the tent to relieve himself, and he fell for a mile.

Now, a day after all his agony, here was Jimmy, with a belly full of Cheerios, sunk back into a pillow, watching Leeza. Tick, tick, tick. On the TV, a mother and daughter—both heavily dipped in hairspray and mascara—were shouting at each other and crying. Jimmy was engrossed.

"Turn it up," Bean said.

The American Merganser is the most common duck in Southeastern
Alaska. It is an unusually silent bird; despite years of observation, this
author is quite certain he has never heard it utter a sound.

—The Pemberton Guide

*M*artin came back to school for a couple of days, then started missing class again. It got so that Bean measured her work by whether he was sitting at his desk. She knew it was silly, with twenty-five kids to look after, but the absences threw her off. She saved her best Debbie stories for when he got back. Someday, he would tell her his secrets. He had to matter to somebody.

At recess she went to the attendance office and asked for his address. "You ought to clear this with the counselor," the secretary said, but she handed Bean a slip of paper.

After school Bean walked down Folsom Street. She followed house numbers past a botanica, a check-cashing joint, and offices for immigration help. The sidewalk teemed with life, even though it was midafternoon. It was the shift change of the unnoticed. Waiters and cooks and busboys spilled into the street with slicked-back hair. They jostled shoulders with the early risers—window washers, gardeners, and hospital attendants—who came home to look after their own children, soak their own feet, tidy their own houses.

She stopped on the corner of Twenty-fourth Street. Three of its four corners were liquor stores. An orange awning flapped on the fourth: POLLO SUPREMO. A black man in sweatpants parked his shopping cart and picked through the trash can out front. A young Latin man strode past Bean in an untucked polo shirt, showered, confident, going places. A Chinese mailman, bag slung over his shoulder, stopped house to house. Women in scarves and big-buttoned coats toddled along, so old that they were beyond detection of race or color.

The street's vitality made up for its shabbiness. Most of the passersby were young, some poked their friends in the ribs. A few held bottles or cans in brown bags, but most of them seemed to have a destination. There was no need to pretend this neighborhood was anything more than it was: a place to recall many years later, after their kids had gone to college or found good jobs, a way station that would attest to how far they had come.

Bean came to a lime green, two-story building with a high stoop that jutted into the sidewalk. Its walls were covered in cheap siding. She climbed the stairs and faced a square of buzzers with eight apartment numbers. There were no names, and she had no number for Martin. She started pushing buttons. After a few minutes a woman dragging sacks of groceries around her ankles climbed up the stoop. She glanced vacantly at Bean, took out a key, and entered. Bean stuck her foot in the door.

The hallway smelled of cooking oil, garlic, and some kind of insecticide—roach powder, perhaps. Bean crossed the landing and realized she was walking almost on tiptoe. She felt edgy, like she might glimpse too much, see someone's life turned inside out. Poverty betrayed privacy. It had always been that way. Family fights, romances, and tragedies were public events.

There were four doors on the first floor; two of them were open. The apartments were single-room, as far as Bean could tell. She glimpsed an old man in a rocker listening to *ranchera* music in the first room. Across the hall, a middle-aged lady in slippers stirred onions over a hot plate. Bean heard scrambling feet that sounded like children, and she walked on, as if stepping through glass.

She knocked on the door where the noise had come from and pressed her ear to the wood. She heard a television station of cartoon sounds blaring in Spanish. There was no answer. Suddenly the television turned off. She waited a few seconds, then knocked again.

"Martin?" Bean said.

She heard a sound like something heavy being moved near the door and detected a break in the light in the door's peephole.

"Martin, soy tu maestra," Bean said. "It's your teacher."

There was some whispering of tiny voices, a disagreement.

Bean stood facing the door. A white-haired woman in the last apartment across the hall opened her door three inches and stared at her. Bean bugged her eyes out at the lady and knocked again.

"Martin?"

Bean thought she heard a faint *"sí."*

"It's Miss Debbie."

Bean looked over her shoulder at the cottonhead watching her. She suddenly felt ridiculous, talking to a door, introducing herself as an imaginary duck. She put her ear to the door in time to hear some recognition. "Miss Debbie." More little whispers.

Bean had to make a decision. The cottonhead had receded. But now the onion lady had popped out for a look. They were like prairie dogs. Bean walked toward her, trying to look as casual and unofficial as possible—probably the pose every border cop, narc, or child-welfare agent went for. She was three paces away when the onion cooker pulled back and shut her door.

At that moment the door burst open from the street. The outdoor light was strong, and Bean was blinded as someone approached. Her eyes recovered just as a man brushed past, lugging a plastic bag, but the shadows hid his face. He stopped at Martin's door, extracted keys from too-tight boot jeans. He was husky with a droopy mustache and acne scars on his coffee-colored cheeks. His hair was tucked into a cap that said "s. l. potosí." There was canned food in his bag; he held a cigarette in the other hand. He was about Bean's age.

She walked up to him.

"Hello, I'm Martin's teacher," she said. She stuck out her hand.

The man looked at it and just nodded. He glanced down the hall, as if to see if Bean was alone. He fingered the key for the door and looked like he was about to slip inside.

"Wait," said Bean.

He stuck the cigarette in the corner of his mouth, opened the door, yanked the key out of the lock, tossed the cans inside. Then he extracted the key and raised its jagged edge toward Bean's face.

"Do not call here more, please," he said, jabbing the key inches from her cheek. "Do not call here more." He opened the door only wide enough to slip through.

The room where Martin waited was absolutely silent.

Bean went to S.F. General to see Jimmy. The structure of his face was becoming more plain, as everything extra fell away. His cheeks had caved in, their bones protruded. His crew cut had thinned, turned wispy and dull. He wore a bandage over one eye from the injections to combat CMV. The port implanted in his chest looked like a Styrofoam peanut on a string. It ran to a Band-Aid over his heart.

Bean looked at her pared-down friend. It wasn't just his physical features. Parts of his personality had eroded. When she walked in, he just stared at her for a moment. She had expected a blast from his quick tongue, some gossip about a sexy orderly or a dig at some Nurse Ratched's expense. But it didn't come. He watched her with his good eye, alert but quiet. He seemed to be saving his energy for what mattered. She wondered what that would be.

Jimmy took a sip of water and struggled as best he could to sit up, until Bean found the button on the guardrail that raised him automatically.

"Hey, Jelly," he said. "What a relief." A stage whisper. "I thought it might be Peter." Lately Peter's pep talks were more than Jimmy could bear.

He tilted his head left and right to stretch his neck. He was sore from lying in bed. Bean slipped behind him and rubbed from the back. His skin looked like gray parchment and didn't snap right back when pulled. At first, she kneaded too hard and Jimmy flinched. Then she tried just using her fingertips. He seemed to like that.

She lowered the bed and the guardrail. "Roll over," she said.

Jimmy flopped onto his stomach. His half gown pulled to one side and gave her a view of his white butt. It looked like a deflated soccer ball. She recalled how Jimmy talked hopefully about "getting my butt back," as if it were something he'd misplaced. It was his metaphor for regaining health, a last nod to vanity. The funny things people worry about when the doctors are shaking their heads. Bean tried to remember what Jimmy's butt had looked like when they were children, all pink and plump. Why couldn't the hospital give a person a decent gown?

At first, she felt shy over the intimacy of her touch. Jimmy had always been cheek kisses and hugs. Before that, it had been Indian burns and noogies. But when they were really young, they had frolicked like puppies, spilling over each other, never worrying about touch, what was right or wrong. Their bodies were pretty much the same, the same strength, the same speed. They slung an elbow around each other's neck and called themselves Burt and Ruthie.

She remembered playing sardines with the kids in the neighbor-hood. It was a simple game, like hide-and-seek, only better. One person hid and everyone else sought. Whenever someone found the hider, he quietly entered the hiding place. The game ended when the last seeker—often on the brink of tears—finally found all the other kids packed together under a tree or inside a shed, like sardines.

Playing sardines with Jimmy was a problem. He loved the game. But whenever he had to hide, he got excited and started to giggle. It gave them all away. Bean remembered one time, at Jimmy's house, when she'd ducked into the doghouse in the side yard. It was a pretty good hiding place. She remembered tingling with anticipation on the crumpled-up carpet, amid the smell of cut plywood and grass clippings, the clingy dog air, the darkness broken by a shaft of light from the little door leading out.

Then Jimmy found her. He crawled in and nearly bumped her with his head. Bean said "Shhh" before he could scream. They huddled quietly for a while, relishing the snugness of well-hidden prey. But when another kid passed by, Jimmy couldn't tolerate the suspense. He began to giggle. Bean pinched him at first, then stuck her hand over his mouth, but that cut off his air and made him gasp. She let go and he giggled again. "I swear, Jimmy," she threatened. Alerted, the kid crawled in next to them.

Now Bean lightly rubbed Jimmy's neck. It was getting dark and she glanced at the window. They were on the seventh floor, and she half expected to see a canyon of city buildings. Instead, she saw herself, reflected in a pool of light from the bedside lamp. She was grown-up now. Her arms were strong. She looked like a nurse. She rubbed his back with the flat of her hands, careful not to dig, watching his distinct ribs rise and fall with each breath.

"Oh yes," he said.

She looked at his backbone poking out from the slit in his gown, the sharp shoulder blades, the clumpy vertebrae, the cup of his pelvis. It reminded her of an egret skeleton she'd found with Bob at Bolinas beach a while back. Its long neck was stripped clean and sun-bleached. Bean had run her fingers down the ridge, counting the vertebrae. Bob had fretted she might catch something.

Now she put her thumbs on both sides of Jimmy's spine and moved them up and down. He moaned some more.

"Heaven," he said.

As she rubbed, Bean relaxed and started to talk. Not colorfully or indignantly like she might at the Patio. But softly, in a monotone. As if recounting a dream. She talked about Bob's proposal, Hanna's departure. She said she was worried about one of her students.

Jimmy grunted at each of her setbacks. "You've been busy, Jelly Bean" was all he said.

Bean feared she'd really messed things up, she told him. She didn't know what to do about any of it.

She reached down and squeezed the backs of his arms, where the triceps used to be. Jimmy used to work out at the gym, not all the time, but now and then. All gone.

"Hey, Bean," he said.

"Yeah?"

"If I get through this . . ."

"When," she said.

"When," he said.

Jimmy and Peter had been talking for a long time about a bike trip in the San Juan Islands, near Seattle, he told her. Now Peter was saying he wouldn't go. He wouldn't even talk about it, said it would be too hard on Jimmy. But did Bean know what? Jimmy was going, with or without him.

Bean returned to his neck. There was loose skin around his Adam's apple.

"Good for you," she said.

So maybe Bean could think about going with him, Jimmy went on. Sometime in the spring, if everything cleared up? Maybe sometime in May? It was supposed to be amazing, he told her. You went from island to island. They had nature trips where the killer whales practically jumped into the boat.

Bean noticed that Jimmy's catheter was stretched taut as he lay on his stomach. It looked like it might tug on the hole in his chest. She raised him enough to give it some slack.

"Bean?"

"Yeah?"

"Could you do the thumbs again?"

Bean returned her thumbs to his backbone.

"Some people have everything," she whispered.

She ran her hands across Jimmy's devastated body and found herself thinking about Andrew. His shoulders like oranges. Those narrow hips. She pined for his body, in all its careless vitality. Andrew was the antidote to all this disease and despair. He was life, bold and beautiful. A buttery twinge in her groin. She imagined Andrew trying to call her—his big, square fingers working the phone pad—only to get the wrong number again and again.

"Would June be better?" Jimmy was talking over his shoulder. He couldn't see Bean's face, how she was locked in a reverie.

"For what?" Bean said.

"The bike trip, you yo-yo." Jimmy thought a minute. "If I can't do the biking, you know, I could just do the boat part," he said.

Bean tied the little straps of his gown in back. She tried to picture his demolished body pumping a bike up a hill. She had an urge to bend down and kiss him between the shoulder blades. She leaned forward.

Jimmy groaned. "Oh, what am I thinking?"

Bean straightened her back.

School wasn't out until mid-June, Jimmy told her. And Bean would need some time to prepare. They should go in August.

Bean ran a light hand over the back of his head.

"August is a good month," she said.

Not a single chair that Hanna had bought at auction was comfortable. For the next several evenings, Bean found herself pacing the cramped living room, wondering what to do with herself. She flipped channels on the TV, took baths, ate cereal for dinner. She found herself growing tense at the end of the school day, dreading the prospect of another meal alone.

She'd talked to Lois a few times on the phone.

"Oh, honey, I was just thinking about you," Lois said into the phone at the Hair Flair. "Guess what? I figured out the coffeemaker."

Lois sounded relieved to hear from her. As if all was forgiven. It wasn't, of course, just understood. Over the phone, Bean grew impatient with Lois's stories. They were always the same, like when you shook up a snowglobe.

She sat in her bedroom, her children's books encircling her. First Mick. Now it could happen to Jimmy. She wouldn't have anyone to look after. And the vice versa of that was too much to think about.

Near her overflowing laundry hamper, she noticed the sticker-covered box that Mick had come in. It was time, she decided. Another calamity was coming and she needed to make room for it.

After school one day, she caught a streetcar, then transferred downtown to a commuter bus for the North Bay. She took a seat amid all the sagging workers.

She sat with the box on her knees, looked sidelong at the other passengers snoozing and reading, and felt alone. Was she the only one on this bus ever to cradle her loved one's ashes in her lap during the evening commute? Had any of them seen their best friends waste away? Had they never lost a family before? She hated them. She could guess at their days. They were ordinary, unscarred. These riders had made their presentations, eaten lunch, scored points with the boss, lost clients, toasted a departing coworker. They had gotten dates, made weekend plans, pilfered office supplies, gossiped, toiled, and groused. By the time they had caught the 6:15 bus, they were a little older, a breath closer to death, but all they were worried about was dinner.

They were going home.

So, finally, was Bean. Her errand would take her right into the old neighborhood. How long had it been? Five years, not since her college graduation day.

As the sun settled into the yellow hills, she recalled how her mother, in a spasm of maternal duty, had insisted on having a brunch for Bean and her friends on graduation. When the day came, Bean showed up nearly an hour late, dragging along her roommate, Peggy, and a punked-out girl who was really more Peggy's friend. Her mother greeted them with lox, fresh bagels, and frittata. She wore an apron, for chrissakes.

When it came time to leave for the ceremony, Bean and her friends were giddy, flapping around in their red nylon gowns, joking about what they were wearing—or not wearing—underneath. Bean's mother snapped a few pictures of them. And then Peggy said, how about a picture of Bean and her mom? When her Stepford mother slipped an arm around her waist, Bean froze. She didn't return the embrace, didn't smile, despite Peggy's prodding: "C'mon, Bean, you old sourpuss." Bean stared back. *We're not that kind of family.*

And yet, they once were. She still remembered how it felt to doze in her mother's lap during a long family vacation to San Diego. That was back when she drifted off so easily. She had reveled in partial slumber, next to her mother's bosom, smelling of talcum and salt, staring stupidly into the weave of her mother's sweater. Back then, it felt like she would be safe and loved forever.

Hugging her box, Bean stepped off the bus in Muir and into the familiar streets. The other commuters set off briskly, in search of a drink, the news, dinner, a kiss. She kept pace with them for a while, then watched them disperse. They cut down backstreets, opened picketed gates, climbed onto illuminated porches. Dogs spilled out of one house as a man with stooped shoulders and a briefcase pushed open the door. A plastic Big Wheel sat on the lawn; flowers from an early spring saluted in the garden.

She walked more slowly now. There were other ways to her destination, but she felt tugged by gravity down a particular street. It might have been the pull of memory, or even hope, but it felt like instinct.

The two-story house with a wraparound porch stood back from the street, behind a small lawn in the shade of Dutch elms. It was an old house, built in generous times. Bean stood by the mailbox and looked up the path to the front door. Her mother lived downstairs; she had converted the upper floor into a rental apartment. Bean knew every inch of that house.

She remembered coming home from school and slapping the rope swing dangling from the elm so that it convulsed wildly over a dirt patch she had scuffed with her feet. She remembered climbing those six steps, using two hands on the fat doorknob, opening and slamming the white door with its scalloped windows. She remembered singing out "I'm ho-ome," as if everything hinged on her arrival, and listening for a response. She recalled sucking in the smell of her house, running stubby-footed upstairs to her room with its big blue bed or to the bathroom with the lion-paw tub.

Bean clutched her box. The rope swing was gone. A Toyota sedan, a few years old, sat in the driveway. Her mother's? The front rooms of the house were dark, but there was a light on in the back, near the kitchen. Such a kitchen: big enough to dance in. There were tall ceilings everywhere and leaded windows that faced the garden. The house had its quirks, of course: creaky wooden floors that announced one's movements better than any alarm, built-in bookcases that had been painted so many times that their doors never quite closed. Her parents had slept downstairs. Bean and Chip slept upstairs.

Her toes almost touched the flagstone path, but she couldn't move any closer. The house was under a force field. But she couldn't walk away, either. A man passed her on the sidewalk. She pretended to admire the garden. She looked over her shoulder at the Pelligrinos' old house and saw that their driveway offered a clear sight line. Plus, it was shielded on both sides by a four-foot hedge. Bean looked around quickly, then slid across the street and ducked into the little driveway. There was a patch of green grass, split by concrete tracks for car tires. She checked for dog shit, then sat down, cross-legged, her box beside her.

She sat for a while, watching the sunlight play out its last rays on the house's front windows. The light gave a golden tint to the windowpanes and the reflected orb crawled along the glass, then spilled orange and pink overhead. The roses in the front yard had started to bloom. Her mother was crazy about roses. When the lights came on, she'd be able to see into the house. She thought she could make out a figure in the kitchen, but she couldn't be sure. She brought her knees up to her chest, rested her chin on them, and waited. After a while she wished for a sweater.

Every few minutes a car rolled past, but Bean stayed focused. After half an hour—or an hour, possibly two—she started in surprise. A car's passing headlights swung round in the street and suddenly trained on her like a spotlight. The driver, apparently oblivious to her presence, thrust the car into the driveway, in a brutal arc. Bean gasped, grabbed her head, and tumbled off to the right. A tan Volvo station wagon rolled over her former perch just as she slammed into the hedge, scraping her arms on the gravel and hitting her head on the pavement.

The driver turned off the car, popped open his door, and shouted at her. It wasn't Mr. Pelligrino.

"Holy shit," he said. "Are you all right?" It was a man in a tweed cap, forty-five-ish. "I could've killed you."

It was an accusation.

"Yeah," Bean said. "Whew." She hadn't seen him coming.

"What?"

"I didn't see you coming."

"It's my *driveway*, for crying out loud."

She picked herself up, was glad to feel nothing wet coming from her head, took a few uncertain steps, and headed down the street.

She got twenty paces along when she remembered Mick. She turned and went back to the driveway. The box was wedged beneath the undercarriage of the panting car. She tugged at the box until the cardboard ripped and a little gray cloud floated up around her.

Scooping the ashes back into the jar, Bean heard through an open window as the driver told someone—his wife?—about his nearly horrible experience.

"What kind of a country is this?" he demanded. "Goddamn homeless people everywhere."

Dubbed "sea parrots" by early sailors, puffins are better equipped for swimming underwater than flying. Taking off from the water is always a dicey affair; they frequently run along the water's surface, crashing into swells in the struggle to get aloft.

—The Pemberton Guide

Bean set off down darkened streets to a dirt road bordered by Scotch broom. She passed a vacant ranger station. Her head had started to throb and she felt gravel burns on her hands, but she held the broken box tight to her chest.

Not much had spilled.

When loved ones die, you lose more than the people. You lose their jokes at the breakfast table. Their peeves and delights. You lose the moments when life's predicament stymies them, when a movie or snatch of music or an unexpected kindness fills their eyes with water, and like a reflex, your own. You forfeit a partner in chores, in pain, in dragging yourself from bed, in picking seeds from a watermelon, swimming in the surf, sipping coffee in a diner, wondering how to fill a Sunday afternoon, then realizing, with satisfaction, you already have.

You lose their reviews and puns and tirades. Their boredom, their fears, their moods. The muscles they are proud of, the ones that ache. Their most embarrassing body part. The dent left by their head on a pillow, their hair in the sink, their slippers in the corner. You are robbed of what you stole from them: their cotton shirts, their pithy sayings, their extravagant stories. You have no one to ask you when you were coming home.

No matter how busy you are by day—holding meetings or sliming fish or teaching students—that is the only question that really matters, Bean knew: *When are you coming home?*

You even risk losing grief's ultimate refuge: your memories. Memory is an organic thing; it must be stoked and tended, like a fire. Lovers divide up that duty. They strengthen memories by passing them back and forth to each other over time, telling and retelling the best stories at parties, embellishing—surely—but also preserving, enshrining. To safeguard a memory, it has to be summoned and retold. Eventually the old story supplants the original event, but who cares? When she faltered, he would recall. She might exaggerate, he would indulge; both would remember. Memory is a balloon that lovers swat to each other like children; it must never touch the ground.

Memory is everything. However slippery, it tells us who we are, where we have been. With any luck, it suggests a future.

Now Bean was custodian of it all, the sole proprietor of her lost love, and of whatever happened next. Had someone really loved her? Or had she imagined it? Had she loved, too? History was hers to distort, rewrite, or forget.

She walked up a hill to a levee. Phoenix Lake stretched out before her—still, dark, hemmed by trees that sloped over the water, stirred only by skeeters in moonbeams.

Bean suddenly wished Hanna were there. She squatted and opened the ripped box. She pulled out the urn, which squeaked against the packing peanuts. She was careful to keep the lid on.

The metal urn was heavy and flared, and she lifted it over her head. It crossed her mind that she might look like a demented tennis champion. She held Mick up until her arms ached. She lowered the urn and kissed it. She tasted ash on her lips. Then she pinched the lid off the jar and poured the contents into the lake.

The ashes looked almost white as they fell. They clouded the dark water only briefly.

Debbie and Shirley were watching clouds roll by
When Debbie exclaimed, "Why do people die, why?"
A western wind blew through the trees
And the water felt chilly around Debbie's knees.
At last, Shirley whispered, "Listen, my dear,"
And Debbie cocked an ear for all she could hear.
But she heard only quiet and told Shirley so,
Till the magpie hushed her and said listen some mo'.
Debbie closed her eyes and put a wing to her ear
Till it came through, still faint, but clear:
Criiick, said a frog, and reeek-reek said a cricket;
Splish went a fish, and a deer chomped in the thicket.
The sounds burbled up and abounded and grew.
They reminded Debbie of a song she once knew.
An old tune that felt like cold lemonade,
Warm nests and chestnuts and naps in the shade.
Her heart lightened a moment, yet she still didn't see
Why such creatures must one day not be.
"We have loved their music," Old Shirley said.
"It comes wrapped in silence, they'll someday be dead.
Our lives are the same, we're not here for long,
And that's why we listen so hard to their song."

Debbie thought for a moment. Then two, then three.
"It still sucks," she said.
"Yes," said Old Shirley, "it does."

Bean and Hanna had spoken only twice in three weeks. Hanna had returned Bean's call to tell her she'd arrived home safely. And Bean had dialed her up one Tuesday evening after drinking a beer. She'd worked out a question ahead of time.

"I was wondering if you knew where the cord is to the frying pan," Bean said.

"What cord? You just put on the pan and fry."

It wasn't going well.

"No," Bean said. "I mean the skillet. The electric one."

The cord was where Hanna said it was, inside the pan. Bean thanked her. She had no plans to actually cook.

Now it was Friday night. Bean had drawn out the school day as long as she could. She slouched on the sofa, trying to ignore the phone until she had to pick it up and dial, or she would explode.

"Hanna?"

Hanna said hey—friendly, but not too.

"Um, how are you?"

Hanna was doing fine. She sounded so far away.

"Really?"

"Yes," Hanna said. A pause. "I'm going to play cards tomorrow."

"Oh, who with?"

With some friends, Hanna told her.

Friends. Bean could use some of those. She struggled to keep Hanna talking.

"What kind?"

Hanna was confused. "What, dear?"

"What kind of cards?"

"Well, hearts, I suppose."

Bean was crying. She felt the tears on her knuckles.

"I wish I could be there," she gasped.

There was a long pause and the line crackled. "Is everything okay, Bean?"

She liked it when Hanna called her Bean. A teardrop hung on her nose; she brushed it away with the back of her hand. "Yes," she said.

"Well, good," Hanna said. A pause. "Because I've been thinking about you."

An opening. Bean lunged through.

"Jimmy's in the hospital," she declared.

"Oh, dear," said Hanna.

The rest came out in a flood. Jimmy's tumor. Him all alone, without family. Peter not knowing what to do. Breaking up with Bob. And Martin—the little boy who didn't talk—she was worried about him.

"Oh, Hanna, I miss you so much," she said.

Bean buzzed around her little apartment, trying to make sure everything was the same as it had been before Hanna left. She emptied the garbage, which was groaning with frozen-dinner tins and microwave burrito wrappers. She put new boxes of Kleenex on every surface she could find. She scrubbed the bathroom and the kitchen counter. At the newsstand, she picked up a couple of magazines for the coffee table. She stocked the medicine chest with a few discreet items Hanna required.

On her way back from these errands, she paused at the front stoop and considered the patch of ground where she and Hanna had planted the black-eyed Susan. Bean had never tended it. She poured water on it now and tried to fluff it up a bit, but the plant was twisted and brown, near death.

When her chores were done, Bean snapped off her rubber gloves, tucked her hair in a baseball cap, and drove the milk truck to the airport. She got there an hour early, as if to atone for past mistakes.

There was time to witness how other people handled separation. She watched a man with a briefcase take leave of a woman in a silk dress. The woman leaned into him as he delicately fingered her hair away from her eyes. No tears. They were confident they'd see each other again as planned. Tomorrow. Next Tuesday. Whenever.

Why didn't that woman fret? Didn't she love him? Didn't she know that he might step into that airplane chute and never come back? Love made cowards of us all. It made us brave in the big moments, when eternity was on the line. But we squandered that gift in a million private fears, doled out in the half-light of our bedrooms, worrying that we might lose our most precious someone.

Growing older meant worrying more about others than yourself. Bean had never thought twice about flying on a plane, though the turbulence in Alaska could be harrowing. The little puddle jumper to Homer or Anchorage was always buffeted around. Her thoughts: *Well, this makes sense as a way to die. At least it will be fast.* She'd assess her seatmate as a partner in their inevitable destruction. Would they share a prayer, or would it be like a really scary amusement ride—no time to contemplate, just a few moments of animal fear, looking into the contorted features of a stranger?

But when Mick had boarded the plane for McKinley—the very last time she saw him—she had considered the craft's fragility. It was folly to climb into such a contraption for any reason other than burst appendix. To push that heap of metal and gasoline into the sky to contend with Nature's worst—it was crazy, like walking your dog on the freeway. She watched the plane take off and fretted that she might never see Mick again.

She had been right, of course, but it wasn't because of the plane. Bean didn't know what message to derive from that. It was either *Treat every good-bye like a final farewell* or *Quit borrowing trouble; it'll come soon enough.*

She was starting to sound like Jimmy.

A gate began disgorging passengers. Bean watched as mothers arranged children, who stood on tiptoe in search of a certain face. There were boyfriends hanging back, leaning against the reservations counter, trying to look cool. There were retired couples seeking grandchildren, now and then adjusting their eyeglasses as if they didn't entirely trust their vision. There was an assorted corps of two dozen others, waiting with Bean, hoping against odds that the one they'd come for had successfully negotiated the horror of modern transport—tickets, taxis, traffic, turbulence—and would slip out of the accordion chute with a story to tell.

The hearts of those waiting expanded in their chests as each face appeared and was reclaimed as one of their own. They wore half smiles and felt the tickle of anticipation, like children playing a pop-up game. *Come to me,* the waiting crowd thought. *Hug my shoulders. Make me laugh. End my loneliness.* The travelers strode in with confidence, presenting the gift of themselves.

The stream of deplaning passengers thinned out and Bean started chewing a fingernail. *Come on, White Hair.* After forever, it appeared: the tuft. Hanna had her back turned; she was wrestling with her carry-on bag.

Bean threw her arms around Hanna, clogging up the last of the line.

"Darn wheels catch on everything," Hanna said.

Bean tried to breathe normally. She couldn't say anything, so she just laughed.

Hanna pitied the black-eyed Susan sitting in the mud puddle, but she set about her duties in a positive way. She entered the apartment like an on-call surgeon, efficiently doffing her coat, stowing her bag, and stepping into the kitchen. Bean felt so comforted, she settled into the couch just to watch Hanna move. The old woman chatted as she worked, organizing the groceries they'd picked up on the way home, squishing her nose in distaste at mysterious items in the back of the refrigerator, mopping the counter with a sponge, complaining about all the rain in Vancouver, and wondering what Marguerite would say when she surprised her at the store.

The next morning Hanna went with Bean to the hospital. Peter arrived after they'd been there a few minutes. He visited almost daily and looked drawn. He said he felt better now that Hanna was back.

Jimmy had been losing weight. The skin around his face was Saran Wrap tight. His elbows looked too frail for his arms, and his Adam's apple bulged from his throat. He had lost about half his hair. When he tugged at it, it came out in clumps. The nurses offered to shave his head.

In the hallway, Peter told Bean of an encounter with one of Jimmy's doctors. The radiologist, who was in charge of zapping the brain tumor, had sharply upbraided Jimmy the other day. "You can't keep losing weight and get this treatment," he said. "I can only do so much. You've got to keep your weight up."

Peter was angry. He wanted to get Jimmy out of the hospital. Bring him home. Jimmy would be more comfortable with some decent sleep and home-cooked food. Everyone knew that hospitals were the worst place for the sick.

Bean and Hanna offered to help, and Jimmy was discharged the next day. For the next couple of weeks, they read to him, changed his linens. When it came time for diapers, they did that, too. Hanna taught Bean how to make the bed with hospital corners. Bean tried to show Hanna how to hook up Jimmy to the IV machine, but the apparatus had a computer pad and Hanna was afraid of making a mistake. It was tiring work and everyone felt wrung out.

After reading to Jimmy and hooking him up one evening, Bean followed her nose into the kitchen. Garlic and melting cheese wafted throughout. She peeked into the oven. It was Mick's lasagna—the distinctive wads of fresh spinach poking out; the ricotta, cheddar, and mozzarella; paprika sprinkled on top. The memory lasagna! How did it get here? It was too horrible to think of.

Hanna came in the back door, scissors in one hand and parsley from Peter's herb garden in the other. Bean pounced on her.

"Hanna, what the hell are you doing?"

Hanna took a half step back.

"I'm making dinner," she said, blinking fast. "Stop shouting at me."

"Mick's lasagna?"

"What?"

Bean had her nose in Hanna's face. She flapped her arms. "That's Mick's lasagna. I saved it."

"What are you talking about? It's *my* lasagna. I made it myself yesterday."

A pinprick, and the air rushed out of Bean.

"Oh," she said. "Okay, then."

But Hanna slammed the scissors down on the counter and raised one twisted finger. It felt like a Gypsy curse was coming.

"No, it's not okay," she blared. "You threw his ashes away. His *ashes*. Didn't bother to think somebody might have wanted them to say good-bye. God forbid, they might provide his mother with a little peace of mind." Bean stepped back, but Hanna crowded her. "You take a week to figure out what you're going to do with him. I say, maybe we should bury him in Vancouver. You say, 'No, I want him cremated.' All right, I think, everybody says it's the wife's decision. Maybe we can scatter him somewhere special. Then you do it *without* me. Like you were dumping an old tub of cottage cheese. I'm talking about my son's *ashes*. Don't come to me about a casserole."

Bean was backed up against the counter.

"And another thing," Hanna said. Her eyebrows were almost touching. "Who do you think taught Michael how to make that dish in the first place? It sure as blazes didn't come from *your* cookbook."

Bean was gathering her papers after school and overseeing the ten-minute detention of two boys who had been picking on a third, when a short Mexican woman entered her classroom. She was Bean's age. Her black hair was cut short in bangs but hung long all the way down her back. She wore a black uniform and white shoes and a decal on her chest said WELCOME TO ROYAL SUITES, with the name Carlota in the middle. She approached tentatively, like someone testing a DO NOT DISTURB sign.

"Señora," she said.

Bean sighed. She had been hoping to leave as soon as school was out. She had been up with Jimmy the night before. The IV machine kept beeping at her for doing something wrong. In the end, she got the air bubble out of the tube, but only after Peter woke up and had a look. He was barely sleeping at all; he looked almost as bad as Jimmy.

The woman introduced herself in Spanish as the mother of Martin Lagos. She was worried about her son because he had stopped talking at home. A year ago he was soaking up English like a sponge. A regular chatterbox. But now, well, it seemed like all the words had been knocked out of him.

Martin was on another of his absences. He hadn't been to school that week. It was Wednesday.

"What do you mean knocked out of him?" Bean said, slow and hard, in English.

The woman shrugged. She handed Bean a paper. It was a first-grade teacher's evaluation of Martin from Mt. Davidson Elementary, across town. It was a document that should have been on file at César Chávez. Bean's eyes bounced down the page. Martin had been a "good student, with imagination."

Martin's mother took back the paper, carefully folded it, and tucked it away. She crossed her arms as though she'd done her job. Bean stiffened. She looked her in the eye.

"Who is the man I saw at your apartment?"

The question startled her. Bean repeated it in Spanish. The woman seemed not to know that Bean had come by last month.

"My boyfriend," the woman said. "He works nights."

"You need to keep him away from your child," Bean said.

She looked at Bean vacantly.

Bean put her hands on the woman's shoulders. "Listen to me," she said. "You need to leave him and go live somewhere else."

The woman's face was unchanged.

"He's hurting Martin." Bean was shouting now. The woman tightened the jacket around her shoulders and looked for the door. Bean said it again in Spanish. It came out "Your boyfriend is doing damage to your son."

The woman backed away and slipped out the door as fast as she could.

Bean got the number for Child Protective Services from the office. After a long wait, a social worker came on the line, heard her story, and asked for evidence of imminent danger to Martin. Bean had none, except for the speech problem. CPS would send somebody over to Martin's house as soon as they could, the social worker told her. But it might take a few days; they were spread rather thin.

Jimmy stopped making sense that week. Bean gave up trying to anchor him to daily life by quizzing him on what month or day of the week it was. He knew that he should know the answers, and it pained her to watch him struggle. At times, she suspected he would be hard-pressed to recall her name. But he still knew she was a friend, and he stared at her with a blank, docile look, which meant he had no energy left for anything but pulling oxygen into his bony chest with the im-planted port sticking out like a mattress tag.

On Friday evening Jimmy tried to get up, apparently to go to the bathroom, got tangled in the tubes from the IV tree, and fell down in a heap. Peter rushed in first, followed by Bean. They lifted Jimmy back into bed. He was as light as a bird.

Peter swabbed a cut on Jimmy's forehead, where he must have grazed the sink. Peter was oddly calm. He had yielded to disequilib-rium. For as long as Bean had known him, he'd been so meticulous. Until Jimmy got sick, she'd never seen Peter's hair without gel, his face unshaved, his clothes unpressed. But illness makes the ultimate mess, throwing everyone out of sync, displaying no respect for night or day, a person's private spaces, dreams, or fears. She liked Peter more now.

Death, Bean saw, arrives like a bossy, drunken aunt. She sits at a man's bedside, squints at the ruins of his face, and asks horridly crass questions like "Who's going to look after your sweetheart now?" or "Didn't you always want to take piano lessons?" She might reminisce for a moment with the poor fellow, scrutinize the photos out of his beloved scrapbook. "Here you are with your first dog," she says. "This was how you looked when you had a family, chased a ball, dove into a lake." With flabby arms and a stained muumuu, the death-aunt shifts her bulk on the bed, carelessly squashing a life-sustaining tube. She watches the man's dinner arrive and tut-tuts as he tries to swallow, gags, then pushes it aside.

"Well, dear," she says after a while, "I'll leave you to the details."

Jimmy started breathing in double time around 3 P.M. Bean had just changed his IV fluid and Hanna was sitting in the corner, keeping her company. Jimmy's chest heaved, and he sucked the air through teeth that looked big and yellow against his crumpled face. Hanna went to get Peter. He was in the kitchen with his mother, who'd flown in from Dallas. Peter called the nursing service. Jimmy was in distress; he needed morphine.

The home nurse didn't arrive until after 7 P.M. She'd been delayed, then got lost, calling twice to report her trouble. Paulette—chunky with a mop of red hair—was new to all this, an apprentice. After four hours of watching Jimmy fight to breathe, Bean didn't want any apologies. She wanted Jimmy to rest easily. Paulette finally bumbled in with her medical bag but forgot what she needed in her car. She came back in, then said, "Now, who's going to learn how to do this?"

Under Jimmy's hospice program, the nurses were supposed to teach techniques to the "primary caregivers." Bean and Hanna and Peter had all endured the rituals, learned how to clamp, inject, connect, program. Peter was an expert, Bean proficient, Hanna baffled.

Jimmy writhed for air.

"This gets connected to this," Paulette said.

Peter was wild-eyed.

"Just give him the shot," he said.

Paulette said they were all going to have to learn it sooner or later; that was how the system worked.

"Fuck the system!" Peter shouted. "Give him the goddamn morphine, now!"

Paulette shrugged and stuck the needle into Jimmy's port. His lungs sounded like he'd been stabbed in the back. The amber fluid raced in.

Hanna adjusted a moist washcloth on his head. "Let go, child," she whispered. "It's all right. Let it go."

Peter stood bedside, holding Jimmy's hand, his other hand over his own mouth.

In three seconds Jimmy's breathing had stopped. Everyone leaned in closer to see. His brown eyes were wide open. Ten seconds passed, and everyone dropped their gaze. Then in a horrid burst that would haunt Bean for days, Jimmy heaved a huge breath, his gums yanked past his teeth, straining to live but succumbing to the drug. The pain-killer killed him.

Bean and Hanna moved into the kitchen as if floating on a tide. They sent Peter's mother to the bedroom. The house was oddly quiet. Then Bean heard some whimpering. She stuck her head out into the hallway. Paulette was wiping her eyes and shaking as she stuffed a stethoscope and other devices into her bag. She saw Bean and apolo-gized. "It's just that I've never seen anyone . . . *go* before." She started to hug Bean, thought better of it, blew her nose, and went outside.

Hanna started to make arrangements. She called the funeral home to come get the body. But they said they could take Jimmy only if there was a pronouncement of death. "I'm telling you, he's dead," Hanna barked.

Bean raced out to catch Paulette. She found her sitting in a Chevy Nova, staring into the rain, crying some more. Bean tapped the glass and Paulette rolled down the window.

"We need a pronouncement of death," Bean said.

Paulette, sniffing, said she wasn't qualified for that. They needed a doctor.

Bean looked needles at her. "We need a pronouncement of death," she repeated. Paulette wiped her nose on her sleeve and signed. From the kitchen, she phoned her supervisor. She took instructions. "Uh-huh. Uh-huh. Uh-huh."

Bean was sure she knew the other end of the conversation. No pulse. No breath. No response to stimulus. That's death. You can do it.

Bean sat with Hanna in the next room. She noticed a bunch of jars stacked in the corner. Jimmy's glazes. Down in the garage was a pottery wheel and kiln he'd barely used. He might have gotten good at it, too.

They watched as Paulette hung up, fished out her stethoscope, untangled it from the blood pressure sleeve, then dropped them both on the floor. She said darn, groaned to bend over and pick them up, looked at her watch, took a deep breath as if to brace against a bad smell, then hustled off like a demented Florence Nightingale to Jimmy's room. Toward Death. Or toward what she was pretty sure was, in fact, death.

Bean and Hanna sat on the couch, holding hands. Bean listened hard and heard the blood pressure sleeve being pumped up one last time around Jimmy's arm.

They were quiet a minute, then Bean asked Hanna what she was thinking.

Hanna was looking into space.

"I just hope he hasn't taken a turn for the worse," she said.

Hanna asked what Bean was thinking.

"I was thinking he might sit up and say boo," Bean said.

Bean and Hanna looked sideways at each other. It was hard to say who started it. But at the very moment Jimmy was officially dead, the two of them sat together, holding hands, and chuckled. Then Bean couldn't stop giggling—it was just like Jimmy in the doghouse—and Hanna held her head in her lap.

Peter read a few lines at the funeral—short and sweet—about Jimmy's brief adventure in ceramics. He told how Jimmy kept going to class long after the aches and pains had crept up on him. So many ashtrays. Everyone suspected that Jimmy was getting kickbacks from the tobacco companies. Then Peter said he felt like one of Jimmy's creations—not an ashtray—just a better man.

Jimmy's parents sat in the front row. Bean sat next to his mother, whom she remembered best for ice-tray Popsicles and the way she called children "kidlets." Her makeup was all crooked; maybe it was hard to apply with all that blinking going on. She tore at a tissue in her fist. Jimmy's father sat stiff-backed throughout the service. He tried to look like a soldier, with his tight-knotted tie, nodding gravely as a handful of speakers passed to and from the pulpit. But Bean knew he was just a real estate broker who'd once had an affair that ended abruptly after he came home with fingernail scratches on his face. Jimmy's dad was on a first-name basis with everyone in Muir. But here, in Jimmy's world, he was among strangers. He hadn't bothered to get to know Peter, and it made Bean so mad, her teeth clenched.

Bob showed up. Hanna must have called him. He sat in the back and pulled his beret off his head. He was really losing his hair now. It gave him a clean, honest look. After the service he made his way up to Peter and wrapped his arms around him in a hug. Before Bean could say or do anything, Bob was gone.

That Saturday Bean got up early and rode the streetcar downtown. The sun was still climbing over the hills, but there were joggers out and pickup basketball games on the blacktops. Bean had taken sixty dollars out of her bank account and planned to spend it frivolously. Her birthday was Sunday, though she hadn't mentioned it to anybody, not even Hanna. She hoped a new pair of jeans or a sleek swimsuit or some CDs of the country stars Bob had introduced to her might scatter her dread.

She got the idea from Hanna. Hanna had gone on a spree a couple of days before Jimmy died. She came home and arrayed her goodies on the kitchen counter. They were from Woolworth's, practical things—aspirin and a heating pad for her arthritis, a comb and brush set for Bean, work gloves for Bob.

Bean had ignored the mention of Bob. She didn't own him, after all. But why all the stuff?

Hanna dragged on her cigarette. She answered as if in a trance.

"Sometimes, when it's so quiet in the house I can't stand it anymore, I go to the stores," she said. "The music, the clean aisles, everything at your fingertips. It makes me feel like things are possible again."

Bean examined the comb and brush set. The box had a picture of a teenage girl from the 1950s staring into a hand mirror. It was amazing that Woolworth's stayed in business. She noticed Hanna's raincoat slung over the chair.

"I just hope you're careful, Hanna," she said.

"Careful?" Hanna said. She played senile better than anyone.

Now, as she walked through the shopping district, Bean thought of past birthdays. Her mother had always given her the wrong gifts. Not just the wrong size or the wrong color or style. The wrong idea. Colossally wrong.

> *When I was three, I was hardly me.*
> *When I was four, I was not much more.*

When she turned nine, and all she wanted to do was climb trees and ride her bike, she got an Easy Bake oven. She was supposed to stay inside and make little cakes with a lightbulb. The next year, after her dad moved out, she got an embroidered sweatshirt. It fit pretty well, except it had two words stenciled on the chest: TICKLE ME. She stuffed it in her bottom drawer. The misfires continued. There was the *Teen Diet Guide* when Bean hit junior high and had discovered the vending machines. At thirteen, she got a painter's easel, even though the only talent she'd ever shown was for writing.

She stepped out of a shoe store and was heading up Powell Street toward Macy's when someone grabbed her arm.

"Hey, Bean," he said.

Fear and then recognition.

"Chip," Bean said. "Oh my God."

It had been years since she'd seen her brother. He was fuller now; his face was round with flesh. His hairline had shifted, but there was still plenty of hair—dirty blond, the same as Bean's. He wore a down jacket that gave him a Michelin tire look. It was too warm for a jacket like that.

She paused a second, then stepped forward, threw an arm around him, and hugged him. The back of his neck smelled stale. Greeting Chip was like hearing good news and bad news at the same time. It had been that way for a long time.

He was very excited. "Is this the most unreal thing that has ever happened, or what? Just the other day—was it last week?—I'm thinking, I wonder what old Bean is up to. I wonder what she's doing. I wonder where she's got to."

"Alaska," Bean said.

"Fuckin' Alaska," he said. "Right. How was it? Pretty cold, right? And now here you are."

"In the flesh," Bean said. The sidewalk was getting crowded and he gestured them into a Starbucks. Bean moved slowly, like she was waiting for something she didn't want to hear. They ordered lattes and he let Bean pay. When he sat down at a round table, his leg began to jiggle. His fingernails were chewed to the quick.

"So you're back now? It's so great to see you, Bean. Really great. Hey, Bean, remember when I gave you that Baby Ruth bar when you learned to read? Remember that?"

"Yeah," Bean said. "I remember."

"Well, welcome back to Heartache City, that's all I can say. Everything keeps changing around here. First everyone's getting rich selling dot-com this and that and ordering snacks for delivery over the Internet. Then—*kaboom!*—everybody's starving and getting evicted. It's all Chinese to me. But we felt it—at Mowbray and Strut—you know, the furnace guys. We felt it even though we didn't have any fancy stock options. They were cutting back my hours, so I took disability. I'm not ashamed to say it. My back was sore, anyway. But you can't live on disability. It's a big lie."

He jiggled some more and spilled a little bit of coffee from his cup. He was talking awfully fast. Bean clutched her cup.

"Did I tell you how great it is to see you?" he said.

He was using again; she was pretty sure.

"So, you seen Mom?"

Bean shook her head.

"Anyway, so the disability runs out and Seth invites me to go in with him on our own service—heating, ductwork, the whole bit. You remember Seth?" A vague image of a greasy-haired stoner. "Well, he's pretty sure he can do it, him and me, if we can raise some capital. Guy's eager to sell the business; he's too old—Seth got him down already. He's really something, that Seth.

"So we'd be equal partners if I can come up with the cash. Doesn't that sound great?"

Everything was great today. "Partners," Bean repeated absently. "Great."

"And I did have the money, almost all of it, if you want to know the truth. But then I started hanging with this girl, Melanie? She's AA and here I'm thinking, Uh-oh—and it turned out I was right. Big-time. I take her to Acapulco for a week—thought it might get her over the hump at first—and, wham-bam, she burned through it all. I'd stop seeing her, but there's something about her mouth. And it's not all her fault."

Bean was following about half of it. *This is my brother*, she thought. *We used to take baths together. He taught me to read. He is my father's son*. Yet he didn't have the slightest clue about Mick. Or Jimmy. Or anything else going on in her life. They were strangers, and the fact appalled her.

When I was five, I was just alive . . .

"Why don't you ask Mom?" Bean said.

"What?"

"For the money."

Their mother never denied Chip anything.

"I can't, Bean. I'm already in the hole to her. You know, like I told you, it's the economy."

She looked at him. He was glancing around and shaking a sugar packet, still jiggling.

"Did I tell you how good it is to see you?"

"You, too," Bean whispered.

"And if you could just help me out. I'd pay you back. With interest. I believe in interest and you could pick the rate. Just tell me."

She felt a bit nauseous. How much of it would go up his nose or for more trips with Melanie?

"How much?" she asked.

"Seventy-five hundred is the deal."

Bean raised her eyebrows.

"Well, I'm lying. The deal is five thousand dollars," he said. "But I've got to pay some bills."

"I don't have that kind of money," Bean said.

"What? I thought everybody made it big in Alaska—all that OT in the season."

She thought of her trips to McKinley, the funeral, the drive home, and setting up an apartment. Until Mudhole sold the house, she was just getting by.

"I'd like to help you, Chip, really I would."

His face clouded, and the sudden bitterness scared her.

"Yeah," he said. "Everyone would like to help old Chip."

He stood up and jarred the table with his thigh. More coffee on the table.

"I just remembered I have somewhere I need to be," he said. "Take care of yourself, Bean."

She watched him leave. A warm breeze slipped past him as he pushed open the glass door. It was too warm for that jacket.

The Snowy Owl's plumage is so well insulated she is unable to transfer body heat directly to her eggs. Each year, before laying her first egg, all the soft feathers on a patch on her belly fall out. Only by applying this bit of naked skin—called a "brood patch"—to her clutch does she manage to incubate her eggs, turning them regularly to distribute the warmth.

—The Pemberton Guide

*T*he phone rang. Bean lay in bed, waiting for Hanna to answer it. She had barely slept, waking up hour after hour, taunted by the red digital numbers on the alarm clock. Now that it was time to get up, she felt like she could sleep forever. She used the crook of her arm to hide her eyes against the sunlight streaming in. The phone bleated again.

"Hanna!" Bean shouted.

No reply, just Fred, clawing at the door. Hanna went to Mass on Sundays; was it really that late?

Another ring. Bean crawled from bed, stomped across the floor in her underwear, yanked open the door, stumbled over the dog—"Shit, Fred"—and swept up the phone on the kitchen counter.

"Yeah?" she said. Whoever it was deserved a little discourtesy. She leaned over the counter and propped up her heavy head with her palm. The chrome toaster reflected her face with a fun-house distortion that wasn't at all funny.

A deep male voice. "Lois?"

She jolted upright, ran a hand over her face, as if that would clear her mind.

"It's Andrew!" He announced himself like a prize.

She pictured his lean face, his strong body like a coil. She swallowed.

"I'm her," she said, already out of sync. "I mean, this is she."

"Remember me?" he said, a smile in his voice. "From the Y? And after?"

"Oh yeah," Bean said. As if she could forget those narrow hips. "How are you?"

"Oh, hey, I'm fine," he said. "I was just sittin' here thinking about you. Well, first I was sitting here trying to figure out your number. But now I'm thinking about you."

"Oh, um, how've you been?" She didn't know anything about him. Except what he looked like naked. This was their longest conversation.

But maybe she could talk to Andrew. Maybe he was just the person. He had unlocked one door for her; maybe he could fix the rest of her life. Here was someone who didn't know Chip or Mick or Jimmy or Bob or Hanna. Hell, he didn't even know Bean. He just wanted to be with her, Lois. They could go start with a cup of coffee somewhere. Take a walk.

He had asked a question. Bean heard the silence and scrolled backward. Andrew wanted her to come over. She pictured his overheated apartment with its dirty clothes and dingy bathtub.

"I've been thinking about you *hard*, Lois," he said.

It was the role of a lifetime, of course. When you were Lois, you could talk like a truck driver, waggle your breasts, drain your men and not look back. Of course, it might not work like before. The mask could slip. The fear would return. It would be worse than ever to see the disappointment in his face: "What's wrong, Lois?" Besides, she didn't have anything to wear; she didn't own any fuck-me boots.

"I . . . I can't," Bean said.

"Oh," he said. Disappointed.

"It's my grandmother," she blurted.

"What's the matter with her?"

"She died. Yesterday. I have to go help out. To Alaska."

"Oh man, I'm sorry, Lois," he said. "Seriously."

"Well, what can you do?" Bean said. She winced, too breezy.

"I'll let you go, then," he said. "Lois?"

Bean swallowed. "Yeah?"

"I know we don't know each other that well. But I just want you to know that I think you're a beautiful person."

Bean hung up and again caught her wavy reflection in the toaster. Her hair was stringy. Her eyes rested in dark scallops. She was puffy. Her outsides had finally caught up with her insides. She looked as bad as she felt.

"Fuck off," she mumbled.

It was Sunday and it was her birthday. She had no plans. She opened and closed kitchen cupboards mindlessly. Nothing in the larder, sweet or salty, promised any solace.

Now we are six, clever as clever . . .

She picked up the phone on the counter and punched in a number. It rang until a woman's voice said, "Hello." Bean hung up, snatched her windbreaker, rushed out of the house, boarded a streetcar, then transferred to a bus.

She rode through a tunnel painted with a rainbow, her fists clenched on her thighs. She leaned her forehead against the window and gave it a few sharp thuds. Was she a fool to do this? It felt like a last chance. Staying away from her mother seemed harder than facing her.

She got off in Muir. She walked with her head up, looking straight ahead. She followed the time-etched route to her childhood home, but she registered little. She reached the two-story house with its wide porch set in the shade.

She walked across the flagstones, past the roses. The heavy front door needed painting. She took a breath and, almost involuntarily, looked back from where she had come. It wasn't too late to walk away. She rang the doorbell.

The door swung open wide and the woman on the other side of it wore a smile, which froze instantly. *She's expecting someone,* Bean thought. *A quiet afternoon of cards? A date? Well, she got me instead.*

Bean waited, arms at her side. *Are you my mother?* She was slightly taller than Bean, still slim, though her weight had shifted. Her grayless hair was combed and her face was made up.

"Bean," she said. Surprised.

"Hi, Mom," Bean said, overly friendly so it came out sarcastic. Inside, it felt good to be recognized. She feared her anger might melt, and then she would cry. But she must not cry.

"My God," her mother said. "Come in."

Bean felt the cushiony hall carpet beneath her feet, took in the familiar house smell of Murphy's oil soap and stale flowers. She saw a corner of the piano where she'd tried to get an octave out of too-short fingers. She saw the air vents on the hallway floor, where the heat chugged out on a winter morning. Her mother led her into the living room, which had always been for company.

Her mother sat on the edge of the love seat and seemed to wait for some kind of announcement. Bean kept silent and forced her to ask. It was the way things had been for a long time. "What are you . . . ?" Her voice trailed off.

"Doing here?" Bean said.

She wasn't sure. She had pushed it out of her mind until now. It always felt so bad to have a birthday when your life was a mess. Another year of struggle behind. No clarity, but that of a ticking clock.

"It's my birthday."

She was twenty-seven years old.

"Yes," her mother said, "I know."

Silence. More silence. Make her say it.

"Happy birthday."

Bean nodded. Time to get on with it.

"I live here now," she said.

"What? Where?"

"San Francisco."

Her mother nodded.

"How long?"

"Since September."

Now Bean's mother was quiet. "Bernal Heights," Bean said. "It's near the Mission."

Bean imagined what her mother was thinking: *I barely hear from you in six years, then all of a sudden you appear on my doorstep and tell me you've been living in the City for eight months?* She hoped she was thinking that.

But Bean's mother just nodded and her mouth went from an O to a dash. She looked like she wasn't going to ask any more questions. Like she didn't care. She fiddled with the diamond ring on her left hand, still there after all these years.

"I take it your marriage didn't last," she said.

Bean had a hard time looking at her mother straight. When she did, she noticed little lines around her eyes, despite the application of foundation. She had once been the most beautiful woman in the world. Now she looked old, only worse, because she was trying not to.

I take it your marriage didn't last.

She made it sound like destiny. The curse of the fuckup daughter.

Bean thought of the photo of Mick and Lois together. It gave her the usual pit in the stomach; she had to stop doing that. Was there a glint of triumph in her mother's eyes?

"It didn't *last*, Mother, because he *died*," Bean said. "Mick died." Her chest tightened and she held her chin up to keep from gasping. "That's the reason it didn't last. He died."

Her mother's voice softened. "I'm so sorry to hear that," she said.

But her body wasn't sorry; her arms weren't sorry. She sat there on the edge of the love seat.

Bean decided to give some information. She presented the complicated details of her own life in a neutral tone, without passion or pain. She didn't want her mother to know what still hurt, what she had surmounted, where she was lost. It felt good to toss around heavy, scary words like *death* and *cremation* and *McKinley* and watch her mother react.

Her mother had never met Mick, but Bean needed her to know how it was with them. Bean sat in the familiar house and told her mother that he was the best thing that ever happened to her. Then she leaned back a bit into the chair as if she had just laid a winning hand on the table.

"It's especially sad to lose someone so early in a marriage," her mother said.

It sounded like an affront. Like their marriage didn't count.

"What's that supposed to mean?" Bean said.

Her mother pinched her temples with one hand. "Obviously, I can't say anything right," she said.

They looked at each other a moment. Then Bean went on with her story. She was back for good now, teaching school. She looked around the room. There were no family photos where there used to be—on the mantel, on the table with the lamp.

Silence.

"I have a dog now," she added.

Her mother listened and said, "Oh," "I see," and "Good for you." But she seemed distracted. Bean felt like a Jehovah's Witness keeping her from dinner on the stove. She kept talking until her mother sighed. "There's a lot of catching up to do after so much time," her mother said. Then she looked at her watch.

Bean wanted her attention.

"I saw Chip yesterday."

That did it. Anything about Chip. Chip this, Chip that. He was well into his thirties and he could still suck up all the oxygen in the house. Bean had never had a chance.

Concern on her mother's face. "Where?" she asked.

"On the street, near Union Square," Bean said. "He's a bum, you know."

Her mother's eyes flashed. "He is *not* a bum. How can you say such a thing? He's your brother!"

"He hit me up for cash."

Her mother's composure had slipped; it was satisfying. She wasn't exactly shouting now, but she was pretty close.

"Why are you here telling me this?" she demanded. "What do you want? After all these years, just walking up to the door. What are you doing here?"

"I don't know," Bean said.

"You want me to wish you a happy birthday? Fine. Happy birthday. You want to tell me your sad story? All right. I'm sorry about your husband. Truly sorry. But you know what, Bean? You're not the first one to have your marriage fall apart—"

"I told you, it didn't fall apart," Bean said, raising her voice. "He *died*."

"Whatever," her mother said. She was standing now and had stopped looking at Bean. If there had been anyone else in the room, she would have appealed to *them.* "My point is, you just walked out of my life six years ago. Six years? Who are we kidding? You checked out on me a long time before that. A long time. And now you find out that it's hard out there. And bad things happen. And people leave, and people die. And so you come back home and you ring the doorbell, and you expect me to make it better."

"I don't expect anything from you," Bean said.

"Well, Bean, that's actually good. Because you know what? I don't expect anything from you, either."

Bean felt like she was standing on an ice floe, one of those snowy rafts that breaks away from the glacier, tugged by the swift current. Her mother didn't expect anything from her. There was no future between them. And they were dissolving their past, here in this house, with the familiar furniture as mute witness, the air vents, the piano. Bean noticed the armchair that used to be in her room; it sat in a corner of the dining room. Her father had held her in that chair.

"You gave up on me because I wouldn't wear your stupid dresses," she said.

"I didn't give up on you, Bean. You so plainly chose your father. You completely iced me out."

"And then you ran him off."

Bean's mother swept up a stack of magazines from the coffee table and cracked their edges even on the tabletop. She lay them back in a neat stack.

"Is that what you think? Is that what you think?" Her voice grew husky. "You know nothing about love. You come here and say, 'Oh, by the way, I've been married for three years and now my husband's dead.' But you know nothing."

"I know what I know," Bean said.

"Do you? Do you know what it feels like to wake up and put on your face and be pretty sure you can make it through another day?

And then you open the front door and there's a world that rips your heart out because your husband is in it with somebody else, and starting over, new children and all. And suddenly, you and everything you thought you'd built—together—it's all just litter on the sidewalk. You don't know much."

She looked over at Bean. "Let me tell you something. Your father was a lovely man. And you'll never hear me say otherwise. But he was weak, Bean. When things got hard, he wasn't there. And that's what matters in life, Bean. Being there. At least, I used to think it did. He left it all to me. Who do you think drove Chip to the rehab clinic? It wasn't your dad. If only he'd been more of a father to that boy."

"Here we are, talking about Chip again." Bean sank into the sofa and pulled her knees to her chest.

Her mother lost a beat. "Well, that's the way it is when you're talking about a family," she said. "It's all balled up together."

"It's time to look at me," Bean said softly. "See *me*, Mom."

Her mother took a fresh look.

"What *are* you? I don't understand you, Bean. You jumped into a cesspool, for heaven's sake. Sometimes it's hard to believe you're mine."

Bean was curled up, but her defiance shot through. "I'm sorry I am who I am," she said.

The phone rang. Her mother twitched and looked to the hallway. But she didn't leave. That was something. After four rings it stopped. Her mother heaved a deep breath and snatched a tissue from the end table. She looked like she wanted to cry but was too dried out.

Bean just hugged her knees and rocked.

The phone started ringing again.

Her mother turned toward it, then stopped. She bent over Bean and put her cheek on Bean's head. Her face looked like all the interior supports had been removed. Wrinkles and makeup remained.

The phone kept ringing.

Her mother wiped her nose.

"So why did you jump?" she said.

"What?"

"Into the cesspool."

For a second, Bean wanted to tell her mother about shadows and fear and becoming somebody. But it was too late for all that.

"I told you," she said. "They dared me."

Her mother frowned and went to answer the phone.

A fog rolled up off the ocean as Bean rode back to the city. Everything felt broken. Seeing her mother had only made her feel lonelier. When the bus passed the Marina, she suddenly yanked the cable for a stop. She strode past the kite fliers on the green and crossed over to the Palace of Fine Arts. She circled around the cupola and came to the pond, where she and Bob had fed the ducks. Schoolkids were staring into the water.

She'd ruined it with Bob, of course. Every relationship that she'd ever had went awry. Got ugly or weird or pathetic. She angered and disappointed the people who tried to love her.

Something about the children caught her attention. They watched the ducks and swans dive underwater.

> One day Debbie got tired
> Of singing, and thinking up rhymes.
> She wanted to sleep,
> So she dove down deep,
> And she's been gone an awful long time.

She walked on. Twenty-seven years old. Mick had liked to surprise her on her birthdays. One night she came home to find a king crab on the stove, its thorny arms reaching from the pot like some body-snatching ghoul. Another year it was the bonfire he'd arranged with Lois and his buddies; they ate halibut cheeks, drank beer past midnight. Lois, strutting like a sandhill crane, trying to get everyone to dance.

Now birthdays were just a reminder that she was getting older, more peculiar, farther from love.

When you had someone else, you could cut the remorse, soften the hard look back. She'd done it for Mick. He had his bad times. The night he ruined Mudhole's nets. He stood there, hands and face covered with mosquito bites, pacing up and down, saying what the hell was he was doing, trying to be a fisherman. She let him talk, then steered him into a cool shower.

She lay him on their bed and fetched cotton balls and ammonia. She dabbed the welts and said soft things. He let her tend to him. He was a fourth-grader in a Cub Scout uniform, paying for his mother's mistake. A high-strung kid without a dad. There would be a little sting at first, Bean told him.

Afterward, he'd fallen asleep, bent like a jackknife. Bean had slipped off her clothes and spooned behind him. She smelled the sea and the ammonia, and she slept well.

The fog poured over the dry hills of Marin like a thick brew. She was drawn to it. It would engulf her. It was a vast comforter of eider down. A foghorn let out its mournful blast.

She moved steadily into the mist. It brushed her cheeks, but she didn't feel cold. Tourists passed her in huggy pairs or in big bus groups. Clusters of Japanese snapped one another's pictures. Bean walked into their scrapbooks without breaking stride. A European couple with sweaters around their necks strolled along, holding hands. She pressed on, forcing them to break apart so she might pass.

At the entrance to the bridge, she walked past the round building with its Japanese sign, GIFUTO SHOPPU. There was a pay phone outside the shop. She put in two quarters and called home. The phone rang until the machine picked up. She heard her own cheerful voice and hung up. What could Hanna be doing?

She trudged up the red stairs of waffled steel, past warning signs: GAPS IN BRIDGE, BIKERS BEWARE.

The bridge looked cold and hard, nothing like the inviting backdrop of a million photos. Its towers were cut off by the engulfing fog, its fist-sized rivets and braided steel cables recalled a battleship. Hundreds of cars blasted by on their aggressive flights home.

Bean started down the pedestrian walkway. The wind had picked up in her ears, and her hair hovered like sea coral. She couldn't see more than thirty feet. A jogger with a back-turned cap materialized in the fog before her, whisked past, and vanished again. She moved to the red-painted rail and peered over. Breaks in the creeping clouds revealed the fierce tug of the bay currents.

A flag at Fort Point snapped in the wind, ten stories below. This would suffice. She leaned against the rail. She was near a joint in the roadway and could feel the traffic shake the bridge. She felt a little dizzy. Her body didn't want to lean against the railing, but she forced herself. Her feet clenched and tickled as if afraid of what the rest of her might do.

Where did those currents lead? Bean turned and looked west, where the great bay disappeared into the ocean. She saw the craggy cliffs of the Marin headlands: grass-tufted, so close, but untouchable. Somewhere out there was a lighthouse, she knew.

Farther out there were islands. You could see them on a clear day. Desolate rocks, surrounded by frigid water churned up from the seafloor by Alaskan currents. There were riptides between the rocks. Great white sharks bred beneath the surface.

But birds lived there, too. Millions of them. Pelicans and cormorants and terns. Gulls like street fighters. Storm petrels no bigger than your finger took cold comfort amid the pebbles. Bean and her third-grade classmates had been there. They'd crouched in a bunker used by biologists to spy on the squawking, nesting, crapping colony.

Mrs. Harper had brought them there. It had been *her* show-and-tell. Mrs. Harper, in her knit sweater and black pedal pushers, her glasses dangling.

In the fog's blank canvas, Bean glimpsed her beloved teacher. She seemed to be reaching out. As if Bean were one of the forgotten creatures, to be rescued from the side of the road.

A car horn blared and receded, covering the causeway in a scream. She walked farther down the bridge.

The cars had their headlamps on now, and the towers cast round pools of light on the walkway. Near the first tower, there was fencing above the railing. It was cyclone mesh, maybe ten feet high, aggressively ugly. Suicide fencing. The city had installed it years back, hoping it might persuade the desperate to go home and die privately with a gun or some pills.

They had erred, of course, by making the fence stiff on top. If it were flimsy, it would have been much harder to scale. Who would let this fence stop them? Maybe if you were really sick, or crippled. But Bean could scale it, easier than an oak tree. In fact, the fence might make the whole thing easier. Once she was up there, nobody could reach her.

She wondered if Mick was watching her now. She'd had such a hard time conjuring his face lately, but now she was pretty sure she felt him looking over her shoulder as she assessed the obstacles. She didn't turn around. If she looked back, the spell would be broken. She could hop a fence. She'd done it all her life.

Fewer people walked by. The fog blew and shed glimmers of San Francisco's lights. The distant city seemed glamorous, but part of another world. The wind blew stronger and she realized she was freezing.

That felt real. The beauty, the hurt. She stopped to consider it all and clutched the fence like one of those sad monkeys at the zoo.

Would Mick catch her as she fell? That would be best, of course. She would plunge and he would swoop beneath her and it would almost be like flying. Would she feel the water? How cold would it be? The pressure could crush your ears; she remembered hearing that. She wouldn't have to swim, would she? All this fretting—the years made us meek. She hadn't paused long at the cesspool. "Jump," they had shouted. And she did. Now she looked around. No one.

It would make so little difference. Hanna would look after Fred; he wouldn't miss a walk. Peter had friends to help him mourn Jimmy. The school would have to find a substitute for her, but classes let out in a couple of months. Bean could slip away, and it would be like she had never been there. Twenty-seven years erased. There might be a small item in the *San Francisco Chronicle:* WOMAN FALLS TO DEATH. A shame for that to be the written record of her life. But the paper wouldn't say much, maybe put a few paragraphs next to the comics. She had seen those stories. Her mother would read it. One last mortification for Mom.

Bean wondered what it would be like to have someone call her Mom. If only she and Mick had managed to pull it off. There had been that one time when her period was late, and she thought: maybe. But it was a false alarm. The sperm knew to stay away.

If she had a daughter, she could start over. She could give her what a kid should have. Not an Easy Bake oven or a TICKLE ME shirt. The real stuff. She could send her off in the morning with an embrace: "Have a ripsnorter." At the end of the day, she could welcome her home and tend to the bites. At night there would be time for Debbie stories. Her little girl would fall asleep knowing she was the most important creature in the world.

Bean's raw fingers dug into the cyclone fence. The foghorn blew from Alcatraz. Two desperate notes from a bassoon.

She shot a look to the top of the fence and waited for a sign from her feet, a spasm that would send her clambering over. She was never going to hold that curly haired girl. And no one would ever read her duck stories. She would tend her wounds until she was eighty years old, fat as a cow, regretting and apologizing with her last breath. Then some bumbling nurse named Paulette would be left to decide whether she was alive or dead.

It would be so easy to just stop. No more slights and taunts, no more rotten birthdays and sleepless nights. No more missing people. Just nothing.

She tugged on the fence. It gave, just a little. With her head bowed and her feet planted, she tugged again. The fence relented some more, and she heard a faint clang.

There had to be a time when you took hold of your life, didn't there? A time when you occupied your body, spun out your own plans. A time when you said, This is what I want, and no one can stop me. All anyone can do is slow me down.

Hang on, Snoopy.

She felt a surge run up from her ankles. A familiar but somehow foreign feeling. What was it? Not fear or shame, not hope or joy. But kin to all of them. It was a feeling with a howl in it. She pumped her arms in rhythm and the fence clanged and convulsed in both directions.

There was a way out; there had to be. Look at Hanna. She'd lost it all. A husband, a son, a home. She lost everything. But the difference was that Hanna seemed to *have* everything, too. It was with her all the time, as if she had a magic pocket in that damn raincoat.

She felt eyes on her. A couple of teenagers, pierced and spiky, had stopped their mountain bikes in the path and were watching her. One of the kids had the same close-cropped hair as Jimmy.

A couple weeks before he died, Jimmy had pulled out the last of his hair with his own hands, like cotton candy. Bean didn't know what to say, so she asked if she could rub his head. As she ran her fingers over his smooth, warm scalp, she knew she had to ask him. "Jimmy," she whispered, "don't you ever feel like just *stopping*?"

His eyes locked on hers. Lucidity came and went, and you could never be certain of him.

"It's a *process*," he said. He stretched out the word and made it sound holy.

Her arms ached and her hands felt stuck to the fence. The kids were still staring; one of them had his mouth open, like he was looking at a crazy woman.

She let go of the fence. She took a couple of steps in their direction.

"What the fuck are you looking at?" she shouted. Her voice was deeper than she'd ever heard it. It had rocks in it. She flapped her arms wildly at the boys. "Get off my bridge!" she shouted.

The one with Jimmy's hair looked alarmed. He hopped onto his pedals, turned, and rode off. The other followed.

She headed for home. My bridge. Jimmy would have liked that. He would have said, "Way to go, Jelly." That's what Jimmy would have said.

The largest waterfowl in the world, the trumpeter swan was hunted to the brink of extinction for its handsome white feathers, which were used in ladies' hats.

—The Pemberton Guide

*T*he house was dark when Bean got home, and Fred was ready to burst. She let him fertilize the black-eyed Susan, then saw the flash on her answering machine.

It was a message from Hanna. Where was Bean? "They only gave me one chance to call, dear," Hanna said. "I guess this is it."

She sounded agitated. "There's been some confusion," Hanna continued. "I need you to come get me out of jail."

Bean reached the district station on Valencia at 10 P.M. She scurried between a couple of squad cars parked out front, up the steps, and through a glass door. A bored-looking black man with stripes on his arms picked up the extension and called the arresting officer.

A redheaded patrolman, forty-five-ish, in a too-tight uniform, came through the saloon doors to the bench where Bean waited. He smiled pleasantly, bent over until Bean thought a button might pop, and gently whispered in her ear.

"Sweetheart, why don't you come with me," he said. "I'll take you to your mother."

Bean looked at him like he was crazy. "What?" she said.

He said it again, in the nicest of tones, but slower, as if she spoke a foreign language.

Was this the way cops talked? Bean shrugged and got up.

"Was it hard to get here?" the cop asked as he ushered her through the doors, his hand pushing just so slightly on the small of her back.

Bean shook her head. "I took the bus."

"All that way?" he said. "All by yourself? My."

Bean squinted at the cop. He wasn't hitting on her, and she didn't think he was being sarcastic. So what the hell was up?

"Yes," she said. "And I've been dressing myself for quite some time."

Now it was the cop's turn to double-take her. After a moment, he said, "Your mother is quite a woman."

"She certainly is."

They had reached the jail. Through the green-painted array of bars, Bean could see Hanna sitting on a bench. Two hookers, one with black tights, the other with platform shoes, stood in the adjacent cell. Hanna popped up when she saw Bean. With the cop's back to her, Hanna silently, frantically waved her arm in a big wheel around her ear.

The cop offered Bean a seat, picking up a cup of coffee already sitting there. "Now, we're not normally in the business of locking up older ladies," he said. "Especially not ones who are so . . . special. And I'm really sorry to be bothering you. It's probably not so easy to get away from home. It's just that the store manager, well, he insisted on pressing charges."

Bean looked across the way at Hanna. Their eyes met, and once again she did the crazy sign with her hand. One of the hookers looked at Bean and did it, too.

"What is it she's charged with, Officer?" Bean asked.

"Shoplifting," he said. "A computer."

"A computer?"

"IBM laptop. A ThinkPad, if you know your hardware."

Bean stared at him.

"No, of course you don't," he mumbled.

Bean got the story from the cop. Hanna had gone into a used-computer store downtown and chatted up the clerk. He had explained about memory and disks and compatibility with various printers. A kid with acne but plenty of savvy, the clerk recommended a few of the machines for sale in the front window. But when he told her the prices, Hanna gave a bug-eyed look and left.

An hour later, when the clerk was helping a couple of college kids with a repair, they heard a crash on the floor near the door. He rounded the counter and saw Hanna standing over a laptop, which was half swaddled in a black cloth, some kind of coat. The computer's lid had flipped open and the liquid crystal display was smashed. Hanna stood there, rubbing her hands. She pointed to the computer on the floor and told the clerk she had brought it in for a repair. But the store's price tag was still on it, and there was a big dust hole in the display case where she'd swiped it.

The clerk grabbed her arm, then locked the door. At that point Hanna claimed to be very disoriented and asked where she was, and why was she surrounded by all those radios? But the kid didn't buy it and called the cops. When the policeman arrived, Hanna said she had to hurry home because her daughter, who happened to be retarded, would worry and would not have anything to eat for dinner.

The black-eyed Susan trick. So that was how they were going to play it.

Since nothing had actually been stolen, and the cop could see that Bean was "a very nice girl," he said he was inclined to release her mother on her own recognizance.

It was Bean's turn to be dense. "On her own what?" she said.

A few signatures later, Bean and Hanna were on the bus headed home. Hanna's cheeks were flushed. Bean was too glum to give a lecture. She just waited for Hanna to apologize.

"Well, never in a million years did I think *that* would happen," Hanna said as the bus rumbled up the market street.

Here it comes, Bean thought.

"It's the darndest thing. I mean it's really unbelievable," Hanna said. Indignation rose in her voice. "Those computers are so ridiculously expensive. How do they expect us to get one?"

It was getting to be too much. "Some people save their money," Bean said.

But Hanna was studying her hands now. She flexed her crooked fingers, and her face showed distaste. She wore a powder blue running suit and white sneakers. Had she been planning to outrun the cops?

"I need to pick up some Ben-Gay," Hanna said.

"Well, when you pick it up, don't forget to pay for it," Bean said.

A few blocks from home, it occurred to Bean to ask Hanna why she wanted a computer in the first place. Hanna thought for a minute, then shrugged.

"For your birthday," she said. "So you could keep track of all those stories you've been dreaming up. You know, about Shirley and the duck."

Lately, Bean had been practicing some of her stories on Hanna. She hadn't thought Hanna was paying attention.

Bean was relieved to see Martin arrive at school on Monday. The other children jostled their way through the door, like salmon spilling into a cannery bin, cowlicks and scrapes and odd, whimsical postures, tugging on their windbreakers, an arm draped over a new best friend, strutting in new basketball shoes.

Then came Martin—all purpose and seriousness—miscast as a schoolboy, like Burgess Meredith playing a child. He knew how to be invisible when it came to the other kids; he didn't brag or fight or raise his hand. He had no enviable clothes, comic books, or collecting cards. He just went to his chair, his face a little dirty, his brush-cut hair like a furry swim cap. No one spoke to him or touched him. He was a foreigner among compatriots.

The other children had found a common language. It shifted according to circumstance; even the bullies could be accommodating. They detected the linguistic abilities of the other children and sized them up in a heartbeat. If one thought the other's English was too weak, they spoke in Spanish, and vice versa. Sometimes conversations sloshed between languages like a tide. .

But the kids had given up on Martin. No matter what they said to him, he gave monosyllabic replies, if any at all. Bean wondered if anyone had ever gone completely mute from household trauma. A mute kid. She thought about what that meant. No sing-alongs with stuffed animals from television. No Christmas carols, "Happy Birthdays," or alphabet songs. No wordplay, chats with imaginary friends, nonsense poems. It meant he couldn't thrill to his own vocal cords, create an echo on a sunny mountainside or in a dank tunnel, bounce his own being off the world and hear back a tinny murmur, repeating, diminishing: "I am. I am. I am."

During recess, Bean phoned Child Protective Services again. She'd arranged to speak with the investigator who had followed up on her call. The woman said she had interviewed the boy's mother in the home and saw no evidence of abuse of either Martin or his aunt. That's all she could say. She would be completing a form that said "does not meet the state requirements for intervention." Bean would receive a copy. Bean peppered the woman with questions. Had the boyfriend been there? Did Martin talk to her? Did she examine him? The woman sighed, and her voice turned sharp.

"Maybe you and me ought to switch jobs," she snapped. "In fact, come on over. I've got a backlog of cases *with* evidence."

Bean hung up and returned to class. She stood before them all, but her eye was on the corner of the room where Martin sat, attentively, waiting for a Debbie story like the rest of them. Bean looked hard at him.

Talk to me, she thought. *Talk to me.* He dropped his face and looked at the floor.

That day Bean invented something called individual conferences. They would last only a few minutes, a chance for each student to tell her what he or she had learned about volcanoes. Bean started off with Qin, a smart Chinese girl who always seemed to teach Bean something new. She sat through the girl's recitation in a corner of the room, keeping an ear on the decibels of the unsupervised classroom; she knew she had only a few minutes before the din became intolerable.

"Thank you, Qin," Bean said, cutting her off in the middle of continental drift.

She called Martin over to her chair. He sat down, or sat up, really, since he had to hoist himself onto the chair and his feet swung freely. He looked uneasy.

"Martin, instead of talking about volcanoes, why don't we talk about Debbie the Duck?" Bean said.

Martin brightened; it sounded like a good deal.

Bean hastily sketched out a plot in which Debbie kept bumping into a scary monster in the Impenetrable Forest. She would be walking by, minding her own business, when he would pull her in and hurt her. He was tall and smelly and strong.

Debbie was very quiet when he hurt her. But she sang a song inside. It went:

Oh you mean monster,
You can break my knee, but I'll still be
Debbie the Duck.
You can slap my bill, but I am still
Debbie the Duck.

Sometimes the monster raged. Sometimes the monster slept. But Debbie was always ready with her song. She sang it to herself, and it made her think of flying free.

You can shake my brain, but I'll remain
Debbie the Duck.

Bean asked Martin to make a rhyme.

"Burn," he said in a croaky voice. "Burn."

Oh God. "Mmm," Bean said. "Let's see."

You can burn my . . .

"Back," Martin whispered. "Back."

But I'll just quack . . . Bean stopped short. Martin wiped his nose with his wrist. Bean looked at the class bordering on mayhem. She was pretty sure Martin would not let her touch him. She swiveled his chair around, so he was facing away from her, and she yanked up the back of his three-day T-shirt. His smooth coffee-colored back had four blackened discs of puckered skin, each smaller than a dime. She dropped the shirt and swung him back around before he knew what happened.

"Thank you, Martin."

Bean stood up. She felt her blood racing through.

———

At lunch Bean left her sandwich on the table of the teachers' lounge and spent ten minutes on the phone. The afternoon lessons took forever. One boy deserved detention for tripping a girl, but Bean let it go. When the bell rang, she said she wanted to speak to all the kids who'd had a conference with her that morning.

"Let's see," she said. "That would be Qin and Martin."

Qin was standing at Bean's hip before she knew it. Martin hung back.

Bean looked down at Qin, trying to think. Her own heart was pounding in her ears.

"Qin, I just want to say, that was an excellent conference," Bean said. "Especially the part about tectonics. Thank you." Bean stuck out her hand. The little girl in the plaid skirt was pleased but uncertain as to protocol. She stuck her own hand up. Bean pumped it, then spun her around and sent her off.

"Martin," Bean said, waving him closer with a hand.

Martin shuffled over. Bean took a deep breath. Was she really going to do this?

"Martin, how do you usually get home?"

Silence.

"Is it the bus? No. Walking? Yes? Walking?"

Martin nodded.

"Today, Martin, we're going to do something a little different." Bean was whispering in his ear.

After school Bean walked with Martin down the long hallway. She tried to stay two steps behind him but ended up prodding him along. When they pushed open the door to the outside, it was a golden afternoon and the sun temporarily blinded them.

Martin looked back at Bean, who had stopped at the door, and she pointed with a jerk of her head. An old lady with white hair that stood straight up was leaning against the jungle gym. Hanna waved. Martin walked toward her unsteadily.

Bean watched the handoff and turned to reenter the door when she ran into the principal, coming out. Emilio Gutierrez had run César Chávez for years. He was a Latino rights advocate and known as strict by kids and teachers alike.

"Hello, Ms. Jessup," he said.

Bean swallowed. "Mr. Gutierrez."

"My, it's nice out," he said. Bean nodded.

They both looked at the only thing to see in that part of the schoolyard. Hanna taking Martin by the hand and guiding him away.

"Who's that with the boy?" Gutierrez asked casually.

Bean's throat grew tight. She was never good at this. She could talk around things all day, but don't ask her to lie outright. It messed up her timing. She was either earnestly fast or deceitfully slow.

"Caseworker," she replied.

Gutierrez grunted. They watched the unlikely pair—born worlds and ages apart—toddle off, hand in hand. The principal excused himself and ducked back into the building.

Bean tried to grade papers for ten minutes, then hurried to catch the bus home. Riding along, she felt alternately elated and horrified at herself.

Martin was in the kitchen with Hanna when Bean came up the stairs. Hanna had emptied half the cupboards and put the contents on the counter and on the kitchen table. Two boxes of cereal, Fig Newtons, crackers, a salami, and two cans of soup.

Hanna smiled indulgently, as if she were baby-sitting a neighbor's kid or a grandchild. Martin was propped up on the counter amid the riches. He had an oatmeal cookie in his hand.

Mixed in with all the food, Bean noticed, were two cellophane packages of white underwear on the table. Shorts and T-shirts for boys, a package each.

"We picked up a few things," Hanna said. She seemed happy, calm. The way she looked after a good find at a garage sale. Bean wondered if she'd paid for the underwear. Then she realized it didn't matter anymore.

Bean put her hands on her hips, looked at Martin, and said, "Well." Her heart was racing. What was she doing? All those school warnings— never hit a kid, never be alone with a kid, never shout at a kid—and she'd gone and stolen one.

Martin nibbled his cookie.

"Do you like our house, Martin?" Bean asked.

The slightest of nods.

Fred was sniffing vigorously at Martin's dangling feet. Bean assumed it was in anticipation of Martin's dropping a few crumbs. But then she realized the dog was sniffing Martin himself. She knew what the neglected boy bouquet smelled like and wondered what stories Fred could extract. At first Martin shied away; then he leaned over and touched Fred's wet nose.

Bean lifted Martin down and took him over to the couch. He stared at the dark television, as if waiting for it to spring to life. Hanna took a seat opposite, in the rattan throne. Bean slipped onto the couch beside Martin. She had grown fond of the couch, the one thing she had bought for the house. It was where she did her best thinking. She leaned her head back and looked at the ceiling, Martin beside her, sunk into the deep pillows, his legs parallel to the floor.

Hanna broke the long silence. "So what's next?"

Bean realized she had no idea.

She put a video on the TV for Martin. *Breakfast at Tiffany's.* Hardly kids' fare, but it was the only movie she owned. Martin sat engrossed by the cocktail party scene, when everyone was crammed into Holly's apartment, smoking and sipping highballs and making out in the shower. Bean stepped out onto the stoop for a cigarette. She sat and looked at the traffic around Precita Park and saw children drift by on Rollerblades. She switched her grip on the cigarette, pinching it between her thumb and forefinger. Might as well smoke like an outlaw. She wished she had a western to show Martin.

The police would call it a crime, of course. She was making decisions that would track her for the rest of her life. Yet there it was. She thought about Mick getting lost on McKinley. Had he lain awake somewhere in the snow, broken back and all, wondering what came next? Had he rued his choices? Did he think about her, did he fear the night? Bean pulled her sweater around her as the evening cooled.

When she came back in, the phone rang.

No one moved for a moment, then Hanna picked up the remote and silenced the TV. Bean and Hanna froze to give their ears full advantage as the answering machine picked up.

It was Gutierrez, the principal. The mother of one of Bean's students, Martin Lagos, had reported her son missing. He never made it home from school. Gutierrez had gone back to César Chávez at 7 P.M. to meet her. He recalled seeing a boy meet his caseworker. He was sure that was it. But Mrs. Lagos said there was no caseworker. "Do you know what in blazes is going on? Please call me immediately." His voice filled up their living room. "I've got no choice but to call the police."

Bean looked over at Martin on the couch. He'd heard his name and he seemed to know there was a problem. Hanna was in the kitchen. She lit a cigarette.

"Do they know where you live?" Hanna asked.

"The school? Of course they do," Bean said.

"So what now?"

"I don't know," Bean said. "I've got to think." A pause. "I guess we've got to get out of here."

But go where?

There weren't many options. She couldn't impose on Peter. No one from school. Her mother's? Out of the question.

"I know where," she said at last.

They all piled into the milk truck, Fred included. Just as Bean slid her door shut, a squad car appeared in the rearview mirror. A cop with reddish hair—could it be the same one who had busted Hanna?—stepped out and walked, stiff-legged, toward Bean's stoop. He was ringing the bell when Bean finally wrenched the stick into gear and pulled away from the curb.

Bob's eyebrows almost flew off his face when he opened the door and saw Bean, Hanna, Fred, and little jug-eared Martin standing around his welcome mat.

He'd barely seen Bean in weeks; somehow she was always too busy. But he stepped aside and they trooped in. He filled up a bowl of water for Fred, found a cookie for the kid. Bean crossed over to the window as soon as they were in and peeked through the blinds. Hanna lit up a cigarette right away; as she moved about, Bob kept slipping an ashtray beside her. The ashtray was uneven and poorly glazed; it looked like Jimmy's work.

"Am I glad you're home," Bean said. She slung her arms around his neck and kissed him full on the lips. It was an extravagant gesture for Bean—over the top, really—and Bob looked irritated. It probably didn't help that Martin was staring at him with obvious fear.

"Would somebody mind telling me what's going on?" Bob said. The television set in the living room blared *Jeopardy!* A carton of mu shu pork sat next to an untouched stack of pancakes and plum sauce, ready to eat on the coffee table. Fred trotted over for a sniff.

"We're fugitives," Hanna said. She seemed to like the sound of it.

Bob looked at Bean.

"We are *not* fugitives," Bean said, shooting Hanna a look. "We're just not home."

Bob saw Fred in the other room, closing in on his pork.

"Fred, no!" he commanded. The dog backed off. "Would somebody kindly tell me what the fuck is going on?" He was staring at Bean.

"Bob," Bean said in reproach. She tossed her head in the direction of Martin.

Ten minutes later Bob had as much of the story as he wanted. He looked at his watch. He argued in a hushed voice as Martin watched his show and ate one of his pancakes.

"All right, there's time to turn this thing around," he told Bean. "You take the kid back. You say you were helping him with his homework. You took him to the goddamn symphony. You went to look at the tide pools. Anything."

"I can't do that."

"You give him back tonight, you're a flake. You don't, you're a kidnapper." His voice rose. "For chrissakes, Bean."

Bob pulled some beer out of the refrigerator and gave one to Bean. She took it but didn't open it. Hanna didn't drink, but she asked for one, too. They sat around the kitchen table. Bean looked away; she was smoldering inside. Finally, Bob said, "So, what am I missing here?"

Hanna jumped in. "Let's gas up the truck. We could be in Vancouver in a few days. I know people there. It's another country. There'd be all this paperwork before they got a whiff of our trail."

Bean looked at Hanna like she'd suggested shooting her way out of Dodge City.

"Hanna, in case you've forgotten, you've got a record," she said. "This isn't something you can just slip into your raincoat."

Hanna shut up.

"I just need some time to think," Bean said. She put her palms to her face and rubbed it like a magic lamp.

Bob's patience was running thin. He whispered to her, "There's really nothing to think about, Bean. The answer is simple."

"Goddammit Bob," she said, standing up. "There's everything to think about."

Bean crossed over to him and put her nose in his face. He looked startled and worried, and that just made her angrier. She burst.

"Can you just get out of your boring little world for a moment and see what's happening here?" she said. "Can you forget your one way to do things, your goddamn shoes in the oven, Old Spice rut, and just see what this is? This is life, Bob. If we can't help this kid, what's the point of any of it? Why bother with the rest, you and your little velvet box?"

Bob was wincing slightly, taking it like a private under a frothing sergeant. Hanna had backed into a corner of Bob's kitchen. The only one who didn't seem to mind all the shouting was Martin, who was either accustomed to it or mesmerized by the TV.

Bean knew she was being cruel, but she felt like she was fighting for her life.

"Nobody was there for me, Bob. Nobody let me know I mattered. When they saw me at all, it was always, 'What's wrong with Bean? What are we going to do with Bean?' "

Bob's thick arms were wrapped around his chest in a hug. He waited till she was through. When he finally spoke, it was as if he were talking to a child.

"We're all sorry for whatever happened to you, Bean. But this isn't about you. It's about him." He tipped his head toward Martin. "You can't steal a kid."

"You're all sorry? Oh, thank you. Thank you for your pity. Thank you especially, Bob, for sleeping with me. Brav-o. I could tell it wasn't easy."

Bob and Bean were facing each other across the kitchen floor. They both shot a look at Hanna, who looked like she wanted to crawl into a cupboard and shut the door. Bob was set in place like a hydrant, and he blocked the way out of the kitchen.

He spoke slowly. "I *do* pity you, Bean, but not for the reasons you think."

"Oh, here it comes," Bean said.

"I feel sorry for you because you don't know how to commit. You don't know how to make it count. You're always finding ways to blow me off and disappear, and then we start over. How long has it been, Bean? A month? Five weeks? I don't see hide nor hair of you, then you suddenly appear on my doorstep with a stolen kid and tell me you're running from the police."

Bob took a step toward Bean.

"Jesus, look at yourself, Bean."

Bean had run out of things to say.

"Look, I need help," she said. "What are we talking about here? You and me? Or the kid?"

"All of it, Bean," Bob said. "All of it. Look at how you treated Hanna. Kept her around when you needed her. Kicked her out when you didn't."

Bean looked at Hanna. Hanna was studying the Formica countertop, running a crooked finger from one speck to the next. When Bean saw Hanna wasn't going to speak up, she started to cry.

"I fixed that with Hanna," she said. The tears were coming out, and they made her mad. "Hanna, I fixed that, right? Jesus Christ, Bob."

Bob opened his bear arms and Bean felt herself pulled by gravity into their embrace.

"Stealing this kid is not going to fix your life, Bean," he said.

Bean cried quietly, her face pressed into his chest. When she spoke, it was in a little girl's voice. "Can we just not talk anymore?" she said. "Just not for a little while, please."

Bean sat on the couch next to Martin to watch the news. It was an odd feeling—tuning in the familiar newscast, with its spinning logos and puffy-haired hosts—to see if you had made the show. Was this what criminals did—committed horrible acts, then settled in front of the tube to see what society had to say for itself?

When the news ended with no word of Martin, Bean returned to the kitchen, where Hanna and Bob sat at the table like old friends. A pile of blueprints lay scattered on the table between them. Bean ripped off a paper towel, ran some water over it, and wiped her face.

"How's the boat coming?" she asked.

"Almost done," Bob said. "Just the detailing. And the mast."

"Show me."

Hanna wanted to see it, too. Bean wrapped one of Bob's sweaters around Martin, who had dozed off in front of the TV, and carried him down the back staircase. Bob's workshop was a garage he rented halfway down the alley. The boat took up virtually every inch of the one-car garage. The mast was unattached and ran the length of the wall. Bob was still shaving it round. It was a beautiful little boat.

The garage smelled of turpentine. Bob had been painting that afternoon.

Bean was impressed. She squeezed past the bow and walked around the boat to admire it. "So this'll really float? I mean, it's safe and all?"

"It'll hold up in the bay," Bob said. "We're not talking open ocean."

Bob and Hanna went back upstairs. But Bean said she wanted to stay. She heaved Martin up onto her hip, then approached the cradle holding the boat. She stepped among the planks and hoisted him in. He awakened, and she nestled in behind him, sitting on the floorboards. She smelled his little-boy smell, the staleness of his clothes, the salt of his neck. She put her cheek against his bristled head and wrapped her arms around him.

A siren approached. Bean felt her insides tighten. She cupped Martin between her knees and listened as the horrible wailing drew nearer. The repeating shriek came right up to the garage door and matched Bean's beating heart. She pulled Martin closer. He didn't make a sound. The siren peaked, then eased into a decrescendo. Red lights flared across the back wall of the garage and receded.

The street outside grew quiet, and moonlight spilled in through a glass portal that ran across its upper length. Bean rocked Martin slowly and whispered to him as he dozed.

They could pretend they were ducks in Phoenix Lake, she told him. All the frogs swam by and sang to them. You had to listen hard to hear them, but they were there. And the fish leapt out of the water to look at them. And the trees stirred softly in the breeze. The water was calm. Their hearts were happy. They were home and they were safe.

Martin rested against her, and she thought of his scarred little back pressing into her stomach and breasts. He was breathing deeply now, and she wondered if his eyes were closed. She wanted to rock him to sleep. She wanted him to float away on this boat in the beautiful lake.

"I always figured you'd be a girl," she said.

She leaned back. She smelled the cut wood and the paint, and she thought about Bob working so long on his boat, building and sawing and planing and measuring. All so he could have something he truly wanted.

She saw a tiny patch of sky through the garage window. She thought she saw a star. It might have been a distant streetlight, she wasn't sure. Maybe it was Mick. Could he see her in this boat, with this child? Would he think Martin was theirs? Would he understand?

Or maybe it was Jimmy, a brand-new light in the firmament. He would still be learning his way around. Would he find his own path, or would someone have to show him, give him an imprint, like a trumpeter swan? Could you get lost in heaven?

"You rescued me," Jimmy had said. "That's got to count for something."

Bean started to nod. She fell asleep knowing that she was looking after someone and believing that somewhere, someone might still be looking after her.

Some curlews will die in storms, others will fall prey to predators, still others will succumb to disease or exhaustion. Yet the undeniable, amazing fact is that most will survive.

—The Pemberton Guide

*A*t dawn Bob and Hanna came downstairs. They'd been up all night. Both of them were moving heavily. Bob's face was stubbled. Hanna's eyes were bloodshot.

"Bean?" Bob said gently.

Bean woke up and felt Martin smashed against her legs. Her back was stiff with pain. She shifted the boy's weight and tried to sit up.

"What time is it?" she said, hair shaggy in her face.

"It's time, Bean."

Bean stumbled upstairs, and Bob followed, carrying Martin in his arms. She poured herself the last inch of coffee in the machine. It scalded her tongue and she gasped. She really had no choice. In the fickle morning light, she was struck again and again by an image of Martin's mother, dressed up in her Royal Suites uniform, looking desperately for her son under hotel beds. Bean stepped heavily to the phone and pulled out her address book. She started to dial, then stopped. Hanna and Bob were staring at her. She took the phone into Bob's bedroom and shut the door.

The phone rang only once. Martin's mother jumped on it.

"¿Sí?" she said.

Bean told her that Martin was well, that she was looking after him. She hadn't meant to steal her boy. It just turned out that way.

Martin's mother cried with relief. "*Gracias a Dios,*" she said. She went on, sobbing in Spanish, saying Bean had no right to do what she did. *No hay derecho.* She was hard to understand, with all the crying, but Bean got the gist. Then she said that her boyfriend wasn't living with her anymore. She'd kicked him out last night. Bean figured it had been easier with the police there.

Bean mumbled that that was a good move. When she hung up, she realized she was shaking. She came out of the bedroom and put the phone in its cradle.

Bob shot her a look. "Were you talking all that time?" he said.

"She kicked out the boyfriend," Bean said. "She needed to talk."

"Damn it, Bean. You just told the cops where you are. Where *we* are."

Hanna put her hand over her mouth.

Bean hurried Martin into Bob's truck and headed for the Mission District. She drove with her left hand on the wheel, her right arm around his shoulder. Partly to comfort him, she told herself, partly to be able to shove him down if a cop drove by. She drove as fast as she could, jerking around the corners, hopping over the crests of the steep hills. The dogs were after her. It would be so much better to get Martin home before the police found her. She tried to distract Martin by telling him that the boyfriend was gone and that his mother missed him very much. Martin didn't react to the news, he just sat up a bit when his neighborhood streets appeared.

A squad car was parked in front of Martin's building. Bean sucked in her breath, yanked Martin to the seat, and rode past, not daring to turn her head. Two blocks down, she slid into a bus zone and righted Martin. He was so docile.

She had been racking her brain all morning for something to say to him. She couldn't bear to tell him to be brave. Or to call her if he needed anything. Or to rest assured, things would get better. She couldn't guarantee anything, and she wasn't going to lie. Martin seemed to know this, too. He didn't ask for anything. He opened the door, slid down the bench seat, and poised his beat-up tennis shoes for the jump.

Bean looked around quickly and hopped out her door to help. She threw her arms around Martin to lift him down. It was all the hug she was going to give. A militant streak ran through her. *Hugs can be lies, too,* she thought; *you walk on alone.*

He turned on the sidewalk and looked up at her. She smiled as best she could. She wanted to tell him something. To plump up his heart. To feel understood. But what? She couldn't think of a thing.

Martin looked up at her, wide-eyed.

"Quack," he said.

Bean felt a shiver run down her body. All those nights spent working on her rhymes. Someone had heard.

"Quack?" he said again. And then he smiled. It was the first time she'd seen it; maybe it was his first smile ever. His teeth were perfect little pearls.

"Quack," Bean whispered. She ran her palm across her eyes, and when she looked up again, Martin was on his way.

He walked down the block, one shoelace flying, the label on his T-shirt poking from his neck. She watched his little body wait for the light at the corner. She listened hard. She hoped he would quack all the way home.

———

She drove straight to school. What was the point of hiding if the police were going to come after her? At least this way they wouldn't bother Bob and Hanna. If Hanna got another arrest, she'd be in serious trouble. And Bob, he didn't deserve this.

The sun was just beginning to burn off the morning mist. As soon as Bean pulled into the parking lot, she turned off the engine and lay across the bench seat. As she dozed, she wondered if the school would protect her from the cops. She imagined that Elena would come out with her microphone and, instead of her usual number, would sing a protest song for Bean. All the colorful murals would spring to life and the chocolate-skinned men in straw hats would defend her with machetes.

At 8:15 Bean awoke to the sound of car doors slamming as kids arrived for school. She stumbled into the brilliant light, hair ajumble, clothes wrecked. She walked the familiar path to her classroom, eyes straight ahead. She was arriving at the same time as the gossip about her, and she heard the whispers swirl.

She reached her classroom and slipped her key in the door. Before she had it open, Mr. Gutierrez was behind her.

"You have three minutes to leave the school grounds," he said. "I've been obliged to have the office call the police."

Bean felt her face flush. Instinctively, she dropped her gaze. Then she dipped into one of her precious minutes to raise her eyes and stare into his. She saw little marbles of anger and fear.

Bean turned and walked away. Elena and some other teachers came up to her as she reached the parking lot. They asked questions. She just shook her head, got into Bob's truck, and drove away.

An hour later she slipped into the Park Bench Café, around the corner from her apartment. She had pulled Bob's beret down low on her head and tucked her hair into her collar. She was rethinking the part about making it easy for the police. They hadn't found her yet. She could leave town. Maybe even leave the country. For that, she needed to get into her house. She needed clothes, money. There didn't seem to be any cops on her street. But that didn't mean they weren't there. They might be waiting inside. Maybe she could get Hanna to check the apartment.

She'd need a car. Bob's truck was too conspicuous. Besides, he used it for work. And Fred. She couldn't just leave Fred. She sipped a hot espresso, hoping it would clear her head. Within minutes, she was racing down Sanchez to Bob's place. She turned a block early, when she spotted it: a squad car parked across the street from his stoop. Bean drove back down the alley and parked on a side street.

She trotted round to the garage, reached above her head, and tapped on the glass. The door unhitched and Bob shoved it open. He was wearing baggy blue jeans, and white paint was speckled all over his sweatshirt. The paint fumes almost knocked her over.

"Jesus, Bob," Bean said. "You need air in here. You're gonna forget your own name."

"I figured I could get my painting finished," he said. "Since we're stuck here." Practical Bob.

"Bob, I've got to get out of here," Bean said.

"And go where?" he asked.

"I don't know," she said. "Boston."

"Why Boston?"

"I have family there."

Bob was incredulous. "What family? You mean your dad? Like he's going to be any help."

"Never mind. The less you know, the better."

Bean looked over at Hanna. She was sitting on a milk crate, with Fred insinuating himself into her lap. One of her clawed hands dug into his fur. Her other fist was wrapped around a cigarette pack and lighter.

"Hanna," Bean said, flapping her hand at the fumes. "Don't you dare light that."

But Hanna and Fred just stared at Bean. All in all, they made a pretty sad-looking crew. Bob with paint on his nose, where he'd scratched himself, standing there looking like you could knock him down with a sigh. She'd turned them all into criminals. Their looks froze her mind, and she felt more miserable than ever.

She tried a diversion. "So, how much you got left?" she asked Bob.

"What?" he said. Totally distracted.

"The boat. How much more painting you got left?" Bean said. She squeezed around the cradle near the stern.

Bob suddenly got alert. "Just a little," he said.

If only they could sail off somewhere. Just disappear. Start fresh.

She continued to circle his boat. It seemed to make Bob uncomfortable.

"I hope you're not thinking of sailing away somewhere," he said.

"Don't be ridiculous, Bob."

He was even more riled. "Would you mind just sitting down? Sitting down right there."

But by then Bean had rounded the stern and seen it. The boat's name. It was written in fanciful white cursive across the back of the blue-and-white-trimmed boat. *Celes*—— There was a "*tine*" stenciled, ready to paint. She looked over at Bob.

He looked back, his face as wide open as a summer tent.

Bean didn't know what to say. "You gonna finish that?" she asked.

"If you don't have any objections," he said.

"That name is going to hound me to my grave."

"It's a good name," he said.

Bob came around and stood next to Bean, and they both looked at the stern. They weren't touching, not really. But Bean felt the hair on her arm lift to meet his. She was stuck, wondering whether to pull closer or push away. She crossed her arms.

"So you really think this'll float?"

Bob nodded solemnly. "One way to find out."

She couldn't tell if they were still talking about the boat, or her, or them. She wished she felt his confidence.

"Suppose we get stuck out there, between Angel Island and Alcatraz, and it takes on water?" she demanded. "You got a pail?"

The fish ran in the strait between the two islands, where the cold ocean water met up with the warm bay. Mrs. Harper had shown them the place; if you squinted on a bright day, you could see the liquid fault. It was where the birds lingered.

Bean blinked and she felt stared at. Hanna's little snap eyes. Fred's begging look. Bob was beside her, but he was probably peeking, too, sidelong. She needed a cigarette. And some coffee. And, God, just a minute to sort things out.

She felt Bob touch her hand. She dropped her arms and her fingers disappeared into his thick mitt. It struck her as the best thing he could do. Better than a kiss or a hug.

"She'll float, Bean," he said.

The police took Bean downtown. Bob and Hanna followed in his truck. Bob had objected when they insisted on putting handcuffs on her, but Bean just held out her wrists.

At the station, the sergeant looked slightly embarrassed as he locked Bean into a cell. They were waiting on a statement from the kid's mother, he told Bean. Apparently, she had gone to work, with Martin in tow. Bean felt a pang for the woman, scrubbing toilets while her son watched.

The cell was a lot like the one Hanna had been penned up in, though Bean was alone. The quarters were tight, but not much smaller than her trailer in Eyak. At least there wasn't a mildew smell. She stretched out on the bunk, where a wool blanket lay folded at the foot.

She stared at the shadows cast by the steel bars onto the ceiling. The exhilaration of her previous day dripped away. She was so tired. *So this is it,* she thought. *The end of the line.* The only thing missing was harmonica music.

It had been silly, really, to think she might run to her father. Hank would have given Bean a bed for a few days, and then let Margie and the kids do their magic. Hank never put his foot down. He never cared enough. He never disciplined Bean or Chip any more than their mother demanded. Hank didn't know what he wanted. That's what their mother said, adding, "I'm afraid it's genetic."

Bean adjusted the flat pillow under her head. The cell was bathed in light from a urine-yellow plastic fixture in the hallway. Her mother was the other extreme. She cared too much—about Bean's clothes, what the neighbors thought, making friends at the club. Everything had mattered except what was important.

Lying there, Bean wondered if she had been too hard on her mother. Her mother had loved Hank. And the shocker was, she *still* loved him. It was obvious when she talked about Hank's new family, and feeling like litter.

Bean rolled over and thought about all that frittata her mother had made for graduation. If only there'd been a way to talk to her differently, so it wasn't always about Bean coming up short. She wanted to tell her what it felt like to see her husband on the coroner's gurney or to watch her best friend fade away.

Maybe, if her mother would just not talk right away, Bean could even tell her about Martin, and why she had to do it. But it would never happen. Her mother would hear that Bean was in jail, and that would be it—the ultimate confirmation.

Bean found herself wishing someone else would get arrested. Hanna had had a couple of prostitutes to chat with. Hours passed, and Bean wasn't sure anymore if it was day or night. There was a draft in the station, and she reached down for the blanket at her feet. She pulled it over her and the wool scratched her neck and smelled of cigarettes.

As she fell asleep, Bean Jessup, jailbird, composed a rhyme.

> *Even a duck*
> *Can tuck*
> *Herself in:*
> *Just curl*
> *And unfurl*
> *Up to your chin.*

She was awakened by a cop carrying a grease-spotted bag. She had forgotten to be hungry until she smelled the Big Mac and fries. She tore into the food. A few minutes later the cop returned. They had finally heard from Martin's mother. She wasn't going to press charges.

"You're in luck," the cop said. "She's probably an illegal."

Bob came to pick Bean up.

At home, there was a phone message waiting from the principal. Mr. Gutierrez had fired her. If he had his way, he said, she would never teach again. On Saturday Elena Ortiz brought Bean's things to the house in a box.

Despite it all, when Bean awoke the next morning, she felt curiously lighter.

She lay on her belly, one eye open, the bedclothes twisted between her legs. She could get up and have a day. Or she could roll over. It really could go either way. She peered over at the blinds, trying to guess the weather on the other side. Fog? Sun? She couldn't tell. She heard Hanna banging around in the kitchen. Would her coffee be strong enough? Would she make eggs this morning? Bean sat up. Hanging on; it wasn't much of a philosophy. She padded to the door and opened it to see what Hanna was making for breakfast.

That afternoon she applied for a job at the Park Bench Café. She learned to work the hissing, sputtering machine that had so frightened Lois. Sometimes in the middle of whipping up a latte, she thought about Lois and wondered how she was doing. She wondered if Rhonda's heart problem was any better. Mudhole had sold the house, God bless him. She thought of them all, then she let them go. She wiped the counter clean.

I've been letting go of things all my life.

She considered getting a tattoo. The girl who worked the register had one. It was a wreath of blue thorns and flowers that twisted all the way around her arm. She wore tank tops to show it off. Bean wondered what she might put on her own shoulder. She'd been through a lot and she figured her body ought to show it.

On a bright Saturday in May, she and Bob hauled the *Celestine* down to the Marina and put it in the water. He was so proud, he would have popped if you poked him. Bean tossed their knapsack lunch into the bow and crawled aboard. Bob hoisted the sail and they set out into the bay among the mammoth ferries and yachts.

When they climbed out of the boat at Angel Island, the ranger who tended the harbor came out for a look. Bob told him about building the boat, more than he wanted to know—from lumber to caulk, soup to nuts. Bean stood at Bob's elbow, in the shade of his thrall. She watched him like a stranger might, and felt vaguely jealous.

They shared a picnic on the bluff overlooking the docks. The pears and the cheese were soft. If it weren't for the crackers, they wouldn't have made a sound. Between bites, Bob looked at Bean, and Bean looked at the view.

Finally he spoke. "You know, you were pretty good with that kid," he said.

Bean nibbled a cracker. "I went a little crazy," she said.

"Yeah, maybe. But even when I was shouting at you to give him back—I dunno. I was rooting for you."

She looked over at him. His broad, bashful face. His scalp getting sunburned.

"Well, maybe between the two of us, we got it right," Bean said.

The words hung in the air between them: the two of us. She regretted them.

Bob shifted his weight on his haunches and wiped his forehead with his wrist. He was deciding whether to try again with Bean. It was so obvious, she felt embarrassed.

"Bean—" he said at last.

She met his glance. Those artless, see-through eyes. She smiled. Ever so slightly, and only once, she turned her head side to side.

They both knew they would never return together to Angel Island.

Hanna stayed. She didn't talk anymore about helping Bean get back on her feet. And she didn't talk about leaving. She just stayed and made herself useful. When Bean came home from work, Hanna was bent over the stove, spooning gravy over a pot roast or slicing onions with her clawed hands.

On warm afternoons Hanna took Fred to the park. Or she reached for her raincoat and announced that she was going shopping. Sometimes she came home with things. Sometimes she just told Bean about what she'd seen. Bean didn't ask many questions.

"I saw the most interesting bootscraper today," Hanna said one night. "Looked like—what do you call those?—an armadillo."

"You mean a hedgehog?" Bean offered. She thought she'd seen a hedgehog bootscraper before.

"What?"

Hanna had gotten lazy with her hearing aid; it irritated her ear and when the battery ran down again, she had just slipped it into a drawer. As a result, they conducted their conversations at a shout. Bean felt the reproaches around them at the movies. But she didn't care.

"I'm pretty sure it was an armadillo," Hanna hollered.

The armadillo never showed up on the stoop. But every once in a while Bean found little presents on the kitchen counter—a chew toy for Fred, nail clippers for Bean. No note, no bag, no receipt. Bean shrugged. What was the point of lecturing a seventy-two-year-old woman? And who was Bean, anyway? She had her own rap sheet to worry about. She ripped open the gift and went to work on a hangnail.

In the mornings she went to the Y for a swim. As always, the water soothed her and lightened her mood. She took great satisfaction in feeling her arms grow stronger, her hips slimmer. She stopped buying junk food and shopped for staples at the health-food store down the street. Bulgur wheat, lentils, humus. Hanna initially was baffled by all the strange ingredients. She poked at the tofu like it was a jellyfish on the beach. But eventually she found a cookbook in a used-book store and learned how to make stir-fry.

Bean walked slowly in the street and imagined she was a foreigner. She wore dark glasses, pulled her shoulders back, and lingered at the sidewalk florist. She made random comments to herself in Spanish. She pretended that someone was filming a movie in which she had a modest but critical role.

The landmarks of her life gradually blurred: César Chávez Elementary, Bob's house, the distant hills of home. They were not part of where she was going.

She lived deliberately. She made "must remember" lists in her head. She took time with zippers and opened boxes of crackers by sliding a finger under the tab. She locked herself out only once—when Fred had been bursting to get out—but Hanna came home before too long. She stopped getting piles of parking tickets. She didn't hide in her bedroom.

Sometimes sadness engulfed her. She recalled Mick's smile—impossibly bright—or felt his arms around her, spooning. Or she heard one of Jimmy's wicked wisecracks, and she laughed abruptly over kiwis at the market.

Without them, she had no one to run to. There was no rest or refuge. It was as if an arctic tern had finally reached the South Pole only to discover there was nowhere to land. No time to think. Must turn back. Must keep flying.

Her life was in her hands. Would she ever fall in love again? How would she earn a living? She already missed the students. Had she made a difference in any of their lives? Just one life; that would be enough. Would she ever sit on the porch and watch her child at play?

They were hard questions and she couldn't answer any of them. But with each day that passed, they didn't feel like pleas or prayers anymore. They felt more like mysteries. She would adjust to whatever the answers were, if they came at all.

One afternoon, on a Thursday, she came home from work, picked the phone off the counter, and marched past Hanna and Fred into her bedroom. She clicked the door shut and extracted a crumpled piece of paper from the dresser drawer. She floated over to the bed, sat down, and punched the number into the phone.

It rang. Her heart went boom-boom between rings.

"Hullo?" he said.

Her back straightened. Images of him springing like a coil in the pool and rocking his narrow hips atop her.

"Hello, Andrew?" she said.

"Yeah?"

"This is Lois. Except I'm not Lois. Not really."

She stole a quick breath.

"My name is Bean."

She hadn't really believed it would go anywhere. A relationship built on a lie; it was doomed from the start. So when Andrew sheepishly told her that he was with someone else—who, as it happened, was there right now—it stung only a little. By the time she hung up, Bean was almost relieved. She had made the call. That was the important thing.

She stole one of Hanna's cigarettes, went out to the front stoop, and leaned against the railing. Hanna, who was bent over a pile of green beans at the kitchen table, kept quiet.

Bean lit, drew, exhaled. So she wasn't going to be Lois again. That was for starters. There were so many things she had been and wasn't anymore. A wife. A daughter. A sister. A friend. A lover. All gone. She wasn't Little Blue, or Burt, or Captain V, or even Celestine. She wasn't a sidekick; she wasn't a teacher.

Once you started paring away, it was hard to know when to stop. You could go all the way back to when you were six years old, standing on the edge of the cesspool, with everyone daring you to jump in.

She was someone quite different now. Her perfect little body today had scars and folds and calluses. Sorrow had flooded her life. She felt it again now, swamping her toes and pulling beneath her, like escaping surf. But she stood up to it. No tears, no wobble. That was something.

The last warm rays of the day gilded the Victorians across the street. The purple-blue sky bore streaks of red. A couple of schoolgirls in plaid skirts and kneesocks crossed beneath her, whispering secrets. It was the kind of day's end whose tenderness almost embarrassed the people who lived there.

In a flash, Bean knew that if she could remember that sky, those girls, that secret, things might turn out all right. Not forever, but for now. That would be good enough, and maybe even wonderful. She flicked away her cigarette and sat up. There was a thumping in her chest. She thought she could hear it.

Tomorrow she would buy an armadillo bootscraper. Next Tuesday she would sign up for a writing class at the junior college. Beyond that, her calendar was open.

Acknowledgments

My father, Harold Marquis, provided early encouragement and read more drafts than one could reasonably ask. Julie Marquis eased the research process with wisdom and humor. Colleen Fitzpatrick lent thoughtful advice, as did Beatriz Terrazas, Ellen Levine, Emily Haynes, and Jane Rosenman.

I wish to thank my Alaskan guides, including Joy Landaluce, Sue Shellhorn, Kelly Weaverlang, Marleen Moffitt, Martha Nichols, Michele Fisher, Franc Fallico, Ken Hodges, and Brian Okonek.

I am also grateful to Karen Zapata, Paul Reinhertz, Linda Barnett, Rafa Nuñez, Bob Mecoy, Allison Jones, Jim Cotton, Matt Marquis, Kathy Lind, Dave Marcus, Phil Peters, and Jeff Marquis.

This project might not have advanced without the support of many others, including Rick Berke, Ben Roth, Mrs. J. D. Haley, George and Carolyn Marx, Erika Andersen, Ellen Grossman, Chris Hedges, Anne Bernays, Bill Kovach and the Nieman Foundation, David McCall, Nancy Marquis, and Martin Niedermair. In ways large and small, they delivered.